Pain

By L.

Copyright © 2012 Lorraine McInerney

All rights reserved.

L.H. Cosway Books.

ISBN: 1481060139

ISBN 13: 9781481060134

Cover image by Anatoly Tiplyashin.

Cover design by Romantic Book Affairs Designs.

This is a work of fiction. Any resemblance to persons living or dead is purely coincidental. No part of this book may be used or reproduced in any manner whatsoever without written permission from the author.

Books by L.H. Cosway

A Strange Fire (Florence Vaine #1)
A Vision of Green (Florence Vaine #2)

Tegan's Blood (The Ultimate Power Series #1)
Tegan's Return (The Ultimate Power Series #2)
Tegan's Magic (The Ultimate Power Series #3)
(Feb. 2013)
Crimson (An Ultimate Power Series Novella)

Painted Faces

For all the men who are women and the women who are men, the men who are men and the women who are women. And those of you who are a little bit of both. You colour my world.

..when in the fast embrace their limbs were knit, they two were two no more, nor man, nor woman – one body then that neither seemed and both.

- Ovid, *Metamorphoses*.

Prologue

Christchurch, New Zealand, 1998.

He was eight years old when his obsession began.

He was so much more than just a boy in a dress. He had been doing this for six years, and still he managed to keep it a secret. He was an only child and his father was forever absent, so the secrecy came easy. Nicholas had been searching for his old cowboy costume in the attic when he'd come across the boxes, full to the brim with his deceased mother's things.

He had exactly three memories of her. The first was how her bright blue eyes always lit up and shone when she saw him. The second was how she would fill the house with pretty music when she sang and played piano, and the third was of her crying, always crying in the bathroom when she thought nobody else was around.

Nicholas had taken her dusty old possessions and made them his life. He would sing like she sang in the video recordings he had of her. He kept them hidden under his bed and watched them over and over again. He would wear her dresses and jewellery and spend hours putting her make-up on his face. In time his habit would evolve into a need to entertain; a desire to express his fascination with the female form by impersonating it. But for now, it was all about her. The woman who brought him into the world and died before he had the chance to get to know her.

Over the years he had come to realise that other people didn't do what he did; they didn't spend hours at a time trying to replicate the memory of their dead mother by becoming her. He wondered if this was what grown-ups referred to as grief. It seemed odd for him to feel sad for a woman he had only three memories of. For some reason he felt like he loved her inherently, despite never having truly known her.

But it was loneliness too that spurred his unlikely habit. His father was a cold man and only spoke to him when it was absolutely necessary, while Nicholas was a child who thrived on conversation, on attention. At school he acted out, making fun of the teachers and always interrupting lessons simply because he craved someone to acknowledge him, to have people know he existed. He found that if he behaved badly, he could be the centre of attention.

He was friends with all of the prettiest girls. The other boys would call him a queer, but he didn't care. He liked being around the girls too much to give it up. He loved how sweet they smelled and how soft their lips were when they let him kiss them and put his hands up their shirts. He relished how they told him he was the most handsome boy in the whole school.

He was twelve the first time he got beaten up. He lay on the ground and let the boys punch and kick him because he didn't know how to defend himself. They spat names at him like faggot and nancy-boy. That was one of the last times they got away with it, because he soon learned how to kick and punch back, how to use his wit as a defence to their name calling. He never bothered trying to show them that he was none of the things they called him. Bullies didn't care about the truth, they just wanted an easy target.

He was fourteen the first time somebody discovered

his secret. It was a Saturday and he was alone in the house. He put his Karen Carpenter CD in the stereo and let it play on full volume as he twirled around in his mother's red velvet dinner dress and her black high heels with the silver buckles at the front. He tried to match exactly how Karen sang. His friends from school all listened to Backstreet Boys and The Spice Girls, but he thought Karen had the most perfect, sweetest voice in the world.

He was holding a hairbrush, which also belonged to his mother, to his mouth as a pretend microphone in the front living room of the house, oblivious to the world, when he turned around to find a man standing there watching him. It was Kelvin, a friend and work colleague of his father's. Nicholas felt like a bomb had exploded inside of his chest. He was caught. This would change everything.

He really didn't like Kelvin. There was something about him that made the tiniest hairs on his arms stand on end. Why did it have to be this man who discovered his secret? He was a bad man, Nicholas could feel it.

Kelvin was old and stern like Nicholas' father, and he wore his ever present business suit. He stood holding a stack of folders in his arms. He smiled at Nicholas just before he set them down on the coffee table.

He dangled a set of keys from his hand. "Your dad asked me to drop these documents by today, he gave me the key to the front door," said Kelvin.

Nicholas was mortified as he stared at the man. *Leave*, he silently begged, *can't he just leave and pretend he never saw any of this?*

The end of his happiness was upon him. Kelvin would tell his father what he had caught Nicholas doing, and his father would call him an abomination, burn all of his mother's things and throw him out onto the streets.

His throat was dry as he managed a reply that was barely a whisper. "I'll – I'll tell him you came by."

Kelvin nodded, but still the stupid man wouldn't leave. He took a seat on the couch and crossed one leg over the other.

"So, what exactly are you supposed to be doing?" he asked, his eyes gleaming with an intention Nicholas couldn't quite pick out. A single tear spilled from his eye and ran down his face.

"Please don't tell my dad," he begged fervently, as more tears followed.

"Oh, of course not. I wouldn't dream of it," Kelvin replied. "Now, come and sit with me. I'm sure we can come to some kind of an arrangement."

Desperate to convince Kelvin to keep his secret, Nicholas took a deep breath, wiped at his tears with his fingers, and went to sit down. His beautiful secret, the one that had brought him so much joy, would never be a happy, childish thing again.

Chapter One
Can I Call You Viv?

Dublin, Ireland, Present day.

The mascara stings my eyes as it drips down my cheeks. It's a good thing I'm not wearing lipstick or I'd look like some sort of circus clown. A lunatic escaped from the asylum perhaps. I could certainly give Alice Cooper a run for his money.

A sudden downpour of rain is soaking through my clothes, leaving my skin full of goose pimples, my curly hair a soggy mess and my boots squeaking with the liquid that has gotten inside. I'm the picture of a modern woman who doesn't own a car and doesn't possess the forethought to carry an umbrella.

This is what we call summer in Ireland ladies and gents. One minute the sun is beating down on you, making you all sweaty, and the next it's lashing rain. Either way, you're going to end up damp. I'm carrying what feels like about a million plastic shopping bags, though in reality it's only three. The bags are most likely adding to my appearance of being an escaped psychiatric patient. Is it just me, or do the psychologically unstable always seem to carry plastic bags around?

I live in an apartment block just off Aungier Street. It's a bit of a dive truth be told, but at least it's central. I fumble for the keys in my handbag which is slung over my shoulder, as a couple of the local kids walk by me, snickering at my struggle. I want to tell them to go fuck themselves, but of course societal rules prevent adults such as myself from swearing at children. I suppress a snort at the idea, it would again add to the façade I'm unconsciously cultivating of being off my trolley.

Finally, I manage to retrieve the keys from their hiding spot at the very end of my bag - wouldn't you know - beneath a half empty bottle of spring water and a half eaten bar of chocolate. I live on the third floor and the building doesn't have an elevator. I have to trudge my way up the stairs, soggy clothes, plastic bags, open handbag (since I'm too lazy to zip it back up after finding the keys) and all.

As I mentioned, the block is a bit of a dive and I don't have the nicest of neighbours, so I always tend to hurry getting from the front entrance up to my apartment. Just as I'm slotting in my keys, the door from the recently empty apartment next to mine flies open.

I'm curious to see who my new neighbour is this time. A single mother with three little brat kids who'll make an unholy racket day and night perhaps? Knowing my luck it'll be something like that. Only it isn't, instead a very smartly dressed man emerges. He has a crisp white shirt on, the first two buttons casually undone, expensive black trousers and black dress shoes. Well, well, well, perhaps Nora and I are going to have a respectable neighbour for once.

Myself and my best friend Nora have been living together for almost three years now in our two bedroom apartment in the city. *Not* as glamorous as it sounds, let me tell you. In those three years we've lived next to a junkie couple, a single mother with two obnoxious children, and a young husband and wife with a baby who, when the baby wasn't crying the building down, would have noisy rows at two o'clock in the morning.

The couple moved out about three weeks ago, providing myself and Nora with some much deserved peace and quiet.

The man I'm currently staring at looks like he belongs in this place about as much as an Indian tiger belongs in the Dublin Zoo. He has jet black hair, sort of midway between long and short, ice blue eyes and a classically beautiful face. His physique is lightly muscled in that kind of athletic way, and when he smiles at me politely his whole face lights up. His eyes are all shines and sparkles.

"Hello there," he says, shutting the door behind him and locking it with his key. His accent is mildly Australian, not Irish. He steps toward me, holding his hand out for me to give it a shake. I give him a look that's probably somewhere between confused and exasperated, as I clearly can't get my hands free for the shake he's waiting on.

"You must be Freda, your flatmate Nora invited me in for a cup of tea earlier. Lovely girl." He says.

Oh, I'm sure she did. Nora is quite the opportunist when it comes to men, and I'd say she thought this fellow was a fine specimen. Even within this short conversation, I've noticed something sort of electric about his personality, something addictive. His eyes pull me in, like they hold secrets that could make my boring old life so much more exciting. You don't come across men this alluring very often.

"Fred, you can call me Fred," I tell him stupidly, placing the plastic bags down on the floor so that I can finally shake his hand.

Our palms touch, our fingers entwine, and I can't believe I'm admitting this, but the tiniest tingle goes through me at the contact. Of course, he doesn't know that, and thank fuck, because he'd probably think I was some kind of a pervert. I mean, who exactly gets tingles when they shake a person's hand? You might as well say, *Hello, you'll be starring in my dirty dreams tonight, Mr Blue Eyes*. Not creepy in the slightest. Perhaps it's been too long since I last had a boyfriend.

I let go first and try to ignore his magnetism. He laughs, a wonderfully low sound that vibrates through to my toes. "Okay Fred, you can call me Vivica."

Our eyes connect and we both smile at his joke. It's funny, but not funny enough to solicit a laugh. "Cool, if we become close friends can I call you Viv?" I respond.

He mock flicks his hair over his shoulder, a very feminine gesture, and puts on a sweet Marilyn Monroe voice. "You can call me whatever you like, Frederick." The gesture suddenly opens my eyes to a certain fey aspect in his demeanour, maybe he's gay. He certainly dresses well enough.

"Why thanks, I'll keep that in mind, Viv. It was a pleasure to meet you. I hope you're finding the place to your liking."

"Oh it's a palace fit for a queen, Freddie, a real find."

I take note of his obvious sarcasm. He still faces me, walking backwards down the hall, twirling his keys around his fingers. Clearly he has somewhere he needs to be.

I laugh. "Well, that's good to hear. Drop in for tea any time."

He nods and leers at my wet top, where my purple D-cup bra is blatantly visible through my cream t-shirt. "Damn it," he says humorously. "Did I miss the wet t-shirt competition, *again*?" The way he's staring at my top makes me 99% sure he isn't gay.

"Ah you did I'm afraid, in Dublin we put on some great ones too. We all gather down by the river Liffey and dive in with our clothes on. When we climb out the junkies on the board walk give us marks out of ten."

He smirks at me. "If that's the case then you must have gotten an eleven. Sounds like a real classy affair Fred, I'll make sure I don't miss the next one."

"Come along whenever you like. We always welcome newcomers." I tell him, running with the joke.

He salutes me then, smiling at me fondly, and disappears around the corner. It's only at that moment that I realise he still hasn't told me his real name.

Inside our apartment is empty. Nora must have gone out somewhere. I drop the shopping bags in the kitchen and go in search of some fresh clothes and a hair dryer. Once I feel like the living again, I unpack my baking ingredients.

I have two jobs. One is working in a charity shop down the road three mornings a week, a handy little number. The other is baking for a cake shop in the city that prides itself on fresh homemade produce. I make all of their cupcakes. In fact, I've been told that I make the best cupcakes in Ireland, though since it was my mother who said it she might have been slightly biased.

Baking cupcakes for a living has its ups and its downs. The up side is that you get to put a smile on people's faces, even if you're also putting a few extra pounds on their backsides. The down side is that you have to get up at four o'clock every weekday morning to bake the things and have them down at the cake shop by eight-thirty. I have a bicycle with a carriage affixed to the back of it. I put the cupcakes in boxes, stick them in the carriage and deliver them to the shop. Oh yeah, and when I call it the cake shop, I'm not avoiding telling you the name. It's a cake shop called The Cake Shop. So hip and modern, you know.

Another bad thing is that I have quite the sweet tooth, so baking cakes all the time sort of indulges it a little too much. In terms of size I'm a small fourteen, which isn't so bad I suppose, but I could always stand to lose a bit of weight. Oh, and I'm talking UK sizes, not US. If I lived in America I could go around telling people I was a 10. Even though there's no actual difference, it would please me no end.

I put my purchases away, ready for tomorrow morning's batch. I bake sixty a day and most days they sell out down at the shop. I divide them into five sections toppings wise, as follows; twelve lemon, twelve orange chocolate, twelve strawberry, twelve toffee and twelve vanilla. Sometimes I'll shake things up a bit with a few red velvets or mint. The oven in my apartment is probably the most expensive thing in the place. It took me two years to save up for it.

There's something therapeutic, I find, about baking the exact same thing each morning. I could do it with my eyes closed. I tend to listen to music when I bake. I enjoy old punk stuff like *Dead Kennedys* and *Social Distortion*. I know, it's an unusual mix, punk and cupcakes, but it works for me. The fast paced punk music gives me an extra bit of a pep in my step at such an early hour.

Of course, I only listen to music with my earphones on, because Nora works as a bartender in a night club in Temple Bar and sleeps in. She'd probably have a coronary if I played my music at four o'clock in the morning, since she only gets home after two. I think she has a secret desire to take a hammer to my electric mixer.

We have opposite routines, me an early bird and she a night owl. But in the same way that the punk rock and cupcakes work for me, our opposite routines work for us. She's my best friend and I love her to bits, but I think if we had to spend all of our time together somebody would end up with a broken nose. And it wouldn't be me.

I flake out in front of the television for a while, watching the afternoon soaps. It's five o'clock when Nora strolls in the door, carrying a little beige and white striped bag from the evil department store that is Brown Thomas. I *cannot* stand the place. It's Dublin's answer to Harrods of London, and I swear to God every single employee is a replica of the bitchy attractive girl you knew from school.

I always get a sick satisfaction as I mosey on past on a Saturday and see the anti-animal cruelty protesters outside, giving out hell because the store sells items made from real fur. The aggravated faces of the girls who work beyond the big glass front windows make me happy in a twisted but very fundamental way.

"So, what did you get from Satan's lay-by this time?" I ask her, as she goes to the fridge and pulls out a bottle of water.

"I'm roasting," says Nora, ignoring my question and sitting down on an armchair with the cold bottle pressed to her forehead. She doesn't like me commenting on her penchant for spending what little extra money she has on stupidly expensive items, such as tiny pots of eye shadow from the Mac counter. I know we're twenty five year old women and genetically predisposed to want to spend money on things we don't need, but come on.

"Yeah well, you're lucky you didn't get caught in the downpour earlier. I was effing soaked," I tell her crankily.

"Mm hmm," she mumbles, fanning herself with the material of her blouse. She picks up her precious bag and peers inside, before pulling out a silky neckerchief looking thing. It's pale blue, reminding me of the colour of Vivica's eyes, or whatever his real name is.

"So, did you meet our new neighbour Vivica?" I ask her jokingly. The joke goes right over her head though, because her brown eyes dart to me.

There's something like disappointment in her expression as she sighs and says, "Don't tell me he's got a girlfriend living with him, that will just completely ruin the fantasy I've currently got going on."

I'm tempted to torture her and draw the whole thing out, but I like to think I have a kind nature, so I don't. "Nah, at least he never mentioned one. We talked for a minute out in the hallway. I told him everyone calls me Fred and he joked and said I could call him Vivica."

Nora eyes me and smirks. "Sounds like you two had quite the cosy little chat."

"Yep, that was right before he pushed me up against the wall and took me right out in the open. I was going to tell him that I was a lady and didn't go in for that sort of thing, but my birthday's coming up in a couple of months so I thought I'd allow myself an early present."

"Shut up Fred!"

She throws a cushion at me. I pick it up and throw it right back at her, knocking her sleek ponytail slightly off kilter. I laugh as she scowls and takes great pains to set it back to rights.

I suppose this is a good time to tell you a little bit about Nora. She is absolutely *obsessed* with her appearance. Not so much in a vain way, but more in a control freak sort of way. Everything has to be neat as a pin. Just so. Clean as a whistle. She has straight dark brown hair, deep sultry brown eyes and a tan. She's one of those Irish people who have a slight Spanish look to them. Some say that this "look" came about when Spanish ships arrived in Ireland hundreds of years ago and the Spanish began "mating" with the local talent. So historically accurate aren't I? I suppose Nora's great-great-great-great grandfather could have been a Spanish sailor.

Nora is also one of those stick thin people with an abnormally fast metabolism who could eat a whole buffet table and still not put on a pound. She's around a size eight. If *she* lived in America she could go around telling people she was a four. Anyway, if Nora's metabolism is an Olympic gold medal runner, mine is one of those slugs that you step on by mistake when it's cold and damp out. We have very different bodies, although the one benefit I get from being a "bigger girl", as they say, is that I'm not lacking in the chest department.

I think Nora is secretly pleased that I'm the "fat one", because it means she tends to get more attention when we go out together. Yes, despite my ample bosom the men always seem to flock to her, however that might have something to do with my more *abrasive*, shall we say, personality. If a guy came up to Nora in a club and said, "You must be lost honey, because heaven is a long way from here," she would eat that shit right up. If the same scenario were to occur with me, I'd cock my head to the side, tell the guy to "piss off" and be on my merry way.

When I look back at her she's still scowling at me for messing up her ponytail. "Just because you can get out of bed and have perfect hair, doesn't mean we all can," she says in a pissed voice.

Somebody's having their time of the month, I think. I have curly golden brown hair, and yes, because of the curls I don't ever really attempt to do much about taming it. I take a lackadaisical approach to hair care, and let's just say that I know it drives Nora up the wall.

I roll my eyes. "Nora, your self-pity monitor is beeping, it's telling me you're feeling sorry for yourself over something trivial and need to get a life."

She shakes her head, finally having gotten her ponytail emergency taken care of, and takes a drink out of her water bottle.

"Anyway," she says. "Back to the topic of our new neighbour. His name is Nicholas and I asked him to join us for dinner tonight before I go to work, so you need to cook something."

"He never mentioned dinner," I tell her. "Are you sure this didn't happen in one of the many fantasies you've had about him since meeting him earlier today?"

She lets out a sigh to end all sighs. "Can you refrain from taking the piss for just one minute Fred, please, I'm really not in the mood."

"Fine I shall *refrain* Nora dear. I shall also *refrain* from cooking you dinner just so that you can impress the man candy next door."

Nora had a fancier upbringing than I did. It never fails

to amuse me when she comes out with these random posh words. A small smile tilts up the ends of her mouth. I can tell that she doesn't want to be smiling but can't help herself. "All right then, continue being a piss taker, but please just make the dinner, will you?"

I grin. "I will make the most fabulous dinner you have ever tasted. It's a rare dish, not many have heard of it, *sausage a la mash*."

She throws the cushion at me again and dashes into her bedroom, slamming the door shut before I can return the favour. I roll up my sleeves and go to have a look at what there is to make for dinner. I don't actually intend to make sausage and mash, because we never have guests over and I kind of want to impress this Nicholas character. I bet when he was a teenager he was the one everybody wanted to have as their best friend. As I said, he's sort of magnetic. Or maybe I'm just being a romantic idiot.

But even if he's well out of my league boyfriend wise, I'd still like to be his friend. I mostly only have two proper friends, Nora and our gay pal, Harry. Yes, we have a gay friend. It makes me feel more normal when I can see that my life is full of stereotypes. If I didn't have such a bad attitude and a habit of swearing I could be a reject from a future chick lit novel written by Bertie Ahern's daughter. After all, I do have the hopeless love life and the low self-esteem.

Anyway, Harry and I bonded over some apple strudel when we met at The Cake Shop about two years ago, and he's been a regular feature in my life ever since. Like me, Harry is a little on the chubby side, and we tend to get along due to our obsession with fine food.

As I pull out some ingredients, preparing to make my

special spaghetti bolognaise recipe, my thoughts drift to Nicholas. I could become his cool gal pal who he comes to for advice about life and women. He'd talk to me of his current super model girlfriend and how they are having relationship problems. Then he'd rest his head on my lap and I'd brush his black hair for him and tell him how women are complicated creatures and that he needs to give her space and love. I'd come out with sappy little nuggets of wisdom such as, *Nicholas, true love is like a flower, it needs care and sustenance in order to grow.* It will be cheesy in the most wonderful way. How sad is it that the idea of playing that kind of a role in his life actually excites me?

I lose myself in the motions of cooking. Yes, not only do I bake, I'm also a dab hand at savoury dishes. In the world that exists inside my own head I am the perfect woman. About an hour later Nora emerges from her room, wearing a tight black dress and blue ballet flats. She also has her reading glasses on, so I can tell she's going for the whole sexy but intelligent look.

At this current moment in time I have on comfortable jeans and one of those oversized jumpers that are all the rage at the moment, with no plans to go and change. Nora's about an eight or a nine on the much touted scale of attractiveness, which you come across in films from the good old US of A. She's got a chance of becoming Nicholas' new squeeze.

I'm a comfortable six, and sometimes I like it that way. It means I don't have to bother trying. The art of laziness is something I perfected many years ago. Often it's nice to just sit back and be a spectator for other people's love lives. I might not have a boyfriend, but I have cupcakes, and those tasty bastards haven't let me down yet.

All right, so now you're probably wondering about my past loves. Let's just say that they have all gone down like lead balloons. Crashed and *burned*. No happy ever after endings for me, I'm afraid. I have had a grand total of two boyfriends in my vast twenty-five years. The first lasted six months and was fairly normal; we basically figured out that we just couldn't really stand each other in the end.

The second, well, he turned out to be quite the psycho kettle of fish. When I told him I wanted to break up with him he stalked me for a whole year. This is the main reason why I don't have any kind of online presence whatsoever. I don't need that piece of work finding me again. I won't go into any more details, because thinking about both of those short relationships tends to give me indigestion.

Nora says she's going to go and knock next door to see if Nicholas is ready to join us. I wave her off and stir the bolognaise concoction in the pot as it heats over the stove. Not two minutes later the both of them burst into the apartment, having a good old laugh about something. I'm still standing by the cooker, finishing up the spaghetti.

"Look Fred, Nicholas brought a bottle of wine. Wasn't that nice of him?" says Nora. I glance over my shoulder as she waggles the bottle in her hand and places it on the dinner table.

"What a treat," I exclaim with mock excitement. "You're a real prize, Viv. How much did that cost you, 8.99 down in Londis?"

"Don't be rude, Fred," Nora scolds. "I need to pop to the loo, you two chat amongst yourselves," she says, full of contained glee at having a male of the species in the apartment.

I hate it when people tell you to *chat amongst yourselves*, because whenever they do I can never think of anything to talk about. So I remain silent and turn back around, focusing intently on the food. A moment later I can feel the heat of Nicholas' body behind mine. He puts both his hands on my hips and rests his head on my shoulder, looking over it at the food.

"Smells delicious Fred," he comments, casual as you please. Like this is normal behaviour for us and we barely know each other.

I stand stock still, my body immobile. Okay, so either he's one of those weird overly familiar guys who touch on people they hardly know, he's gay, or he's actually coming on to me. I'm thinking it's one of the first two.

"Yep," I mutter.

"The wine cost twenty Euros, and I got it from the off licence down the road," he says.

"Oh, very la di da Viv, you must be a big spender."

He laughs and his breath tickles my neck. "You like calling me Viv, do you?"

"What can I say, feminine blokes really do it for me," I reply, trying to keep my cool at his proximity.

"I can do that, if it's what you're into. In fact, I can be whatever you want me to be. I don't think it is though. I think you're the kind of woman who likes a man to take the lead." He softly jerks my hips back and presses into me ever so slightly. My eyes go wide. What the fuck is this about?

I twist around, lifting the spoon I'd been using to stir the bolognaise and pointing it right at him. A speck of tomato sauce splats down onto the floor. "*Okay.* Listen here, back the hell up or I'll knee you in the balls."

He takes a step back, putting his hands in the air in surrender, his face the picture of amusement. "Sorry Freda. I thought you were making all the passive aggressive comments because you were into me."

"Yeah well, you thought wrong. Now sit down at the table and make nice before Nora comes back out." Perhaps we're not going to have such a normal neighbour after all. I'm thinking he might be a sex pest.

"Yes sir," he replies, grinning like a fool. He really is far too handsome for his own good. When he pressed into me I felt like I was on fire, in a good way. Although at the same time I wanted to squirm with discomfort. I've never been the "touchy feely" type.

He keeps on looking at me, holding my gaze. I want to look away but I can't seem to manage it. "What colour are your eyes anyway? They look gold in certain lights," he says, his voice low and intense.

I shrug, all bashful. Jesus, one compliment and I've melted into a pool of sweat on the floor. "Hazel I guess."

"They're lovely," he says. "You're lovely."

My breathing catches. "Thank you for establishing my loveliness, Viv. Now, do you like garlic? Because there is a *lot* of garlic in this bolognaise."

He smiles, showing me straight white teeth. The kind of teeth you only see on movie stars. "I love it."

"Good," I reply, just as Nora emerges from the bathroom.

Deciding to take the piss to cover up my embarrassment at Nicholas' compliment, I say, "You might want to crack a window in there Nora, you were in for a while, number two was it?"

Her face goes bright red. I love embarrassing her. I take back what I said earlier about having a kind nature. I'm a cruel, cruel lady.

Nicholas' laughter fills the entire room. He looks to Nora. "She's just fabulous, isn't she?" Now *that* was the statement of a gay man if ever I heard one. It's in contention with the look he gives me, his icy blues eating me up. Good God, can somebody please loan me a burqa?

"Unfortunately yes," Nora replies, giving me a harsh look, a look that says *shut up and stop embarrassing me in front of my future husband!*

I cut up some focaccia bread and place it in a bowl with little dishes of balsamic vinegar and olive oil, for dipping, because I'm fancy like that. When I put them on the table Nora immediately digs in. Oh no, don't wait for me or anything. After all, I'm only the lowly cook who's facilitating this dinner date for her.

As I dish up the spag-bol, Nora dives right in with the old predictable questioning. "So Nicholas, what do you do for a living?"

He takes a piece of bread, dips it in olive oil and shoves it in his mouth. I notice him savour it for just a second and feel proud because I baked the bread myself. I have this weird fascination with watching people derive pleasure from the food I've made.

"I'm a cabaret performer," he answers simply, taking both of us by surprise. I would have guessed he worked in business or banking, since he's such a snappy dresser.

"Oh really," says Nora. "How interesting, what exactly does that entail?"

"It's a whole act, a bit of music, a bit of comedy, a bit of interaction with the audience."

"Do you sing?" she asks, intrigued.

"I most certainly do," he winks at her, just as I place the remainder of the food on the table and sit down. "Wine Fred?" he asks, lifting the bottle and glancing at me.

"Of course, Viv," I answer, twirling some spaghetti around my fork.

His gives me a brilliant smile and pours the liquid into my glass. I take a sip. It's nice, he has good taste.

"And have you lived in Dublin long?" Nora continues with her interrogation.

"Just arrived. I've visited a couple of times though, it's a great city. A friend of mine manages a new club here and offered me a regular gig performing, so I jumped at the chance. I've been travelling from country to country for years, going wherever the work took me. But I think I'm ready to settle down somewhere, for a while anyway."

"Nora's in the night club business herself," I put in. "She bar tends, you two will be able to exchange stories about all the drunks."

Nicholas looks to Nora. "Oh really, where do you work?"

"Temple Bar," she sips delicately on her wine. The delicate part is for Nicholas' benefit. If we were alone she'd be knocking it back like a good thing.

"Ah. The club I'll be performing in is on Capel Street. For a moment there I thought it was fate and we'd be working in the same place," he says charismatically. Nora goes all goofy eyed. He turns to face me. "So tell me about you Fred, what do you do?"

Before I can answer Nora butts in, probably wanting his attention back on her. "She's a baker, she makes cupcakes."

Nicholas grimaces. "Early mornings, I presume?"

I nod. "Very early mornings, it's the one flaw in a perfect occupation. I also work in the charity shop down the road. It sells all sorts of clothes and knick knacks."

"Two jobs, I'm impressed," he says, grinning.

"I'm an industrious young lady." I quip.

His eyes zone in on me, some sort of interest lying in their depths. "Oh, I bet you are," he murmurs, looking at my chest again. I'm half tempted to click my fingers in his face and tell him to look at my *eyes*, but that would be too cliché, even for me.

There's quiet for a couple of minutes, as we eat with Nora looking between the two of us suspiciously. She thinks there's something going on that she doesn't know about. There is *nothing* going on.

"This is brilliant, you're a great cook," says Nicholas, breaking the silence. "I haven't had a meal this tasty in a while. Can I take you home and you can cook all of my food for me?" he jokes.

"Of course you can, just put a cardboard box under the sink and I'll sleep in there."

"Nonsense," Nicholas chides. "You'll share my bed, I wouldn't agree to anything less."

"Great, so I can be your cook and your bed warmer, what a convenient set up."

Nora laughs nervously, our banter is making her uncomfortable, but I'm the only one who knows her well enough to be able to tell.

"My thoughts exactly," Nicholas agrees. "I could fall asleep on those wonderful breasts each night. I couldn't think of anything more relaxing."

At his words I actually spit the wine I just drank right out of my mouth and it sprays all over the table. Shit. Nicholas is shaking with laughter and Nora's laughing too, though in a slightly more hesitant manner.

"I can't believe you just said that about Fred's boobs," she remarks, a hint of flirtation in her voice. She gives his arm a friendly slap. "You're terrible."

"Yeah, just *terrible*," I say sarcastically.

"I wish I had ones as big as yours Fred," she continues with a pout. "Mine are like little fried eggs."

"I happen to admire all shapes and sizes." Nicholas gives her a dashing smile which seems to lift her spirits. God, Nora is one of the best people I know, but for some reason she can turn into a total stereotype when she's around a man she's interested in.

"What, even square and rectangular ones?" I ask. "You are a true connoisseur, my friend."

He laughs loudly. "Triangles too, oh and octagons. I'm an equal opportunist for breasts."

We finish up eating, and thankfully nobody mentions my chest region for the rest of the meal. Nora glances at her watch and begins rushing around, grabbing her things for work.

"I lost track of time in such good company," she says to Nicholas, slipping on her coat. "I hope you'll visit again."

"I'd love to," he replies, giving her a peck on either cheek. She blushes and slips out the door.

Nicholas strides confidently toward the table and starts helping me clear away the dishes.

"You can go now you know, I've got this," I tell him.

"I'd like to stay for a while, if that's okay with you?"

I shrug my shoulders. "Sure, if you want. But be

warned, I usually go to bed pretty early, so there'll be no late night shenanigans, if that's what you're after," I tease.

Nicholas puts his hand to his heart. "Ah you wound me, beautiful lady. I had been hoping to romance you. Late night shenanigans are not my forte."

I ignore the "beautiful lady" bit and continue with the cleaning up. Once the dishes are washed, dried and put away we switch on the television and sit down on the couch. I slip off the flip flops I'd been wearing and tuck my feet up under my legs. Nicholas' hand slowly drifts over to me and he picks up a lock of my hair, splaying his fingers through it.

"This is some great hair Fred. It's so silky, I'd love to get it in a wig."

I cock an eyebrow at him. "I think you might have a few kinks in your armour there, Viv."

His grin borders on devilish. Yes, devilish. "Lots of kinks, lots of quirks, my sexuality is multi-faceted."

"Right. And wigs are your thing." I say. "Each to their own, I guess."

His smile is confidently secretive.

"Isn't it supposed to be chinks in your armour?" he ponders.

I snicker. "Well, that wouldn't have worked as good as kinks."

He grins. I focus back on the TV, even though I'd much rather study his pretty face. After a minute he pokes me in the side.

"Hey, stop that," I complain, but he keeps on doing it. Each time his touch lingers a little longer than the last. Soon he begins full on tickling me, and I laugh involuntarily. I fight back, finding his ticklish spot in his stomach, and he laughs too. I try not to think about how toned and nice his abs feel. He takes the lead in our tickle war when he climbs on top of me and holds down my wrists with one hand, while tickling my stomach with the other. I squirm beneath him, unable to take the torture.

He stares down at me and abruptly stops the tickling. His hands are still holding mine captive. A heavy tension fills the air and I suddenly realise what a compromising position we've found ourselves in. His expression turns serious. "You're very pretty, Fred," he says, matter of factly. Then he brings his face closer and traces his lips along my ear. "I'd really like to fuck you."

I flinch at his words. "Christ Nicholas!" This is the first time I've spoken his proper name out loud to him. He lets go of my wrists as I shoot up from the couch.

He leans back, sitting up with his legs spread apart, absolutely comfortable and at home. His lips tilt up at one side. "We're both adults here Fred. Are you really that offended by my proposition?"

I unnecessarily focus on straightening out my top. "Um, what...yes, of course. I hardly know you."

"You've been flirting with me all night, darling," he replies gently.

I furrow my brow, momentarily confused. "Have I? Oh my God, you're seriously mistaken. I absolutely have not. I was being friendly, joking around. Do you say you want to...to have sex with every girl who talks to you?"

In the back of my mind I know I've sort of brought all of this on myself, and I guess the way I spoke to him this evening could be mistaken for flirting, but only vaguely.

"No, not all of them," he replies. "But I can tell we'd be very compatible in bed. What's the problem if I'm direct about it?"

I shake my head at him, my mouth hanging open in wonder. I've never met a man like this in my life.

"This coming from the guy who said he wasn't interested in late night shenanigans," I say, trying to make the whole thing back into a joke so that I don't have to deal with my own embarrassment. I may act like a snarky bitch at times, but that's mostly a front for the scared, shy girl who's hiding behind her. Never have I had a man say words like this to me. And really, I'm ashamed, because I wish I had the confidence be the kind of girl who would simply reply, "Okay let's get it on then," before hopping right into the sack.

He gazes at me for a long moment, before looking away and running a hand through his dark hair. "I apologise. I just thought we could keep each other company for a night. We're both lonely, it makes sense."

I look at him and protest, "I'm not lonely." What I really want to do is ask him, *Are you lonely?* I don't understand how he could be. He's handsome and confident and has everything going for him.

"You seemed lonely today, all soaked from the rain with your shopping bags in your hands."

"I was more annoyed than lonely."

His eyes study me. "All right, my mistake. You're not lonely Fred. I better go, I've got my first show tomorrow night to prepare for. You should come along. I already mentioned it to Nora. The club is new, it's called The Glamour Patch, it's not too far from here."

"Oh, sure. Yeah I might come. I'd like to see you perform." I pause and bite my lip. "By the way, you probably should have put the moves on Nora instead of me, she likes you if you hadn't noticed."

His expression is warm. "I noticed. I'm not interested in Nora, Fred, I'm interested in you." And with that bombshell, he leaves the apartment.

Chapter Two
Punk Rock and Cupcakes

The next morning I'm up at the crack of dawn to get my cupcakes made, business as usual. It's Friday and I'm really looking forward to the weekend when I can sleep a little later in the mornings. The first thing I do is put the oven on to pre-heat it. I'm in a Green Day *Dookie* sort of a mood, so I fire up "Longview" on my mp3 player and let the drums and heavy bass wake up my vacant brain and tired, puffy eyes.

Once I've gotten the cake mixture all ready, I set out the baking trays. I put the paper cake holders into the little grooves and then spoon a dollop into each one. I pop them in the oven and go about preparing the toppings. I don't make my cupcakes in the traditional fancy smancy way with an icing bag, instead I just dump on the toppings for a more rough and ready rustic appeal. People seem to like the whole lucky dip nature of it, because you could get one with lots of icing or one with just a small bit.

The smell of cake fills the apartment by the time I get around to making myself a cup of coffee.

I turn off my music and sit down by the television to flick through the stations, keeping the volume down low so as not to wake Nora. If there's one thing I've learned about that girl after having lived with her for three years, it's that you do not mess with her sleeping pattern. People who work at night are quite cranky about getting their shut eye. My mum once worked the graveyard shift in a twenty-four hour supermarket, and I tell you the woman was like a monster if you woke her before her time.

It's just after seven forty-five when I get myself dressed and load the finished cupcakes into their boxes. I keep my bike out in the small storage garage at the back of the apartments. Once the cakes are secured firmly in the back carriage, I hop on and make my way over to The Cake Shop, which is located smack dab in the centre of O'Connell Street.

My favourite thing about early morning cycling is the fresh air. Well, it's as fresh as you're going to get in the city. Out on the road I zoom down Aungier Street, past George's Street, and turn right onto Dame Street. I fly by the morning traffic and people dressed in suits and office wear as they scurry like ants through College Green to their various destinations. My music blasts through my earphones, the sound track to my life at this moment in time being Green Day's "When I Come Around". I take a left turn off College Green onto Westmoreland Street and head over the O'Connell Bridge to O'Connell Street. That's my morning cycle in a nut shell.

Pulling up outside of The Cake Shop, I secure my bike with a chain lock before removing the cupcake boxes and heaving them inside. I have to make two trips to get them all in. There are a good few members of staff about, but I'm not real familiar with a lot of them. The place is full with the breakfast crowd, having their morning coffees and pastries.

I don't have to get here before the place opens at eight, as the manager Patrick (a friend of mine from my Culinary Arts college course) told me that cupcakes are more of a mid-morning/lunch time sort of item. So eight-thirty is my delivery time. Early morning customers go for fancy little French numbers, like croissants, fruit Danishes and brioche. A nugget of bakery wisdom for you there.

Having Patrick as a connection is actually how I got the job here. It's a bit of an unconventional set up, but I abide by all of the health and safety standards, even though I work from home. Anyway, with a Culinary Arts degree I'm well over qualified for the work I do. I just don't possess the nerves of steel it takes to work in a professional kitchen.

"Fred!" Anny shouts energetically in greeting as I step in the door. She's one of the workers I am familiar with and a real nice girl, for the most part. She comes on nights out with me and Nora the odd time. Although, between you and me she might have a bit of a penchant for drinking too much and having thrilling one night stands with men she's never met before.

She's one of those people who are fun to drink with, but you wouldn't really want her as an everyday friend, as she's sort of hyper and will talk your ear off given half the chance. Remembering Nicholas' gig tonight, I decide that she might be interested in coming along.

"You up for going out tonight?" I ask her, as I snap on some plastic gloves and put the cupcakes into their display cases at the front of the shop.

"Great minds think alike, I was just going to ask you the same thing," she exclaims. "What did you have in mind?"

"Our next door neighbour is putting on a show at some club, he asked us to come see it," I tell her, finishing up with the cakes and stacking the empty boxes to bring them back out with me.

"Sounds like a plan," she agrees. "I'll pop 'round your

place at about eight or so. We can have a few drinks first. Wet the old whistles," she elbows me in the side, with a very nudge, nudge, wink, wink tone to her voice.

God. She's the only one who'll be getting up to any nudge, nudge, wink, winking. I never go home with people, and Nora does only very rarely. If you didn't know us well you'd probably think we were wizened old shrews. I like to think of it as being selective, as in selecting *no one*. In some ways I haven't outgrown the age of sixteen, when you're too insecure and nervous to take up the advances of prospective "suitors", as my granny would have called them.

At this, somebody creeps up behind me and pinches me on the bottom. Without even turning around I know who it is.

"Harry, I'd recognise the pinch of those chubby little fingers anywhere. In for your usual breakfast is it? Six cream donuts and an extra-large mocha Frappuccino?"

Harry comes to stand beside me and Anny, hands on hips. He works as a teller in the bank down the street and tends to come in here for his morning coffees. "Nope, sure you've probably eaten them all," he remarks. "I'm on a diet, so I'll just have two custard Danishes and a chocolate croissant to go. Oh and a small Frappuccino."

He's joking, obviously. We like to tease each other about being big fat pigs, though neither one of us is obese. We're more what you would call "cushioned", in the sort of way that shows we enjoy the finer things in life.

"I was just saying to Anny that me and Nora are going out tonight to a gig, you want to come with us?"

Harry places an arm around my shoulder and kisses

me on the cheek. "I wouldn't miss it. I'd resigned myself to a night of dinner for one and a DVD rental. A gig sounds like much more fun."

"It will be," I tell him. "Come to ours at eight for pre-outing drinks. I better be off, my shift at the shop starts at nine."

"Right, see you later then," says Harry.

"Bye," Anny waves as I exit the crowded cake shop.

Cycling back over to George's Street where the charity shop I work in is located, some bastard in a Mercedes honks his horn at me because I block him from pulling out around a corner when he'd had the chance. I go one-handed on the bike and give him the classic middle finger. I can't see his face properly through the glass of the car window, but I like to imagine his expression would have shown him to be appropriately shamed. Sheepish, even. Although it's more likely that he got angrier and made some similar gesture back at me. An Italian style chin flick perhaps.

I situate my bike outside the shop and lock it up. You probably think that I'm one of those women who give their bike a name, like Bertha or Betty. Well I most certainly am not. I find that sort of carry on highly irritating. Not to mention annoyingly self-important. Oh look at me, I'm so wonderful that I have to give every item in my life a human attribute. A girl I went to school with did that with her shoes, each pair had a different name. She called her comfortable flats her Marys and her sex kitten high heels her Tatianas. I told her that her Tatianas sounded like an Eastern European prostitute. She didn't talk to me again after that.

Inside the shop my co-worker Theresa is sorting through some of the new donation bags. Because all of the proceeds go to charity, we get people giving us bags of old clothes and such that they don't want anymore. Oh and by the way, I'm not a volunteer. I do get paid for working here, just a little over minimum wage, which isn't so great, but at least it's a job.

The shop is an outlet for one of the big charities, I won't mention the name. I wouldn't say it in front of Theresa if asked, but my personal opinion is that most large charitable organisations are fronts for evil money making administrators and hot shot CEOs. You'd be astounded by how small a percentage of the money donated actually goes to those starving African babies. I suppose you could call me a sell-out, because even though I know all this I still continue to work for the place. What can I say, I have to pay my rent.

Theresa's been working here for almost a decade. Unlike me, she's innocent enough to believe that her work is contributing towards the greater good. She's in her sixties and has that whole kind of hippy floaty look going on, with her long skirts and grey hair in a plait down her back. She's a lovely woman and we get along, although I think the generational gap means that we misunderstand each other at times.

Like when she asks me about what I did over the weekend and I tell her about my antics with Nora and Harry and how we drank a whole bottle of tequila together, she'd draw the wrong conclusion and think I was trying to tell her I have a drinking problem. She comes from a very upper middle class background and doesn't get the whole casual abuse of alcohol that the "young people" get up to these days.

"So, what treasures have there been bestowed upon us this time, Tessy?" I ask her, shoving my coat behind the counter and going to sit down beside her. I always love looking through the donation bags. However it's a good thing I'm not squeamish, because there can often be some questionable looking stains on the clothing. And sometimes they're quite – fresh.

"Morning Freda. Oh the usual, old clothes, some books, children's toys," Theresa responds. She has a problem with calling me Fred. She doesn't understand why I'd want to go by the name of some middle aged van driver when I could go by a pretty name like Freda. I told her I like to be economical with syllables. Another example of me saying something to her, and she not getting it in the slightest.

I pull out various items and fold them neatly into a pile. "Wow, take a look at this bad boy," I say, showing her an extra-large man's Hawaiian shirt. The bright colours hurt my eyes. "I don't think I've ever actually seen one of these in the flesh before."

Theresa eyes me with a wan smile, her head tilted to the side. "You're a bit of an odd duck, aren't you Freda," she says, her glasses hanging too low on her nose.

"Quack," I reply, deadpan.

We spend the next hour taking inventory, while intermittently serving customers at the register. I work here part time, Wednesday to Friday from nine to one o'clock.

At around twelve forty-five the shop door swings open and in walks Nicholas, wearing aviator sunglasses, a crisp navy shirt and dark designer looking pants. He casually strolls over to the cash register, slipping the glasses up to rest on his messy black hair.

He puts his hands out, gesturing around the shop.

"Look at this place, so vintage, so cute," he says.

"Theresa, I'd like you to meet my new friendly stalker. His name is Vivica," I joke.

Theresa's standing over by the bookshelves, adding some new items to the display. She smiles vaguely and waves hello to Nicholas, although she looks slightly confused. "That's nice," she says and turns back to the books.

"What brings you to this neck of the woods, Viv?" I ask, noticing the attractive beads of sweat on his forehead. The man even makes sweat look good.

"I've been exploring the city," he says. "I remember you saying you worked in a charity shop down the road last night. I took a wild guess and figured it was this one."

"Well, your skills of deduction did you proud. What can I do for you?"

"I was hoping you'd join me for some lunch. There's a Mexican place across the street."

I have to consciously close my mouth, because my jaw's in danger of dropping to the floor. He wants to take me to lunch. Perhaps he's decided I could be his cool gal pal just like I'd hoped. The operative word there being "pal", since I acted like a virgin on her wedding night trying to fend off her randy husband with him yesterday. There'll be no more propositions of that variety for me, I'm guessing.

"Ah, you discovered my one true weakness. I'm incapable of turning down free food." I tell him.

"Who said I was paying? I thought you'd jump at the chance of escorting a fine young damsel such as myself out for a meal."

I snicker, grab my coat and fold it over my arm, since

it's too warm out to wear it. I shout to Theresa that I'm going to head off and that I'll see her next Wednesday. She waves me away, engrossed in neatening up her bookshelves. Nicholas presents me with his arm and we dash across the road to the Mexican restaurant. The waiter greets us at the door and ushers us to a table for two at the back.

"So, are you all nervous for your big Dublin début tonight?" I ask him, while perusing the menu.

He glances over at me. "I get the pre-performance jitters like everyone else, but once I'm on stage they all float away. I become another person, a persona I suppose you could call it."

"I invited my friends Harry and Anny to come along. I hope you don't mind."

He grins, those sparkly blue eyes shining again. "I don't mind at all. The more the merrier, that's what I always say. Except if it's an orgy; you've got to be picky in matters of group sex."

"Oh, I completely agree. You can never be too careful in a gang bang."

"Sometimes you end up with too much gang and not enough bang," says Nicholas.

"I've never had a taste for too much gang. I much prefer the latter," I laugh.

"Ah, we have that in common then," he replies in a low voice, just as the waiter comes to take our order. Nicholas gets the quesadillas. I go for the tacos with guacamole on the side. I love guacamole; I could eat buckets of it and never tire of the stuff.

Today I'm wearing a black sleeveless top with lacy trim. My bra strap is loose. It falls down my arm, and my eyes catch on Nicholas as I'm righting it. He tilts his head to the side and watches the movement of my fingers with rapt attention. Just then the waiter returns with our drinks. I decided to go wild and order a margarita. I know, alcohol at lunch time. Perhaps Theresa's correct in assuming I have a drinking problem.

I take a long gulp of the cool icy liquid, and ask, "Whereabouts in Australia are you from anyway?"

He sputters his water ever so slightly. "Oh no you didn't! You have just made a big offence, Fred, *huge*."

"What? What did I do?" I'm confused now; he gives me a look of mock indignation.

"Think about it," he teases, "think about what you just asked me."

"I asked you where you come from," I state, my brow furrowing in annoyance.

"Yes, but you assumed I'm Australian. That's awful Fred, completely and unforgivably awful." He's having a real good time with this, I can tell.

"You *sound* Australian," I interject. "Although your accent is sort of vague, *sorry* for being presumptuous. So enlighten me, where do you hail from oh wise one?"

He shakes his head, feigning indignation. "New Zealand, you twat. That's like me saying, *so Fred, where in England do you come from?*"

I take another gulp of my drink and wipe my mouth with the back of my hand. "That is *so* not the same, Viv. Irish and English accents are miles apart. Australians and New Zealanders sound the same."

"That's a terribly ignorant statement to make. I'm shocked and disappointed. There is a very distinct difference. If you had a good ear you'd be able to tell."

"Well I'm sorry that I don't go around learning the

vague nuanced differences between accents of countries across the world. What an uncultured oaf I am," I declare.

Nicholas shakes with laughter. "You are a fucking hoot, Fred. I'm officially making you my new best friend. It's quite an honoured and sought after position, I'll have you know. So far I have a grand total of four friends in Dublin. You've currently just snagged yourself the top spot."

"Oh stop, Viv, I'm welling up here," I reply drily.

The waiter comes with our food and I dig in, scooping up big chucks of guacamole with a spoon. It's the best thing to eat on a hot day like this, cool and tangy.

"So then," I begin, after a minute of quiet eating. "Where in *New Zealand* are you from?"

"Give the lady a round of applause," Nicholas mocks. "She got it right. I'm a city boy, Christchurch to be exact."

"No way!" I say, open mouthed, taco in my gob and all.

"Way," Nicholas replies. "Why is that a surprise?"

"Oh I was just thinking of that movie, you know about the lesbians who offed one of their mothers because she was trying to break up their relationship. *Heavenly Creatures.* Peter Jackson directed it. That's set in Christchurch and it's a true story, I love that film."

"Fair enough, bit of a tangent there Fred, but I agree. Winslet was great in it."

"So um, brothers and sisters, have you got any?" I ask.

Nicholas shakes his head. "No, I'm an only child I'm afraid. My mother died when I was six, so it was just me and Dad. He worked in the stock markets, a very serious character. There weren't a lot of laughs in our house."

"Where is he now?"

"Died of a heart attack when I was twenty-one, that was seven years ago. All the years at that stressful job finally did him in."

"That's horrible, I'm sorry," I say genuinely.

He brushes me off with a wave of his hand. "Don't be, he was an awful father. We didn't get along. I moved out the moment I turned eighteen and never looked back. Tell me about your family Fred." He picks up his quesadilla and takes a bite.

I let out a sigh. "God, where do I start? They call me the menopause baby because my mother got pregnant with me when she was in her late forties. I'm the youngest of four siblings; three sisters, one brother. My parents are now in their early seventies and live in the Dublin suburbs where I grew up. My brother Tony is the eldest, he's forty-seven. He's got a wife and three kids. I don't see him much because he lives down in Waterford now. My sisters are all in their late thirties or early forties. You could say I was a bit of an only child myself, since my siblings were all basically grown by the time I came along."

"I bet you were like a fresh start for your parents. They didn't have to go through the empty nest syndrome since they had you to take care of."

"Hmm. They like to annoy me by saying that I ruined their plans to retire early to the south of France and leave their child rearing days behind them. But they love me really, at least that's what my therapist says," I joke.

"They sound like funny people, that must be where you get it from," Nicholas observes.

I raise an eyebrow and smirk. "You actually think I'm funny?"

"You're hilarious. I don't think I've stopped laughing since I met you."

"Most people find me irritating after a while. Wait and see, you'll soon tire of the shit jokes."

His face turns serious and he puts his hand on my wrist. "Hey, you're great Fred. I think you're great. Now drop the pity party," he chides.

"I am not having a pity party. Nora has pity parties. I have pathological self-deprecation. It's an incurable condition, so don't make fun."

He squeezes my wrist once before letting go; the skin there gets all warm for some reason. Despite my ambitions to be the "friend" of a cool customer like Nicholas, I'm not sure if my insecure female heart can take it. I'm doomed to feel butterflies at his touch, like a desperate old maid eager for any human contact she can find, who gets tingles when people brush past her on a crowded street.

Nicholas pays for the food once we're finished, even though I offer to pay for half. He says he owes me since I made him dinner last night. We chat as we walk back to the apartment building, stopping to have a look around the markets at the front of the arcade. When we get home, we part ways and agree to have a drink together after his gig tonight.

Later on while deciding on what to wear, I pick out my dark purple 40's tea dress and a pair of silver ballet flats. I don't go in for high heels, because really, for me it's like putting my feet inside a torture chamber. Nora can wear heels until the cows come home and still be dancing like a good thing at three in the morning, but not me.

Since it's the summer I shave my pins in the shower, in preparation for going bare legged. If heels are torture chambers for the feet, tights (panty hose for those of you on the other side of the pond) are torture chambers for the belly. They always seem to roll down when I bend over and bunch up around my stomach and hips.

Nora pops out to grab us each a bottle of wine (yes I said *each,* when it comes to drink our eyes are bigger than our livers) and gets back just in time for Harry and Anny's arrival. Harry hasn't got a notion how to dress well; he could do with getting a few tips from Nicholas. He's wearing baggy beige cargo pants, red Converse and a too small Family Guy t-shirt under his bright blue blazer.

"So, where are we headed for your neighbour's performance?" he asks, opening himself up a bottle of West Coast Cooler.

"Some new club called The Glamour Patch," I shrug. "And are you serious with that drink? I use that shit as a mixer, it's mild as fuck."

Harry almost chokes on the liquid as he knocks it back. "The Glamour Patch?" he coughs.

"Uh, yeah. Have you heard of it?"

He looks like he's holding back a massive grin. For some reason he plasters on a straight face. "Oh, I most certainly have. You're in for a great night. And mind your own business about what I'm drinking; we all don't intend to end up blind drunk with our knickers around our ankles."

I shove him in the arm and laugh. "You're missing out

then."

He looks me up and down, like a class A bitch, though I know he's only messing. "Mm hmm."

Harry likes to tease me and pretend I'm a slut, and I relish it because it allows me to forget that in reality I'm actually a bit of a prude. Oh I can talk about sex like it's my specialist subject on *Mastermind*, but when it comes down to it I'm not that experienced. I've never had a partner who made my skin boil with need. It's all been rather "meh" to be honest.

I get through about three glasses of wine by the time the taxi arrives to take us to the club. We all huddle in, sufficiently merry and irritating the driver by chanting, "Turn up the radio, would you, I fucking love this song," when something by Rihanna comes on, even though my sober self would turn her nose up at such mainstream music.

He drops us at the club, where lots of people stand outside, chatting, laughing and smoking their cigarettes. It's only when I take note of the clientele that my suspicions begin to pique. There are a *lot* of men, and the few women present mostly have that whole short haired indie look going on favoured by lesbians. Yep, I'm almost certain this is a gay bar. Which begs the question, what kind of "act" exactly does Nicholas put on? We pay the ten Euro entry fee, a bit steep, but I'm hoping the show will be worth it.

I pull Harry aside and hiss, "You devious mare, you knew this was a gay bar, didn't you!"

He almost falls over laughing. "Guilty as charged. I wanted to see the look on your face when you finally copped on. I thought you'd know since PantiBar is only a few doors down. So tell me about this neighbour of yours, I'm much more intrigued by him now, is he a dish?"

I take Harry by the arm and lead him over to the bar. "Oh not only is he a dish, he's a gourmet five course dinner, with champagne." And, I believe, probably bisexual, since he very blatantly came on to me but also works in a gay club. Not that I'm judging or anything. As far as I'm concerned he can have sex with a blind midget if that's what floats his boat.

"Sounds promising," Harry says, motioning the bar tender over and ordering us two Sex on the Beach cocktails. I know I shouldn't be mixing my drinks, but these are like summer in a glass and Harry is paying, so it's an offer I can't refuse.

Nora and Anny have disappeared into the bathrooms, probably to check their make-up. They're still too drunk and oblivious to have noticed that the men in here are far more interested in each other than they ever will be in them. Their only hope of scoring is if they're up for trying out a night of lesbian passion.

I keep gulping back the cocktail and scanning the room. I can't see Nicholas anywhere and I'm just about ready to burst with curiosity as to what his show is going to be like. You might have a hunch. I might have one also, but I'm keeping my lips sealed until I can verify it with my own two eyes. I spot Nora and Anny emerging from the hallway that leads from the bathrooms.

They bump into two guys with snazzy haircuts who immediately start chatting animatedly to them. When I see the blond one gesture to Nora's sparkly stilettos I imagine he's complimenting her on her outfit. Typical. She probably thinks they're chatting her and Anny up.

I'm sickly anticipating the moment when realisation hits her, like a peeping Tom waiting eagerly for a glimpse of underwear through their next door neighbour's bedroom window.

I'm just finished the last drop of my cocktail when *Scissor Sisters'* "I Don't Feel Like Dancing" starts blasting from the speakers with its catchy beats. The thing about this song is that in contrast to the lyrics, when I hear it all I want to do is dance. Perhaps that's the point. Also, I have one of those futile crushes on the front man Jake Shears. He's just got this irresistibly pretty face.

Harry and I give each other "the look" in silent agreement that we're going to take to the floor and dance our little hearts out. He grabs my hand, flips it over his shoulder, cocks his head to the side and drags me away from the bar. We probably look quite...special, with our uncoordinated movements, but I'm having fun, so who cares what I look like.

We continue in this manner for about three songs before we're both out of breath and a pool of sweat slicks itself down my back. As far as I'm concerned, a night out isn't a night out if your dress isn't sticking to you by the end of it.

At the back of the club is the performance area, where there's a big stage with tables and chairs all around it. The place is fairly packed, but we manage to snag a small table right at the front, just as Nora and Anny decide to join us. Anny runs off to get a round of drinks for us from the bar. Nora has a bit of an irritated look on her face. Damn, I must have missed her moment of revelation.

I tip my head to her and laugh. "You look like you

just sucked on a lemon."

She folds her arms over her chest. "Nicholas is gay, isn't he," she says, her voice dripping with dejection.

I shrug, again remembering his proposition from last night. "Not necessarily. The jury's still out. There's hope for a Christmas wedding yet," I tell her.

She narrows her eyes at me and turns to glance around at the stage. A man in his mid-thirties with a slick of bleach blond hair steps out in front of the red velvet curtains that obscure the back of the stage from the front. He has a microphone in his hand. There are several wolf whistles and cat calls as he waves to a few individuals he knows in the audience.

One man shouts something rude up, but I can't make out the words properly over the noise of the crowd. I think it had something to do with "nice arse" and "suck". Who knows. The guy with the mic smirks and with a breathy voice says, "I might take you up on that later, sugar." He's wearing a purple shirt that's almost the same colour as my dress and shiny black trousers.

He spots me sitting just shy of the stage. "Oh honey, look at us all coordinated," he gestures between his shirt and my dress and the audience laughs. I give him a little sweeping bow.

Then he addresses the whole club, all business. "Welcome to The Glamour Patch, this evening we have some great entertainment lined up for you still to come. But now we have someone very special, our headlining act all the way from Christchurch, New Zealand. I'm sure some of you have witnessed this act before, so it needs no introduction really. I'll let the performance speak for itself," he finishes, and with a flourish bounces off the stage and disappears into the crowd.

A slow mischievous beat starts up. The music sounds familiar but I can't quite place it. It's one of those anticipatory song intros, beginning slowly and then slapping you with the big reveal. It's all too appropriate as I can't wait to see Nicholas take the stage.

Anny slams four drinks down onto the table, just returning from the bar. "I didn't miss anything, did I?" she asks, all out of breath.

Nora shushes her and yanks her down into her seat. My eyes return to the stage just as the curtains are drawn back to reveal Nicholas, a microphone in hand, and my God do I have a hard time containing my surprise.

Chapter Three

A Sweet Transvestite

His black hair is gelled back into a style akin to Jamie Lee Curtis when she did the striptease for Arnold Schwarzenegger in *True Lies* in her bra and underpants. His face has full on make-up, ruby red lips, smoky black eye shadow with false lashes and pale foundation. On his feet are patent, black six inch heels.

My eyes travel up his legs to find he's wearing hold up stockings and skin tight black sequins hot pants. Finishing off the outfit is a tiny black waist coat that does little to hide his ripped stomach and muscular tattooed arms. He's also wearing a pair of lacy gloves that go up to his elbows. He's a fucking drag queen!

I had my suspicions, but having them confirmed makes my stomach twist with an edge of discomfort. The discomfort is only due to the shock of seeing my new very handsome male neighbour decked out in women's clothing and a face full of makeup. But then, once I come to terms with the idea, (which doesn't take very long) I feel as though all of my Christmases have come at once.

This is astounding, amazing, so incredibly thrilling. Only today a world travelling cabaret performing drag queen took me out for lunch and named me as his new best friend. The idea plunges my black and white world into a vibrant techni-colour rainbow.

The music is still going, building up the tension. It's only when Nicholas' ice blue eyes land on me do I recognise the song. It's "Sweet Transvestite" from *The Rocky Horror Picture Show*. The guitar bit kicks in. His lips tilt up at the side in a smirk as he strides confidently across the stage. When he's standing all too close to where I'm sitting, he starts to sing.

At this the crowd goes wild, shouting and cheering. I enthusiastically join them. Nicholas struts his stuff in those heels so effortlessly that it puts the best of us women to shame, his hips swinging from side to side as he walks.

He goes over to the other side and sings to the crowd who are cheering him on. He's got a brilliant singing voice, all deep and husky. There's a half sleeve tattoo on his right upper arm and another one on the inside of his left forearm, full of details I can't make out from this distance.

Coming towards the end of the song he makes his way back over to me, stops slap bang in front of my table and goes down on his haunches, his legs spread wide with one arm resting on his bent knee. The pose gives me a good view of the bulge at the front of those tight hot pants. I see he doesn't partake in "tucking" then. My throat goes a little dry. He levels me with his intense stare when he sings the last verse.

The lyrics burn right into me, and I shiver all over when he says the word "tension". Okay, this is messed up. I'm getting all hot and bothered over a man who's more comfortable in makeup and a pair of heels than I am. He leaves me then and goes to the centre of the stage to finish off the number. I'd been so consumed with watching Nicholas' movements that I'm only now noticing the full house band playing behind him. There's a drummer, guitarist, bass player, keyboard player and even a guy with a saxophone.

The song ends. Nicholas fans his face and flutters his

false eyelashes, then he turns to peruse the audience. "What an opener, huh?" he says. I expect him to put on a high pitched female voice, but he just talks the way he normally does. The crowd cheers.

"I suppose I better introduce myself formally. The name's Vivica Blue, they call me Blue after my big blue eyes. *Not* because of my rumoured stint as a blue movie actress. That's all idle gossip." He finishes with a grin.

Somebody whistles enthusiastically. Vivica! He hadn't just plucked that name out of the air when he'd told it to me. He glances at me with a quick wink, and I'm smiling like a fool at the extra bit of attention.

When I look to Nora her face seems a little pale and her lips are drawn in a thin line. I see all of the fantasies she's built up about Nicholas shattering to the ground in just that one expression. I have a very open mind about most things; men dressing as women doesn't bother me. Nora has much more "traditional" values. She's not some crazy religious freak, but let's just say that her idea of a fetish wouldn't go any further than a pair of furry pink toy hand cuffs.

I listen back to what Nicholas is saying. "This place is going to be my new home so I hope you'll all be very welcoming. I'd also like you to make the acquaintance of the new house band. They're called The Wilting Willows. Give them a big round of applause." Noisy clapping ensues.

Nicholas scratches the back of his neck. "So I'm not sure if any of you saw me perform in Edinburgh last year," only one guy shouts to say that he did. Nicholas laughs and makes a face. "Great, one person. As you can see, I'm very popular. Anyway, I performed this next song over there for the first time, and it requires something of a prop," he reaches down as one of the club workers hands him a chair. He carries it to the centre of the stage before putting it down.

He turns and nods to the band, indicating he's ready to start. He reaches just behind the curtain to the side of the stage, pulling out a black bowler hat and placing it slant ways on top of his head. The intro begins and Nicholas says, "This one's from the masterpiece that is *Cabaret*, it's called "Mein Herr". I hope you'll enjoy it."

He lifts one leg and settles it on the seat of the chair, intimating a very feminine seductive pose. As he lifts the mic to his mouth and begins singing the lyrics to the song, I get a flashback to the movie starring Liza Minnelli. God help me but Nicholas has her every movement and gesture down pat.

He sits down on the chair, then crosses one leg over the other and twirls his high heeled foot around several times to the beat of the song. Next his leg goes up into the air as he stands, before going back down to the floor. He thrusts his hips in, out, in, out with his hands resting on the top of the chair.

After he's finished the song he whips off the bowler and pulls a furry Russian style brown hat out from behind the curtain. He also has what looks like a long orange dress coat strewn over one arm.

"I hate to cover up this magnificent body," he jokes. "But the next song I'm going to sing requires an outfit change," he puts the furry hat on his head and slips into the coat, buttoning it up all the way.

I know what the next song is before he's started singing, because the band is doing a fairly good imitation of an intro that normally requires a full orchestra. "Don't Rain On My Parade" by Barbara

Streisand from the movie *Funny Girl*. He really knows how to pull out all the icons. He works his way through the song, completely owning the stage and belting out the lyrics with a power to rival Barbara's original rendition.

Over the course of the next hour I'm treated to music from the likes of Shirley Bassey, Julie Andrews and Judy Garland, to name a few. Nicholas even gets a few members of the audience up onto the stage to sing with him. He tries to persuade me up at one point, but I get embarrassed and determinedly decline.

By the time he's finished singing he's sweated half his make-up off. He sings "Maybe This Time", another number from *Cabaret*, as his closing song and takes three bows before hopping off the stage and into a crowd of adoring fans. Most of them are men. He seems entirely comfortable and at ease with himself as he takes their compliments and chats with them about the show.

My drink has long since dried up, so I leave my friends and make my way over to the bar. I slide my bum onto a stool and ask for a mojito. A few minutes later I hear somebody taking the stool beside mine just as a familiar voice asks, "Well, what did you think?"

I turn my head to the side to find Nicholas sitting there, his waistcoat is unbuttoned and he's swapped his hot pants and high heels for a pair of loose jeans and boots. He's ripped off the false eyelashes so the only make up left on his face is a hint of red lipstick and some smudged black eye liner. I stare at his bare chest for a minute and have to make a conscious effort to drag my eyes away.

"It was brilliant!" I exclaim, mustering as much

enthusiasm as I can. "I was a little gob smacked when you first walked out in that get up, but I was kind of expecting it given the venue."

Nicholas laughs. "I knew you'd like it; I just had a feeling. Although when I waved hello to Nora a minute ago she seemed less than impressed." He makes a sad little frown at me.

I shake my head. "She's just put out because she had you down as her new potential love interest. Little did she know you'd turn out to be gay," I say this last part to see what his response will be. I'm way too curious about his sexual orientation.

He nods for the bar tender to pour him a shot of whiskey and levels me with a funny look. "You think I'm gay? Even after what I said to you last night?"

I sip on my drink. "Well, I was thinking maybe you were pulling my leg or something. Besides, apart from Eddie Izzard, I don't think I've ever heard of a straight drag queen."

He smiles wryly before knocking back his shot. He stares up at the ceiling when he mutters, "Yeah well, you're looking at one."

"You're joking right? You have to be at least bi."

"Nope. I only have eyes for the ladies," he states, all of a sudden he seems slightly pissed off. Oh God, am I acting insensitive and rude? Surely being a straight guy who likes to dress up as a woman would have left a few scars along the way. I hope I haven't touched on any of them.

"Sorry, sometimes I don't think before I open my mouth. That was rude of me."

A soft smile touches his red stained lips. "It's okay, no offence taken. I'd offer to buy you a drink but you seem all set. What is that anyway?" He shifts his stool closer to mine and takes a sniff of my drink. Our arms touch.

"Ah, minty," he says. "Mind if I have a taste?"

I raise an eyebrow as he lifts the glass to his mouth. "Not at all, you've never had a mojito before?"

His smile turns mischievous. "I have, but I wanted to have a taste of yours. Put my lips where your lips have been."

"You're such a pest," I laugh, swiping my drink away from him.

"That's quite a fetching outfit Fred. Can I take a loan of it next week?" he jokes.

"After the way I've been sweating in it tonight you don't want it, trust me. This club is stifling hot."

"Not necessarily. The sweat is an added bonus. I can sniff on it while I have some private man time," he says with an over exaggerated leer.

"Ugh, even I think that's disgusting Viv, and I work in a charity shop. Dealing with "soiled" clothing is a part of my job," I elbow him lightly in the ribs.

He gives me a wary look. "I hope you wash your hands regularly." He pauses. "Just how soiled are we talking? I have to admit, I'm morbidly curious."

"Don't worry, the dirty clothes get laundered before they're put on display. But if you're looking for details, I've seen everything from questionable white stains to yellow ones and all that comes in between."

"What comes in between white stains and yellow?" Nicholas asks with a smirk. "In my experience they both come out of the same...pipe. I'm not aware of any in between in that area."

Oh, he's trying to out shock factor me. Well, he's met his match. "I'm not sure, possibly pre-cum." I knock back a long gulp of my mojito. If I weren't so drunk I wouldn't have had the courage to say what I just did.

Nicholas almost falls off his stool he's laughing so hard. "Fuck, that was a good one Fred."

I lift my glass to him. "I'm available for special occasions and corporate events."

"I'll spread the word," he says and nods hello to someone behind me. I turn around to find that Harry, Nora and Anny have just approached the bar.

"Ah, friends," I say, grabbing Nora around the neck and giving her a rough hug. She pulls away in annoyance.

"You're drunk," she says, looking me up and down.

"That's the point," I reply, gesturing to my drink and turning back to Nicholas.

"You know Nora already; these are my two other friends Harry and Anny."

Harry steps forward and shakes Nicholas' hand. "Great show! I was singing along to every song, you did some of my all-time favourites."

"Well I do aim to please," Nicholas answers graciously.

"Fred," Anny interrupts. "I want to go to Coppers but Nora won't come, help me to convince her will you?"

I throw Anny a cynical glance. "I haven't been to Coppers since I was eighteen, desperate and too young to know better. I'm sorry but I agree with Nora. That club is a glorified cattle market."

"I'm intrigued, what is this place you speak of?" Nicholas asks, leaning close to my shoulder.

"It's this awful club where people go to pick someone up if the rest of their night has been unsuccessful. Like a last chance saloon if you will. God Anny, I thought you were better than lowering yourself to the level of Coppers," I say, digging in the old screw when in fact I know well that Anny will fuck a door knob with enough alcohol in her system. And she doesn't like going home without at least having gotten a good snog and a grope in.

"I want to go for the music," she replies, a blatant lie. "I'm in the mood for some dancing."

"Yeah, that and a dose of chlamydia," Harry puts in. I raise my hand to give him a high five.

"Shut up Harry!" Anny laughs, elbowing him a little too hard. He shoots her a warning stare.

"I think you should show me this place Fred," says Nicholas. "I want the whole Dublin night out experience; the good, the bad and the ugly."

I smirk at him. "You're serious?"

He has another shot in his hand now. I hadn't even noticed him ordering it. Nora's right, I am drunk. "Oh, yes," he replies, finishing it off in one gulp.

The idea of going to Coppers with all of my single friends is depressing, but when I add Nicholas to the equation it almost seems like a fun idea. We could be there in an ironic capacity, making fun of all the desperados.

"All right then. I wouldn't want to be an inhospitable host, since this is my city and you are but a newcomer."

"Oh yeah, she agrees to go when Mr Make-up asks her," Anny slurs, a bottle of beer in her hand.

"Shut your face Miss "I Want to go to Coppers for the Music", before I shut it for you," I say to her jokingly. But I am sort of annoyed at her name for Nicholas. I barely know him, yet I find myself feeling awfully defensive of him. If he's offended by what she's said it doesn't show on his face.

"I'll just go and grab a t-shirt," says Nicholas, gesturing to his open waist coat and bare chest. He returns a few minutes later in a clean grey t-shirt, shoving his wallet into the back pocket of his jeans. He hasn't bothered to wash off the barely there make-up though. It looks good on him, like he's some sort of eye liner wearing rock star. There's a short guy with brown hair beside him. I recognise him as the drummer from the house band, The Wilting Willows. He's got silver eye shadow on. I notice Harry taking an immediate interest.

"This is Sean. You all don't mind if he comes with us?" Nicholas asks.

I put my arm around Sean's small shoulders. "Not at all. You do know that we're going to Coppers right?" I say to him, conspiratorially.

"Yeah. Sure I'll go for the laugh," says Sean in a mild Dublin accent similar to my own.

"You've got the right attitude my friend," I reply as I lead him out of the club and into a taxi. We have to go in groups of three since none of the drivers will allow six people in one car. I find myself sitting in the back seat, wedged between Nicholas and Sean. Nicholas is a little too close for comfort.

"You really don't know the horror you're about to witness," I say to him on the drive.

"Life's all about new experiences," he answers mysteriously. His hand is leaning flat against the seat beside my thigh. His fingers brush my leg ever so slightly, which is something I wholeheartedly try to ignore.

Five minutes later we're on Harcourt Street,

surrounded by guys in jeans, crisp shirts, and stinking of the latest overpriced aftershave. Not to mention a string of girls in skirts too short to be decent and shoes that should be made illegal for being so uncomfortable looking. One girl in a tight blue dress is getting sick out on the road. Her high heel gets stuck in the tram tracks and she struggles to try and pull it free. Her friends drag her back to the path just in time before she gets run over by a car.

Coppers is short for "Copper Face Jacks" and it's in an old Georgian house on a street filled with similar buildings. In my opinion it's a waste to have such a den of iniquity in a historical building like this one, but what can you do. We go through entrance and pay the fee. Well, Nicholas insists on paying for everyone, although Harry, Anny and Nora are already inside since their taxi had been ahead of ours.

A heavy beat blasts my ears, with some guy singing about being sexy and knowing it. Yeah, sure. The activity of going around *telling* people you're sexy sort of negates the whole point of *being* sexy. It's supposed to be something other people notice about you. (When your brain starts having these pointless arguments about meaningless pop songs, that's when you can safely say that alcohol has set up shop in your system for the night.)

Nicholas pulls me close and shouts into my ear over the music, "I thought you were exaggerating when you described this place, now I see you were actually putting it mildly."

I laugh as my eyes drift over the masses of young men and women, scrambling for each other on the dance floor. Desperately seeking a small piece of affection, affection that's all about gratification and nothing about love. Not that I know much about the latter. I've never been in love. It's sad but it's true. I think the most I've ever been in has been low grade lust. Pathetic. The next song to come on is some new one by Lady Gaga.

"Come on," says Nicholas. "Dance with me, I love me some Gaga."

I want to ask him if he's sure he isn't gay after that statement, but I let it slide. He pulls me into the sweaty masses, and I try to lose myself in the beat. The only way I can do dancing is jokey or not at all. I cannot do serious. I cannot do sexy. I can do a good robot though, and that's what I end up doing. Yes, I do the bloody robot right there in front of the most beautiful man I've ever met. He laughs at me, at least that's something, even if it's just polite laughter.

Nicholas is determined to get me to dance with him properly. Like any *normal* adult woman would be able to. He grabs my hips and turns me around, slipping his arms tight around my waist so that his front is pressed all along my back. He sways me back and forth with him, but my body has gone rigid and despite the alcohol in my system I'm as self-conscious as I can possibly get.

His breath is like hot, humid air on my skin when he breathes, "Relax," into my ear. "Follow my lead," he continues.

I try to follow his lead, God help me I try. I think I just about get used to the rhythm. One of his hands leaves my waist to travel to my neck where he lifts my curly hair up, allowing his fingers to get lost in its thickness.

"You still dreaming about that wig, Viv?" I shout to him over the music.

His hand returns to my waist and he seems to hold me even tighter then. "No, I'm dreaming about all of this golden brown honey draped over my pillow."

For the life of me I cannot think up a response to that. No witty retorts spring to mind like they usually do. All I can think is that I'd love that too, to lie in his bed with him, the sheets all messed up, as though we were lovers in some arty French film.

I can feel Nicholas' laughter against the back of my neck. "What, nothing to say to that Fred?" he asks huskily.

"You got me. I'm completely speechless."

His mouth is close to my ear again, and it's hard to think straight when he does that. "I'd like to see you speechless, breathless, panting..."

Embarrassed to the core by his words, I pull away from him and mouth "bathroom" before running off. In this moment I desperately need some distance between us. My inhibitions are so ingrained in me that even the most lethal brew of Poitín couldn't strip them away. Poitín (if you've never heard of it) is an Irish variety of moonshine that can contain as much as 95% alcohol. Needless to say, my insecurities are crippling; I'm just really good at hiding them. In the toilets I find Nora leaning against a cubicle door with her arms folded.

I nod to the cubicle. "Who's in there?"

Nora sighs. "Anny. She's getting sick. Too many vodkas and red bull."

"Ugh," I bang on the door when I hear her heave into the bowl. "Anny you deserve to be sick after drinking that filth." A glass is never the same again after it has played host to Red Bull. You can forever get a slight hint of the taste.

She manages a whispered, "Piss off Fred," and for a second I feel bad for her.

I go over to the sink and splash some water on my face. "So, why are you being such an ice queen with Nicholas all of a sudden?" I ask Nora.

Another sigh, but no answer.

"If you sigh one more time I'm going to drag you into one of these cubicles and dunk your head in the toilet," I warn her.

"I just don't get it," she finally replies, turning to check her reflection in the mirror.

"What's to get? He's a straight guy with a penchant for dressing up as a woman. He's also got one hell of a singing voice."

"He's straight?" Nora asks, eyebrows almost disappearing into her hair line.

"Yeah, he told me earlier that he was. Think Eddie Izzard and replace the comedy with singing."

"Oh." She pauses, a thoughtful look on her face. "I still don't get the whole drag queen bit. He's so bloody handsome, why can't he just be normal?"

I point a finger at her. "You have to get over your hang ups Nora. Human beings don't always fit into a perfect box the way you want them to."

Her eyes narrow. "You're just loving this, aren't you? People have to be weird for you to want to be their friend."

"Very true, and you're my best friend, which makes you the biggest weirdo of them all."

Just as I'm finished washing up I cup both my hands under the running tap and then splash the water right into Nora's face, before running out of the bathroom. She screams as the door slams behind me. A devious thrill runs through me. She can be so uptight. I love pissing her off sometimes, for entertainment purposes if nothing else.

Needing some air, I go out to the smoking area where I'm greeted by a calming cloud of nicotine. I've got a bit of a habit for socially smoking. I'm about to ask some girl if she's got a spare cigarette when I spot Nicholas, Sean and Harry all puffing away like chimneys over in the corner.

I march up to them and pluck Harry's smoke from his fingers, before shoving it between my own lips. "Give me that cancer stick," I say. "I'm saving you from getting the black lung Harry, be thankful."

"I couldn't help myself, I haven't had one in months," Harry admits guiltily.

"You're welcome. I'll just finish this off for you, Good Samaritan that I am."

Harry rolls his eyes and smirks at Sean, who grins back. Oh I'm definitely sensing a vibe of attraction between these two.

"And you Vivica," I gesture at Nicholas, who looks cooler than a block of ice with a smoke dangling from his lips. "I expected better of you, leading these two young boys astray."

Nicholas pulls the smoke from his mouth, letting out a long draw. "I like to corrupt," he replies, hidden meaning in his guarded expression. Is he pissed that I ran off on him when we'd been on the dance floor?

I don't say anything, I just continue enjoying the cigarette I appropriated from Harry. I can feel Nicholas' eyes on me. When I look at him again he's not staring at me anymore. His eyes are trained on the dirty floor, a sort of sad expression on his face. A thin girl with long, silky black hair and perfect skin sidles up to our group, her sights quite clearly set on Nicholas. As you might expect, I take an instant disliking to her.

"Hey, could I get a light from you?" she asks him.

He lifts his eyes from the floor to look at her, and then pulls his lighter from his jeans pocket. "Sure you can," he smiles. She leans forward, giving him a good look at her cleavage. Harry and Sean are deep in conversation, but my attention is riveted on the exchange between Nicholas and this girl.

"I love your accent," she says, with drunk unfocused eyes. "Where are you from?"

His smile transforms into a smirk, and his mischievous baby blues glance at me for a brief second. "Australia, have you ever been?" he lies.

"No, but I hear it's lovely," she answers, sucking in a drag of her smoke.

Nicholas touches her lightly on the elbow. "Excuse me for a moment, I'll be right back."

He walks over to me and whispers, "Do you think she's trying to make me her last chance saloon for the night?"

"I would say that's a definite yes," I answer him.

"Shall we have a little fun with her?" he continues.

"You really are the corrupting type," I say to him with a holier than thou expression.

"In or out Fred," he states.

"Oh, go on then, you've twisted my arm," I grin.

"Great," he takes my hand and guides me over to the black haired girl, who gives me a blatant catty look and turns back to Nicholas.

"So, I never quite caught your name, I'm Nicholas and this is my Irish cousin Freda. I'm here visiting her."

The girl loses the cat eyes with the false information that I'm Nicholas' relative and therefore not a threat. "I'm Niamh, it's nice to meet you Nicholas – and Freda."

"Likewise," says Nicholas, before raising my hand to his mouth and giving my knuckles a lingering kiss. Niamh looks confused for a minute, but then she seems to shake it off.

"Oh my God, so cool, are you wearing eye liner?" she asks, stepping up close to run her finger just below Nicholas' eye.

"I am. Freda enjoys putting make-up on me. I'm like her little toy doll."

Niamh's nose crinkles as she glances at me. "You put this on him? Why?"

Not so "cool" anymore then. I try to sound as mysterious as possible. "Oh, it's just a little game we like to play. I do his make-up for him and he does mine. It's a cousin thing."

"And then we do some French kissing," Nicholas adds.

"Eh, what?" says Niamh, stubbing her smoke out on the nearest ash tray.

"Kissing cousins, have you never heard of it?" Nicholas asks her.

"No I've heard of it, you two are a pair of *freaks*," she says, taking a step back.

"We were wondering if you'd like to join us for a *ménage à trois*?" Nicholas steps forward.

"Fuck no, get away from me," she says cuttingly and runs off.

I burst out laughing. "She completely fell for that. You're an evil genius," I tell him.

"One of my many talents," he brushes fake dust off his shoulder.

"Why did you do that though? She was hot and definitely up for a night of debauchery," I eye him curiously.

"I don't know, she smelled like stripper perfume. It put me off," he replies.

"What on earth is stripper perfume?"

"You know, the stuff you get in the Euro shop for 2.99. Completely awful."

I feel a little self-conscious at the knowledge that he notices how girls smell. Has he caught a whiff of my sweaty self yet tonight? God I hope not.

"It does sound awful. When I was a kid I had friend who would put rose petals in jars with water and sugar to make perfume. She'd get this rash on her neck because of it."

Nicholas laughs and shakes his head. "The ideas we come up with when we're young."

"Don't even talk to me. One Halloween I was obsessed with John Travolta in *Grease* and made my mum make me a T Bird's jacket so I could dress up as him. She ended up getting a black bag, cutting two holes for arms and writing "T Birds" on the back with Tipp-Ex. Then she found me an old black wig that one of my uncles used to impersonate Elvis at a fancy dress party. I thought I looked the shit."

Nicholas is holding onto his stomach he's laughing so much. "Oh God, you're killing me. Please tell me you have pictures."

I grin. "I think Mum might have some in a family

album somewhere."

"I must see this evidence, it will make my life complete. You're the perfect friend for me Fred, you the drag king and me the drag queen."

"Hey, I haven't been in drag since I was ten. It was a gruelling business. I decided to go for early retirement."

When my eyes flick to the side I catch sight of Harry and Sean's "deep conversation" which has now transformed into furious snogging against the wall. I give a wolf whistle and go over to pat Harry on the shoulder.

"Be sure to use protection," I whisper loudly. He raises one hand to give me the finger, not once breaking the kiss.

I step back and stand beside Nicholas, who's making a show of watching the two and stroking his chin ponderously. He makes his fingers into a square in front of him, creating a frame around Harry and Sean.

"I think I'll call this one "Love in the Modern Environment", hand me my camera would you darling?" he puts on a false Spanish photographer's voice.

"Right away, Rodrigo," I chirp.

Nicholas peers over my shoulder. "Oh. Somebody looks pissed at you," he whispers, just before Nora stomps up to me, dragging a recovering Anny along with her.

"Did you have to pull that stunt with the water?" she asks. "Look at my top, it's soaked through."

"Sorry, I was caught up in the moment," I explain, unable to hold in the touch of sarcasm.

In the same way I don't think before I speak, sometimes I don't think before I do stupid things. It was only water, but as far as Nora's concerned her outfit is ruined for the night.

"Well whatever, I'm sick of this place and Anny's just plain sick, so I'm going to stick her in a taxi and then head home."

"Yeah I think I'm ready for bed myself," I reply with a big noisy yawn.

Nicholas grins at me. "Can I join you?"

"To go back to the apartments yes, in bed no," I say, pointing a firm finger at him. I keep getting these little shocks of nerves every time he says something flirtatious, and my immediate reaction is to shoot him down for fear of him finding out that I fancy the pants off him.

He smirks. "That's what I meant," he looks at Nora and jokes, "she thinks a lot of herself, doesn't she."

Nora suddenly seems like a deer caught in the headlights with Nicholas talking to her. "Um, yeah." She pauses and a cruel gleam comes into her eyes. "Unfortunately, she's often misguided."

And with that slam dunk she turns around and pulls Anny along with her. She's really snippy with me tonight. She's also taking a lot of her disappointment that Nicholas isn't the dream guy she thought he was out on me. I tap Harry on the shoulder and tell him that we're leaving. He waves me away without a care.

"Well, that was a little bitchy," says Nicholas, as we trail a couple of feet behind Nora and Anny.

"Nora can be harsh at times. I like to look at it as her being brutally honest."

"Or brutally jealous," he remarks.

I snicker. "Oh yeah, she's got so much to be jealous of. I splashed a load of water on her in the bathroom, so she's still annoyed about it. She's mad anal about her appearance."

"Did you just suggest anal?" he asks, pretending he didn't hear all of what I said, the sly dog. "That's very forward of you Freddie, but I'll have to decline. I haven't got the conviction for such an endeavour tonight I'm afraid."

"Hardy har har," I roll my eyes at him.

When we finally get outside Nora's putting Anny into a taxi. Nicholas and I wait on her by the side of the road. There's no point in the three of us getting a cab back to our block since it's only a five minute walk away. Anny's taxi drives off and Nora approaches us. I'm not in the humour for her bad mood so I simply say, "Come on, let's get home."

Our walk to the apartment is quiet, with only one or two jokey remarks from me and Nicholas. Nora is as silent as the dead. The only saving grace is that it's not a long walk. Nora goes on ahead of us when we get to the building and hurries straight to our apartment. I stand outside Nicholas' door with him to say goodnight.

"Well, thanks for a colourful evening. I can't wait to see you perform at the club again. I'm thinking I might make the place my new regular haunt. There's certainly something to be said about surrounding yourself with a bunch of men who are more interested in what dress you're wearing rather than what's underneath it." I'm rambling, I don't know why. It's possibly due to the intense look on Nicholas' face right now.

"There was at least one man who wanted to see what's underneath the dress," he comments drily.

"Oh you silver tongued devil!" I mock, in an effort to push away the tension that seems to be filling the air between us.

Nicholas slots his key in the door. "Do you want to come inside and see my place?"

He opens the door just slightly, and I really should be running straight to my own apartment, but my eyes land on something red and feathery looking, and like a child who's just caught sight of the ice cream van, I'm compelled to go after it.

"I'd love to," I say, stepping right inside. The feathery red thing turns out to be a cushion made entirely of the softest feathers I have ever laid my hands on. But the most fascinating thing is what the cushion is sitting on, a lime green velvet *chaise longue*. I feel like I've just stepped inside a boudoir that's decorated in a mix of outlandish psychedelic colours and old world vintage. The lounge area is a lot bigger than mine and Nora's place, I notice.

I sit down on the lime green creation and plop the feathery cushion on my lap so that I can pet it. My tipsy self enjoys soothing textures.

"I've never been in here before. None of our previous neighbours were the friendly type. It's fucking huge. I have to admit Viv, I think I've got apartment envy."

He smiles and pops the kettle on. Tea seems like a good idea. I need something to clear my foggy head. "Feel free to visit any time," he says.

The place might be bigger than ours, but it's also a whole lot messier. There are unpacked boxes all over. Most of them appear to have women's clothing in them. Show costumes I'm thinking. Over by one of the windows are three wigs sitting on those plastic mannequin heads. Eyeing the ginger one I joke, "I can't wait to see you as a red head Viv, why didn't you go for a wig tonight?"

He sighs as he pours boiling water into tea cups. He never asked me if I wanted tea, but I don't mind him assuming because I'm quite thirsty.

There's a strange, almost calculating look in his eyes. Then his face goes blank and it takes him another few moments to answer me. "I had to go bare bones because I haven't yet hired a dresser." He brings the cups over to the coffee table where I'm sitting and drops down beside me. "I'll let you in on a little secret, I'm awful at choosing costumes and doing my own make-up. I've always had an assistant to do it for me."

"Wow, there must be money to be made in the drag queening business if you can afford an assistant."

He raises an eyebrow. "Not really. I inherited a lot when my father passed away. It's caused me to accumulate expensive tastes. I should probably be more frugal."

"Is that what you're doing by living here? Any sane person with cash to splash would run a mile from this dump."

He glances around. "It's not so bad. I think it's got character. I've always tended to select my living spaces in older buildings, places that feel lived in are oddly reassuring to me."

"If by *lived in* you mean an aged whore with cracked skin and some sort of downstairs infection she can't get rid of, then you're right, this building has *plenty* of character."

Nicholas grins. "You have a wonderful way with words Fred, disgusting but wonderful."

"Why thank you. So tell me more about this assistant predicament. I thought you looked amazing tonight.

You can dress and do your make-up fine, what's the problem?"

"I've just gotten used to having somebody else do it over the years. I suppose you could call it a combination of habit and laziness. I'm also terribly disorganised, if you hadn't noticed." He gestures around his apartment.

"Ah, now we're getting to the crux of the matter. I think I should stage an intervention. No longer will Vivica Blue require the services of an assistant/dresser/make-up artist, from here on out she will do it all herself," I laugh. "You need to learn to get organised if you want to survive in the cut throat business of gay night club performance. Harry tells me the gays can't abide by clutter."

He doesn't say anything, but he seems to be regarding me strangely.

"What?" I ask.

He sips on his tea. "You're something of a job collector," he replies ponderously. "How would you feel about a third?"

I look at him, incredulous. "Are you asking me to be your assistant?"

"I might be," he smirks. "How are you with make-up?"

I shrug. "I get by."

"And what about fashion?" he goes on, eyes roaming over my dress. "You seem to have good taste. I like the whole 40's vintage thing you've got going on tonight. Yes, there's definitely potential. How about a two week trial period?"

"You forget that I work in the mornings. I'm not sure I could survive one job at night and another where I have to get up at the crack of dawn."

"Yes but that's weekdays. My gigs are Thursday through Saturday."

"I'd still have the late night on Thursday and the early morning on Friday." I disagree.

"I'll pay you double time on Thursdays to make up for it." He's not backing down.

Thinking of the extra money I could earn just for helping to select some outfits and putting on a few false eyelashes is extremely tempting. I could certainly do with the cash.

"Why are you so determined for me to agree?"

"I don't know. There's something about you that comforts me. Perhaps the fact that every second word out of your mouth begins with an F."

"As if you're any better," I laugh.

He winks. "Exactly, that's how I know we'll get along. Besides, you *are* my new best friend aren't you?"

"I am. But don't tell Nora, she'll only get jealous." I take a sip of tea, the warm liquid sobers me a little, although I wish it wouldn't. Being in the presence of Nicholas in all his sexy glory is easier when I'm tipsy.

He sits there silently, nursing his own cup, not saying a word. His searing eyes haven't left me. For some reason I don't feel like being the one to break the silence.

After a while Nicholas asks softly, "So will you agree? I promise you'll have a ball. The job is a piece of piss."

Staring at all of the unpacked boxes scattered around the room, I'm not so sure about that. I'm hoping he turns out to be one those people who just live in organised chaos.

I let out a heavy sigh and nod, unable to refuse. The idea of being around Nicholas on a regular basis makes my heart beat quicker.

His eyes grow even hotter at my acceptance. "That's brilliant, you can start tomorrow."

"I hope I don't fuck it up on you. I won't have a clue what I'm doing."

"Just be your fabulous self and you won't," he says sincerely, coming over to shake my hand. "Welcome to the wonderful world of Vivica Blue," he goes on, smiling down at me. This hand shake is a threshold moment. With this strangely beautiful man in my life, I have a feeling it will never be the same again.

Chapter Four
Ollo the Ferret

I wake up the next morning at ten-thirty, feeling wonderfully refreshed with my full eight hours of sleep, in spite of the alcohol I drank last night. Unfortunately, the sensation is misleading, because when I sit up the dizziness hits me. I go into the kitchen and get myself a pint glass of cold water. Nora won't be up until around one, because she has to work for the next three nights in a row and will be getting every bit of shut eye she can grab during the day.

It's sunny out again and I want to take advantage of that, so I grab a quick shower, pop on a comfy blue cotton sun dress and some flip flops and head out for a white mocha from Starbucks. The nearest one is on Dame Street, which is a short walk, but I'll go the distance for such creamy goodness.

As I pass by Nicholas' door I stop a moment and consider asking him if he'd like to join me. I argue with myself back and forth in my head before I finally take the plunge and knock.

There's silence for a minute, but then I hear movement. It sounds like he's getting out of bed. Oh no, I hope I didn't wake him. A floor board creaks just before the door opens and Nicholas peeks his head out, squinting his tired eyes at me. He appears to be topless, but he could very well have no clothes on at all since he's hiding his bottom half behind the door.

I've never understood the appeal of sleeping in the nude, but slim people seem to be mad about it. Us heavier types tend to avoid doing anything with our full bodies on show, even if we're the only ones there to witness it.

He seems momentarily disgruntled, but when he sees it's me his whole face lights up. Let me tell you, having a man like this look so pleased to see you first thing in the morning is a nice little boost to the ego.

"Fred, what a pleasant surprise," he greets me. "What time is it?"

"Around half past eleven. I was wondering if you'd like to join me for some mid-morning caffeine to get the old motors running."

"That sounds like a great idea. Give me a minute to make myself decent," he replies.

"I knew it! You're in the nip behind there aren't you."

He grins. "Bare as the day I was born darling, now don't go getting all riled up at the visual. I'll be right back."

He closes the door over a little and disappears. I stand in the hallway waiting for him. Five minutes later he returns, pulling a black t-shirt on over his damp hair. I shamelessly ogle his abs before quickly looking away in case he catches me.

"That has to have been the quickest shower in all of history. I think I was only in for about a minute and a half."

He locks the door to his apartment and we continue out of the building. "You should inform the Guinness book of world records," I tell him.

"Oh I have every intention," he replies with a smirk.

When we get out onto the street Nicholas links his arm through mine, in a friendly sort of way. We saunter down George's Street, dodging the crowds of weekend shoppers who are out in their droves. Just before the

Starbucks on Dame Street is the Central Bank, which is always coated in a sea of black clothes, studded belts, and brightly coloured hair dye on Saturdays.

It's a prime hang out spot for the Goths and Emos, not to mention the hipsters. I'll let you in on a little secret, I used to wish I could fit in with this crowd when I was a teenager. Whenever I go by I always get a little pang of nostalgia. Most of them are in their mid to late teens, but you can always spot the odd person in their twenties who just refuses to grow up. I'm looking directly at one of those people right now, and I know him well.

Jonny O'Connor was in my class in secondary school. I always used to think of him as being the only punk in the village. He'd dress all in black and have these massive gelled spikes sticking out of his head. I admired his bravery, because in the town where I grew up the most acceptable items of clothing were Nike tracksuits and gold sovereign rings. He was something of a hero of mine back then, but he never really lived up to his potential, since he can be spotted outside the Central Bank every Saturday without fail. I also think he might be unemployed. Not because of the recession though, just due to laziness.

He's standing in the middle of a group of seventeen or eighteen year old girls, just shooting the breeze. They probably think he's a legend. I'd say he buys alcohol for all the under-age kids and then joins them on a bender.

I momentarily consider stopping to say hello, but then I think it might be better to keep my head down. If you think I can come across as brash then you haven't met Jonny. He's certainly got a mouth on him.

We were never really friends at school, since I was a bit of a loner. He was a loner too, but a loner who was always in the spotlight for acting out. One time he went mental at a teacher because she was reprimanding him for not having his homework done. He picked up his chair and threw it at the blackboard. He almost got himself expelled for that.

My plan for keeping my head down doesn't go so well. Jonny's booming voice echoes at me, "Freda Wilson's a cunt!" When I turn around I see him pissing himself laughing. The girls he's with glance at me curiously.

Nicholas grins at me and asks, "A friend of yours?"

"Not even close," I reply, taking a few steps over to Jonny and his harem. Jonny's got the tail end of a joint stuck between his pursed lips. "Now what way is that to speak to someone?" I say as I approach him. Nicholas is just behind me.

"You've got one haven't you," says Jonny crudely, his eyes all glazed over. I've stopped to chat with him a few times over the years when I've passed by here, and he strikes me as one of those people who started smoking marijuana way too young and now their brain doesn't work as fast as it should. It'll take him longer than average to answer a question, for example.

"Didn't you know? I was born with a bit of a downstairs mix up," I joke, but my voice is a little terse. People like Jonny piss me off, because he's pissing his life away. He frowns at what I've said. It takes him a minute to process the joke, then a sly grin forms on his face.

"I always wondered why you never got with anyone at school, thought it was just because you were fat."

Okay, so I know I've got a bit of meat on my bones, but it hurts when people point it out. My last boyfriend (the stalker one) told me I had the kind of body every man dreams about, and that real men aren't interested in stick insects. They want boobs, bums and hips. It was one of the nicer things he said to me. My cheeks are flaming red with embarrassment due to the fact that Nicholas is standing right beside me and has witnessed Jonny's remark. The teenage girls giggle.

I give them a massive smile and point at Jonny. "You do know he's forty, right?"

One girl instantly pales and asks, "What?"

"Yep, he goes around telling everyone he's only twenty-five so that he can get off with younger girls." I lean closer and whisper, "He's a bit of a paedo."

"Oh my God, gross," says another member of the group, before dragging her friends away.

When I look at Nicholas I notice that he's frowning at Jonny, his blue eyes have narrowed to slits.

"You really are a cunt Freda, now they'll go around telling everyone what you said. It's not even true." Jonny gripes.

"You should have thought about that before you called me fat. Besides, can't you find women your own age to hang around with? Those girls can't be any older than seventeen. You should steer clear, you don't want to go getting a name for yourself."

He takes a drag out of his joint and then throws it to the ground. "I couldn't give two shits Fred," he eyes Nicholas. "Who's this?"

Nicholas suddenly wraps his arm around my waist and announces, "I'm Fred's boyfriend, and I don't appreciate you speaking to her like that."

Oh my goodness. My heart is going ninety. Fred's boyfriend? He's clearly trying to help me save face in front of Jonny.

Jonny lets out a big crooning, "Ooooh, so sorry to offend. I shan't speak to your precious girlfriend like that then." He looks back at me, shaking his head. "See ya Freda. Tell that Nora friend of yours I said hello. She's hot."

And with that he hops over to a group of guys, grabbing one of them around the neck to get him in a head lock. Some people never grow up.

I turn back to Nicholas. "You didn't have to say that, you know. Jonny's an idiot, always has been. I don't care what he thinks of me."

"How do you know him anyway?" Nicholas asks, ignoring what I've said.

"We went to school together. He was the resident trouble maker."

We start walking again and go in through the front door of the Starbucks. Nicholas holds it open for me and I duck under his arm to get by. My chest brushes off his and a small smile makes his blue eyes crinkle.

"I thought he might have been an ex of yours," says Nicholas.

I give him a look of mock outrage. "I might not have the highest of standards, but the ones I do have certainly surpass Jonny O'Connor. You saw him preying on those teenage girls, he's a total creep."

I order my white mocha and Nicholas asks for a latte. The girl goes to make our coffees and a silence ensues. For some reason I can't think of anything to say and Nicholas is standing all too close, his arm braced against the glass display cabinets. I can smell his shower gel and it makes me want to run my hand over the bit of dark stubble growing on his jaw.

"So you're not seeing anyone then," he says, breaking the silence. I hadn't realised he was still pondering my relationship status.

"Um, no. My last boyfriend was three and a half years ago," I reply, and then regret having been so honest. I'm kind of embarrassed about my lack of a love life. Nicholas strikes me as the kind of person who, when the urge comes upon him, simply goes to a bar, picks up a woman and takes her home to have his wicked way with her.

He lets out a long whistle. "That's some dry spell Fred. I'd be worried you might have grown back your virginity."

"I'm just picky," I reply defensively. "And I wish it was possible to grow back your virginity. The first time I had sex can be summed up in two words beginning with A: awkward and awful."

"Yep, first times are a bastard," he says. "Probably because we haven't a clue what we're supposed to be doing. We're all fingers and thumbs."

The girl puts our coffees down on the counter and Nicholas insists on paying. "Fingers and thumbs eh? Sounds...dirty." I reply.

The girl comes back to give Nicholas his change and looks at me funnily, having heard what I said. I give her a wide grin. She can do what she will with that.

"It's filthy," Nicholas goes on. "I can't wait to show you what I can achieve with my fingers."

I almost choke on the creamy white mocha as I take a gulp. My face must look like a strawberry right about now.

He pats me on the back, laughing. "Easy there, Fred. I don't want to have to give you the Heimlich manoeuvre.

Oh wait a minute, I kind of do. It might give me the chance to cop a feel."

I regain my composure and throw back, "You're fucking obsessed Viv. If you're that keen on them then by all means go ahead and have a squeeze. Get it out of your system."

I'm trying to be breezy. *Breezy, breezy, breezy.* When really if he did touch me I'd melt into a jittery mess of flesh and bones.

His eyes sparkle with delight. "Can I hold you to that? I want to do it at a time when I can give them my full attention. Some place private." His grin is a mixture of anticipation and mischief.

My eyes almost bug out of their sockets, and I try to remember to be breezy. Breezy I say! "Oh, of course. Just give me some warning before you dive in. I can't guarantee I won't throw a punch if you catch me off guard."

He laughs and takes a sip of his latte. "So where to now? I was looking for Stephen's Green the other day on my explorations, but couldn't seem to find it. I ended up at some train station."

"You must be fairly bad with directions, because you can't really miss it. Come on, I'll show you."

I lead him towards Grafton Street, where it's all bustle and noise. The buskers are out in full swing, trying to lure a few sheckles from the tourists.

There's a living statue dressed in yellow from head to foot with his face painted gold. When a little girl throws a Euro into the basket at his feet he springs to life. He gives her a wide smile and a slow bow. She giggles and runs shyly back to her mother who's waiting close by.

"It must be stifling in all that fabric and paint," I

mention to Nicholas as I peer up at the living statue, before dumping my empty coffee cup in a rubbish bin.

"We all paint on a face to show the world," Nicholas replies philosophically. "For some of us, that's quite literal." He takes a brief pause. "When you're passionate about something, you don't mind suffering a little discomfort."

I give him a wry glance. "Have you had to suffer for your passion?"

He nods gently, his eyes roving over the crowds as they push by us. "More than you would think."

There's some sort of sadness tingeing his words. I keep looking at him, wondering what kind of suffering he might have endured.

But then he plasters on a bright smile and jokes, "Those high heels can give you blisters like you wouldn't believe."

I accept his change of tone, because I hardly know him well enough to probe for details. "Tell me about it, that's why I avoid them like the plague."

Nicholas quirks an eyebrow at me. "You never wear heels?"

"Not if I can help it. Me in heels never leads anywhere good, usually it ends up with me injuring myself and others," I laugh.

"It's all about practice and technique, you know. I'll teach you, that way I'll get to see those shapely legs of yours in a pair of stilettos someday."

"Never going to happen. And I take it that by "shapely" you mean legs eight-eight as opposed to eleven."

Nicholas shakes his head at me like I'm a naïve child. "You really do have pathological self-deprecation, don't you," he comments. "When I saw you weren't wearing any tights last night I had to do a good job of keeping from slipping my hands beneath the hem of your dress to see if your skin feels as soft as it looks."

I shove him away from me, flattered but indignant. "You have sex on the brain twenty-four seven Viv. I think you might need therapy."

"Perhaps I do," he grins. "Don't get me wrong I'm no Russell Brand, but I do have quite an avid interest in shagging."

"Enough said, I'll be steering clear of you and the myriad of sexually transmitted diseases you might have contracted over the years."

"No need to worry. The closest I've ever come to an STD was a kidney infection," he replies humorously. "I always put a rain coat on the little fella before heading into a storm."

At his words, I let out a long snort followed by furious giggles. Yes, a snort. God help me. I cover my mouth with both hands and try to gain some composure. "You do realise you just referred to your penis as "the little fella", that's not very reassuring Viv." Although from the view I got of him in those hot pants last night, I don't think he has anything to be worried about.

He shrugs, his eyes all alight at having made me laugh so hard. "Perhaps you *should* be reassured. If I had a small *appendage* I'd be too self-conscious to even broach the topic of size."

"Fair point," I say, just as we reach the top of Grafton Street, where a crowd has gathered to listen to Dave McSavage belt out a few jokes.

If you're not Irish then you've probably never heard of this piece of work. He's a semi-famous comedian who regularly busks around Dublin, singing songs and making fun of the people who pass him by. I never stop to watch him for fear of him making a joke about big boobs and/or well-endowed bottoms.

One time when I was walking by he made the wrong joke about the wrong guy, a guy who stopped walking, turned around, approached McSavage and gave him a punch smack dab on the nose. Needless to say, the man has a pair of balls on him to keep on doing what he does after that episode. At the moment he's accusing a dad with two little kids of being a kidnapper to the swift tune of his acoustic guitar. The dad hurries away looking embarrassed as the crowd laughs uproariously.

Nicholas laughs quietly by my side. He has a lovely low and husky sort of laugh. He folds his arms over his chest, creating a delightful strain in the t-shirt fabric across his pecs. I only realise that I'm staring when I hear him give a short cough to garner my attention.

My eyes flick up to his. "What?" I ask, my voice containing all the guilt of a murderer caught with a bloody knife in her hands.

"Enjoying the view, Fred?" he replies.

"Um, no. Yes. Maybe," I sputter like a complete and total fool.

He leans in close to whisper in my ear, "If you play your cards right, I'll let you cop a feel some time too."

I notice that we've just arrived at the entrance to the park at Stephen's Green, so I quickly take advantage of that fact by announcing, "Well, here we are," while in my head I'm hearing his words repeat over and over, *I'll let you cop a feel, I'll let you cop a feel.*

"So we are," says Nicholas.

There are people everywhere, soaking up the bit of

heat. There's something you should know about Irish people, once there's even a hint of sun in the sky we'll be out in our fucking droves, our pasty pale skin all on show.

The annoying thing is that when you live in the city you'll always come across the less than savoury males going around topless. They walk around with thick gold chains around their necks, showing off their skinny birdlike chests, most likely sporting a prison tattoo somewhere on their skin. It's a gut curdling sight, in my humble opinion. A group of said males are currently lying on a patch of grass close by, numerous open cans of beer spread out around them.

Nicholas spots me eyeing them with thinly veiled disgust. "Now, now Fred, don't go coming in your pants or anything," he jokes.

"I think I just did a little sick in my own mouth," I throw back.

We pick a spot of grass and sit down. A minute later a park attendant walks up to the group of guys and tells them to move along. They put up a bit of an argument at first, but then they finally pick up their beers and leave.

My eyes are grateful for the small mercy. Their tattoos make me remember the ones I saw on Nicholas last night. I never had the chance to get a proper look at them.

I eye the one on his forearm; it says *Dolores* in fancy black lettering and there are little shaded shooting stars all around it.

"Who's Dolores?" I blurt out. Not because I'm eager to know if she's a past girlfriend, but more because my internal filter is on the fritz as per usual.

Nicholas gives me a warm smile. "My mother, all of my tattoos are dedicated to her." He presents his arm for me to study the details. I run my finger over the slight bumps created by the ink beneath his skin.

"What about your other one, the half sleeve?"

He shifts in his place and pulls up his t-shirt to reveal an intricate picture of a woman with long black hair that covers his entire upper arm. She's looking away as though she's shy, her hair covering up most of her face.

"That's my mum. I got it copied from a photograph I have of her," he says, as my eyes take in the beauty and craftsmanship of the tattoo. I don't think I've ever seen one so intricate before. It's really detailed, all black and shaded grey, no colour, as though taken from a black and white picture.

"She was beautiful." I say in awe, taking in his mother's appearance and realising exactly where Nicholas' beauty comes from. "I wish I had the guts to get a tattoo. I think I'm frightened of the permanency."

"Yeah, a lot of people feel that way. They think they won't always like what they get. I suppose it's all about conviction. If you choose something that means a lot to you then you're not going to regret it. I lost Mum when I was so young. It's nice to have a little reminder of her always on me."

I stare into his eyes for a second and get caught, like a fly in a spider's web. There's deep, deep pain in him somewhere, underneath the flirty, confident surface. Is it strange that I suddenly feel like pulling it all out of him so that I can spread it before me and study the cracks? Like the little broken pieces of a lost relic, you try to put them together to create something that you can understand.

I drag my gaze away from him and my eyes land on something brown and furry scuttling around on a blanket where a woman is lying on her stomach reading a book. It's some sort of animal. It takes me a minute to see what it is.

"She has a ferret," I burst out, ruining the serious moment between us. "I'm going over." I hop to my feet and start galloping towards the woman, like an overly enthusiastic child. "Oh my God, I'm so sorry for disturbing you, but I just had to come say hello to your ferret," I declare.

The woman lifts her head from her book and pulls her sunglasses up to rest on her dark brown hair. She's got a real nice tan and when she says, "Oh yes, he's so cute isn't he," I notice she's got an Italian accent.

She also has massive cushion-y lips like Monica Bellucci. She looks like she's in her late thirties and is very well put together. I knew she had to be foreign. No Irish person would have a ferret for a pet, let alone be eccentric enough to take it out to the park with them. This bizarre action immediately makes me want to befriend her.

I kneel down on the grass as the ferret stares up at me with shiny brown eyes. I lift my hand to slowly pet him and he actually lets me. My fingers drift over his silky fur. I'm so consumed with the ferret that I hardly notice that Nicholas has come over to join me and is currently chatting with the Italian woman.

"What's his name?" I ask her excitedly.

"I call him Ollo," she says, turning away from Nicholas for a moment to answer me.

I look back at the ferret and immediately begin crooning his name to him as he scurries between my legs. I laugh with such joy you'd think I was a bit of a simpleton. When he runs off to huddle inside the woman's bag I stand back up to join her and Nicholas, who is currently talking to her about the town she comes from in Italy.

He seems interested in what she has to say and I can't help feeling a pang of jealousy. She's got those really firm, high boobs that look like two ripe peaches. They'd make an attractive couple, I think to myself sadly.

"Thanks for letting me play with Ollo," I say, in an effort to join their conversation.

"It's no problem," says the woman, who Nicholas proceeds to introduce as Dorotea. She's been living in Ireland for a couple of years and works as a hairdresser in Peter Marks. I nod and smile politely, but suddenly I feel like I've got a brick in the pit of my stomach with the realisation that Nicholas might have exchanged phone numbers with her while I was so ridiculously amused by playing with Ollo.

I probably have an awfully dejected expression on my face as I imagine the two of them doing the horizontal tango in Nicholas' bed. I've not yet seen it, but my mind conjures up a vision of black silk sheets, dark wood and debauchery.

"Are you okay, Fred?" Nicholas asks with concern.

"I'm fine. I just remembered that I promised I'd bake my mum a sponge cake for a dinner party she's throwing tomorrow, so I have to be getting back to the apartment." This is a massive lie, but I don't think Nicholas cottons on.

"All right, I'll come with you," he says, and we say goodbye to Dorotea and Ollo. It can't be healthy that I'm so upset over the prospect of him with another woman and I've only known him two days. I'm going to make a fool of myself over this man, I can just feel it.

"You must have visited a lot of countries over the years for your work," I say to Nicholas on our walk home, thinking of how he knew the town where Dorotea comes from.

"I have. The first place I went when I left home was France." He smiles nostalgically. "I wanted to live in Parisian Bohemia, experience the life of a tortured artist. I spent two years there before I moved on. I haven't lived long in any one place since. I've gone from Germany to Spain to Italy to America. I've not seen much of Asia, but I've been almost everywhere in Europe and the US."

"It must be hard, never putting down roots anywhere," I comment.

He looks at me with interest. "That's not what people usually say. Normally when I tell someone about all of the places I've been to they'll say something like *wow, your life must be so exciting doing all that travelling.*"

I shrug. "I suppose it would be exciting for a while, but then you'd just be jaded with it all. That's what I think anyway."

"Oh Freda," he smiles. "You've hit the nail on the head. I was so completely jaded, almost irreparably so. But then my friend offered me the permanent job here and I thought, why not go and live in Ireland, it is after all, supposed to be the friendliest country in the world."

I laugh and sarcastically reply, "*Supposed* being the operative word."

He glances at me sideways. "You don't think your people are friendly? I've had nothing but smiles and welcomes since I arrived here."

I reach over and pinch him on the cheek. "That's just 'cos you've got such a pretty face, Viv. I doubt you've ever gone anywhere and not received an enthusiastic welcome."

He turns away with a sheepish grin and a slight blush. Oh my God, is he bashful? It's so out of place on him, and therefore completely adorable.

I decide to change the subject and ask him what Paris is like, since I've never been, and for the rest of the walk he paints me a picture of the city with words.

Chapter Five
Be Italian

I leave Nicholas at his apartment and he tells me to call in at around eight tonight to head over to The Glamour Patch for his gig. I'm incredibly nervous about my first stint as his assistant. It still seems rather surreal when I think about it.

I go inside my own place to find Nora sitting on the couch, furiously typing on her laptop. I throw my handbag on the kitchen counter, before slumping down beside her. She's on Facebook, wouldn't you know, gossiping with some girl she was friends with at school. Nora and I went to different secondary schools. She attended a private all-girls school, while I went to my local mixed public school. I've met a few of her old friends, and by God are they the bitchiest girls I have ever come across.

I think there's something that happens to girls when they're all cooped up in a classroom with no males to keep them occupied year after year. Instead of vying for the affections of the absent boys, they resort to separating off into groups and making up rumours about one another. All sorts of back biting and viciousness takes place.

I mentioned earlier that I don't have an online presence, so I'm not on Facebook like Nora is. To be honest, the whole process of putting your entire life out there for other people to have a nose at gives me a sick feeling in my stomach. This lesson was learned the hard way. My stalker ex-boyfriend used to go on my MySpace page (yeah, remember MySpace?) to see what

I was up to and where I would be on any given day. I was so fucking dim back then. I would basically provide people with my every movement, down to what I had for breakfast. I wouldn't be surprised if I mentioned a bowel movement once or twice.

I can joke about it now, but it was so scary when it was happening. Aaron would show up randomly in places where I was and begin hassling me to rekindle our relationship. Nora doesn't know anything about this whole episode, since it happened before we decided to move in together. I barely even like thinking about it myself, never mind actually putting it into words and reciting the entire story for my best friend.

Needless to say, I deleted every piece of information I had put up about myself online once I realised Aaron had been following me. It's a good thing I learned my lesson before Facebook became all the rage. People are even worse now than they were back then.

It's sad to think how humanity has been reduced to being more comfortable communing through the medium of a keyboard, rather than having a real life conversation. Okay, so I'm ranting. I'll get off my soap box.

I scan down Nora's chat window to discover that her friend is informing her of the recent job loss of a girl from their old class. Nora's soaking up the gossip with barely contained relish. This is one instance where I find myself thoroughly disgusted with her behaviour.

"You need to step away from the internet, Nora," I say to her.

Sometimes she'll spend her entire day off from work trawling through the pages and photographs of ex-boyfriends and old acquaintances. It's like a drug or something. Her eyes become all glazed over like she's been lured into a technological cult.

"I'm talking to Saoirse, Fred. Leave me alone."

"Tell Saoirse I said she's a cruel bitch for spreading rumours about some poor woman who's fallen on hard times."

I have never met Saoirse, but Nora talks about her a lot and I get the impression she's a bit of a cunt. This impression is mainly derived from the fact that she and Nora never have a conversation that doesn't involve intense bitching about someone else's bad luck or public embarrassment.

Nora stands up from the sofa and carries her laptop to the kitchen table, away from my prying eyes.

"You shouldn't be nosing at other people's conversations," she tuts. "It's your own fault if you don't like what you see."

"Very high and mighty talk coming from someone who's dissecting the misfortune of a woman she hardly knows for the sake of having something to gossip about," I say.

We're not normally so snippy with one another, but I'm still annoyed at her for being a bitch to Nicholas, and she's still annoyed at me because Nicholas' penchant for dressing up as a woman hasn't caused me to write him off as a freak. It's also getting on her goat that Nicholas has been paying far more attention to me than he has been to her.

We've been friends since we were sixteen, and over the course of the nine years that have passed since then Nora has never been overlooked by a man in favour of me. I'm the one who guys like to have as their friend. She's the one they want to lure into bed. It's always been the way of things. I can't really blame her for being a little muddled up over the recent turn of events.

"So, where were you all morning?" she asks, her eyes still glued to the screen of her laptop.

"Out having coffee with Nicholas. We went to the park and guess what? I saw a woman there with a ferret. She had it with her as if it was the most normal thing in the world. I was well impressed."

Nora scrunches up her nose at me. "You were impressed because she had a ferret with her? Is that even legal? I thought those things could bite you and give you rabies."

"Don't be so melodramatic. Besides, this one didn't bite. He even let me pet him and he kept running in and out between my legs like a four year old all jacked up and hyper on sugar."

One end of Nora's mouth turns up in a half smile. "I hope you're going to have a shower after that, who knows what kinds of fleas it might have left on you."

I throw my head back and roll my eyes. "I'll take my chances. Oh, I have other news," I continue.

"What's that?" Nora asks, as her fingers are tap, tap, tapping away at her keyboard.

"Nicholas offered me a job working as the assistant for his shows. You know, helping him choose his outfits and putting on his make-up. How cool is that?"

Suddenly her tapping ceases and she looks up at me. "Are you serious?"

"Yes, why wouldn't I be?"

"Um, one because you already have two jobs, two because you have no experience in that area, and three because, well, it's just a little odd, don't you think? Why would he offer the position randomly to you when he could do a couple interviews and hire someone who actually knows what they're doing?"

Her reasons disgruntle me. "Maybe he doesn't like doing interviews," I say. "And for some reason he thinks I'm the funniest person ever, he said he likes having me around."

I add on this last bit to get a rise out of her. It's not very successful. She lets out a derisive snort. After having lived with me for almost three years, she finds what other people would term 'funny' as me being an irritating, loud mouthed bitch.

"Perhaps he's laughing at you, rather than with you," Nora suggests with a cheeky grin.

"Meh. I'm not bothered either way." I lie "You should see his apartment. It's chock full with boxes of wigs and women's clothing. I can't wait to have a look through it all."

"You really need to find yourself a decent hobby Fred," she remarks, returning to her bitch-fest with Saoirse. Her comment makes my stomach sink to the floor, like when you pop a balloon with a pin.

Telling myself that my interest in Nicholas' woman clothes is perfectly normal, I make a sandwich for lunch and head into my bedroom for a bit of a lie down. I open my window and let the city noise drift in.

I tend to get a little antsy when it's too quiet. It's like my brain has made this strange evolution that helps it to adjust to the stress of living in a city. If there isn't at least some kind of ambient noise in the background I get freaked out. My favourite is the hum of the oven as it's baking a cake or a nice lasagne. That way you get the comfort of the noise and the prospect of a bit of grub on the horizon.

The sounds of traffic and people talking patter in through my window. I finish eating my lunch and then lie back on my bed, slipping off my flip flops. Before I know it I've drifted to sleep and I'm dreaming of Nicholas wearing boxer shorts, high heels and a lacy black bra over his muscular chest.

He's wearing make-up too, but not much; a little mascara and some dark lipstick. For some reason I am incredibly turned on by the sight. He's half boy, half girl. All gorgeous. His hair is messy and his eyelids are lowered. Bedroom eyes, my aunty Margaret would call them. She reads a lot of erotic romance novels, so she's always coming out with these random phrases that you'd never use in real life.

I'm lying on his bed, and it's the one I imagined he had when I thought of him and the Italian woman Dorotea having sex, draped in midnight black silk sheets. I don't know why I subconsciously think that silk sheets are sexy, because in reality they'd probably be really uncomfortable, sticking to all the wrong places.

I'm only wearing my underwear; the purple bra I had on the first time I met Nicholas and matching pants. He steps up to the bed and leans one knee on the mattress. I crawl over to him and trace my fingers over one of his bra straps, sensuously lowering it over his shoulder. His scorching blue eyes burn a trail along my cleavage and he smiles as I raise my hand and lower the other strap. His hand reaches to one of my breasts and lightly squeezes. Then everything goes slightly hazy.

I wake up and there's a little puddle of drool on my pillow. I glance at the clock to see I'd been napping for a couple of hours. My cheeks flame with embarrassment when I remember the contents of my dream. I never considered myself to be kinky, but the idea of Nicholas in a bra is oddly appealing. Perhaps I have a slight touch of lesbianism in me that I never noticed before. Nora better watch out.

I quickly throw on a long black gypsy skirt and a light grey t-shirt, run a brush through my hair and dab on a bit of make-up. I don't have time for dinner, but my stomach is full of butterflies for my first night as Nicholas' assistant so I don't have much of an appetite anyway. It's just gone five past eight when I knock on his door. He answers immediately, looking flustered.

"There you are," he says. "I need your help. I just can't decide which outfit to wear tonight."

I step into his apartment. "What time do you go on stage?"

"Around ten or so," he replies, leading me into his bedroom where there are several dresses strewn across the bed. I'd been completely wrong when I'd visualised it. It's made from light pine wood and the sheets are grey cotton. A lot more practical than black silk, I imagine.

"Well do you need particular outfits for particular songs?" I ask. "Like when you put on the Barbara get up last night for "Don't rain on my parade." Or have we got free reign to pick out what we like?"

Nicholas runs a hand through his hair. "Free reign, I guess. I wanted to pull out all the stops for my first performance last night, but really the outfits don't have to match the songs. Very few people are sober enough to notice anyway." He seems a little sad over that.

"Well I definitely noticed. You were smokin'," I reply to try and cheer him up. I admit I haven't known him for long, but I haven't yet seen him like he is now, all worried and anxious.

He gives me a smile that lights up his entire face. "Of course *you* noticed," he says. "That's why you're my new best friend."

I squeeze his arm and begin looking through the assortment of outfits.

"How about this one?" I ask, holding up a slinky red cocktail dress.

"Too eighties," Nicholas replies, shaking his head. He's pacing back and forth, slightly manic. Perhaps he's one of those crazy geniuses. Before going on stage he has a breakdown, but once he steps out in front of the audience he becomes Vivica Blue: androgynous boy-girl with a voice capable of singing like a legend.

"Okay, so what decade are you thinking? Please don't say nineties," I joke, imagining some of the awful dresses women wore back then. The grunge style is probably the only one I admire from that period.

"Something classy, let's say...." he drifts off and rushes out of the room. I can hear him rifling through an unpacked box out in the living area. He comes back in wielding a wonderful dress consisting of black satin with silver and gold beading.

"Twenties," he says, completing his unfinished sentence.

"Oh I like it, do you have any bobbed wigs? That would totally complete the look."

Nicholas' eyes shine with excitement. "I most certainly do." He leaves the room yet again, before returning with a short blond wig. "I'll look just like Jane Horrocks when she played Sally Bowles in *Cabaret* on Broadway," he declares. "Fred you're a genius. I knew I wouldn't regret hiring you."

"Hey, I hardly did a thing," I say, raising my hands in the air. "It was all you. You really don't need an assistant, you know."

He stops fussing over the wig for a minute to look at me. "Getting ready for a performance is no fun when you haven't got someone to share it with, and I want to share it with you, Freda."

I like the sound of my full name on his tongue. "Well, I'm not complaining. This is a dream job. I feel like one of those pretentious stylists you see on television makeover shows, who get paid thousands to tell some woman how to match her blouse with her skirt."

Nicholas laughs as he carefully places the dress and the wig inside a plastic zip cover. He hands it to me as he grabs what he needs before we leave for the club. He has one of those big silver boxy make-up sets. You know the ones that look like treasure chests, and you open them up to reveal layers upon layers of eye shadows and blushers.

Out on the street Nicholas hails a cab and within minutes we're hurrying in the back entrance of The Glamour Patch, past the Saturday crowd who are queuing up to get inside. He quickly greets the manager, who turns out to be the guy from last night who introduced Nicholas' performance, the one with the bleached hair and purple shirt.

"Phil, this is my assistant Fred. She'll be helping me get ready for my gig," he says.

I shake Phil's hand as he smiles at me warmly. "Fabulous hair Fred, it's a pleasure to meet you," then he rushes off to his office.

"Saturdays are busy, busy, busy," Nicholas sings as

we step inside a small dark room. He flicks the light switch to reveal a dressing table shoved up against one wall, with a massive mirror, two chairs and various free standing hangers. I pop Nicholas' outfit onto one of the hangers and put his make-up box down on the table.

"So, where do we start?" I ask, hands on hips.

Nicholas has a navy backpack with him, which he drops down onto the floor.

"Hmm, how about a drink first? I'm a little more nervy than usual. I think I need something to settle me down."

"Do you normally get nervous before a show?" I ask.

"Sometimes I do, sometimes I don't. Perhaps it's because you're here. I want to impress you."

My eyes widen in surprise. "Really? But I was here last night and you were fine."

He smirks. "You didn't see me before the show."

"You really don't have to be worried about what I think; I love your whole act. You can't do much wrong in my eyes," I try to reassure him. In the back of my mind I'm truly flattered that he wants to impress me. I must have made quite the impact on him. It's strange because I thought I'd been acting like a fool half the time.

A second later Sean, the drummer from The Wilting Willows and snogging partner of Harry, ducks his head in the door.

"Hey Nick, you all set for tonight's gig?" he asks, with a big grin on his face, a clear sign that he got some decent action last night. I'll be giving Harry a call tomorrow to get all the details. I'm always strangely intrigued to hear about what two men do together in bed. Needless to say, I'm quite an avid follower of

Harry's love life.

Nicholas is leaning against the wall, arms casually folded across his chest. "I sure am, be a dear and grab myself and Fred here a drink from the bar, would you?" he glances at me wickedly before bringing his eyes back to Sean. "Two mojitos, if you don't mind."

I'm suddenly struck with the memory of him taking a sip of my mojito last night, saying he wanted to put his lips where my lips had been. A little shiver runs through me and my stomach clenches.

Sean gives a salute and a wink before heading off on his errand. I sit down on one of the chairs. It's the swivel kind, and like a child I can't help myself but to swing back and forth on it.

"You're going to make yourself dizzy," Nicholas comments, watching me from his spot by the wall. His voice is warm. It makes me feel weird and sweaty.

"I used to love doing this when I was a kid, spinning around until I couldn't balance and fell onto the floor." I tell him. "I think I might have given myself a concussion once."

Nicholas laughs gently, before stepping over to the table to open up his make-up case.

I stop swinging to peer at myself in the mirror. My hair looks wild, as usual, the soft twisty curls falling over my shoulders. My eyes are alight with excitement. I hope Nicholas doesn't realise how pathetically delighted I am to be here right now. I feel sort of unworthy of being involved in such an exhilarating profession.

Most people want to be performers at some point when they're young, whether it's being a singer, a dancer or an actor. I never did. I just always knew I wanted to work with food. I'd play games where I was running my own imaginary restaurant, with all my dolls and Barbies acting as patrons. I was an eccentric little git.

That dream never came true in the way I wanted it to, but at least I'm doing something with food. Although aside from making colourful little cupcakes, I haven't got a creative bone in my body. I'm happy to sit back and enjoy the creativity of others. Luckily, as Nicholas' assistant I have a front row seat.

Nicholas takes the chair beside mine and I scoot over closer to him to have a look at all the eye shadows, so shiny and colourful like a rainbow. Nicholas begins retrieving lipsticks, concealers and blushers, and all variety of things that I have no clue about and probably should since I'm supposed to be the girl in this situation.

"I'll take the lead tonight," he says. "Once you get used to my routine you'll be doing all of this yourself." He sets a pair of black false eyelashes down on the table, the final item.

"Okay, so do you normally dress first and then put on your make-up, or vice versa?"

Nicholas gives me a little grin and tuts. "Make-up first, my clothes are expensive. Some are one of a kind. I can't risk ruining them." He hands me a bottle of red nail varnish. "Would you paint my nails for me Fred?"

"I'd love to Viv," I reply with relish, taking the bottle from him and turning in my seat so that I'm facing him. I take his hand into mine, his fingers aren't too soft, but they aren't rough either. His nails are clipped short and are very clean.

I put his palm resting flat on my lap, fingers spread out. I momentarily regret it, because having his hand so close to my lady parts makes me a little breathless. I push back the desire to swoon and focus on the task. Nicholas seems to lean forward ever so slightly, watching my movements intently as I paint his nails a glaring shade of fire engine red.

I get lost in the painting, and when I glance up I almost knock the bottle over. He's way too close, his eyes eating me up, his lips parted.

"What?" I ask. "Did I make a mistake?"

I know I didn't make a mistake. I just need to distract him from whatever thoughts are running through his mind right now. He looks like he wants to rip my knickers off.

"No," he answers simply. "I have to admit, for some reason I find you incredibly sexy, Fred."

His words cause my breath to gush out in something close to a gasp. *Distract, distract, distract*, chimes my embarrassed brain. "You might need to pop in to Specsavers for an eye test Viv," I try to make it sound like a joke, but my nerves make the sentence come out all shaky.

His smile is half evil sexy, half tender. "I've got perfect twenty-twenty vision, I'll have you know. How about I lock the door so that we can have a quicky? If we're going to work together I need to get this urge out of my system to fuck your brains out."

"Ah, I have a true romantic on my hands," I mutter half-heartedly. No, my underwear is not distinctly more...damp. No siree. Jesus, he has a blunt way of putting things that causes my brain to go a bit loopy.

"I never claimed to offer romance Fred, but I'm fairly confident I can provide you with the perfect sexual release. It has been three and a half years, after all."

He's smirking at me now.

"Best friends don't do that sort of thing," I say, putting on a fake haughty voice. "It wouldn't be proper."

Thankfully I'm saved from this tension filled conversation when Sean returns with our drinks. He plops them onto the table and then runs off, mumbling something about finding a missing lucky drumstick.

I take a sip of the cool drink, hoping the alcohol might settle my nerves. The dressing room didn't seem very big to begin with, but now it feels positively minuscule. Nicholas sips on his drink too, his eyes never leaving me. I glance at the clock on the wall.

"It's past nine, Viv. We'd better get your make-up started if you don't want to be late, late for a very important date," I ramble, quoting the white rabbit from *Alice in Wonderland* for absolutely no reason at all, other than the fact that he turns me into a nervous wreck.

He sets his drink down on the table and clasps his hands together. "All right then, have your way with me," he says, pouting his lips.

"I thought you said you were going to take the lead and I'd just watch for my first night?"

Nicholas shrugs as he shoves his dark hair into one of those tight cap things you wear under a wig. "Might as well throw you in the deep end. Do your worst."

I furrow my brow. "Okay, um, I'll start with foundation." I pick up the tube of pale concealer. It's almost a perfect match for his clear skin tone. I squirt some onto a little applicator sponge and begin smoothing it over his cheeks and forehead.

"I find it better if you use your fingers instead of the sponge. It gives a more natural finish," he suggests.

I swallow hard and put down the applicator, before squeezing foundation onto my fingertips this time. I always use my hands when I'm doing my own make-up, but I thought that was just me being too lazy to go out and buy the proper bits and pieces.

His skin feels gorgeous. His face is clean shaven; the stubble he had this morning is gone completely. I find myself getting a bit of a crick in my neck as I stand over him, trying to apply the make-up. In a bold move I perch myself lightly on one of his thighs. God help him I'm no Kate Moss. I hope I'm not *too* heavy and give him a dead leg. He doesn't say anything, but I can tell he's intrigued by my actions.

"My neck was hurting bending over," I explain.

"Mm hmm," he mumbles, his gaze locked on my breasts, which are currently right at his eye level.

I move on to powder and then blusher, dusting it lightly over his cheeks.

"Thank God for thinly padded bras," Nicholas comments, just before he flattens one hand out on the small of my back to pull me closer and pinches me right on the nipple through the fabric of my t-shirt with the other. You'd probably expect me to jump right off his lap in surprise. Only I don't. I sit there, trying my hardest not to piss my pants at how scarily erotic the moment is. He's still doing it, and my eyes are captured within the blue prisons of his irises.

I let out a long breath. "What are you doing?" I whisper.

"Giving you a thrill," he answers darkly.

"Very kind of you Viv, you can let go now."

"Say please," he throws back.

I grit my teeth. "Please."

He grins happily and releases his hold. I almost miss the pinch of his fingers. I should probably head down the road and purchase myself a vibrator to relieve the way Nicholas makes me feel, all hot and needy. Capel Street is sex shop central, after all. A little tip for you there, if you ever find yourself in Dublin with a bit of free time on your hands. Ahem.

I've always wondered what lies beyond all those blacked out windows, but have never had the nerve to venture inside. The front displays have all these mannequins decked out in tacky fetish wear. When passing by I tend to ponder the fact that nobody I've ever seen go into those shops has the kind of body you'd want to see in a black leather bikini with furry red trim.

I silently stick on Nicholas' fake eyelashes and he stands up to go and get changed. He pulls his t-shirt over his head and begins unbuckling his belt. When it comes to his physique, chiselled is the only word I can think of. I quickly avert my eyes as I hear his trousers fall to the floor with a billowing thump.

He begins laughing, but I'm still not looking. "You're going to have to get used to the sight of me sans clothing, Fred. It's part and parcel of the job."

I drag my eyes up to him. Good God, he has nothing on but his boxer shorts now. And then he doesn't even have those on, as he whips them off and pulls a pair of dark red satin knickers out of his bag. I am looking anywhere but at his nether regions. Anywhere! Don't get me wrong, I'm curious, but I think if I took a peek the image would be branded into my brain and every time we had a conversation I'd just be visualising his man bits.

"So you go the whole hog then, with women's underwear and everything?" I ask, eyeing the slinky satin pants. He pulls out a pair of tight men's briefs as well, probably to wear underneath and keep everything – in place.

He nods. "I might not be as flashy as traditional drag queens, but I do like to think of myself as being authentic. Although I don't stuff my bra or put on a lady voice. I also don't tuck my dick. I'm not trying to fool people into believing I'm an actual woman in that sense. I think being somewhere in between male and female is just as intriguing."

He slips on the briefs and then the knickers, blessedly covering himself up. Unfortunately, they don't hide much, and it doesn't take a very wide stretch of the imagination for me to picture him without them. Sometimes I can't seem to control my filthy mind and where it wants to wander. This job is going to give me a heart attack at twenty-five, and it's only my first night.

He slips on a matching bra, which is kind of pointless, since he has no tits to speak of. It makes me wonder if he gets his jollies out of wearing it. I mean, it's not providing any lift or aesthetic function. Nobody's going to see it beneath the dress, nor will they see the knickers.

"Um, can I ask another question?" I venture.

"Go ahead," he replies, adjusting himself in the knickers.

"Well, I was just wondering about how you classify yourself. Are you a drag queen, or a transvestite or a cross dresser? Or are they all one and the same thing?"

Nicholas shrugs. "Everybody has their own opinions on it I suppose. For me, a drag queen dresses as a women purely for performance and that's what I think of myself as being. A transvestite or a cross dresser could be a man who wears women's clothing because it's a fetish."

"So it's not a fetish thing for you?"

He smirks. "Nope. Cross dressing is often related to sexual preference. I like to be a man in the bedroom, but a woman on the stage."

"Oh," I say, my cheeks going a little red.

"Don't be afraid to ask me things. I'm willing to answer all of your questions Fred."

I nod, but remain quiet after that.

Next he puts on his sheer hold up stockings, before slipping the dress on over his head. I zip it up for him at the back. Then he sits down in the chair by the mirror to tackle the wig. I help him get it on right. As I'm doing this my fingers absently drift over the skin at the back of his neck. I hear him pull in a sharp breath, so I try not to touch him again. He slips on a pair of glittery purple heels and we're done.

"Well, how do I look?" he asks, turning his made up face from side to side. He looks like a really hot woman. It's unsettling, but also titillating.

"If I was into girls, I'd do you," I tell him honestly.

He leans forward conspiratorially. "Psst, I'll let you in on a secret Fred," he glances sheepishly from side to side. "I actually have a cock. Don't tell anyone, it would ruin my reputation. But feel free to do me any time you want."

"Good to know," I answer quickly, picking up my half-finished mojito and knocking it back.

"Record timing," Nicholas goes on, noting that it's only ten to ten. He has a couple of minutes before he goes on stage, and he begins doing warm ups with his voice, readying himself to belt out a few tunes for the crowd in the club. I marvel at how he can reach the really deep low notes as well as the tippy top high ones.

A few minutes later the club manager Phil peeks his head in the door. "You ready to go Miss Blue?" he asks with a grin.

"Ready as I'll ever be Philip," Nicholas answers, getting up from his seat. He takes my hand and leads me out toward the back of the stage.

"Will you stay and watch the whole show?" he asks me, nearing the noisy revellers beyond the red velvet curtains. The place seems even more rowdy than it had been last night.

"Of course I will. I'll even sing along," I tell him excitedly.

He keeps his tight hold on my hand as we step up behind the curtains. I can hear Phil out front, telling a few jokes to the audience before announcing the act. When I look at Nicholas his body seems to be vibrating with nerves and anticipation. He absently runs his thumb back and forth over my wrist. The movement makes me feel all warm inside.

When Phil declares, "Ladies and gentlemen, I give you Miss Vivica Blue," Nicholas lets go of my hand, smacks a quick kiss onto my cheek and rushes out to the stage as The Wilting Willows play the opening bit to "Cell Block Tango" from *Chicago*. Mostly it's Sean doing a great job of creating the beats of the intro on his drums. Nicholas begins speaking the lyrics, and I'm eager to see how he'll tackle such a big number. I've seen the movie, and I can remember there being at least five or six women singing this song all together.

Some members of the audience are chanting the lyrics along with him. There are lots of little stories within this song, each woman telling her tale of why she killed her boyfriend or husband. I watch from behind the curtains, entirely fascinated as Nicholas strides from one side of the stage to the other, reciting each story, putting on a slightly different persona with each new character he impersonates. His outfit actually matches pretty well with the song, despite the fact that he said it wasn't important that it did.

He seems more mesmerising to me than he had last night, perhaps because I have such a bird's eye view from my spot backstage. My heart beats quicker and I find myself getting lost in him, in her, in the persona he takes on. Am I attracted to the man behind the costume? Or do I want the man *in* the costume? It's hard to tell. I think I like the entire package. Nicholas can be so masculine at times, but he also shows some feminine traits. For instance, I can talk to him and joke around as though he were one of my girlfriends, yet when he levels his hot eyes on me my throat gets dry and my stomach tightens.

Before I know it he's almost finished his whole set and is getting ready to perform the final song. He skips over to the band and begins giving them instructions, perhaps about the number he wants to sing. They all nod their heads, clutching their instruments. Sean throws Nicholas a tambourine, which he catches deftly between his fingers.

He brings the microphone to his mouth to address the audience. "I'd like to dedicate this last song to a new friend I made recently," he pauses. A new friend? Does he mean me? My palms go a little sweaty at the idea.

He stares into the crowd beyond the stage, with that trademark sexy evil smile. "This one's called "Be Italian" from the musical *Nine*."

I have no clue if he's talking about me or not, but as the song starts up, I begin to doubt it. He hasn't looked at me once. He continues staring at one spot in the crowd.

I crane my neck around the curtain, far too curious about what or who he's looking at. That's when I realise I now truly know the meaning of the saying *curiosity killed the cat*, because when I peer out I catch sight of a pair of big seductive lips and long silky dark hair. Disappointment fills my gut. If I'm a cat right now, I'm more or less road kill. Dorotea, the Italian woman from the park, is sitting at the very front of the audience at a table with two other women. Her eyes are fierce, eating Nicholas up from head to toe.

What is she doing here? He must have invited her while I'd been obliviously occupied over playing with Ollo. It seems I'm not the only woman who isn't fazed by Nicholas being a drag queen. If anything, it seems to be making Dorotea even more pleased with him, as he belts out the song in a faux Italian accent.

I never thought I was the kind of girl who could become consumed by jealousy, but right now I feel like that's exactly what's happening to me. *Of course*, he wasn't going to sing a song just for me. Dorotea is sex on legs. It's probably a foregone conclusion that the two of them will end up in bed together, possibly later on tonight.

I try to pull back my dejection, scolding myself for getting carried away by Nicholas' attentions in the first place. He said it himself that he's a serial shagger. He probably propositions every half decent looking girl who crosses his path.

The song he's singing right now, "Be Italian", is a very gypsy-like, saucy number. He's using the tambourine as he dances, tapping it off his hips, shoulders and thighs. Dorotea's mouth is positively watering. I guess it really is true that performers want everyone to fall in love with them, especially when they're on stage.

Perhaps I'm reading too much into this. Perhaps he's just trying to be playful and friendly by singing a song to her. God, I should probably kill any romantic notions I have been harbouring about this man. It will only see me purchasing a one way ticket to the crazy house.

Nicholas finishes his set with a sweeping bow as the audience cheers him on. He dashes off the stage, his blue eyes sparkling with excitement as he takes me by the hand and pulls me along with him back to his dressing room.

"That went even better than I expected," he breathes as he plops down onto a chair. "Grab the make-up removal wipes from my bag, would you Freda?"

I bend down and pull out the packet of wipes before taking the seat beside him. He's already pulling off his wig and unclipping the cap that was keeping all his natural hair in place. He turns his face to me and I pick off his false eyelashes, before venturing to clean the make-up from his skin. I do so gently, as he closes his eyes to give me full access to remove the mascara and eye shadow he's wearing.

He really is very pretty. Seeing his features this close, I realise what perfect bone structure he has. It makes me wonder what it might have been like for him growing up. Maybe he didn't have such a good time of it. Sometimes the pretty boys find themselves a target of bullying. Mostly because the ones doing the bullying are jealous of their beauty.

"What age were you when you started doing all this?" I ask him curiously, eager to know how it all came about. I mean, did he just wake up one morning and know he wanted to be a singing drag queen? Or did it happen gradually?

He opens his eyes and his expression is serious, but not guarded. "I was in my late teens when I began performing properly, but I started experimenting with wearing bits of women's clothing and make-up when I was very young, eight or nine years old."

I momentarily think about how he must have been such an interesting kid. Then I remember how his mother died when he was only little. "If your mother was still alive she probably would have found the whole thing fascinating," I tell him softly.

He seems to get uncomfortable then and doesn't reply, so I change the subject. "So, Dorotea huh?" I do my best to muster a grin so that he doesn't cotton on to the fact that her presence here tonight has given me a true dose of the disappointments. I had been living in a dream world where I thought I was the only woman in Dublin who had turned Nicholas' head.

He grins back. "I invited her along when we spoke in the park. She's quite something, isn't she?"

"She certainly has the perkiest breasts I've ever seen for a woman in her late thirties," I reply.

Nicholas grabs my wrist to stop the movement of my hand as I clean away the last traces of his make-up. "Is that a note of jealousy I detect?" His face is practically glowing. I want to smack the pretty off him.

"Of course not. I was just commenting on her perkiness. Besides, I think you two would make a very intriguing couple. It'll look like you're one of those young male escorts with a sugar momma."

"Oh my God, you *are* jealous. This is just brilliant," he says, he's so close that the tips of our noses are almost touching.

"I. Am. Not. Jealous. And why would it be brilliant if I were?"

"Because it would mean you're trying to hide the fact that you're attracted to me."

"You really *do* need everyone to be in love with you," I retort.

"Come again?"

I shrug. "When I was watching you on stage I came up with a theory about performers and how they need everyone to fall in love with them, even if it just lasts for the duration of the show."

His grin turns speculative. "How philosophical of you Fred." A silence fills the room as he studies me. "Would it bother you if I said I was planning on taking advantage of Dorotea's attraction to me tonight?" he asks.

"Nope," I reply, trying to emit a casual demeanour.

He narrows his gaze at me. "Are you sure about that? Because you only have to say the word. You are, after all, my first choice for a fuck."

"Jesus Christ," I whisper, shaking my head at him with wide eyes. "You don't mince your words, Viv."

"I take it that you're not going to say the word then," he sighs sadly.

The door to the dressing room swings open and Phil

strolls in, followed by Dorotea and her two lady friends. I knew she wasn't the kind of woman to leave without getting her pound of flesh. Nicholas *did* lead her on by singing such a sexy song and dedicating it to her.

"I have some ladies who were just dying to come back here and see you," Phil announces.

Nicholas is still wearing the dress and heels, but his face is now free of make-up and his black hair sits messily atop his head. I go about clearing up the bits and pieces that have been left strewn across the dressing table, while Nicholas stands to greet his guests.

"Dorotea, I'm so glad you could come," he says as he approaches her. They both give each other kisses on either cheek. Very la di da. I try to ignore the niceties as Dorotea gushes over Nicholas and introduces him to her friends.

On seeing her a second time, I recalculate her imagined age in my head, putting her at a decrepit forty-five rather than a well-preserved thirty-eight. Even though it isn't true, it still makes me feel a little better.

She's wearing a fitted cream dress with matching high heels. She's also got those really long nails, the ones that look like they'd take your eye out. *Very impractical*, my haughty, insecure subconscious remarks. Oh, who am I trying to fool? She looks amazing, and I feel so fucking drab in comparison.

It seems a little ironic that I've inflicted this source of misery on myself. If I hadn't been so taken with the fact that she had a ferret in the park with her then she and Nicholas never would have even met.

"I'm going to go get a drink," I say, pulling Nicholas aside. "Do you want one?"

Dorotea hears what I've said and declares in her perfectly spoken English, "Wonderful idea! Get a bottle of champagne, you can put it on my tab."

"Champagne eh?" I reply, desperately holding back the urge to comment on the exorbitant prices they charge for a hair cut in Peter Marks, and how it must really be lining her pockets.

"Yes, chop chop," she says and claps her hands, as if I'm some kind of a servant. Her friends giggle; you can tell they've had quite a few drinks already.

I glance at Nicholas, who looks like he's on the verge of bursting out laughing when he sees the expression on my face.

I'm not at all impressed by her and her ferret keeping ways any longer, I think to myself.

Chapter Six
Walk of Shame

I leave the dressing room and head towards the bar, where I order a bottle of champagne on Dorotea's tab, as well as three shots of rum for myself. I stand there and knock them all back, not minding the burn so much since I'm too full of satisfaction that I got one over on Dorotea and her "chop chop" clappy fucking hands.

The barman gives me the bottle of champagne in a fancy bucket of ice, as well as four glasses. I carry them all back to the dressing room, where I find Nicholas still in his drag outfit, surrounded by his three admirers. Phil has disappeared off somewhere.

"Well, here you go ladies and *gent*," I announce. "Champagne for my real friend, real pain for my sham friends," quoting the Fall Out Boy song as I'm feeling particularly "emo" right now.

"Ah, great movie," says Nicholas with a smile, thinking I'm referring to the film *25th Hour*. I give him my best moody teenager *you are so old you don't even get what I'm talking about* eye roll, even though he's only three years older than me.

"Pop open the bubbly Doro," shouts one of Dorotea's nameless friends. I imagine she's a hairdresser too, because she has one of those spiky mullets that those in the profession seem to think look good.

"I'm going to head home," I say to Nicholas. "Do you want me to drop your stuff off at your apartment for you?" I glance at the ladies. "That way you'll be free to enjoy your night."

He regards me seriously for a long moment, and I

begin to wonder if he even plans on answering me. It looks like there's a million thoughts passing through his head.

"No I can manage it," he says finally. "Why are you leaving? I thought you were going to stay for a drink."

My head is already spinning a little from the sneaky shots I had at the bar. "I changed my mind. I'll catch you next Thursday shall I? You don't have any more shows until then right?"

"That's right." He pulls over his bag and rummages for his wallet, taking out a twenty and handing it to me. "Make sure you get a taxi home," he says warmly, his fingers absently brushing against mine as I take it.

I try not to feel happy about the fact that he wants to make sure I get home safely in a cab. I silently shove the money in my bag and nod to Dorotea and company.

"Ladies," I say, before grabbing my coat and slipping out the door.

The cab drive is short, but I manage to fit in a good bitch fest with the driver; the two of us complaining about our crappy government and the bastard bankers who screwed us over during the boom years. Dublin taxi drivers love a good rant, but what they love even more is a person who will rant along with them.

"Ah, don't even get me started on those pricks in the banking sector. They think they're fucking untouchable. And they get away with it too, you know why?" asks my balding, slightly overweight taxi driver.

"Why?" I ask, egging him on.

"Because it's all their fucking best buddies who are in power. The Taoiseach and all those ministers are hardly going to prosecute their friends now are they? Politics in this country, it's an incestuous pile of shit. Pricks," he spits. The Taoiseach is the Irish version of a Prime Minister.

"Pricks," I agree, just as he pulls up outside my building.

I pay the fare and hop out. When I get inside the apartment I make myself a big mug of hot chocolate, before getting straight into bed, hoping the warm beverage will make me sleepy. It doesn't work. My brain won't stop thinking about Nicholas and what he might be doing with Dorotea right now. It's a pity Nora's still at work, because I could have gone into her room and nagged her with my story of disappointment and jealousy.

Deciding that sleep isn't going to happen for me at this moment in time, I head into the kitchen and pull out the makings of a Victoria sponge cake. I go to my parent's house every Sunday for dinner, so I figure it will go over well with them if I bring dessert along with me tomorrow. Baking tends to work good to keep my mind off life and the things that are stressing me.

I'm stirring the cake mixture in a bowl and listening to "California über Alles" by *Dead Kennedys* on my headphones when Nora comes in the door, looking tired after her shift. She pulls a stool up to the kitchen counter and sits down, sticking her finger into the cake mix before popping it in her mouth. I've never had a taste for raw cake mix, but it's always been a favourite of Nora's

"You can get salmonella from that you know," I say, pulling off my headphones and nodding to the finger she has stuck in her mouth.

"No you can't," she retorts, going in for another dip. I knock her hand away.

She sits back and eyes me. "So you're baking at night. You only ever do that when you're depressed about something. What is it?"

I sigh and continue to silently prepare my ingredients.

"Come on Fred, I'm ready to hit the sack. This is your last chance to tell me what's bothering you, because in the next five minutes I'll be dead to the world."

"Nicholas confuses me," I confess.

Nora cocks an eyebrow. "In what way? Don't tell me you want to shag him while he's wearing a dress or something."

I shake my head and laugh. "No of course not - well, not really." I admit sheepishly. "It's just that he's always so forward with me. He compliments me and it turns me into a pile of mush. I don't want to fancy him if he doesn't mean what he says. I get the impression he flirts with everyone, but I'm too insecure to handle it. You know what it's like when a man says he wants you, you want him to have never liked any girl as much as he likes you."

"And there was me thinking you weren't interested in him," Nora replies with a sly grin.

"Oh fuck off, of course I like him. You'd have to be blind not to find him attractive."

"I know, he's quite beautiful, isn't he?" she says, for a moment forgetting her gripes about him making his living performing as a drag queen.

"Ugh, you're not helping Nora. Just go to bed."

"Fine," she replies, grabbing her bag and sauntering into her bedroom.

I finish up with the cake and set the timer for the oven to go off once it's cooked. I'll put the jam and cream on it in the morning. After all the baking my brain is now too exhausted to think about Nicholas, and I finally get some sleep.

When I visit my mum and dad on Sundays I tend to pile my hair up in a messy bun and wear the most comfortable clothes I can find. Today that consists of black leggings, boots and an old baggy Green Day t-shirt. We always spend the day eating, chatting and watching television shows, so there's not much of a point in getting dressed up.

I very much regret that as I'm leaving my apartment, carrying a plastic container with the Victoria sponge cake sitting inside it, because I bump right into Nicholas who's standing at his front door. He's not alone either. He's saying goodbye to Dorotea, who clearly spent the night and is looking a little worse for wear. Nicholas' eyes run up and down my body. The fucker, he shouldn't be looking at me like that if he just spent the night shagging another woman.

I don't want either of them to know that this surprise meeting has plunged a heavy brick to the pit of my stomach, so like always, I make a big stupid joke of it.

"My, my, am I witnessing the walk of shame right now?" I declare loudly, plastering a fake happy smile on my face. "This is a classy neighbourhood I'll have you know, you're lowering the tone."

Dorotea turns to glance at me. "Oh my word, you gave me a fright, so noisy," she complains, covering her tender hangover ridden ears with her hands. She doesn't look so great without her make-up on, and there are crusty bits of last night's mascara stuck in the corners of her eyes.

Nicholas has one arm braced on the wall beside his door. He's wearing trousers but no top and his hair is a sexy mess. I hate him for looking so good with such little effort.

I step up to them both, before shouting in Dorotea's ear, "Sorry, my bad." It gives me a sick satisfaction when I see her cringe.

Nicholas is only barely containing his amusement. I turn to look at him. "I take it the champagne went down a treat."

He grins and nods to Dorotea. "It's not the only thing that went down last night."

"You cheeky little devil," Dorotea scolds with saucy outrage. "You never returned the favour; I'll be collecting on that."

I resist the urge to make a gagging noise.

Nicholas' eyes are levelled on me when he replies to Dorotea, "My apologies, but I only visit the lady garden under very special circumstances." The way he's looking at me makes me think he's visualising visiting my lady garden. A shiver runs down my spine.

She pouts and folds her arms across her chest. "That's not very fair."

"Sorry, those are the rules," Nicholas chirps. "Where are you off to Fred?"

I show him the cake I'm holding, realising it reinforces the lie I told him yesterday about baking my mum a cake for a fictitious dinner party. "Visiting the parentals for Sunday lunch," I reply.

"You lucky sod, I could kill for a nice roast. It's the best cure for a hangover."

"Sadly, you're not invited," I say. "See ya later alligator." And with that I flounce off down the hall, feeling quite triumphant with myself.

I hop on a bus out towards Coolock, which is where my mum and dad live in the house I grew up in. Coolock is on Dublin's north side, and it's a pretty bleak place in some ways. The area consists mainly of housing estates and factories.

I'll give you a little lesson on the Dublin class system. In general, the working classes live in towns on the north side, while the middle and upper classes live on the south side. Of course, there are a handful of posh places on the north side, such as Malahide, Howth and Skerries, but mostly it's working class. Nora grew up in Malahide. We met at a summer tennis school and have been friends ever since, despite our very different backgrounds.

Coolock is mainly known for being home to the Cadbury headquarters in Ireland, as well as the Tayto crisps factory. The smell of oil and frying potatoes has always simultaneously made me feel sick and reminded me of home. So basically we produce chocolate and crisps. Perhaps you could blame us for the increasing problem of obesity. Growing up here, you got a thick skin fairly quickly. If you came across as a victim the other kids would rip you to shreds.

This is probably why I developed such a sharp tongue over the years. I needed to be able to put people in their places so that they wouldn't mess with me. I never really fit in anywhere as a teenager. I tended to flit from group to group and often I'd just hang out by my little old lonesome. Sometimes it felt like my mum was my best friend. Feel free to shed a tear for how pathetic I was. In a way it was a good thing, because if I had of been popular I probably would have ended up pregnant at fifteen and living in a council flat for the rest of my days. That or a junkie. A lot of kids grow up too fast here.

I knock on the front door to my parents' house, as their ginger cat Leonard rubs off my legs and purrs loudly. I don't know why they named him Leonard. It's a weird name for a cat. Too human. Perhaps they were making a subversive reference to Leo for lion, since a lion is basically just a huge cat.

My mum answers as usual; her grey hair is nicely blow dried so I'm guessing she paid a visit to the hairdressers yesterday. Every fortnight she goes to get her hair trimmed and blow dried. I'm surprised she has any hair left, she goes so often.

"Freda come on in, ah you baked a cake did you?"

She eyes the plastic container with relish. My mum is a fiend for baked goods.

"I did," I reply, handing her the cake. The house smells deliciously of roast lamb. I go into the living room where my dad is sitting in his favourite chair watching a football match. My dad's crazy about two things, football and golf, so if either of them are showing on the telly there's no prying the remote from him.

He supports Manchester United and is currently wearing his red jersey with pride. I sometimes like to point out the irony of him being in love with an English team and also having a penchant for ranting on about the troubles up north and how the Brits stole a third of our country from us. He just scowls at me and tells me to shut up whenever I do.

It's a prevalent contradiction in Ireland. The boys I went to school with would don their Liverpool football shirts one day, and the next they'd be graffiti-ing the words "Brits Out" on the nearest lamp post or wall.

I put a hand on Dad's shoulder and give him a quick kiss on the cheek in greeting, and then I let him focus back on the game. We sit in silence for a few minutes, as the commentators describe what's happening on the field with fervour.

"Your mother had a fall Wednesday last," my dad comments out of nowhere. This is how conversations with him normally run; silence interspersed with the odd piece of news.

"She never mentioned it," I say. "Is she okay?"

He lets out a breath and shifts in his chair. "Ah, she bruised her ankle. Wouldn't let me take her to the doctor's. She said she was fine."

My dad doesn't say much, but when he does you know it's important. He's clearly telling me this because he's worried about Mum, which means he wants me to talk some sense into her. Out of all my siblings, I'm the one who visits the most. My brother and three sisters all have their own families to take care of, so they don't really have much time to come see our parents.

"I thought she was limping a little bit when she answered the door," I reply. "I'll get her to let me have a look at her ankle after dinner."

Dad nods, satisfied, and returns his attention to the football. Because my mum had me so late, I've always been quite aware of my parents' mortality. Even as a child I'd have these nightmares about one of them getting sick and dying.

Now that I'm older I know that their deaths are inevitable, but it still isn't nice to think about them not being here anymore. When one of them gets even a little bit sick it makes me realise how close they are to the end of their lives. But I always try to reassure myself with the fact that lots of people live well into their nineties these days, which means my parents could have a good twenty years left in them.

Mum's pottering around in the kitchen, so I go in to check on her. She's standing by the cooker, stirring some gravy in a pot.

"Dad says you had a fall," I say to her casually.

She tuts and shakes her head. "It was nothing. I'm fine."

"If it's fine then you won't mind me having a look at it."

Her body stiffens. "Leave it, Freda."

I grab her by the hand and pull her over to a chair, before sitting her down. "Stop being stubborn, Mum." She slumps back in defeat as I roll up her trouser leg and pull down her sock. I can't contain my gasp when I see the big purple and yellow bruise on her ankle. I glance up at her. "This is nothing, is it? Why did you pretend you were fine?"

She gets a little flustered. "Oh, I didn't want to make a fuss," she's deflecting now, I can tell.

"Spit it out, Mum."

She wrings her hands and throws her eyes to the heavens, an expression that tells me she thinks I'm overreacting. "Well, it's just that Dr Richards retired a few months ago and they have this new doctor working at the clinic and he can be a little difficult."

"What do you mean by difficult?" I ask, my temper flaring at the idea of some doctor being mean to my mother.

She worries the hem of her peach coloured cardigan

for a minute. "Nothing too bad, he's just very flippant when you tell him about your ailments and makes out as if you're a hypochondriac."

"The bastard," I say, imagining some hot shot doctor who thinks he's above dealing with the health complaints of elderly women like Mum.

"Language Freda," Mum scolds half-heartedly.

"Listen, I'm taking you to see him tomorrow, and if he gives you any crap he'll have me to contend with."

"You don't have to go out of your way. I know I should have gone to the clinic myself after I fell. I'll get your dad to take me tomorrow."

"Mum, I'm taking you. I'll drop by first thing in the morning. Now you go and have a sit down in the living room. I'll put the dinner up."

She places her hand on my arm, tells me I'm a great girl, and makes her way out of the kitchen.

After a leisurely dinner and a few hours of chatting to Mum about this and that, I say my goodbyes and make my way to the bus stop. A few teenage boys in ridiculous looking tracksuits follow behind me for a minute, and I know they're considering whether or not to jump me for my purse. I turn around and face them, walking backwards.

I eye the one who appears to be the ringleader. "Just fucking try it you little shits," I shout at them.

Surprised at being confronted, they tuck tail and run off. You'll find that most scumbags who mug people are cowards, so you only have to show them you're onto them and they'll scurry away. It's the desperate ones you have to watch out for, because they have nothing left to lose and they'll resort to extremes.

It's around half past six when I get back to the

apartment, and I can hear laughter coming from inside as I slot my key in the door. Opening it I find Nora, Harry, Sean and Nicholas sitting in the living area with a massive pizza box spread out on the coffee table.

"Well, well, well, look at you all shooting the shit," I remark, slightly annoyed that I wasn't informed of this little get together. "What do you think this is, the set of *Friends*?"

"Harry and Sean decided to come over and surprise us with a pizza." Nora explains. "Since you were out they knocked next door and asked Nicholas if he'd like to join us instead."

"Viv you cow," I say, glancing at Nicholas who's currently seated in my favourite spot on the couch. "Would you take my grave as quick?"

He grins widely, patting his stomach. "Sorry Fred, but the pizza was delicious. I couldn't resist. I'm sure I can figure out a way to pay you back." His words drip with sexual intent.

"Be careful there Viv, or you'll end up bankrupt. You already owe Dorotea a visit to her lady garden."

At this Nora almost chokes on the glass of juice she'd been sipping. Harry and Sean eye Nicholas with near identical interest. "Who's Dorotea?" Sean asks. "And what's all this about a lady garden?"

Nicholas makes a motion of zipping his lips. "A gentleman never kisses and tells."

"It's a good thing you're not a gentleman then," I say, sitting down in the space beside him since it's the only seat left. "And I'm sure you did a good deal more than kissing, you trollop." I look to the others. "Dorotea is a sassy Italian hairdresser Nicholas and I met in the park yesterday. She *showed* up at the club last night and

Nicholas took it upon himself to *show* her a memorable evening."

I give him a cheeky wink, all the while my stomach is turning at the topic of conversation. I really do bring the misery on myself sometimes. I was, after all, the one who brought up Dorotea just now. "I caught the two of them saying their farewells this morning. Nicholas mentioned that Dorotea went down on him and she seemed less than impressed that he didn't return the favour."

When my eyes catch on Nora's she gives me a brief sympathetic look, since she's the only one who knows how stumbling upon Nicholas and Dorotea after a one night stand would hurt me. Especially after my brief confession late last night. Okay, so I know I'm a fool to be hurt by it since I barely know him, but Nicholas is just one of those men who can make you fall head over heels with a simple heartfelt smile.

"Oh, this is juicy," says Harry. "Come on, give us the details Nicholas."

Nicholas shoots me an expression that's half amused, half put out. He absently trails a finger down my bare arm, stopping just before my wrist. "She was very – how do I put it? Enthusiastic. Although I could have done without all of the noises. She was a moaner in the true sense of the word. I'm surprised you didn't hear her through the walls. Couldn't shut her up."

He leans forward. Harry, Sean and Nora instinctively lean towards him in anticipation of what he might say next. "And get this, she had no hair down below whatsoever. I wasn't complaining, but it kind of threw me for six when I saw it. Most women have a landing strip at the bare minimum. She was like a porn star."

"Oh my God, I think you just traumatised me for life," Harry jokes. "As a gay man I have to admit I'm quite squeamish when it comes to women and their downstairs business."

"That's awful Harry," says Nora. "It's just a vagina, why would it make you squeamish?"

"It's the unknown," Harry replies. "The unknown can be frightening to a delicate flower such as myself."

I snicker. "Delicate my arse. You can suck a dick, but you can't take the idea of a hairless vagina."

Nora grins happily and crosses her arms, delighted that we're teaming together to defend our womanhood.

"Ugh, please don't tell me you've got one as well," says Harry, leaning into Sean as though he might expire.

"What a vagina? Or a hairless one?" Nora puts in.

"The latter," Harry replies, making a funny shape of displeasure with his mouth.

"I get a Brazilian wax every couple of weeks," Nora answers boldly. I'm surprised she's being so open; then again, personal hygiene is one of her best subjects. As I mentioned before, Nora's about as anal as they come. If there's a pun in there, I apologise. I've never accompanied her on her trips to the salon, because the idea of sitting there with my legs akimbo while some stranger goes to work on me with hot wax makes me shiver with trepidation.

"Is it wrong that I'm really enjoying the turn this conversation has taken?" asks Nicholas, leaning in close to my ear. "I think vagina is one of my favourite words." Nora and Harry are still arguing back and forth, so they don't hear him whisper to me. "I bet you have a really pretty one Freda, like a flower."

"You're a pervert," I say, pulling away nervously. "And if you think vaginas look like flowers you must have a very unique way of seeing them. What do you do, close one eye and squint?" I joke and rub at my arms, hoping he doesn't notice the goose bumps.

"If I had you in my bed, I definitely wouldn't be closing my eyes," he continues, unnerving me.

I let out a shaky breath. "Nicholas...you have to stop..." words fail me for once, and that hardly ever happens. The temptation to give in to his suggestiveness and flirting is too much. I can't let myself go there, because I know that one night is all he's ever going to want from me. Unfortunately, that's not something I'm capable of giving him. If I slept with him even once I'd probably end up following him around like a psycho lovesick puppy for the rest of my days.

At the sound of his name he lets his fingers trace over my thigh. "You should call me Nicholas more often, it kind of makes me hard."

"Please shut up now," I grip the edge of the couch. Nora, Harry and Sean are completely oblivious to the torture I'm currently undergoing.

"When I pinched you – last night – what did you feel?" he asks.

"Nothing," I answer through a tight jaw.

His fingers travel up my thigh, and dance in between my legs for a brief second when he goes on, "You felt nothing here?"

"Seriously Nicholas, back off or I'll punch you."

He raises his hands in the air in surrender, but doesn't move his lips from my ear. "One final thing," he whispers. "When I was inside Dorotea last night, I closed my eyes and pretended it was you."

My hand moves of its own volition, probably more out of shock than anything else, and I slap him hard right across the face. The room falls silent, and everyone's looking at me like I'm some kind of crazy person.

"Oh God, I'm so sorry. I didn't mean that," I falter when he turns his face to reveal that he's shaking with laughter.

"It's okay Fred, for such a pretty little thing you've got some strength in you. Ow," he rubs at his jaw.

"What happened?" Nora asks, looking worriedly between the two of us.

"I think I offended Fred's sensitive nature," Nicholas answers.

"It's nothing," I say. "I'm going to my room for a bit."

I stand up and march straight to my bedroom without saying another word, in an effort to hide my blazing red cheeks.

Chapter Seven
Apology Cupcakes and High Heels

About a half an hour later I hear people leaving, then my bedroom door opens and Nora and Harry come in. Nora sits down on the edge of my bed and Harry sits at the end of it.

"Nicholas and Sean have gone home," Nora says, breaking the silence. "Do you want to tell us exactly why you slapped Nicholas? Because he was keeping pretty much schtum about it once you left."

I turn over onto my side and huff, "I don't want to talk about it."

Harry pulls on the toe of my sock. "Come on, spill the beans Fred, you didn't just slap him for no reason."

I tug on a curl, making it go straight for a second before allowing it to bounce back to its natural state. "Ugh you guys, this is *so* embarrassing." I pause, looking each of them in the eye. "He told me, and I quote, that when he was inside Dorotea last night he closed his eyes and pretended it was me."

Nora makes a confused face. "Inside?" she asks, slow on the uptake, before her eyes widen in shock and realisation. If I wasn't so depressed I'd have a good old laugh at her reaction. "Wow, I'm not surprised you slapped him," she finally says.

"Maybe he's one of those sexy psychos," says Harry. "You know like the vampires out of *True Blood*. They talk all explicit and then they drink your blood and give you the best sex of your life." He lets out an evil cackle.

"He's not a sexy psycho, Harry. He just wants to have his way with me before leaving me high and dry."

Harry smirks. "I don't think he'll be leaving you dry..." he trails off.

I crawl forward to slap him upside the head. "Hey! I thought you were supposed to be squeamish about vaginas."

"As if." He rolls his eyes. "I was trying to come across all innocent for Sean's benefit."

"That's devious," I say. "I like your style. So tell me, what's the story between you two?"

"They had a night of wild drunken passion and now they're madly in love," Nora answers sarcastically.

"Shut up Nora, just because *you're* a dried up old hag," Harry quips.

Nora is *not* happy with that statement. Her expression has gone icy. She turns her attention back to me. "Seriously though Fred, I think Nicholas really might be into you in a big way. He was talking about you a lot while we were having pizza before you got home."

My curiosity piques. "Oh really, what did he say?"

"He was just asking questions about you, what sort of music do you like, what's your favourite movie, who was your last boyfriend, the kind of questions that show he's interested in you. He was also gushing over what a great job you did as his assistant last night, and that he's thinking of keeping you on."

"He was probably just being nosy," I tell her flippantly, trying to ignore the butterflies in my stomach.

"Ugh, if you want to be all modest then fine. I've told you what I think, so take it or leave it." Nora brushes some lint off her lap.

"Oh, I was going to ask you," Harry puts in, "if you'd be interested in coming to Electric Picnic at the end of

August. Sean and I are organising a group trip."

"You and Sean really are diving in head first, aren't you," I muse wryly. "Organising events and what not. Who have you invited so far?"

Electric Picnic is an arty farty music festival that goes on in Stradbally Hall in County Laois at the end of the summer. I went once about two years ago, drank too much and ended up being sick half the time. It served me right. I wouldn't mind giving it another chance though; I haven't been to a good festival in ages.

"So far on the list is yours truly, Sean, Nora and my brother Colm. Oh and I asked Nicholas if he'd like to come earlier and he said he was in." The idea of Nicholas going further piques my interest.

"You know your brother irritates the pants off me Harry," I say.

Harry's older brother Colm is his complete and total opposite. He's very straight laced and works in some high end financial services job down in the IFSC, which is Dublin's premium financial district, inhabited mainly by posh wankers who have a very high opinion of themselves. Harry's parents are always comparing him to his brother, since he only works as a lowly bank teller and Colm's a high flyer.

Harry let's out an amused laugh. "He only irritates you because he's always asking you out on dates, and you're always shutting him down."

Oh yeah, did I fail to mention that? Harry's brother also has a bit of a thing for me. I probably would have given him a chance by now if it weren't for the fact that he bores the tits off me. He once talked to me for a half an hour about a new tie he bought for work in some fancy men's boutique on Dawson Street, lamenting whether or not he should have allowed the shop girl to talk him into getting a pinkish shade of peach. He was worried his workmates would slag him off about it. Oh yeah, and he ogles my boobs every chance he gets. Not in a fun and flirty way like Nicholas does, but in an annoying, almost on the verge of drooling sort of way.

"I suppose I could just try to ignore him for the duration," I sigh. "I heard Crystal Castles are playing this year. I really want to see them live. Just make sure Colm's tent is set up far away from mine"

"So you'll come then?" Harry asks excitedly.

"Yes, when are you buying the tickets?"

"I'll get them on my credit card next week. That will give everyone the chance to throw the cash my way."

The idea of spending over two hundred Euros on a weekend ticket makes me feel slightly ill, but I need something to look forward to since I haven't got any sun holidays on the horizon. I suppose I can bring myself to part with the money.

Nora leaves to go and get ready for work, while Harry stays in my room and regales me with stories of his night of passion with Sean. I have a hard time holding in my laughter when he describes him as being "a little jockey with a big whip". Sean's probably only about 5"2, but he has that whole sort of cute Frodo Baggins thing going on.

I get an early night and try to push thoughts of Nicholas and the things he said to me earlier in the evening out of my head. It's no use though. His words echo through my mind, making me feel like getting up and taking a cold shower.

In the morning I deliver my cupcakes, before heading out to collect Mum and taking her to see her GP. The new doctor she doesn't like turns out to be a guy in his early thirties with a D4 accent. (D4 refers to "Dublin 4" which is an upper middle class area where people talk with pretentious, highly irritating accents, a whole lot of "loikes" and "oh my Gawds") He cracks a few shit jokes, and I can immediately tell that he thinks he's in fucking *Scrubs* or something. His thinning brown hair is cut and styled into one of those wannabe David Beckham mullets. My mum looks at him as if he's an alien from another planet, it's comical.

"So, what appears to be the problem, Mrs Wilson?" he asks, while scrolling down her file on his computer screen.

"I had a fall last week and bruised my ankle," Mum answers.

Dr Knobhead turns around in his swivel chair. "Well, we'd better have a look at that," he says, before proceeding to poke and prod at Mum's bruise. He determines that nothing's been broken and prescribes her a few painkillers and some healing salve to put on it every morning and night.

The thing that annoys me throughout the whole process is that every time Mum lets out a whimper of pain as he's prodding her, he glances up at me and gives me an amused shake of his head, as though she's overreacting. It really pisses me off.

I find that a lot of doctors become fairly desensitised to other people's pain after a while. Years on the job, seeing sick people day in day out, turns them into emotionless automatons. I'm sure there are some truly caring doctors out there, but I haven't yet come across one if there are.

Their sympathy always seems so disingenuous. Dr

Knobhead clearly got into the profession for the money and the ability to brag about devoting his life to a good and noble cause. If you hadn't noticed thus far, I'm partial to the odd rant every now and again.

On the short walk back to the house Mum tells me of the recent scandal with my sister Eileen, who's making her husband Jim sleep in the spare bedroom. I jump to the conclusion that she must have caught him having an affair, but apparently she's going through some kind of a crisis of identity.

She called Mum up the other night in tears, going on about how she's wasted half her life taking care of her kids and her husband. She wants to get away and do something new, have an adventure. It annoys me how she only ever calls our parents when she's got something to complain about.

"Jesus, who does she think she is, Shirley Valentine?" I ask Mum jokingly.

Mum suppresses a grin and slaps me lightly on the arm. "Stop that Freda, you know Eileen's always been the sensitive type."

"Temperamental you mean," I reply, thinking how it was a good thing she was in her teens by the time I was born, that way I didn't have to live through her dramas. Though I can imagine my toddler self giving her bemused looks whenever she went off on one.

Mum has her arm linked through mine, and we walk slowly to account for her ankle. I stay and have lunch at the house with her before catching a bus back to the city.

The next few days pass in their usual routine fashion. The weird thing is that I don't see hide nor hair of Nicholas and when Thursday comes around I begin to wonder if the slap I gave him made him think I was a nut job he should steer clear of. Now that the shock factor of what he said to me has worn off, I feel a little guilty. Perhaps he has the same issue with censoring himself as I do, and that's why he said what he did.

When I get home from my shift at the charity shop I grab the extra cupcakes that I set aside this morning, ice the word "sorry" onto them, put them on a plate and go to knock next door. Bringing baked goods as a gift for people tends to soften them up, even if they're supremely mad at you.

I made the effort with my appearance today, blow drying my hair and putting serum in it to make the curls extra silky. I'm also wearing the outfit Nora says suits my body the best; a little white vest top tucked into a high waisted navy pencil skirt. The skirt is made from good quality elasticated fabric, so it clings to the parts you want, while the dark colour hides any problem areas. In other words, the hips are emphasised and the stomach is disguised, providing an hour glass shape. If it weren't for Nora I wouldn't have a notion about any of this stuff.

I knock on Nicholas' door and when there's no answer I begin to feel a little sinking disappointment in my belly.

I press my ear against the wood and listen closely, and I'm almost certain I can hear faint music coming from within. With this piece of evidence that there's somebody inside, I continue knocking. Perhaps not a wise move if Nicholas really does hate me now, but I shrug and keep going. In for a penny, in for a pound.

A minute or two later I hear the lock flick over and the door opens. Nicholas stands before me with ruffled hair, wearing lounge pants, a t-shirt and a silky black Asian style kimono, the kind designed for women. It has pretty flower patterns all over. He looks like he's been in bed all day and it's almost three o'clock. His face seems haunted. I try to ignore his mismatched outfit and the fact that he's not looking his usual dapper self.

I cheerily lift the cupcakes up to show him. "Apology cupcakes, if you'll accept?"

"Ah Fred, you're a sight for sore eyes, come in. And what's this about an apology? I wasn't aware we were having a quarrel." He puts his hand on my lower back as he ushers me into the apartment. His touch burns right through to my skin.

"Well, I thought that because I hadn't heard from you since the happy slapping incident you were giving me the cold shoulder," I say, placing the cupcakes down on the kitchen counter.

"Nonsense, a little bit of a slap between friends is all in good fun," Nicholas teases.

I take the liberty of putting the kettle on to make tea, before going over and opening up one of the windows. The place feels muggy, as though he's been in here for days, wallowing in misery like a hermit. My ego would like to assume he's been depressed over my reluctance to hop into bed with him, but I'm clever enough to know that this is something else entirely.

Nicholas sits down on his *chaise longue* and rests his head on his red feathery pillow. He stares out the window I just opened, with some kind of torment in his eyes. I silently finish making the tea, before bringing it over to the coffee table, alongside two lemon cupcakes. One for each of us. Perhaps the bright yellow icing will lift his mood some.

Nicholas brings his attention back to me. "Oh look at these Fred, how delightful." He picks up a cupcake and takes a delicate bite. I sit beside him and place a hand on his shoulder.

"Are you okay Viv? You seem a little out of sorts."

He glances at me and licks some icing from the corner of his mouth. "I'm just going through one of my low periods. I'm either happy or I'm sad Fred, there's no middle ground with me. The life of a travelling performer can be a lonely one, sometimes it gets you down."

His words send a dart right through me. I feel bad at having thought Nicholas was always the spirited flirt he often comes across as. I remember him telling me he was lonely when we first met, now I know he wasn't just faking it in the hopes of a sympathy shag.

"Do you have, like, manic depression or something?" I blurt out rudely, not having fully thought the question through.

Nicholas smiles softly. "Something like that. But thank you for bringing the cupcakes, they've cheered me right up."

I hate that he doesn't specify. Though to be honest, I think we all have a little tendency towards depression. It's a modern thing. Most lives move too fast for human beings to be properly happy these days.

"Hey, it's my pleasure. If you ever need someone to talk to I'm just next door." I nudge him with my elbow good naturedly. "What's the point of having a best friend if she can't cheer you up when you're down?"

Nicholas releases the full force of his smile on me and it almost takes my breath away. He pulls my hand into his and gives it a squeeze. "Thank you, darling."

I drag my eyes away from him, because his beauty is quite overpowering, even when he's a dishevelled mess like he is right now. His bedroom door is ajar, and I can hear low music streaming through. "Are those the dulcet tones of Leonard Cohen I hear? You are a true cliché of sadness Viv," I joke and he laughs.

He's still holding my hand. He rubs his thumb over my palm. "You're a ray of sunshine, Freda. Thank you so much for taking the time to come and see me."

I get caught up in his stare again, and this time I can't seem to look away. Something clenches deep in my heart at the way he's staring at me, like I'm some kind of saintly apparition. "It's nothing, I like being around you Nicholas," I breathe, my totally honest statement surprising me.

He has a sharp intake of breath and his blue eyes dance. "I really like it when you say my name, you know."

My stark honesty continues when I hurry on, "I'm sorry if I can be a bit abrupt sometimes, or if the things I say hurt your feelings. It's just my way. I can't seem to help it." For some reason I feel the need to get this out, perhaps because today has shown me that Nicholas is not this indestructible, confident person like I thought he was.

"I like your way, don't ever change," he pauses and licks his lips, his eyes drifting to my cleavage. Because I'm wearing the outfit Nora says looks good on me, the "girls" are out a little more than usual. Nicholas' smile turns into a cheeky grin. "Remember when you said I could cop a feel the other day? I think I'd like to take you up on the offer now. It will lift my spirits."

I feign indignation. "You sir, are an opportunistic scoundrel."

He reaches forward and I shift back. "Relax Fred, you'll like this, I promise."

I force myself to remain still for him. After all, I did tell him that he could give them a squeeze to get it out of his system. Just another example of my big mouth getting me into a sticky situation.

His thumb brushes over the bare skin of my collarbone, before his hand traces down to the curve of my breast. My breaths come short and fast. Nicholas notices instantly, and his lips tilt up at one end in a smirk. Finally, he cups me fully in his hand, his eyes studying my body before returning to my face. He squeezes firmly, while his other hand wanders up to do the same to the other one. His eyelids flutter.

"I love this outfit on you Fred; your body is a feast for the senses," he breathes.

His hands slide down my breasts to rest on my hips. He pushes me back so that I'm lying beneath him. I've been rendered immobile. Every touch sears through me, making me want more, making me addicted. He slowly reaches for the hem of my skirt and hitches it up, before pulling my legs apart and wrapping them around his waist. I gasp when he grinds his obvious erection into me. There's far too much fabric between us and I'm entirely too turned on.

His lips claim my neck, as he pushes my hair to the side. I can feel his kisses at the base of my spine. Each one tingles right through me. I let my hands drift up and sink into his soft black hair, then I trail them down over his hard, muscular shoulders. Nicholas' hand feels its way up the inside of my thigh, before cupping me right on the vagina. I gasp. Pant. Lose my fucking mind.

"Are you wet for me Fred?" he asks, his voice sounds like a dark prison that I desperately want to get inside. This has gone way past copping a feel, but I can't seem to bring myself to put a stop to it.

"Mm hmm," I mumble, unable to give a proper response.

"God, you're so fucking lovely," he curses, as he slips one finger beneath fabric of my underwear, finds my clit and begins making these wonderful circular motions.

His touch makes my body simultaneously melt and awaken. My senses go into overdrive. When you're attracted to someone the way that I'm attracted to Nicholas, even the slightest whisper of his fingers against yours makes your body wake up and take notice. Needless to say, him having his hand inside my knickers makes me feel like I'm going to explode.

"You smell great, you feel bloody fantastic," he's almost panting now, burying his face in my hair for a second, before kissing and sucking on my neck.

Sensation flits through me, radiating out from my centre and encapsulating every nerve ending in my body. I haven't been touched like this in what seems like forever. Come to think of it, no man has touched me in quite this way before, with such practised confidence as if he knows exactly how to bring me to the brink of ecstasy.

Then he removes his mouth from my neck and captures my lips in a slow, wet, languid kiss. I let out a long moan that goes right from my mouth into his. He kisses me harder then, sliding his tongue in and out, hard and soft at the same time.

He continues driving me insane with his fingers, increasing his speed to almost make me come but then slowing back down again. Teasing me. He gives me one last soft kiss before pulling back to look at me.

"I want to watch you when you come," he says, his mouth hanging open as his eyes rake over me. "Christ Fred, your lips are like little pillows of heaven, and your mouth, God, your fucking mouth."

I blush and turn my gaze away from him, too embarrassed to maintain eye contact. He takes his other hand and pulls on my chin, making me face him again. His smile is intolerable. "Are you shy? Fuck, that just makes me ten times harder for you."

His hand moves against me faster and I can tell I'm close to the edge now. He holds my eyes as he bends down, places a kiss to my fully clothed breast before biting down hard on my nipple through the fabric. At that my body explodes with perhaps the most intense orgasm I've ever had. I shake against him several times with the release, my eyes wide and looking straight into his.

I have never felt this much sensation with a man before. Most of my sexual encounters have been messy, drunken fumbles. But this was something else, something wonderful. And now I hate myself for having given in, because looking into his eyes as I came did something to me. It made my heart reach out and latch onto his, even if his heart might not want to latch onto mine.

My entire body is happy and limp with the pleasure I've just experienced. Nicholas pulls me back so that I'm lying on top of him, my curves sinking into his hard lines.

His hands travel up and down my arms, leaving a trail of shivering fingerprints all along my skin. I rest my head in the crook of his neck and sigh into him. I'm not going to think about how what just happened is going to seriously change our tentative friendship. I try to think of nothing but how this feels.

"You're so pretty when you come, all wide eyed and surprised," Nicholas laughs tenderly. "I didn't think you'd make me feel so clean Fred."

"What do you mean?" I ask, my face still pressed to his skin.

"Every woman is different," he explains. "Some of them make you feel satisfied, others make you feel high, most just make you feel used or dirty, but you Fred, you make me feel cleansed. There's no guile or ulterior motives with you. You're just in the moment for whatever it might bring."

I make him feel cleansed. That's just too romantic, I don't think my heart can take it. "That sounds kind of sad. Don't any of them ever make you feel love?"

"Some have come close," he answers, but then he goes quiet.

He seems to be lost for a moment, so I try to bring him back to me. "Well, all I know is that was one of the best orgasms I've ever had. I've been plagued with men who didn't know what they were doing."

Nicholas smiles and presses his face into my hair. "I'm flattered. Although since you said yourself that you haven't had a boyfriend in three and a half years, I must not have been up against very stiff competition."

"How do you know I don't have one night stands to keep me tided over?" I fake a sulky tone.

"You don't, you're not that kind of girl. I can tell.

Perhaps that's why you make me feel so clean."

I don't reply. To be honest I feel sort of sorry for him if he feels that way after sleeping with women, dirty and used. Why would he keep doing it if that's what he gets in return? Is the pleasure of the moment really worth it?

I stay quiet and enjoy the feeling of being so close to him, with almost every part of our bodies touching. He keeps running his fingers through my hair. It feels nice, peaceful. I could almost fall asleep.

"I really like you Fred," he whispers, jolting me from the nap I was just about to fall into.

I hesitate before replying, "I really like you too Nicholas. But - do you think this might have been a bad idea?"

I hate to bring reality crashing down on both of us, especially after such a tender interlude, but I'm so scared that we've ruined things now. Never again will I be able to look at him and not think about how he touched me.

"No. I think we both know where we stand with one another." His voice is gentle.

He sits up then and I slide off him, fixing my skirt back down. What does he mean by that? I'm too frightened to ask.

My cheeks heat up, because now that what just happened is over I feel awkward with him. The line between friends and lovers is completely blurred and I'm not exactly sure which side I fall on. I scramble for something to take my mind off it, and then my eyes latch on the glittery purple high heels he'd worn last Saturday night sitting in the corner of the room.

"Hey, remember you said you'd teach me how to walk

in heels?" I say with a forced smile, nodding towards his purple shoes.

"Yes?" he asks.

"Care to show me now?"

Nicholas gives me a humorous grimace. "That might be difficult, since I've got a severe case of blue balls at the moment."

Our eyes lock, and I don't know whether he's saying this because he wants me to get him off the way he got me off, or if he's just being flirtatious. In a last ditch attempt at self-preservation, I joke, "Well walk it off, Viv. A girl needs to know how to wear heels if she wants to make it in the cut throat world of fashion. I plan on developing an eating disorder and entering Britain's Next Top Model next year. This lesson will be the first step to achieving my dream."

He frowns slightly before understanding dawns on him. I'm embarrassed and he knows it. That makes me even more embarrassed. It's a cruel cycle.

Nicholas accepts my challenge when he clasps his palms together. "Right well, we'll have to start you off on a pair of low ones," he walks into his bedroom and comes back out with a pair of plain black two inch heels.

"No way, I want the sexy flashy ones you wear on stage," I say dramatically.

"You're already sexy enough Fred," Nicholas remarks hotly, before bending down on one knee and removing both of my flip flops. Even him touching my foot makes me go all melty, but I try to ignore it. He gives me an evil smile as he slips on the black shoes, like he knows exactly what his touch is doing to me. He slowly runs his hand over my calf, before rising to his feet and tugging me up with him.

He goes over and grabs the purple ones, putting them on his own feet. He's tall enough as it is, but he's even taller with the shoes on, like one of those mythological Amazonian women who chopped off one of their breasts so they wouldn't get in the way when they were shooting a bow and arrow - or something like that. It's actually quite practical when you think about it. Practical but painful. I hope you enjoyed that tangent. There are more to come. I'll keep you posted.

I glance up at Nicholas just as he asks, "Do those fit you all right? You look about a size five, those are a six."

"I'm a five and a half actually, but these are okay. Where did you get them? You're definitely bigger than a size six."

He smirks, clearly thinking of the innuendo that large feet equal large privates. "Why thank you Fred, I didn't realise you noticed. Those were my mother's. I like to keep some of her stuff with me."

I pause in my inspection of the shoes to look up at him. "You keep your mother's things still, after all this time?"

"I do. It's comforting."

In my head I'm thinking it might be some strange psychological attachment related to grief, but for once I don't blurt out exactly what's inside my noggin. Instead I reply, "You must have really loved her."

His smile is a sad one. "I did. Still do. Now the first step is to keep your legs straight as you walk, try not to bend your knees."

Pushing away the thought of how weird it is to be wearing his dead mother's shoes, I try to follow his instructions. "You do realise I'm probably one of the most ungraceful women you will ever meet. I'm not sure it's possible for me to keep my legs straight when I walk. I'll look like I'm trying to impersonate a robot."

"Nonsense. Make sure you put your heel down first rather than your toe. Keep your legs together and take slow, easy steps."

I snicker and comment, "That's not what you were saying earlier on." Damn internal filter, it never keeps working properly for long.

"I know. I'm not usually known for telling women to close their legs, but for this particular activity it's a requirement. Besides, you can spread them for me later."

I raise an eyebrow and shake my head at him. "You should be so lucky."

I take slow steps across the room, just like he told me to. Even though the heels aren't very high, they still feel like skyscrapers to me since I'm not used to wearing them. I wobble a little before finding my feet. Soon I pick up my pace, becoming increasingly more confident in the dead woman's shoes. Weird.

"Um, Nicholas, can I ask you something?" I venture nervously.

"Fire away," he says, before sitting carefully down on a stool in the kitchen area. He crosses one leg over the other, the way a woman would. Sometimes his movements are so authentically female it's unsettling. When I cross my legs I tend to let one ankle rest on my knee, not at all as feminine or dexterous as the way Nicholas does it. Although that might just be because he's wearing the heels, which is putting him into woman mode.

I swallow to try and moisten my dry throat before mumbling, "Well, I was just going to ask you if you could keep what happened between us today to yourself. I don't want you telling people all the details the way you told everyone the details of your night with Dorotea."

"If I recall correctly, you were the one who prompted me to tell," he answers with a wicked grin and a touch of provocation.

"Yeah well...you'll soon learn that inconsistency is the name of the game with me."

"You're certainly inconsistently hot and cold," Nicholas throws back sharply, his expression serious all of a sudden.

"What's that supposed to mean?" I ask, turning on my heel to face him.

He flings his eyes to the *chaise longue* where not long ago he gave me one of the most intense orgasms of my life. "One minute you're all panting and wet for me, and the next you're sarcastically telling me to *walk it off, Viv*. We're attracted to one another, why all the dancing back and forward?"

Great, now I feel guilty. I shrug and let my eyes fall to the floor. "I'm not used to this. And despite the attraction, I don't think we'll be good for one another. Somebody will get hurt, and that somebody will most likely be me."

Nicholas might have the quirk of being a drag queen, but we're still aeons apart when it comes to looks. He's all smooth grace and sexy smiles, whereas I'm big haired, awkward and a touch frumpy. You may well roll your eyes at my low self-esteem. It's a condition for which there is no cure.

He stands now and strides towards me, stopping inches from my face. "I would never hurt you."

I look anywhere but at his beautiful blue eyes. "Perhaps not intentionally..." I trail off.

"Look at me Freda," he grabs my chin and forces me to meet his gaze. "I would *never* hurt you."

His words singe me. Is he telling the truth?

"But I'm working for you now. It's not the best idea for us to go complicating things." I feel like some idiot girl off a soap opera with that shitty line.

He's silent for a long moment. His face is difficult to read. "Okay then," he finally replies.

He unexpectedly waves away our argument and begins chatting about tonight's gig and what he plans on singing and wearing. I'm relieved that he's not pushing the issue, yet I'm also kind of disappointed that he gave up so easily.

I am such a wanker sometimes.

Chapter Eight
Frilly Knickers and Pretty Men

Later that day Nicholas has me unpacking an array of outfits in the dressing room at The Glamour Patch. He hasn't breathed a word about our earlier encounter and subsequent argument. Perhaps he's deciding to move on, realising that I'm a whiny girl who isn't worth his efforts when he could have a porn star like Dorotea when and wherever he wants her. Okay, so I know she's not an actual porn star, but she might as well be compared to me.

Tonight Nicholas is going for a burlesque inspired look that includes a silky red and black corset, frilly knickers (with some tiny black men's briefs underneath to make sure his meat and two veg don't pop out to say hello) hold-up stockings and a pair of black leather high heeled boots. On his head is a bobbed wig, black this time as opposed to blond.

"Why do you always change your look?" I ask him, as I tug the wig into place so that it sits in the right position on top of his head. "Dame Edna Everage always wore similar outfits, so did Lily Savage."

Nicholas lets out a throaty laugh as he touches up his blusher. "Are you seriously comparing me to Paul O'Grady?" He cocks a shapely eyebrow at me.

While I was doing his make-up earlier on I used a brow brush and an eyebrow pencil to make his brows look more structured and feminine. Although they weren't very bushy to begin with. I have a feeling he does some very subtle plucking. You'd hardly notice it when he's in his everyday "Nicholas" mode. But they're just a little too suspiciously neat.

"What's the problem with that? Lily Savage was a staple of my childhood television experience. I have this dream that one day I'll be neighbours with Paul O'Grady. We'll have tea together every morning followed by gossiping and walking our spoiled dogs in the park."

Nicholas raises his hand and jokingly slaps me hard on the arse. "Hey! You've already got yourself one drag queen best friend, you don't need another one. And the problem is that we are very different kinds of performers, plus I can sing."

"And Paul's funnier than you," I mutter huffily under my breath, rubbing a hand over my now stinging bottom.

Nicholas grins happily as he watches me. "I heard that, another word from you and I'll be forced to take you over my knee." He picks up a hair brush and makes a show of fake paddling my behind. I giggle and run to the other side of the room so that he can't get to me.

"Easy there Viv, somebody might walk in and think you beat on your employees."

"I'm sure they'll forgive me, after all, my employee is a *very* naughty girl with a *very* nice bottom," he stares at me through the mirror on the dressing table. If he wasn't in his Vivica Blue costume I'd probably be more embarrassed by the way he's staring at me, as though silently reminding me of his hand being down my knickers not too long ago.

He breaks the moment when he speaks. "To answer your question, I don't really know why I change my look all the time. It's just how I do it. I'd probably get bored if I had to wear the same thing for every gig."

"It definitely keeps things interesting," I tell him with a smile. I don't think I've ever had as much fun as I've had while sifting through all of Nicholas' drag clothes. He has everything from sequins, to silk, to spandex. I'm secretly anticipating the night he decides to don the latter. Nothing will be left to the imagination, and I will be reserving myself a front row seat.

"So I hear you're coming to Electric Picnic with us," I say, casually sitting down on the chair beside him.

"Is that the music festival thing Sean and Harry were going on about?" he asks, dabbing a small bit of gloss onto his lips. I nod silently. "Yes I'm going. It sounds like it'll be fun and I love camping. Are you hinting at sharing a tent with me Fred?" he teases and gives me a camp smouldering look up and down.

I gulp at the thoughts of what sharing a tent with Nicholas would involve. I try to hide my nervousness when I reply, "No, um, I'll probably be sharing with Nora."

His eyes are far too perceptive. "Ah, that's a shame. If it got cold at night we could have cuddled up and kept each other warm."

I push back my initial instinct to tell him I wouldn't mind cuddling him if I could trust him not to drop the hand in the process. Ever since we met I've found him to be overly tactile, always touching the places that send my adrenaline soaring. The small of my back, the spot below my ear, the inside of my wrist..*Okay*, I'm turning *myself* on here. Who would have thought that a drag queen could be my ultimate male fantasy?

"It will probably be sunny, so it won't get too cold," I say, pushing back the imagery of the two of us alone in a tiny tent.

Nicholas lets out a loud guffaw of a laugh, and I don't know what I've said that he's found so funny. I keep asking him for the next few minutes, but he just shakes his head and wipes happy tears from the corners of his eyes. Annoyed by whatever private joke he's harbouring about me, probably something to do with my prudish embarrassment, I sigh and go about cleaning up the dressing room.

Just before he takes to the stage, Nicholas suggests that I go out and sit at the front of the audience to enjoy a drink. He says I worked hard enough today and that I deserve a break. He doesn't have to tell me twice. I grab a glass of white wine from the bar and hustle back to the stage where I swiftly sit myself down at a table of rowdy, pretty men.

I chat with them amiably and tell them that I'm Vivica Blue's executive assistant, even though I have no clue what exactly an executive assistant is, nor what one does. Their eyes all light up when they hear I know Nicholas and they immediately begin to pester me with questions about him and his ambiguous sexual orientation.

In layman's terms, they want to know if he's gay, straight or bi. I'd feel bad having to break it to them that he doesn't bat for their team, so in the spirit of keeping things mysterious I tap the side of my nose and give them the old "Now, now, wouldn't you like to know" routine. I'm sure Nicholas would thank me for preserving his mystique as a performer. The prospect of him being gay or bisexual is likely what keeps the place teeming with male punters on the nights of his gigs.

When Nicholas' set begins he comes out singing Nancy Sinatra's "These Boots Are Made For Walkin'".

He laughs as he sings and gives me a wink, before pointing down at his black leather boots. He's clearly singing the song intentionally to tease me about how crap I am with a heel any thicker than an inch and a half.

After a couple of songs he does a skit where he changes his whole outfit in front of the audience. I'd been wondering why he got me to leave a purple dress and a pair of custom made, red soled Louboutins by the side of the stage before he went on. I spent a while marvelling at how he managed to get a pair in his size. They must have cost him a pretty penny.

He cleverly manoeuvres himself out of the boots, seductively zipping them down while the audience whistles and cheers him on. He slips on the Louboutins and then pulls a shy looking guy in his early twenties up onto the stage and gets him to help him out of his corset. The guy's entire face goes red as a tomato as he fumbles with the complicated buckles, while Nicholas cheekily teases him not to be taking a peek. At long last he's in his new outfit and he continues with the second half of the gig.

For the final song of the set The Wilting Willows sit idly and watch as Nicholas prepares to sing a capella. The entire club is reduced to hushed whispers once Miss Vivica Blue's demeanour turns serious.

"This last song is about love, it's sad but it's real. I'd like to dedicate it to my new home and the wonderful friends I've made, who have welcomed me with open arms and made me feel like I've always been here. This one's called "The Wind That Shakes the Barley".

Nicholas' voice echoes around the silent club, eerily filling the space despite the fact that it's only him singing. I look up at him and he catches me with his eyes, like he always does when our gazes meet. He holds me there, like a prisoner, as goose bumps wash over my skin with the haunting lyrics. He sings each word with meaning, as though he wrote the song himself and felt every moment of the love and tragedy that the story tells. He continues singing, but comes and sits down right in front of me on the edge of the stage.

I sat within the valley green, I sat me with my true love
My sad heart strove the two between, the old love and the new love
The old for her, the new that made me think on Ireland dearly
While soft the wind blew down the glen and shook the golden barley

When he says the word "golden" he reaches down and drifts a hand through my hair. My entire body comes alive, like he's singing for me and only me. Like the hundred odd people packed into the club aren't here at all. It's just the two of us.

While sad I kissed away her tears, my fond arms round her flinging
The foeman's shot burst on our ears from out the wildwood ringing
A bullet pierced my true love's side in life's young spring so early
And on my breast in blood she died while soft winds shook the barley

He's so caught up in the song now, caught up in the story, that an actual tear runs down his face. God, he really is good at this, I think to myself. My eyes go a little watery too. He can put so much genuine feeling into his voice. He shouldn't be singing in some obscure little club in Dublin, he should be on a proper stage, sharing his wonderful voice and his ability to convey emotion with the world. Suddenly, when Nicholas gets to the final verse, people in the audience begin singing along with him.

But blood for blood without remorse I've taken at Oulart Hollow
And laid my true love's clay cold corpse where I full soon may follow
As round her grave I wander drear, noon, night and morning early
With breaking heart when ever I hear the wind that shakes the barley.

When he's finished singing, quiet encapsulates the building, before people rise to give him a standing ovation. Nicholas bows three times, blows me a discreet kiss and disappears behind the red velvet curtains. I say goodbye to the men I'd been sitting with and make my way to the dressing room.

Once there, I find Nicholas sitting by the mirror, having already made a start on removing his make-up. His mood is sombre, perhaps he's still feeling the after effects of the song. It's an iconic Irish Sean Nós song, but I'm surprised he knew it at all since he normally sings songs from musicals or big band numbers.

Then a realisation hits me like a ton of bricks. He sat and sang an Irish song to me, just like he sang the Italian inspired song to Dorotea last week. Oh no. Disappointment fills my gut as I think how despite the heartfelt story of tragic love he told, it was all just a ploy to get me to sleep with him. After all, the same thing worked a treat with Dorotea. I'm such an idiot for getting so taken in by it all. A mixture of sadness and anger fills me as I step forward and carefully remove his wig, not breathing a word.

He watches the movements of my hands in the mirror, as he swipes the make-up wipe across his cheek. I take out all the clips that had been keeping his hair in place beneath the wig. His gaze is speculative, like he doesn't know how to broach a conversation with me.

God, I'm so ridiculously upset with him right now, and it takes everything that's in me not to burst into tears and flee the room like the cliché of a spurned admirer. I really am just another potential fuck to him, some stupid girl he thinks he can manipulate into bed with an emotional song and a fake tear or two. He played Dorotea like a fucking piano. I'm not going to go the same way.

"Why did you sing that song?" I ask him finally, after a silence that was beginning to feel like it would go on forever.

"I wanted to pay respects to the country I'm trying to make my home," Nicholas answers after thinking about it for a second. His brow furrows slightly as he regards me.

"And why did you sit by the edge of the stage and sing it directly to me, touching my hair like it meant something?" I keep my voice steady. It's difficult but I just about manage it.

Nicholas looks at me long and hard now, no trace of his usual humour on his face. "It's a show Fred," he answers low and soft. "I was giving the audience a show."

"So it's all fake then?" I go on, steeling myself for what he might say next.

He looks away and stares up at the ceiling for a minute. "Not all of it, but I do act. It's all a part of the performance. Do you think I mean it when I blow kisses to the men in the audience and flirt with them? I'll admit I feel things when I sing, lots of lyrics hold meaning for me, but 95% of what I do on stage isn't real Fred. I'm Vivica Blue up there, not Nicholas."

"Right, I think I get it now," I reply, my jaw tight.

He puts his hand on mine, stopping me from removing the final few clips from his hair. "Do you Fred?"

"Yes, what you do on stage is a performance, it doesn't mean anything."

"It's entertainment Fred, and I am an entertainer. This is what I do. It's what I've always done. I wouldn't know how to be any other way."

His words hurt me, because I know what he's really trying to say. He's telling me that he can't be changed. He'll continue to shag his way from woman to woman just like he always has. And yes, I'll admit that somewhere in the back of my mind I wanted to be special to him, different from all of the other women who've turned his head. Isn't that what every girl wants? To be loved by someone uniquely, to make a man feel something he hasn't yet felt for anyone else.

The female need for true love is a fickle bitch. It forces itself into your life and shapes your actions, always driving you to find that one guy who'll love you unconditionally. Some of us seek it in the worst of places too, in soulless pubs and night clubs filled with guys who can't see past their own shallow egos, who only see the surface of a woman. They don't look for what's underneath because they don't want that; they want the aesthetic, the long hair and the tight little dresses.

Nicholas is no different really. I want him to be more than just some flirty straight drag queen. I want him to be the one. Unfortunately, I think I'm cursed to be one of those women who sees "the one" in the wrong one.

We barely speak after that, just quietly pack up the last of his things. When we get back to the apartment building he goes inside his place and I go inside mine. Tonight has been a cold slap of reality, if nothing else. I just need to enjoy being friends with Nicholas, let him boost my confidence with his flirting and quit harbouring unrealistic romantic ideas about him.

The next day I'm like a zombie. The noise of the blender as I mix the cupcake frosting makes me want to act out Nora's fantasy and take a hammer to the bloody thing. I think I'm going to have to bake my cupcakes on Thursday evenings before I go to the club with Nicholas and refrigerate them, because getting up to make them in the early hours of the morning is going to mean I'm consistently cranky on Fridays.

They won't be as fresh as they usually are, but at least I won't mess up the icing as badly as I am now. I've just dropped a massive blob of vanilla onto the kitchen floor. I crankily get down on my hands and knees to wipe it up.

When I arrive at the charity shop, Theresa greets me with a nice cup of coffee and it wakes me up a little better.

"You're looking tired today, Freda. Late night last night was it?" she asks, looking fresh as a daisy. The cow. I'm jealous of her full night's sleep. I only got about two hours, since I spent a while wallowing in misery over my realisation that Nicholas isn't going to be the love of my life like I subconsciously wanted him to be. Mournfully, I relived how exquisitely he kissed me and made me come, and then fretted over how I'm not going to get to experience that again.

"Yes, I've got a new job in a night club," I tell Theresa, bringing myself back to the present. I avoid going into detail about being a drag queen's assistant so as to avoid her questions. I don't want to talk about Nicholas right now.

"Goodness, you're going to end up working yourself to death," she tuts like a mother hen.

"Not necessarily. When you add up all the hours I work in my three jobs it's more or less the same as the usual 40 hour week most people do. The hours are just a little all over the place. But I don't mind, it keeps me busy. I'll probably sleep this afternoon when I finish my shift here though. I'm going to be tired until I get used to the new routine."

"True," Theresa agrees. "Oh, by the way, a young man came in here yesterday looking for you."

"Oh yeah, it was probably Harry. What did he look like?"

She puts her hand on her hip and squishes up her face as though trying to remember. You'd swear she saw him ten years ago instead of yesterday.

"Blond hair, medium height, glasses, a bit of a stern expression."

Her answer causes my stomach to drop and air to gush right out of my mouth in a gasp. Christ on a fucking bike. That does *not* sound at all like Harry. There's only one person I know fitting that description, the stern expression gave it away. My ex Aaron. How on earth did he find me? I know Dublin's hardly the biggest city in the world, but he lives in the suburbs and I don't have a Facebook page.

The only people who know where I work and live are my family and my small group of friends. I know this sounds crazy, but I actually Google myself regularly out of paranoia, just to make sure nothing pops up that I didn't manage to erase.

Aaron never hurt me, but he was possessive to the extreme, and *not* in a sexy way. One time he wouldn't allow me to leave his house and he locked me in for several hours before finally agreeing to let me go. I had to sit in his living room and watch as he manically paced back and forth, ranting about how I didn't value our relationship the way he did.

I don't even know why I went out with him in the first place. I was never even remotely attracted to him. He looked halfway between a computer nerd and a poster child for Nazi Germany. He has this starkly blond hair and eyebrows. We met at a college party for some society we were both members of and he was just really pushy, asking me to go out to dinner with him.

If you've ever been to college you'll know that it's the one time in your life when you meet the biggest amount of weirdos. I experienced everything from sociopaths to narcissists to plain and simple psychopaths. The only reason I agreed to go out with Aaron was because I'd been single for so long and wanted to show people that I wasn't a closeted lesbian. Some girl who didn't like me had started up a rumour.

Anyway, I'd only planned on going out on a few dates with him, but he stuck to me like glue. There was no getting rid of him. He'd show up after almost all of my classes, take me to lunch, walk me home at the end of the day. It was *suffocating*.

Now, I know what you're probably thinking. What makes me so special that some guy would be that crazy about me? There lies the rub. There was nothing particularly special about me. Aaron was just one of those guys who fixated on a single girl and became obsessed with her. Lucky me, I happened to be that one girl.

I cannot believe that after three years he's still on the hunt. Suddenly I'm remembering the time after I'd told him I was breaking up with him, and he'd marched into his kitchen and started smashing plates and cups onto the floor like a nutter, calling me a slut and a whore. He clearly has some undiagnosed psychological condition where he develops these attachments to people he can't let go of.

My heart is thumping way too fast and I think I can feel a panic attack coming on. Theresa gives me a strange look as I excuse myself and run to the bathroom. I sit in there for about fifteen minutes, trying to calm myself down.

Various horrific scenarios run through my head. Like what if he's gone even more do-lally in the three years that have passed since we broke up? What if he breaks into my apartment and threatens me with a knife? Or says he's going to kill himself if we can't be together? Actually, I think he tried that one when we were together. As you can imagine, he's not the kind of person you want to have obsessed with you.

Finally, I manage to pull myself together and go back out to the shop, but I'm well and truly shaken for the rest of the day.

Chapter Nine
Lady Suits and Locked Bathroom Doors

Two weeks go by, within which I find myself constantly looking at the people who are walking behind me, paranoid that I'll see Aaron somewhere. Every time a new customer comes into the shop my heart jumps in case it's him.

He doesn't turn up though, and I begin to think that it might not have been him who asked for me that time at all. Perhaps it was just some customer I'd been chatting to who wanted to follow up about a purchase. One who bore a freaky resemblance to my old boyfriend. Yes it's unlikely, but I latch on to the easy explanation as it's the only way to retain my sanity.

When I spend time working with Nicholas we seem to find a platonic middle ground, which both of us stick to rigidly. I think he knows he hurt my feelings before, so he's being very careful not to lead me on again. I'm a one man kind of woman, but he's not a one woman kind of man. Obviously, any tryst we might have had would never have worked out.

I help him set his apartment up properly and unpack all of the boxes, because he wants to have a belated house warming party on Sunday night. His second bedroom is practically an oversized wardrobe now, with all of his costumes stored in it. He gives me a check for my first two weeks working with him, including that first Saturday night, and it's far more money than I expected. I try to get him to write another check for less, but there's no budging him.

"You're a pleasure to be around Fred. Take the

money, you deserve it," he says casually, waving away my protests.

I grudgingly slip the check into the pocket of my jeans and say no more about it. The idea that he's paying me to spend time with him doesn't sit right with me, but I bite my tongue. I'm his employee first and foremost, and that will just have to do.

I have to cancel going to visit my parents on the day of Nicholas' party, because I agreed to cater it for him. I have a chat with Mum on the phone for a while and she tells me how her ankle is all healed up now. She's the only person who knows about my past with Aaron, but I haven't mentioned that he might be looking for me again because I don't want to worry her. She's older now, and I'm afraid the stress might make her sick.

For the party food I make an array of cupcakes, as well as some savoury finger foods. I cook some delicious bacon strips dipped in honey, chicken wings with garlic and chive dip, deep fried jalapeño poppers, and dainty little sandwiches skewered with cocktail sticks. A heart attack waiting to happen, in other words.

I might have gone a little overboard, but I'm not exactly sure how many people Nicholas has invited. He did mention that he'd asked Dorotea to pop by, which is why I have decided to wear the most flattering dress I own. It's tight, black and silky, with short lacy sleeves. It also shows my cleavage in the best possible light. I clip my curls up in a messy French twist, with lots of tendrils falling down.

I am asking for trouble by dressing like this, and I know it. But I'm feeling a little spurned over how easily Nicholas seems to be keeping his hands off me these days. It might be a touch evil, not to mention irrational, but I want to torture him.

Harry and Sean drop by the apartment like I'd asked them to, because I need them to bring the food next door and set it up for me while I get ready. Harry stands in my bedroom doorway and lets out a low whistle. I'm making my eyes all smoky with some black eye shadow, to really bring out the gold notes in their hazel colour. I'm going for broke. These have been a shitty, nervy two weeks, what with the whole Aaron thing going on, so I just need one night where I can feel good about myself.

"The trays are all in the kitchen," I tell him. "Be careful with the chicken wings. They're still pretty hot."

"They're not the only thing that's hot tonight. Fred, I'm worried I'll turn straight if I keep staring at your boobs much longer."

"Good to know," I laugh. He winks and goes to sort out the food.

A few minutes later Nora comes in to see if I'm ready. She's wearing a nice beige shift dress and brown sandals. I notice her give my appearance a sharp look.

"You never make this much of an effort. What's going on?" she asks shrewdly.

"Is it too much?" I ask back, biting at my fingernails out of nervousness.

"You look like a wet dream and you know it," she rolls her eyes at me. "I was just wondering why. I thought you and Nicholas were never going to happen, at least that's what you've been saying this past week or so. A little *too* fervently might I add, like you're trying to convince yourself more than anything else."

I shrug and let out a long sigh. Nora's completely right. I have been trying to convince myself – and failing miserably. "Remember the Italian woman he slept with?" I finally ask her. Nora nods. "She's going to be at the party, so getting dressed up is helping me to boost my confidence."

"Well I hope it works," she replies drily, before we lock up our apartment and head next door.

Phil, Nicholas' friend and manager of The Glamour Patch, answers the door to us wearing a blue shirt with glittery shoulder caps. I've gotten to know him quite well over the past two weeks, and he just might be the funniest person I've ever met. He's managed a ton of different clubs over the years, including one in San Francisco, and has some of the most entertaining anecdotes you will ever hear.

"Fred look at you, hot to trot, come in. I've just been munching on your chicken wings. They're to die for," he leads us into the living area and I take note of who's here.

Sean, Harry and Harry's brother Colm are chatting on the couch. I could kill Harry for bringing Colm along, because I know I'll have to fend off his lecherous advances once he has a few drinks on him. Nicholas is standing in the kitchen with Dorotea and her hairdresser friend with the mullet.

He looks amazing in a midnight blue shirt, a thin black tie and dark slacks. Staring at the tie makes me want to loosen it up and pull it off him (like a temptress in a sexual thriller movie from the early nineties). Other than that there are a few faces I recognise as employees from the club, as well as the other members of Sean's band, The Wilting Willows.

Phil leads us directly to the kitchen and hands us each a glass of wine. Somebody must have brought their karaoke machine along, because there's one all set up in the corner of the living area. Wonderful. I know I'll think it's a good idea to get up and start singing later on. "Starman" by David Bowie is currently playing through a pair of iPod speakers.

Nicholas' eyes catch on mine as I pass him by, and good God do they burn. I feel a blush spread all over my body at how intensely he's staring at me. Like he could devour me. His gaze blazes a fire all along my body, from head to toe. He leaves Dorotea and approaches me. I don't fail to notice Dorotea giving me a look. I roll my eyes at her, and her lips go tight with a scowl. Nora has hopped over to join Harry. Hopefully Colm will set his sights on her tonight instead of me.

I turn around and pretend to be admiring the new painting Nicholas bought to hang up on his wall. It's modern art, so I can't really discern what it's supposed to be, but it's a good distraction. I feel his hand touch lightly on my hip. His warm body is too close behind me.

"I like your dress," he tells me huskily, "and your hair looks beautiful up like that."

I take a sip of wine. "Thank you," I answer, barely a whisper. What the hell is wrong with me? His voice is so dark and sexy right now, I'm having a hard time keeping my cool.

"Dorotea's not happy that you've left her to fend for herself," I comment with a glance over my shoulder, clocking the Italian sex bomb and her friend sizing me up.

"Fuck her," he growls low in his throat. I widen my eyes at his vulgar expression.

"You already have, but why the venom? I thought you

two were best shagging buddies."

Nicholas discreetly massages my hip with his fingers. "She's been calling me non-stop looking to come over. It's driving me insane. Phil mentioned to her that I was having this party when she dropped into the club the other night. She proceeded to call me up and complain that she hadn't been invited. So that's why she's here."

I turn around then, slightly pissed off at his explanation. "Well it serves you right. I mean, look at yourself Nicholas, you're handsome and charismatic. You can't just sleep with a woman and then expect her not to want to see you again."

On the inside I'm wondering if this is how he would have ended up treating me should we have slept together. Would he speak of me so callously, as he has just spoken of Dorotea?

"I'm twenty-eight Freda. I've had lots of experience with clingy women over the years. It doesn't mean I have to like it. But let's rewind a moment, you think I'm handsome and charismatic?"

"You know you are," I answer him with a sigh. "Maybe that's the problem."

He bends down so that his lips graze my ear. "The admiration isn't one sided. I think you look completely fuckable in that pretty little dress."

"Are we back to this again?" I ask, feigning boredom, though on the inside I'm feeling quite triumphant that the dress has done its job. "I thought you'd gotten over your attraction to me. You've been very well behaved."

"I was trying to respect you, but I also don't want to hurt you. You're my friend, and I could see how I was upsetting you, so I stopped. That doesn't mean I don't think about your mouth every night, about how you felt against my hand, how you moaned when I made you come."

"Nicholas, shut the fuck up," I whisper.

Before he can respond I hear Harry calling us over to the living area. I step away from Nicholas and go to sit down on the couch, while he follows and sits beside me. Nora is sitting on the *chaise longue* beside Colm. Yes, that *chaise longue*. I can't even glance at the thing without blushing.

"Fred, you're looking well," says Colm, shamelessly eyeing my cleavage. Harry's brother has light brown hair and is wearing a black shirt with grey trousers. I can smell his designer aftershave even though I'm more than four feet away from him.

"Piss off," I mutter under my breath while I sip on my wine. When I look at Nicholas I notice him trying to contain a smirk, since he heard what I said. Harry heard too. He gives me a look of warning. He has this weird hero worship thing going on with his older brother. Even though Colm is a complete and total wanker, Harry seems to think that the sun shines out of his arse.

"Be nice," Harry mouths at me soundlessly.

"Fine," I mouth back, before turning to Colm. "Thank you, you're looking quite dapper yourself." He doesn't notice I'm using a sarcastic tone, which only further reinforces my negative opinion of him. He thinks so highly of himself that he doesn't even consider it a possibility that someone might be mocking him.

"Do you think so?" Colm asks with a grin, before standing up and coming over to sit in between myself and Nicholas. He just barely manages to squeeze himself in, and I have to bite back my laughter at the bemused look on Nicholas' face.

Sean, Harry and Nora continue with whatever conversation they had been having, and a tall good looking guy comes to sit down beside Nora. He's a bartender from the club, but I don't know his name. Nora turns to shake his hand before giving him a flirty smile.

"It feels like I haven't seen you in ages," Colm says beside me. "When was the last time?"

"Um, Harry's birthday I think," I mutter, knocking back the wine. Perhaps alcohol will make him more bearable.

"Oh I remember now, you were wearing this great pair of jeans," he waggles his eyebrows at me suggestively. Oh good fuck. Here we go.

Nicholas turns to his side to fully take in the awkward exchange.

I need him to go away, so I say, "Viv, would you mind putting together a plate of food for me? I'm starved."

He smiles wickedly. "Not at all, I'll be right back." He gracefully slides off the couch. When he's gone I feel a little better. There's just something about having him witness Colm trying to chat me up that makes me feel ill.

"You call him Viv? I thought his name was Nicholas?" Colm asks in confusion.

"It's a pet name," I answer quietly, watching as Nicholas piles food onto a plate for me. His shoulders look *really* nice in that shirt. In fact, the whole outfit renders him something of a work of art. I'm so distracted by him that I realise I've completely blanked out on whatever Colm had been saying to me.

"So, what do you think?" he says, as I turn to look at

him.

"Sorry, what did you say?" I ask, just as Nicholas returns with the food. This time he sits on the other side of me, in effect turning me into a very uncomfortable human hot dog.

"I was asking if you'd like to come to a dinner party my company is holding next Saturday?" Colm reminds me.

"Fred works with me on Saturday nights," Nicholas interrupts. He holds one of the tiny sandwiches up to my mouth. "Open wide," he says in a low voice. I take a bite out of instinct before I have the chance to fully comprehend what's happening. He's feeding me? Is this situation for fucking real right now?

"Oh, yeah," Colm glances at Nicholas in annoyance for a moment, before quickly wiping his expression clean. "Harry mentioned something about your new job. Couldn't you take the night off? I promise you won't regret it." There go the flirty bloody eyebrows again.

"She can't I'm afraid. Saturday nights are the busiest. I wouldn't be able to spare her," Nicholas answers for me. I stare at him in awe, taken aback. He has a pair of balls on him, that's for certain. I have no intention of saying yes to Colm, but I'd almost do it just to put Nicholas in his place.

I finish the sandwich he's holding out to me, and fake bite at his fingers as a warning for him to back off. Unfortunately, this only seems to excite him. His eyes brighten with mischief.

At exactly this moment Dorotea and her friend come over to join us. Dorotea perches herself on the arm of the couch, leaning in really close to Nicholas. Her friend stands before us with a glass of red wine in her hand. Colm eventually takes the hint and scooches over for her. Now it's an even tighter squeeze. Nicholas surreptitiously pinches me on the thigh and I return the favour by elbowing him in the ribs in warning.

"Freda that's a beautiful dress," Dorotea chirps with a small hiccup. Somebody's had a few.

"Thanks, the same goes for your suit," I reply politely.

She's wearing an all-white lady suit with big shoulder pads, like the one Madonna wore in that video she did with Britney Spears a couple years ago. She looks like she should be holding a high powered business lunch in the eighties. That or attending a *Saturday Night Fever* themed disco. She's still hot though, despite the fashion faux pas. "You didn't happen to bring your furry friend along with you tonight?" I ask.

She leans even closer into Nicholas and slurs, "Is she propositioning me, do you think?"

Jesus *Christ*.

"She's talking about your ferret Ollo," he explains to her slow drunken brain.

She slaps a hand on her thigh and bursts out laughing. "Oh Ollo! My mistake, I thought you were making a double *entendre* Fred. No, I left him at home."

I hold in the reply that's on the tip of my tongue. I want to tell her that I've been given a first-hand account of how *not*-furry her little friend is. But I keep that one to myself. Is it wrong to internally snicker at your own unvoiced joke?

"Aw that's a shame," I say to her, as I happily note that Colm has turned his attention to the mullet lady on the other side of him. He brings a new meaning to the term *any hole will do*.

"Nicholas," Dorotea purrs, "would you help me in the bathroom for a moment? I spilled some wine on my sleeve and if I don't rinse it out it's going to stain."

"I'm sure you can handle it yourself," he answers her dismissively, before standing up to go and refill his whiskey glass. I take the plate of food from him and begin picking at some chicken wings.

Dorotea huffily makes her own way to the bathroom. There's a knock at the door and Phil rushes to answer it, letting even more people in. It's a good thing I went a little overboard with the food. I didn't expect there to be this many guests.

Nicholas gets swept up talking to the new people who have arrived. I slide further away from Colm and the mullet lady to sink into the corner of the couch. It's awfully anti-social of me, but I always seem to find myself doing this at parties at one point or another. I'll slink off into the background and stuff my face with whatever food is on offer, just watching the others interact around me.

I give myself a little imaginary pat on the back for how well I did with the catering. I always tend to veer more towards comfort food as opposed to *haute cuisine*. Perhaps when I'm older I'll have enough money to open up my own little rustic café in a village in the country. People will flock from far and wide to taste my cupcakes and my home made stews, I muse.

Dorotea has returned from the bathroom and is insinuating herself into a conversation Nicholas is having with a group of men I don't know. They must be more workers from the club. She slips her fingers through Nicholas' and rests her head on his shoulder.

Judging from his posture, he seems a little uncomfortable with her touching on him, but he's not pulling away. Perhaps this is just for the sake of good manners.

I force myself not to watch them any longer and instead focus my attention on Nora and the tall guy she's still chatting to. I'm hoping he's straight, because Nora hasn't seen much action with men for a while and she deserves to be swept away by some hunk. It's like watching a movie. I work my way through three chicken wings, two jalapeño poppers, several pieces of bacon and two more glasses of wine, while I observe her flip her hair, touch him flirtatiously on the shoulder, subtly pout her lips etc.

I give her an encouraging wink when I manage to catch her eye. She blushes at being caught pulling out all the stops. Harry and Sean fiddle around with the karaoke machine and before I know it Harry's belting out "I Will Survive" at the top of his lungs. Like me, he hasn't got a note in his head. The guests gather round and cheer him on. I decide this is my cue for a toilet break. I slip inside the bathroom and do my business.

When I'm washing my hands I notice the door handle turn.

"I'm in here," I call out, but whoever it is still continues coming in, the rude git.

I look up to discover Nicholas standing behind me. He maintains eye contact as he reaches back and turns over the lock on the door. Something *I* should have done before coming in here.

"Um, *ocupado, occupé, occupato* – any of those ring a bell?" I joke. I continue nervously scrubbing my hands and trying my best to ignore the way he's looking at me.

"I apologise for barging in, but I've been dying to get you alone all night Freda," he breathes.

He approaches me and presses the front of his body flush along my back, bracing both of his hands against the sink to pen me in. He reaches around me and shamelessly caresses my breast, right before he pulls down the front of my dress to bare the nipple. It all happens so quickly.

"Exquisite," he says, as he stares at my reflection in the mirror, one tit spilling out over the silky fabric.

Suddenly he's flipping me around, leaning down and taking me into his mouth. I gasp at the sensation of his hot tongue flicking at my bare nipple.

"You're not playing fair here," I protest, straining against him.

He comes up for air long enough to bite back, "And you are? Look at this dress, you might as well have a sign over your head that says *fuck me*." His gravelly voice sends a tingle shooting through me and a blush covers my cheeks.

His mouth clamps back onto my nipple and I moan instinctively. His hand wanders beneath my dress and violently slips past my knickers to plunge right inside me. I hold tightly onto his shoulders and my body goes limper with each thrust of his hand. He releases my nipple and buries his face in my neck.

"We've been dancing around each other for two weeks. I can't take it much longer," he sinks another finger into me, moving rhythmically in and out. "God you're so tight and soft Fred, I want to lick you all over."

"You're scandalizing me Viv," I manage to breathe

with a smirk. He smirks right back at me.

"I told you I like to corrupt, and you are the perfect candidate with those innocent fucking eyes of yours."

He watches me as I writhe against him. "What will it take for you to scream my name? Do you need my cock inside you for that?"

"Oh God, shut up!" I gasp.

He pushes my dress up higher, revealing my black lacy knickers. Then he goes down on one knee and presses his face to my mound. He runs his nose up and down, and I swear I could come just from that movement alone. Somebody knocks on the bathroom door and tries the handle a few times. Nicholas swears and removes his fingers from me, before standing up.

He runs the thumb of his other hand over my lower lip, and nips at the side of my mouth with his teeth. "If we weren't in the middle of my house warming party Freda I would so spread your legs and eat you out right now."

I swallow a hard lump of saliva and breathe heavily. I squeeze my eyes shut. I'm full to the brim with need and emotion. God, what's the point of trying to resist him when I'm already half in love with him? Spending the best part of the last fortnight with this man, laughing and joking and getting to know one another has really done a number on me. I want him so badly it hurts. But I want all of him. Not just the sex. I want his smiles and his teasing, his smouldering looks. His sad eyes when he thinks nobody's watching. Most of all, I want his heart.

"We better go back out," I say shakily, fixing my dress down. I take a step toward the door, but he grabs my wrist to stop me. He deftly swings me around to face him before pulling the top part of my dress back up. He has me so frazzled that I'd just been about to walk out into the party with one boob hanging out.

"Great fucking tits, Fred," he says darkly. "I can't wait to suck on the other one next time." He kisses me softly on the lips, his tongue snaking out for just a second. Then he goes to unlock the door, revealing Sean waiting on the other side. He eyes us both and laughs.

"Sorry to interrupt, but I really need to take a slash," he says.

My cheeks flame red as I hurry out, and Nicholas' laughter follows behind me.

Chapter Ten

Karaoke and Seduction

As I'm entering the living area I notice that Dorotea's eyes are on me. Shit! Did she see that I'd been alone in the bathroom with Nicholas? Her gaze is cool and a little hazy, so I can't tell whether she's mad or if she's just one of those stare-y-when-drunk kinds of people. When I first met her I thought she was cool as shit, now she's becoming something of an irritation.

Over the next hour I keep my distance from Nicholas. I actually can't look at him without blushing like a maniac. I sit with Harry and Sean for a while, as I lubricate myself with alcohol in order to numb how my traitorous body won't stop tingling all over. How is it that I manage to maintain my self-consciousness even when I'm half plastered?

Nora's still engrossed in her barman hunk, so I leave her to it. Soon most of the guests begin to leave, probably because a lot of them work at the club and have shifts to get to. Phil seems to have taken the whole night off though. He's currently walking around the apartment with one of Nicholas' platinum blonde wigs on his head, a lacy pink bra over his shirt and a bottle of wine clutched in his hand.

Harry and Colm say their goodbyes because they've got work in the morning. That leaves only me, Nicholas, Phil, Dorotea, Dorotea's friend, Sean, Nora and her barman left in the apartment. Phil hops over to the karaoke machine (which as it turns out belongs to him) and lifts the microphone to his mouth.

"Okay everyone, I know something that will spice up

this shindig. How about we play a game of seduction karaoke?"

"What's that when it's at home?" I ask with a giggle, tipsy as you like.

"Somebody volunteers to be the judge and then we all have to sing to them and try to seduce them," he explains and pauses to burp. "In the end the judge picks out who gave the most seductive performance."

"Sounds like a ball of cheese," I mumble.

"Great idea, I will sing to Nicholas," Dorotea declares with relish, not hearing my comment and clapping her hands in delight.

Phil winks at Nicholas. "Well Miss Blue, do you want to be the judge then?"

"I'd love to Philip," he replies smoothly, before taking a sip from his glass. I'm convinced he's looking at me every chance he gets, but I refuse to acknowledge him for whatever irrational reason. The wine voice in my head is urging me to go over and lick his face, but that would be surreal and I have just enough willpower to hold myself back.

Dorotea stands to make her way over to the karaoke machine, but Phil playfully pushes her back to her seat.

"Not so fast, love, I'm going to go first," he chides, waggling his sassy "no no" finger in her face.

Dorotea huffs and folds her arms as she drops back into her seat. Phil straightens out his wig, which kind of suits him in a weird way, and messes with the buttons on the machine before the intro to a song begins playing. The lyrics to George Michael's "I Want Your Sex" start rolling down the screen and Phil begins swaying his hips from side to side as he jokingly sings to Nicholas, who's sitting comfortably before him with an amused look on his face.

When the song ends I stick two fingers into my mouth to give Phil an ear splitting wolf whistle and everyone claps for him. Dorotea slinks up to the machine and begins whispering in Phil's ear. He laughs and scrolls down his list of songs, searching for the one she's asked for. Once she's all set she shirks out of her white blazer and drapes it over the back of Nicholas' chair, revealing the cream silky blouse she has on underneath. She undoes a few more buttons and fluffs up her boobs. Nicholas laughs and shakes his head at her.

When her music starts playing I roll my eyes at the predictability of her song choice, "I Touch Myself" by Divinyls. She pouts her lips at Nicholas and leans over him so that he can see right down her blouse, as she sings in her deep Italian accent about how she doesn't want anybody else and that when she thinks about him she touches herself.

God, why does the Italian accent have to be so sexy? She's got an unfair advantage here. Although I do feel a little awkward for Nicholas when she levels her deep brown eyes on him and sings the line about thinking she'd die if he ignored her, because he kind of *has* been ignoring her tonight.

He claps politely and allows her to give him a peck on the cheek when she's finished singing.

"Okay, who wants to go next?" Phil asks, as he scans the room. I sink lower into my seat and focus intently on the glass of wine in my hand.

"Fred, how about you?" he says, when nobody else volunteers. Lovely. I let my gaze drift to Nicholas for a moment, and he looks positively delighted at the prospect of having me sing to seduce him.

"No Phil, I can't sing for shit," I tell him, shaking my head.

"Oh come on, karaoke isn't about being able to sing. People with good voices who do karaoke just come across as show-off wankers. It's supposed to be funny!" he exclaims, strutting over and grabbing my hand.

"Funny eh? I thought the idea here was to seduce," I mutter.

"That too," he replies, and leans in to whisper, "sometimes when people think they're being sexy it's kind of hilarious," he nods discreetly to Dorotea. It cheers me up that I wasn't the only one who noticed how corny she was singing that song.

"Oh go on then," I answer, as an idea springs to mind. "Exactly how extensive is this collection of yours?"

"You'd be hard pressed to find a song I didn't have. I've got thousands," says Phil.

I scroll through the artists list and grin when I get to W. The song I want to sing is right there on the screen. I grab the microphone and Phil hits play as I muster up my best British West Country accent.

When life throws you into uncomfortable situations such as being forced to sing in front of a room full of people, all you can do is resort to the lowest common denominator and take the piss. I place one hand on my hip, give Nicholas a cheeky grin and launch right into a rendition of "Combine Harvester" by The Wurzels.

Nicholas' face breaks out into a huge smile as I bop along to the beat, turning from side to side like I'm doing line dancing. I tip my imaginary farmer's hat to him. By the time I get past the first verse everyone's pissing themselves laughing and singing along to the group "ooh ah ooh ah" bits. Well, everyone except for

Dorotea, who either doesn't get the joke or just hates me having Nicholas' attention.

I tell him that I drove my tractor through his haystack last night.

I tell him that I threw my pitchfork at his dog to keep quiet.

I tell him that I've got a brand new combine harvester and that I want to give him the key.

I tell him that we'll have twins and triplets because I'm a man built for speed.

I tell him that he's a fine looking woman and that I can't wait to get my hands on his land.

By the time the song ends everyone is rolling around in hysterics. Nicholas isn't laughing anymore, he's staring at me with such tenderness that it makes me want to squeeze my eyes shut and blink to make sure that it's real.

He stands up from his seat and strides toward me. He cups my cheeks in both hands and looks right into my eyes for what feels like forever.

"You're adorable," he whispers, just before his lips capture mine in a hot, deep kiss. I moan quietly when his tongue slides against mine.

"Well, I think we know who won this round," Phil declares loudly.

I pull away from Nicholas just as I hear Dorotea shout, "*Brutta! Vaffanculo!*"

I don't speak a word of Italian, but I've seen enough Mafia films to know she's said something along the lines of "fuck you bitch". She's staring angrily at the both of us.

Nicholas pushes me behind him and steps forward. "Speak to her like that again and I'll throw you out of here," he warns. Wow, for some reason I wasn't expecting him to stick up for me so fervently.

"What are you doing kissing her?" she demands, gesturing wildly at me with her hands. "I have told you I want you tonight and you do this!"

"And I told you I wasn't interested. It's not my fault you refused to listen."

I guess you can't really argue with that logic. Dorotea stares at him for a minute before turning to assess me. "Why do you want her? She's fat."

My panicked gaze flits to Nora, who's staring at Dorotea with her annoyed face on. Oh no, I can tell she's getting ready to pounce. We might call each other every name under the sun when we're hanging out in our apartment, but that's just good natured ribbing. Nora doesn't abide by anyone attacking me and I her. She gets up from her seat and stands in front of Dorotea.

"Don't fucking talk about Fred like that," she warns.

Dorotea gives her a look up and down that is at once measuring and dismissive. "I say what I like, *brutta*."

I step past Nicholas and pull Nora away from Dorotea. "Leave it Nora, she's just drunk."

"Did you hear what she said? She called me a bitch in Italian. Who does she think she is?"

"I don't know, a hybrid of John Travolta and Tony Soprano maybe?" I make a joke to try and diffuse the situation.

Nora lets out a loud bark of a laugh. "John Travolta! Because of the suit, right?"

I nod.

"What did you say about me?" Dorotea questions. Her eyes have narrowed to slits.

I ignore her and glance at Nicholas, who has suddenly appeared beside me. "We're going to leave, things are getting a little hairy in here." I say to him.

He strokes my cheek. "Don't go, if anyone should be leaving it's her."

"I'm wrecked anyway, I want to go to bed. We'll talk soon though, okay?" I whisper.

"We will," he leans forward and kisses the corner of my mouth. "And you're not fat, you're perfect," he adds on so quietly that only I can hear. My heart melts just a little bit.

Nora exchanges phone numbers with the guy she'd been talking to all night and we head next door to our place, leaving a triumphant looking Dorotea in our wake.

She probably thinks that because we're leaving that she's won. I don't envy Nicholas' position right now, because he'll have to fend her off at some stage later on tonight I imagine. At least I hope he'll fend her off and not give in once she flashes her peachy boobs at him.

Nora throws her keys on the coffee table in the living area and plops down onto the sofa. I slip off my shoes, grab us both a glass of water and sit on the armchair opposite her.

"Here, drink this if you want to lessen your hangover in the morning," I say, shoving the glass over to her.

She takes a long gulp, wipes her mouth with her wrist and eyes me with interest. "So, that was some hot kiss Nicholas gave you. It didn't look like it was a first kiss either. What haven't you been telling me Fred?" Great, I thought she'd be distracted enough by Dorotea's drunken outburst that she wouldn't ask me about the kiss.

I let out a short breath and don't even bother trying to lie. "You're right, it was our second kiss - I think. We had a bit of a fumble in his living room about two weeks ago, but we kind of got into an argument afterwards, so he's kept his hands to himself ever since. Until tonight, of course."

"Oh my God, you secretive little slut. Why didn't you tell me?"

"Because I was embarrassed, and also because I was depressed over the fact that I can't have him the way that I want him."

"Pfft, if a man kissed me like that I'd take him any way I could get him," Nora replies.

"Yeah, yeah, you're a real sexual adventurer," I roll my eyes. Similar to me, Nora is all talk when it comes to sex. "I just don't know if the subsequent heartache will be worth a night with him. He shagged Dorotea and now it's like he can't even bear to look at her. I'd be down in the dumps forever if that were to happen with me. The man is gorgeous, but he obviously has issues. The question is, do I want to put myself on the receiving end of them?"

"Just do it with him Fred. I can almost smell the hormones coming off you. You need to get it out of your system."

This is Nora's drunken solution to my drunken worries. She takes a gulp of water before continuing, "Anyway, did you get a look at Richard? The guy I was chatting to all night? We're going out on a date this Wednesday. He bar tends at The Glamour Patch half the week, and works in The Button Factory in Temple Bar the other half. That's right around the corner from where I work," she gushes.

"Very serendipitous," I tell her drily. "The Button Factory though?" I scrunch up my nose in distaste. "That place is full of music snobs. Make sure you don't mention to him that your favourite album is Mariah Carey's Greatest Hits, or your burgeoning romance will be over before it's even started." I joke. "He is hot though, you'll have to tell me all about what happens on your date."

"Yeah, just like you told me all about you and Nicholas and your living room romp," she says, raising a cynical eyebrow.

"I'm going to get some sleep," I reply, ignoring her comment as I glance up at the clock. "I have to be up in three hours to bake."

"Ugh, I'd hate to be you," Nora chirps. "And by the way, my favourite album is "This is Me...Then" by J-Lo, so get your facts straight," she adds on as I'm shutting my bedroom door.

I laugh and crawl into bed.

When my alarm goes off my head feels like it's been pulverised with a meat grinder. I suppose it's my own fault for knocking back the wine like a housewife on her night off from the kids. I trudge my way through my morning baking routine and go to take a long, hot shower once the cupcakes are cooking in the oven.

I shudder just before I step under the spray, because I can still smell Nicholas' aftershave on my skin from last night. In a weird way, I kind of don't want to wash it off.

I towel dry my hair once I get out and stare at my tired eyes in the steamy mirror. The only thing keeping me going right now is prospect of slipping back into bed when I return from The Cake Shop.

The annoying thing is that after I've delivered the cakes I'm wide awake. I cycle back to the apartment with a tingling heart. I really want to see Nicholas, perhaps because somewhere in the back of my mind I enjoy torturing myself.

I finally decide to give in to the temptation when I grab the ingredients for eggs Benedict and drop into his place to make him breakfast. He gave me a spare key last week so that I could get into his apartment and sort through his costumes when he was out. I still haven't returned it.

I send him a quick text message to let him know I'm on my way. He replies immediately with a simple, "Looking forward to it" and one of those winky faces. I've never fully understood the use of smileys in texts. I always end up using a frowning face when I should be using a vaguely annoyed one, or a smiling one when I should be using a shocked one. Anyway, with a bag of food in my hand I turn the key in the lock and step inside his place.

The apartment isn't looking great after last night's shindig. I drop the food on the kitchen counter and then walk over to the living area where I find Dorotea and Phil all tangled up and asleep on the sofa together. Dorotea's wearing Phil's shirt and he's wearing her blouse. I see the party didn't end after Nora and I had left, then.

I shake Phil by the shoulder to wake him and a second later he stirs and begins rubbing at his eyes. Dorotea groans and wakes up too.

"Fred, what time is it?" Phil asks, looking a little out of sorts.

I glance at the clock. "Almost ten. How are you

feeling?"

"Like I just ate a bowl full of sand. Ugh, I'd be eternally grateful if you could rustle me up a cup of coffee."

"I'll do you one better. I'm making eggs Benedict for Nicholas, do you want some?"

I allow my eyes to flick to Dorotea for a moment. She's currently running her hands through her dishevelled hair in an effort to neaten it up.

"Oh that would be wonderful," Phil exclaims, his face instantly brightening. This is why I love cooking for people; it can magically transform a cranky person into a cheerful one.

Dorotea is looking a little sheepish. She hasn't yet said a word. I decide to put her out of her misery. "Will you have some breakfast too?" I ask her with a polite smile. I can't blame her for how she reacted last night. After all, Nicholas did sort of love her and leave her in the lurch.

A small smile forms on her lips as she replies softly, "Yes, thank you Freda."

I turn and make my way back over to the kitchen to start on the food. Dorotea disappears into the bathroom to freshen herself up. Phil comes and sits by the counter to watch me cook.

"Did you train professionally?" he asks as he takes in my movements.

"As a chef you mean? Not exactly. I did a Culinary Arts degree."

"I thought so, you can really tell by way you work with the ingredients."

I smile and continue cooking.

"By the way, nothing happened between Nicholas and

Dorotea last night after you left. He went to his bedroom in a bad mood and everyone else went home. Myself and herself stayed up and had a few more shots at the karaoke, as well as one too many glasses of wine before passing out on the sofa."

"Good to know," I reply, as a small feeling of happiness rushes through me. Maybe - just maybe - I'm more special to Nicholas than all of the other women he's known. I hold on tight to this morsel of futile hope. "I bet you never expected to wake up with a woman wrapped around you this morning," I tease him.

"Definitely not," Phil laughs, taking off Dorotea's blouse.

Dorotea comes out of the bathroom wearing her white blazer and joins us in the kitchen. She grins and hands Phil his shirt as he hands her the blouse. Then her expression becomes serious as she turns to address me. "Freda, can I please apologise for my behaviour at the party? I was drunk. I was out of line. I didn't mean to be so crazy, but that man, you know, he has a powerful effect on me. On most women I imagine."

"And men," Phil puts in.

We both eye him.

"What?" he exclaims. "I didn't mean *me*. He works at my club. I can't help noticing the way the customers look at him, now can I?"

"I guess not," I answer with a laugh before turning back to Dorotea. "Don't worry about it. All is forgiven." I've never really been the kind of person to hold a grudge. All it takes is one "I'm sorry" and I'm putty in their hands.

I serve them their breakfast and then dish up some plates for Nicholas and myself.

Dorotea takes a bite and says, "You certainly know how to cook Freda." She pauses and frowns as she studies me, then points her fork in the direction of Nicholas' bedroom door. "That one in there, he will break your heart. He only wants the first rush of lust, anything that comes after isn't exciting enough for him. You save your heart, don't ever give it to him. Find a nice man, a good man. One capable of accepting another's love."

Her words give me a little shock of reality, because she's voicing the reservations that I've had all this time. "I'll keep that in mind," I tell her, as I put the plates and cups on a tray and make my way into Nicholas' room. "It looks like his Lordship isn't going to grace us with his presence, so I'll have to bring the food to him." I call behind me.

I use my elbow to push down the door handle and then shoulder my way inside the room. The sight of Nicholas' ruffled mane of black hair and bare chest, not to mention the blanket strewn across his nether regions hits me like a bomb to my long unattended libido.

He couldn't look any more appealing if he tried. I really shouldn't be carrying a tray of food right now, as it's in danger of crashing to the floor. Still, I maintain my grip and set it down on his bedside dresser.

"Morning Sunshine," I chirp. "Get your mouth ready for a taste sensation." I walk across the room and pull his curtains open to allow some day light into the place.

"Morning," he replies with a dazzling smile. "That's a lovely t-shirt Fred."

I glance down at the low cut navy top I have on. Hmm, I wonder why he think it's so lovely.

I smirk at him and hand him his breakfast, before

sitting down on the edge of his bed. I'm very curious as to whether he has anything on beneath the blanket.

He takes a sip of the coffee and then looks down at the plate hungrily. "You're my little breakfast angel," he exclaims. "What are you doing all the way over there? Come sit beside me."

I slip off my shoes and crawl to the top of his bed. We eat side by side in companionable silence.

"Did you sleep well?" I ask past a yawn, just as I set my empty plate back on the tray on the dresser.

"Better than you did, clearly. You seem tired," Nicholas replies, his eyes taking all of me in.

"You continue to forget that you're not the only person I work for. I had to be up this morning to make my cupcakes."

"Aw, poor baby," he purrs and grabs my wrist, pulling me closer to him. "Let's take a nap now, get you caught up on your sleep."

He throws open the blanket and mercifully reveals himself to be wearing boxer shorts. He yanks me under with him and throws it back over us. Then he wraps his arms around my waist from behind and pulls me close to him. I want to feel the affection he's offering, just for this moment. I don't want to resist. So I don't.

"Mr Turner, is that morning wood?" I ask, feeling a distinct hardness press up against me.

"Shut up and deal with it, Fred," he laughs and buries his face in my neck. "You always smell so clean," he mumbles.

"You smell like last night's whiskey," I comment, while keeping to myself that he also smells faintly of aftershave and man.

"You're cheeky," he says and pinches my stomach.

"Ow Viv, that hurt!"

"I'm sorry, can I kiss it better?" He asks darkly.

"You probably shouldn't. Dorotea and Phil are still out in your kitchen. I made them breakfast too, they spent the night on your couch."

Nicholas gives me a confused look. "Now that's something you don't hear very often."

"I know. Dorotea apologised for her behaviour last night and everything. She also warned me not to trust you."

I'm saying this mainly because I want him to tell me that he can be trusted. I want to be able to trust him.

He becomes still all of a sudden. "She did, did she? Do you think you can trust me Fred?"

"I want to. I'm not sure if I should though."

He remains silent then. I wait with bated breath for him to say something to prove Dorotea wrong, but he doesn't. He just runs his hand over my stomach and then up to cup my bra. It's infuriating. I twist around in his arms to face him.

"Hey, can we just sleep?" I ask. I want to see if he can lie here with me and not try to turn it into sex.

He searches my eyes for a moment, and answers, "Sure, come here."

I sink back into his embrace and he trails his fingers up and down my back, paying extra attention to the curve of my spine. I'm so exhausted and his touch feels soothing. Moments later I drift off.

When I wake up again Nicholas has his hands levelled on either side of my head and his torso is resting between my open thighs. My calf length skirt is pushed up around my hips. He's staring at me, had probably been staring at me while I slept! Is that supposed to be creepy or sexy? Perhaps a little bit of both.

He seems pensive.

"What? Was I drooling?" I ask, trying to avoid the serious expression on his face.

His eyes drift across my lips. "No."

"What are you doing?" I whisper.

"Watching you. I enjoy having you here."

"I'm sure you do. Just like you *enjoyed* having Dorotea here the other week."

"We fucked on the couch. She never got as far as the bedroom."

I shift my hips to try and roll him off me, but he stays firmly in place.

"Did you have to tell me that? I spent half of last night sitting on your couch." I make my voice sound disgusted, but on the inside I'm secretly thrilled that she didn't get to sleep in his bed with him. Like I just did. *And*, I didn't even have to go as far as having sex with him.

He eyes me shrewdly. "It didn't mean anything with her, you know."

My breath catches. "Oh."

He sighs. "Losing myself in women I've just met, it's this habit that I can't seem to shake off."

I don't know how to respond to him. In the end I make a joke, effectively ruining the serious moment. "I thought you said you *weren't* a sex addict."

He smiles and keeps on looking at me, silently drinking me in. Then he grins broadly and shakes his head.

"Shut up, Freda," he says hoarsely, before taking my mouth in a hard kiss. I can feel it everywhere, zinging through me. He's pouring all of his unspoken feelings into this one kiss. I can tell. Perhaps I am too, as I match his enthusiasm by nipping at his bottom lip. I expect him to try and take things further, but he doesn't. He pulls away and smiles at me for nipping at him. "Naughty. I like it. Come shopping with me today."

"Shopping for what?" I ask.

"Clothes. I need some new things. Oh and possibly a second hand car."

I stare at him, wide eyed. "You're going to buy a car, just like that?"

"No, not just like that. I'm living here permanently now. I need transportation."

"You do realise that this city isn't very big. It only seems that way when you're unfamiliar with it. You can walk just about anywhere within a half an hour or so. A car won't get much use. But I'll go with you, so long as you buy me a nice lunch."

He gives me a look that's half smirk, half tender. "I'll buy you lunch if you let me buy you a new dress too. Of my choosing."

I scoff at him, but I am intrigued. "Am I obligated to wear this dress that you pick out?"

"No. But I'd like it if you did."

"It's a deal then, and we'll see about me wearing the dress."

I make a quick trip next door to my apartment to brush my teeth and change into a top that hasn't been slept in. When I come back out Nicholas is waiting in the hallway, casually leaning up against the wall. He's got those aviator sunglasses on top of his head again, the ones that sort of make me want to swoon like a loser. He smiles and holds out his hand to me. I smile back and take it.

Chapter Eleven
Mirrors and Changing Rooms

Nicholas shops like a pro. He knows exactly what he likes and what he doesn't like, and he deals with the shop assistant like they're old pals having a chin wag. I've always found clothes shopping to be the ultimate nightmare experience, especially when I was younger.

I've been chubby since the day I was born, so picking out clothing is never fun. Even if I find something that I like, there's always a chance the shop isn't going to have it in my size. And then sometimes when they do have it in my size it just doesn't seem to sit right on me.

We're in a fancy men's clothing store at the moment and I'm feigning interest in those shelves behind the counter where they have every shade of business shirt you could possibly wish for. The shelving unit reminds me of those cardboard charts you get when you're buying paint. Little rectangles of colour.

I glance back to where the shop assistant is helping Nicholas and I'm struck by the contrast between how he dresses when he's on stage and how he dresses when he's being himself. Vivica Blue is all lace, silk and high heel shoes, while Nicholas is sharp shirts and designer slacks. The odd time you'll catch him in a t-shirt and jeans.

Nicholas ends up leaving with several bags of shirts and trousers. As we step out onto the street he says, "So lead the way darling, show me where you like to shop."

"You're not still set on buying me a dress, are you?" I ask, with a sigh that a moody fifteen year old would be proud of.

"Of course I am. Take me to your usual boutiques."

"You do realise that clothes shopping is one of my top three most hated life activities, just below doing my taxes and having a smear test."

"Don't be silly, if I had a body like yours I'd be dressing it up all the time. You could give Christina Hendricks a run for her money."

I snort. "My arse I could."

Nicholas gives me the frown he always seems to give me when I'm being down on myself. He shakes his head and purses his lips.

"Fine, if you won't lead the way then I'll just have to pick somewhere myself."

I trudge along behind him and when we get to Grafton Street he all but drags me inside an irritatingly fashion forward women's clothing shop. Mannequin legs at the front of the store display a whole range of multi-coloured skinny jeans. I've always found half body mannequins to be strangely disconcerting. Like some window dresser chopped off the upper part because they didn't need it.

I become unnecessarily annoyed when Nicholas begins pulling dresses off the racks in exactly my size, despite the fact that I've never told him what size I wear.

Okay, so I'm also kind of flattered that he paid enough attention to notice.

"If you think I'm trying all of those on you've got another thing coming," I tell him, while my stomach growls as if to ask, *where exactly is this lunch I was promised?*

"You're moody today," Nicholas remarks, leading me into the changing rooms. He hands the dresses to the shop assistant as if it's a completely normal thing for a man to be doing. I think it's his confidence that stops the girl from telling him that he's not supposed to be in here.

He opens the curtain to one of the cubicles and gestures for me to go in. I step past him and moan as I glance around. "These things are torturous, look at all of the mirrors. They show every part of your body that you don't want to see." I absolutely despise seeing myself from behind. I can remember the first time I peered over my shoulder in one of these changing rooms like it was yesterday. The horror, oh the horror.

"Let me in and I'll look for you," he grins, one arm stretched up, his palm leaning flat against the wall outside the cubicle.

"Fuck off," I scowl, grabbing the dresses and yanking the curtain closed.

Nicholas' laugh filters through. "Perhaps your moodiness can be attributed to the fact that you never got around to coming last night in the bathroom," he suggests, loud enough for everyone in the dressing room to hear. I could strangle him. The shop assistant up at the front snickers.

"Jesus, would you shut up?" I hiss as I shimmy out of my clothes. I peek my head out past the curtain. "And how do you know I didn't take care of myself when I went to bed?" I whisper at him with a wink. I didn't. I'm still dying for his touch, but my evil side wants to torture him.

His eyes grow hot and he groans. "That's a real pretty picture you're painting for me. Did you?"

I smirk and pull the curtain back over. "None of your business."

"Come on Fred, I'm dying here. Please tell me you thought of me while masturbating. It'll make my day. My year even." He's still talking *way* too fucking loud.

"Are you incapable of whispering?" I ask him quietly, picking out a purple dress, since it's one of my favourite colours. I step into it.

At this he slips quickly in behind the curtain and pins me up against the mirrored wall. The purple dress is sitting at my waist as I haven't yet had the chance to pull it up all the way. He grabs both of my wrists and holds them tight by my sides.

"Tell me," he pleads, now finally deciding to whisper.

"Tell you what?" I grit out.

"About how you touched yourself," he murmurs, eyes glued to my bra.

I look at his lips for a minute before returning my gaze to his eyes. "It was a joke."

He smiles and releases my wrists. "Too bad. Now I've got the image of you with your hands between your legs stuck in my head. You're going to have to do something to alleviate me."

I push him away, although since we're in a tiny box of a cubicle I can't push him very far. "Alleviate yourself," I say, and pull the dress up the rest of the way.

He makes a tut tut noise and raises an eyebrow. "Doing it myself is never as much fun, Fred. You of all people should know that."

"What do you mean?" I ask, as I try to reach the zipper at the back of the dress. Nicholas swipes my hands away and does it for me, before running his fingers down the curve of my spine. It feels...nice.

"My apartment a fortnight ago, lying on my *chaise longue*, ring a bell?"

I let out a huff. "I knew I shouldn't have allowed you to take things that far. I'll never live it down."

Nicholas stands behind me, staring at me in the mirror. It reminds me of how he'd done almost the exact same thing last night in his bathroom.

"It was a beautiful moment, don't regret it. I don't."

I scrunch up my nose. "Beautiful..." I say on a breath.

He places a hand on my stomach. "You certainly felt beautiful."

I drag my eyes away from him and look at the dress I'm wearing, changing the subject. "I'm not sure about this one, what do you think?"

"The colour suits you, and the fabric is pretty. I particularly like this bit," he traces his fingers over the lining where there's a dip in the cleavage.

"You would," I snort, but my heart isn't in it. I want him to continue talking. I want him to keep saying words that make me feel warm inside.

He smiles at me through the mirror. "You know Fred, when you sang that song to me last night, I don't think I've ever seen anything sweeter."

"I was trying to be funny and subversively mock Phil's seduction karaoke." I roll my eyes at him.

"It was the cutest thing ever. You always manage to make me smile."

I look away from his gaze. There's too much affection in it and I can't take it. "Well I'm happy to be of service."

"Hey," he whispers seriously. I glance back up at him. "You'll always be my friend, won't you Fred? Don't let me fuck this up. I need you in my life now. I need the golden eyed girl who can make me smile."

His words are far different than they've ever been. I've

never heard him speak so sincerely.

"Of course not." I muster a grin. "You'll be hard pushed to get rid of me Viv. I'm like a cold sore."

He shakes his head. "You've got a wonderful way with words, disgusting but wonderful," he says, repeating what he'd said to me all those weeks ago in his apartment when he'd first asked me to be his assistant.

In the end, Nicholas buys me two dresses. The purple one and a bright red one. The red one was his choice. It's tight, sleeveless and only goes down to my knees. I make objections about wearing it, putting on a snooty voice and saying I'll look like a Jezebel or a harlot of easy virtue. He tells me he'll get me into it if it's the last thing he does.

We're laughing together as we exit the shop, bags in hand, just as I walk head first into somebody's chest.

"Oh sorry..." I begin to apologise and glance up at the person when my mouth drops open. Immediately, I am not smiling or laughing anymore. In fact, it feels like all of the blood in my body is running distinctly colder. Before me stands Aaron. Yes, *that* Aaron, of the psycho stalker ex-boyfriend fame.

He puts on a big (fake) surprised face. "Hello Fred, wow it's been a long time."

I want to tell him that it hasn't been long enough. "Um yeah." I mumble. "Hi."

"This is such a coincidence, I was just thinking about you."

Coincidence, my arse. "Right well, here I am. It was nice to see you again, but I'm in a hurry."

I try to move past him, however Nicholas chooses this moment to step forward.

"Freda, aren't you going to introduce me to your friend?" He asks, placing a hand on my shoulder. Aaron's eyes zoom in on the small touch.

I could slap Nicholas right now, but then I think I could also use his presence to my advantage. I plaster a smile on my face and wrap my arm around his waist, leaning into him affectionately.

"This is Aaron, Nicholas. Aaron, this is my boyfriend Nicholas." I pray to God that he doesn't decide to expose my lie. Thankfully he wraps his arm around my waist too and goes along with the charade.

"Your...boyfriend," Aaron says the words really slowly, like he's trying to fit them around his big psychotic tongue.

"Yup," I say, as a sweat breaks out on my palms.

There's a long, awkward silence, within which I'm waiting for Aaron to say something testy. When we were together he was the king of the inappropriate outburst. The first time he met my mum he was in a bad mood because the electricity supply at his apartment was on the fritz. When she asked him if he'd like a cup of tea or coffee while welcoming him into her house he told her he despised hot beverages. I mean, who says things like that? Mum just nodded and smiled, while giving me a wary glance. She knew he was bad news from the outset.

Aaron looks like he's on the cusp of a similar outburst right now, one which would reveal the fact that this is no random meeting. But he manages to reel in his temper when he smiles, too widely to be deemed normal, and says, "It's great to meet you Nicholas. Freda," he nods to me and then walks away. He doesn't even say goodbye.

When he's gone Nicholas laughs. "I take it that was an ex of yours then?"

"How did you know?"

"First off because you introduced me as your boyfriend, and secondly because of the way he looked at you, all possessive. I didn't like it to be perfectly honest."

"Yeah well, I didn't like it either," I tell him. "And I'm sorry about roping you in to pose as my fake boyfriend like that. I just needed to make sure Aaron didn't get any ideas about rekindling our relationship. He's never been the full shilling, if you get me. I don't need him trying to worm his way back into my life."

Although from the looks of it, he's already trying. I'm suddenly realising that it really was him who came to the shop and asked for me that time. That means he's been snooping around for at least a couple of weeks now, which can't be good.

"How much of the full shilling is he lacking exactly?" Nicholas asks, as he opens the door to the restaurant that we've just stopped in front of.

I walk inside and the waitress leads us to a table for two. I'm still frazzled and jumpy. My heart is beating too fast. I really, really fucking hate Aaron. Just when I've got a nice little life going for myself he decides to show up again. I also hate myself for not putting him straight from the start. If I had of refused to go on a date with him then I might have saved myself the trouble of becoming the object of his obsession.

I sit down and glance at the menu, before thinking *what the hell*, and I recite the tale of how I met Aaron for Nicholas from beginning to end.

"Sounds like it was a wrong place, wrong time sort of

scenario," says Nicholas. "If you hadn't been at the party then you never would have met him."

"That's true. We didn't have any lectures together or anything. God, I really wish I never went to the party now."

"Unfortunately, you can't rewind the clock. But honestly Fred, if it really was him who showed up at your work then you might have a problem on your hands. You need to keep your eyes peeled. I'll help. I'll make sure he's not hanging around the apartment block. If I do catch him snooping I'll run him off. There's no need to panic, just try to be observant and make sure you've got someone you can call on short notice. I'll be right next door when you're at home."

I stare at him and smile my thanks. It's nice to have someone know about Aaron. Someone who isn't my mother, who can't afford the damage the stress would cause to her health, and someone who also isn't Nora, who would be freaking out left, right and centre. If I told her she'd be calling the police every time she heard a floorboard creak.

By the time we get finished with our lunch it's late evening, and we have to rush to a used car dealership just outside of the city so that Nicholas can pick out some new wheels.

I have no idea what sort of vehicle he wants, but if his home décor is anything to go by it's going to be something out of the ordinary.

My predictions aren't wrong, and we end up driving away in a powder blue Nissan Figaro. It costs just under eight grand and has a sort of fifties vintage look with only two front seats, like a sports car. Not masculine in the slightest, but what else could I have expected from

Nicholas? In a way I think he picks out the car to purposely stick two fingers up to society's accepted view of masculinity. I kind of adore him for that.

Back home we leave the car in the car park at the back of the building and go up to Nicholas' apartment, where I help him put away all of his new clothes. He bought a ton of stuff today. I make fun of him when I find the Calvin Klein boxers at the end of one of the bags by putting them on top of my head and wearing them like a hat. Nicholas grins, gives me a good natured slap on the arse and yanks them off me.

"So juvenile," he scolds, shaking his head.

I stick my tongue out at him and lift up a pile of new shirts to go and hang them in his wardrobe. Just as I'm finished putting them on the rack I spot a stack of old video tapes in the corner.

"What's on the tapes?" I ask, shutting over the wardrobe.

"Tapes?" Nicholas raises an eyebrow as he admires the steel blue tie he bought.

"Yeah, the old ones at the bottom of your wardrobe. Please tell me they have recordings of you as a kid so that I can watch them and you can get all embarrassed."

He smooths out the tie and tilts his head back to meet my eyes. His seem kind of sad. "They're not of me. They're of my mother. She was a lounge singer when she was alive. Those tapes are all that's left of her performances."

"Really? Was she any good?" I ask with interest.

"She was one of the best," he answers, sort of forlorn.

"Perhaps you inherited your singing voice from her then," I suggest.

He gives me a small smile. "Perhaps."

"Can I watch one of them?" I blurt out.

Nicholas' expression becomes more closed off. "I'd rather if you didn't. They're kind of something that I like to keep just for myself."

"Okay, I can respect that." I pause for a moment before continuing, "Dolores was a lucky woman to have had a son like you. I just know she would have been so proud if she could have seen the man you turned out to be."

He stares at me for a long time after I've said it. Like it means a lot to him to be told that. I know he's hardly perfect, but if I ever have a son like Nicholas, who doesn't care that what he loves to do goes against societal norms, and does it anyway, I know I'd be supremely proud of him.

"Thank you Fred," he answers quietly, and comes over to give my hand a squeeze.

For the next few days I spend every evening with Nicholas. Sometimes he comes to my apartment and other times I'll go to his. Nora seems to have warmed up to him again, which makes me strangely happy. Not that she's still interested in him romantically, she knows that I've got a soft spot for him and we're not *those* kind of friends. We might not have the most harmonious of friendships, but we'd never ever touch a guy one of us liked or had already dated with a bargepole.

Nicholas doesn't try to push the boundaries of our relationship like he did at his house warming party, but he has been becoming more and more tactile. He'll randomly pull me into a hug, or trail his fingers up and down my arm while we're sitting on the couch watching television. Sometimes he rests his head on my shoulder.

His hugs make me melt, they are so warm and affectionate.

I've also caught him smelling my hair once or twice. He knows that I notice this and he doesn't even get embarrassed about it. That's another thing that I admire about this man, he is so completely unapologetic for his actions. He is who he is, you can either take it or leave it.

The way he's acting around me is perhaps even more dangerous than when he's overtly sexual, because it's making me want him to stick around. If he decided to leave Ireland and go travelling again I don't know what I'd do.

When we go to The Glamour Patch for his usual gig on Thursday, it feels like we haven't been here in ages. So much has happened over the last week. Normally I'd be looking forward to Thursday because it would mean I'd be getting to see Nicholas again, but I've been seeing him almost every day anyway.

I haven't noticed him going out to pick up other women since he slept with Dorotea. This is another thing that could be dangerous, because if he does go back to his promiscuous ways I will be devastated.

The audience is a little more subdued than usual tonight. The Thursday crowd aren't as rowdy as the crowd you get on a Friday or a Saturday. I'm standing in my usual spot by the side of the stage, watching Vivica Blue do her thing in a long, dark red evening gown, black silk gloves, diamond accessories and a brown wig. She could give Audrey Hepburn a run for her money.

Nicholas glances at me out of the corner of his eye during the show more than usual. We've become so close this past week, just hanging out and doing our own thing in a companionable fashion.

About midway through his act he struts over to the band and begins giving the guitarist instructions, whose name I think is either Liam or Lionel. I can't remember. Whenever Nicholas goes to speak with the band I always know he's asking them to play a song that isn't in the original set list.

When he makes his way back to his microphone stand he turns to look at me for a long moment and smiles playfully. What is he up to?

The band starts playing the recognisable intro to "Every Breath You Take" by The Police. It's not one of Nicholas' usual numbers, and certainly not his usual style. The next time he looks at me I give him a confused glance and in return he nods out to some spot beyond the stage. I look out past the curtain to the audience, but I don't notice anything unusual.

It's only when my eyes travel as far as the bar that they stop dead in their tracks. Sitting with a pint at his side and a serious expression on his face is Aaron. Good sweet Jesus. Would it be wrong to march right up to him and kick him in the balls? Maybe that would help him to get the message. Although I could be pointing a gun at him and he'd still think we were destined to be together. You can never get through to a head case.

His presence tonight shows that he really is unashamedly following me again. Something pinches at my lungs. A mixture of fear and irritation.

Then my brain goes a little loopy and I almost laugh thinking of how he would have had to force himself to swallow down his male pride and come into a gay bar to look for me. A moment later I do actually laugh as the significance of Nicholas' song choice hits me.

He's still singing, talking about how every breath I take and every move I make he'll be watching me. It couldn't be more apt in describing Aaron. For six whole months he hid in the shadows, watching me live my life. Only every once in a while would he venture out to harass me. I don't know which part was more disconcerting, the times when I felt he could be nearby but I couldn't see him, or the times when he'd actually come up and talk to me, making no effort to disguise the fact that he'd been stalking me.

I could hug Nicholas right now, because sometimes you need humour to bring you out of a dark place. I look to him again and he's on the brink of laughter as he sings. To be honest, I kind of wouldn't mind it if Nicholas were the one to be watching every move I make. When you're attracted to someone, extreme behaviour can be sort of...appealing. If Edward Cullen had of been ugly I'm sure Bella Swan wouldn't have been quite so smitten with him coming into her bedroom to watch her sleep at night. We females can be strange, shallow creatures when the mood takes us.

I look back to Aaron and my heart goes haywire, because he's staring right at me now. How did he manage to spot me all the way back here? Perhaps he has some kind of special stalker radar. He picks up his pint, takes a long gulp and stands up from the stool he'd been sitting on. With his eyes still glued to me, he starts walking through the bar and towards the stage. Nicholas is watching him approach with a wary expression. I wonder if Aaron gets that the song currently being played is intended to mock him.

The closer Aaron gets the more panicked I become. For a moment I consider running from the club. Then again, it's probably safer to stay here in a public place. The song ends just as Aaron hops up onto the stage, quick as lightning, and slips in behind the curtains. I fold my arms across my chest and muster a calm expression.

"Fred, you lied to me the other day," he says, crazy as you like, stopping right in front of me. "You thought you could fool me and expect me to believe that some fucking - I don't even know what the fuck that is supposed be out there on the stage – that that freak is your boyfriend?"

My jaw drops open. He's acting indignant, what the hell? Like he has a right to be pissed off. This is ridiculous.

"Are you serious you fucking nut job?" I ask him deadpan. "What are you even playing at, coming here where I work and acting like you have a right to know anything about my life? Our whole relationship was a bloody joke. It ended years ago and you're still acting like we were some kind of star crossed lovers. I've told you this before and I'll tell you again Aaron, I never even liked you in the first place. You made my life extremely uncomfortable for a long time and now you're trying to do it again. And. I. Am. Not. Fucking. Having. It."

I pause and run a hand through my hair, surprised at my own outburst. I didn't realise that I was suppressing so much of my anger until right now. Him acting like he has every right in the world to be here has caused me to explode.

"I need you to come back to me," he says in a dead,

oblivious voice, not even acknowledging anything I've just told him.

"It's been almost four years, can't you just get a clue and move on?" I say in exasperation.

The problem with Aaron is that he's never gotten violent or threatened me. I would have gone to the police if he had been. He's just been clingy, possessive, annoyingly obsessive and a touch mental. He's the kind of person who makes you want to create a resolution where you don't let any new people into your life for fear of them turning out to be like him.

He sighs. "I tried. I had a new girlfriend and everything, but she wasn't you. I broke up with her."

"You're being ridiculous. We're never going to happen ever again, so I suggest you join some online dating agency and keep searching for the one, because it certainly isn't me." I'm already feeling sorry for whatever woman he might foist himself on next.

I hear the clicking of high heels as Nicholas walks off the stage and comes to stand beside me.

He levels Aaron with a hard glare, and even though he's in drag he still manages to come across as threatening, which is a feat in itself. "You have thirty seconds to leave the club before I call security," he tells Aaron carefully.

Aaron looks Nicholas up and down. "Fuck off tranny, I'm talking to Fred."

"No you're not, and if you don't do as I say you'll have this tranny's high heel stuck up your arse in a minute."

Aaron stares at Nicholas before he bursts out laughing. He's never been a laughing sort of a person, so when he does it's highly creepy. "Stay away from my arse, you fucking queer bastard."

"Oh you've got nothing to worry about there," Nicholas retorts and wraps his arms tight around my waist. "Fred's arse keeps me occupied on a nightly basis."

I snicker involuntarily and try to hold in my laughter.

"That's sick," Aaron narrows his gaze at me. "You're not actually with this freak, are you Fred?"

I take great satisfaction in the disgusted look on his face when I reply, "Oh I most certainly am, we're madly in love. You can come to the wedding if you like."

Nicholas squeezes my hip and smiles down at me adoringly.

"Wedding?" Aaron says, slow and steady, his eyes turning to slits.

"Yes, *wedding*." I state. "So you see, there's no chance for you and I Aaron, because I plan on loving, honouring and obeying this wonderful man until the day I die."

I'm laying it on thick and heavy now, hoping he'll be disgusted enough with the idea of me marrying a drag queen that he'll leave and never seek me out again. For a second I have a cute image in my head of me and Nicholas actually getting married for real, with him in a wedding dress and me in a tuxedo.

Aaron's shaking his head back and forth like he can't believe what he's hearing.

"You're both sick," he spits.

He takes a step away and runs a hand over his jaw. He looks like he's about to say something more, but then he just turns and walks away, still shaking his head, like he can't get his mind around the idea.

"I'm already looking forward to the wedding night,"

Nicholas jokes, his arms still wrapped around me.

I smile up at him gratefully and let out a long sigh. "Thanks for coming and helping me with that. I'm sorry you had to interrupt your set for it."

He stoops down so that we're at each other's eye level. He runs a finger over my bottom lip and stares at me with something like longing in his gaze. He shakes it off then, and I kind of wish he'd do whatever it was he was going to do a second ago. I wouldn't even care about how I'd look snogging the face off a drag queen.

"What's a best friend good for if they can't help you fend off a crazy ex every now and again, eh?" he asks fondly.

"Very true, Viv." I shrug out of his hold and swipe him on the behind. "Now go get your pretty self back out there. You've still got another thirty minutes left in your set."

He salutes me and saunters off onto the stage, apologising to the crowd and telling them that he had to take care of some urgent matters of the feminine hygiene variety. I laugh and go to the bar to get myself a drink. After my close encounter with Aaron, I think I deserve one.

On Saturday morning I sit and have breakfast with Nora and she tells me all about how her date with Richard went on Wednesday night. I've been spending so much time with Nicholas that we haven't had the chance to chat until now.

"Yeah, he's nice," she says, while buttering a slice of toast. "I definitely want to see him again, but I'm going to wait for him to call me. I really hate this part."

"I'm sure he'll call," I tell her. "Just don't let your

twitchy dialling fingers get the better of you. I bet you've been fretting over whether or not to call him every night since the date."

She sighs. "Sometimes it's a little scary how well you know me, Fred."

"I know you better than anyone," I joke, putting on a creepy voice. "Perhaps someday you'll open your eyes and see that I'm the one you really want."

She laughs and threatens to fling the butter knife at me. "Shut up. By the way, how have things been on the Nicholas front?"

I shrug. "So, so. Nothing new to report really." Except for how he can reduce me to a quivering mess with a simple look.

She takes a bite out of her toast and I can tell she's not really listening to me anymore. She's too wrapped up in her thoughts of Richard. She hops up from the table and goes to grab her laptop from the living area. She comes back and sets it down, before opening it up.

"Let me show you Richard's Facebook page," she says. "His profile picture is *hot*."

She does some speedy typing and is then turning the screen around to show me a picture of Richard in some kind of forested area with a harness on, the ones you wear when you're about to abseil down a cliff.

"He's definitely rocking the gun show," I comment with a grin as I note his skin tight, short sleeved t-shirt. "I don't know Nora, I might have to rethink my evaluation of him. This picture is halfway to poser town. Are you sure he's not a dickhead in disguise?"

"No need to be so jealous," she smirks and sips on her coffee.

"I'm not jealous," I lean forward and click on the

picture to try and enlarge it, but I end up hitting the wrong button, which brings me back to Nora's page. Her profile picture shows her just before a night out with me and Harry, standing in her bedroom doorway, looking annoyingly well-groomed. I hate this picture of her because it makes her look like a vacuous tramp, and despite how she sometimes comes across, Nora's got a brain inside that head of hers. She just thinks it's cooler to pretend to be shallow.

She's enjoying her breakfast at the moment, so I take the opportunity to sneakily scan down her page and see what's been going on in the virtual world of Nora. Most of the comments are from people she works with, but then I see one that isn't, and I almost shove the laptop off the table in fright. About three days ago, one Aaron O'Toole writes:

Hey Nora! Long time no chat, how are things?

To which she replies:

Hi Aaron, oh same old, same old. Any news with you?

This is followed by a bland discussion about Aaron's job at some engineering company and how he's up for a promotion soon. If I had a Facebook page I would be cutting in on this chit chat with a big, huge, fucking explosive WTF!? I fall back into my chair and stare at Nora, gob-smacked.

She chews and swallows before glancing up at me. "Jesus Fred, you've gone pale. Are you okay?"

I flip her laptop around to her and point a finger at the conversation between her and Aaron. "Explain this." I do my best not to grit my teeth.

"Hey, you were looking at my page, you nosy cow!" she says and immediately signs out, shutting her laptop down.

"How the fuck do you know him?" I ask, my voice scary calm.

"What, that guy Aaron? He's a regular at the bar. I talk to him when business is slow. He added me a couple weeks ago. Sometimes we chat online. He seems nice enough, not much of a sense of humour though."

As she says this it all falls into place. That little scheming rat. Not only does he know where I work, he must also know where I live, and more importantly, who I live with. I clench my fists in anger. How dare he drag Nora into his obsessive quest to get me back.

"Do you know him or something?" she asks warily.

"You need to delete him. Block him. Whatever it is you do online." I tell it to her straight. "He's not just some random regular at your bar Nora. That is my old boyfriend from college, and he is 100% nuts. He's been following me for weeks now. He used to do it years ago too after I broke up with him. I never told you about it because it was a shit time for me and I just wanted to move on from it." I pause to take a breath. Then another realisation hits me. "Have you ever told him anything about me during your chats?"

Nora still seems to be in shock from what I've just told her. It takes her a minute to answer. "Um, only in passing really. He did ask me who I lived with and what they do. Harmless stuff."

"No information is harmless when it comes to Aaron, he uses it all." I slam my hands down on the table in exasperation. "I can't fucking believe this Nora. Do you just go around telling every random stranger you meet all about your life? Have you no common sense at all?"

She looks at me with watery eyes, and I instantly feel

terrible for shouting at her. But she needs a reality check, a big one. Half the reason Aaron has been so successful in sussing out the workings of my life has probably been down to Nora brainlessly feeding it to him over the internet.

She stands up from the table. "Look I'm sorry, I didn't know. You don't need to shout at me." Her watery eyes turn to full on crying, and she dashes into her bedroom. I slump down in my chair and fold my arms across my chest.

I need something to calm me down, so I stand up and begin furiously cleaning the kitchen from top to bottom. By the time I'm done I'm not so consumed with anger anymore. I just can't believe how trusting Nora is of people sometimes, and I can't believe the depths Aaron will sink to for information on me. I need to do something about him, I'm just not sure what that something should be.

I knock next door and Nicholas lets me in. We sit in his bed under the covers, and I tell him all about the morning's debacle. I'm using a lot of hand gestures, which means my anger hasn't quite abated. Nicholas listens quietly, his eyes serious.

"I think you might need to go to the police about this," he says, while stroking soothingly up and down my arm.

"They won't take me seriously. You don't know what the Garda are like in this country. They'll file a few pieces of paperwork, give me a pat on the back and tell me they'll see what they can do. In other words: sweet fuck all. That or I'll get a wanker who'll insinuate I'm overreacting and laugh me out of the place."

"Where does Aaron live? I could go and have a word

with him," says Nicholas, and there is no humour in his voice right now.

Whoa. I'd like to see what Nicholas looks like when he's having words. Probably scary and sexy as hell. He might wear a dress every now and again, but beneath that his body is rock hard strength. He goes to the gym every second day at around lunch time. Sometimes he asks me to join him, to which I usually give him a wry shaking of my head before I turn back to dig into whatever tasty lunch I've whipped up for myself.

"He lives about a half an hour's drive outside of the city, but I'm not telling you where. He's got a screw loose, who knows what he might try and do to you alone in his house."

"Exactly, he'll *try*. Freda, my darling, do you think I couldn't take him?"

I give him an appraising look. "Brawn to brawn you'd win hands down, Viv. But Aaron is unpredictable. He might sit you down in his kitchen and politely offer you a cup of tea, just before he picks up the toaster and throws it at your head."

Nicholas' brow furrows. "I thought you said he was never violent with you."

"Oh not with me, but he'd do a number on the plates in his kitchen cupboard whenever he lost his temper. By now he could have progressed to full on grievous bodily harm."

"Okay, I won't pay him a visit then, but if he shows up at the club again I can't promise you I won't break something, his nose most likely. With some people you need to use more than words to get through to them."

"Look at you, Viv, getting all macho to defend my honour." I poke him in the side. "But if anyone's going to have the pleasure of breaking Aaron's nose, it's going to be me."

"Now that's something I wouldn't mind witnessing." Nicholas pulls me into a hug and kisses the top of my head. "Poor little Fred has had a terribly taxing week. What can we do to make it better for her?" he ponders. His thumb grazes my stomach where my t-shirt has hitched up a bit. I suck in a breath and push away the tingles.

"You listened to me rant when you could have been getting a few extra hours beauty sleep. You've done enough, Nicholas. And thanks, by the way, for listening."

"I'd listen to you read the telephone book, Fred."

I glance at him, amused. "What do you mean?"

"I mean, I like to listen to you. More importantly, I like to watch those pretty lips move. It's kind of seductive."

Out of instinct I bite my bottom lip, drawing his gaze there. He lowers one hand down over my hip and rests it on my backside, which he grips and uses to pull me in closer to him. Drawing my face to his own, he runs the tip of his nose down my cheek to my neck. I swallow. He smells like soap and laundry detergent, with just a hint of aftershave. I reach up and gently tangle my fingers through his hair.

I notice immediately when his breathing quickens and he continues his descent down my body. From my neck his nose travels to my collarbone, then quite surprisingly he just rests his head on my chest. He doesn't even try to feel me up.

"I love how warm and soft you are. All I ever want to do is touch you, but sometimes it feels like not touching you is even more of a turn on." He pauses and looks up at me. "I want to ruin you Freda, in the best way possible."

I don't breathe a word, but I'm practically panting.

He kisses me softly on the fabric of my t-shirt. "I'm sort of enjoying this game we're playing, but we're going to destroy each other one of these days, you do know that right?"

Does he mean destroy in a good way or a bad way?

He doesn't get the chance to elaborate because there's a hesitant knock at his apartment door. He kisses me again on the t-shirt and gets up to go and answer it. I climb out of his bed and straighten my clothes. When I enter the living area I find Nora standing beside Nicholas, looking like shit. Her nose and eyes are all red, like she hasn't stopped crying since she stormed into her bedroom earlier this morning.

"Fred, I'm so sorry. I was such a bloody idiot."

I walk straight over to her and take her into a semi-awkward hug. Nora and I don't really show each other affection, but since she's so upset I suppose I can make an exception. I pet at her hair. "Listen, it's okay. Aaron would have found some way to worm his way into my life with or without you. It's not your fault. You can't be suspicious of every new person you meet." I pull away to look at her and try to make a joke. "You know, I'm probably the one who should be apologising. You had to suffer through Aaron's god awfully dull conversation. You deserve a medal for that."

The joke does the trick and she lets out a sad little giggle. I see Nicholas watching me over Nora's shoulder. He comes over and wraps his arms around the both of us, creating a group hug.

"How's about we forget all about boring, psychotic Aaron for the time being and I take you two gorgeous ladies out for lunch?" he asks.

We both smile at him and nod our heads.

Chapter Twelve
A Brick Through a Window

"Yoo-hoo," comes Phil's sing song voice as I sit in the dressing room and help Nicholas out of his costume.

It was a wild gig tonight. At one point a member of the audience was so drunk and riled up that he climbed onto the stage and tried to grab Nicholas by the crotch. Nicholas was a good sport about it and gracious as ever, but I think he's a little bit upset. He's trying to hide it.

I do wonder why he's upset though, since he often invites people up onto the stage and can be very touchy and flirty with them. Perhaps it was because the guy tonight was really aggressive and got up onto the stage without Nicholas' permission.

"We're having a lock in after closing time," Phil announces. "Do you two want to join us?"

A little thrill of excitement goes through me. I've never been to a lock in before. "I'm definitely up for it," I turn to Nicholas. "What about you, Viv?"

He looks a bit tired, but he musters a grin. "I wouldn't miss it. Count me in."

"Good stuff," says Phil with a clap of his hands. "We're clearing the punters away now. Come out when you're ready."

Phil leaves and I glance up at the clock. It's almost three in the morning. Normally Nicholas' gigs don't run this late, but Phil had another drag queen called Linda Lovely from Brighton doing a once off performance tonight, so Nicholas' slot got pushed back.

Once I have all of his make-up off he stands and shimmies out of the skirt and corset he wore for his show. He's wearing the frilly burlesque knickers again, and I can't help myself but to take a peek. He catches me looking and eyes the bra strap on my bare shoulder, since I'm wearing an oversized blue top that hangs off to one side. I glance away.

By the time I look back he's slipped out of the knickers and into his boxer shorts; the Calvin Klein ones that I wore on my head like a hat. The memory makes me slightly giddy.

Nicholas puts on a nice pair of black trousers and a light grey shirt. His hair is a mess from being squished up under the wig, and I know that he won't fix it himself, so I grab the hairbrush from the dressing table and stand up.

Pulling him down into a chair I say, "Let me brush your hair Viv, it's a disaster."

He sits silently and I comb his hair until it's sufficiently neat. It's cut tight to his neckline, but a lot longer on top. I run my fingers through it after I'm done, because I kind of can't help myself.

He glances at me through the mirror as I stand behind him, a wry expression on his face.

"All done," I say, pulling my hands away.

"Thanks," he grins and then pats me on the bottom.

We head out to the now empty club and make our way over to a table where Phil, Sean and Linda Lovely are sitting doing shots of tequila. Unlike Nicholas, Linda Lovely is still in her full drag get up, which consists of a huge pink wig, a silver dress and rainbow coloured heels. She looks like a fairy godmother from a dream you'd have while tripping on acid. I think I remember Nicholas mentioning that her real name is Dave.

A few members of staff potter about, doing the final clean-up of the night.

"Nicholas Turner," announces Linda Lovely as Nicholas sits down at the table and I take the chair beside him. "I'd forgotten how good you look in a pair of trousers. Two eggs in a hanky." She smacks her lips.

Phil, Sean and I burst out laughing, while Nicholas stands up to twirl around and give Linda a proper look at his goods. She arches her sculpted eyebrow and nods approvingly.

Sean pushes a glass in front of me and pours some kind of fruity cocktail into it from the big jug sitting beside the bottle of tequila. I take a sip and it tastes like lemon and orange heaven.

"What is this?" I ask him, gulping it back.

Sean shrugs. "It doesn't have a name yet. I rustled it up at the bar and put a bit of everything in."

I laugh. "Should I be worried?"

He gives me a nervous look. "Prob...ably not."

"Prob...ably not is good enough for me," I tell him, nudging him in the side with my elbow.

Phil speaks up, "Linda my lovely, tell Nicholas and Fred your juicy gossip."

Linda coughs to clear her throat and proceeds to detail an encounter she had last weekend, with a celebrity she refuses to name, who came into her club in Brighton and had a quicky with her in the toilets. The unnamed celebrity apparently has a wife and two kids. I spend the next half an hour trying to goad her into telling us the name of the celeb, but her lips are sealed as tight as a chastity belt.

At some point Nicholas rests his arm across the back of my chair and begins rhythmically tracing his fingers in circles over my bare shoulder. Every time he does this I pull my top back up to cover my skin, but he just waits for it to fall back down again. It's a weird little game we're playing.

I think I hear Linda Lovely make a comment to Phil, something like, "What's the story between those two anyway?"

I'm tipsy enough not to think too much about the answer to that question or about how transparent we both are.

I'm currently on my fourth glass of Sean's mystery cocktail, which has gone from tasting like lemon and orange heaven to the elixir of the Gods. Every touch Nicholas gives me is so subtle and barely there, yet I'm hyper aware of all of them.

Sean gets up and sets some music playing over the sound system. He's one of those drummers who's always tapping out a beat on whatever surface he can find. Earlier I watched in fascination as he created an intricate rhythm, using his knees as percussion instruments.

I turn to Nicholas drunkenly. He looks like his mind is elsewhere, like he's sad about something. "Viv, the next time some guy gets up on the stage and grabs you like that I'm going to punch his lights out."

He smiles and leans in close to me, pulling himself out of his own thoughts "Very gallant of you to offer Fred. I'll hold you to that."

I take a long swig of my drink, and ramble on, the alcohol making me far too honest. "I could tell you didn't like it. I didn't either." I break out into furious laughter. "Seriously Viv, I will cut a bitch the next time."

By the way Nicholas is paying perfect attention to me, I don't think he's as plastered as I am. In fact, I think he's been nursing the same drink all night. That can't be good. He's going to remember all of my ridiculous comments. The problem is, I'm too drunk right now to care.

I twist my chair around so that I can look at him properly. I put both of my hands on his cheeks, holding onto his face. "You're so pretty Viv, it's not fair. How can you be pretty *and* handsome? Did you sell your soul to the devil or something?"

He puts his hands on top of mine. "Nope, and being pretty isn't the cake walk you think it is Fred," he answers, somehow managing to sound miserable while he's smiling.

I frown. "Why? Because arseholes think they can come up on stage and grab your crotch without asking your permission?"

He laughs and his eyes go all sparkly and crinkly the way that I like them. "Something like that. Mostly it attracts people whose attention you don't want."

I grab a hold of his bicep, for no real reason other than it looks nice and I want to feel it. "I'll be your bodyguard, if you want me to be."

"I want you..." he trails off with a hot expression, and doesn't finish his sentence.

I suddenly notice that Phil, Linda and Sean are up and dancing. Linda totters her way over to me and pulls me up by the hand. I follow her over to the others, bopping along to the music. Nicholas remains seated, watching the show.

I don't think I've ever felt more drunkenly happy, as I allow a six foot tall drag queen in rainbow high heels to twirl me around the empty night club to the beats of "Rock DJ" by Robbie Williams. I laugh so hard when Phil tries to do the splits that I almost cry. When he's standing again Sean jumps up onto his shoulders and Phil gives him a dancing piggy back ride around the room.

Some time later I find myself not dancing merrily with Linda anymore, but slow dancing with Nicholas, while the others return to the table to continue drinking. I can't even remember him approaching me. All I know is that it feels good to have his arms wrapped around my waist, while mine are wrapped around his neck, playing with the ends of his hair.

He looks down at me and whispers, "If you weren't so drunk, I'd ask you to stay with me tonight."

I lay my head on his chest, tired. "It's nearly five o'clock. The night's almost over anyway."

"That's true. I should get you home, you look sleepy."

"Can't I just sleep here?" I ask. "Here is good," I snuggle in closer to him.

"Here *is* good," he agrees, stroking a hand down my hair, "but you need your bed. Come on, we'll see if we can catch a taxi outside."

Nicholas tells the others that we're leaving, but Phil asks us to wait so that we can all go out together. It only takes him a couple of minutes to lock the place up. Linda and Sean are singing the lyrics to "Sweet Caroline" as we stand by the front door, waiting for Phil. I lean into Nicholas, because I'm too wasted to hold myself up.

"Done and dusted," Phil declares, as he saunters into the front lobby and unlocks the door for us.

Nicholas and I are the first to step out, and my entire

body seems to instantly sober when a brick comes hurtling towards us, along with somebody shouting the word "QUEERS!" at the top of their lungs. Nicholas pulls me out of the way just in time for the brick to go smashing through a window instead of hitting us.

I look frantically from left to right to see who threw the brick. Then I spot the suped-up Ford Fiesta with go faster stripes on the other side of the street. Three scumbags are standing by it, while another sits in the driver's seat. Nicholas stands up straight and pushes me behind him, just as Phil, Linda and Sean all spill out the door.

"Which one of you threw that?" Phil shouts.

The three jog across the road, with one of them walking right up to Phil and punching him in the face. Another has a baseball bat, which he swings at Nicholas. Nicholas ducks and kicks the guy in the knee cap. Sean and Linda are huddled around Phil, who's clutching his bleeding nose, while the other two thugs spit a range of threats and homophobic slurs at them.

I get a good look at all of their faces, trying to commit them to memory. The one who attacked Nicholas swings for him again, but this time Nicholas feints to the side and brings his elbow down on the guy's jaw. He drops the baseball bat and lets out a yelp of pain, while Nicholas grabs the bat.

"Now!" he shouts angrily, wielding the bat. "All three of you are going to get into your piece of shit car and drive far the fuck away from here."

The one whose jaw Nicholas just bashed raises his hands in the air. "Okay pal, calm down," as if Nicholas were the one to initiate the attack and not simply defending himself.

Nicholas takes a step towards him. For a second it looks like he's considering hitting him with the bat. "I'm not your fucking pal, you scumbag. Now go before I do something I regret."

The three of them scurry off to their ridiculous car, while mumbling things like, "Fuckin' psycho" and "Bleedin' lunatic". Typical. We all step back inside the club. Nicholas pulls me into his arms and squeezes me tight.

"Jesus, that brick was an inch away from hitting you Freda," he breathes.

Linda is already on the phone to the police, and Sean is pulling some tissue paper from his bag to give to Phil for his bleeding nose.

"That was fucking scary random," I say to Phil, as Nicholas continues to hold me. "Has anything like that ever happened before?"

"Not since I've been managing the place," he answers in a shaky voice. "But we haven't been open very long."

"This is weird. It's like they were waiting for us, like they knew there were still people inside even though it's well past closing time," says Sean.

"Little bastards," Linda hisses, just as she hangs up the phone and goes over to give Phil a hug. "Look what they did to that gorgeous face of yours. The Garda are on their way now."

We all go to sit by the bar and wait for the police, which could take a while, since they're not exactly known for their speedy response times. Forty-five minutes later they mosey on into the club and ask what happened. We all give our statements and I describe what the three guys looked like in as much detail as I can. Thankfully they don't make us go to the station to be interviewed further.

Nicholas calls for a cab to bring us home. I don't think he's released me from his hold since the attack.

"You were so brave, taking them on like that," I whisper to him, as we sit in the back of the taxi wrapped around one another.

"I've been working in gay clubs all my life Fred. This wasn't my first encounter of queer bashing, you know. One time over in London four guys jumped me, broke my arm and my nose. I gave as good as I got though."

"God, I forget how hard it must be. It's awful that you've had to go through that."

"I survive. I always do," he says softly, just as the taxi pulls up to our block.

When we get inside we go to our separate apartments. I hop straight into the shower, needing to wash away the night's events. When I get out I really don't feel like going to bed alone, so I get into some PJs, take my key to Nicholas' place and sneak next door. I find him just getting out of his own shower, with a towel wrapped around his waist.

Our eyes lock.

"I didn't want to sleep alone," I tell him.

He nods to his bedroom. "Go on, make yourself comfortable. I'll be there in a minute."

I crawl beneath his soft blankets and am immediately ten times calmer. A few minutes later Nicholas comes in, wearing boxer shorts and a t-shirt. He slips in behind me, switches off the lamp and pulls me into his arms. I fall asleep to the relaxing touch of his fingers trailing across my stomach.

When I wake up I'm alone in the bed. I glance at

Nicholas' alarm clock on his dresser and the time reads 14.13. I've slept half the day. I stretch out under the duvet like a lazy cat. A few minutes later Nicholas comes through the door, carrying a tray with tea and toast.

"This is about as far as my culinary skills go, I'm afraid," he announces with an exaggerated grimace as he sets the tray down in front of me.

I sit up and the duvet pools around my waist. Nicholas' gaze immediately falls to my chest since I don't wear a bra to bed. "Hey, eyes on the prize Viv," I tease as I pick up a piece of toast and take a bite.

A slow grin forms on his lips. "Sorry, but I'm only human Fred, and those are the prettiest breasts I have ever seen."

"Flattery will get you everywhere," I tell him happily.

"Will it really?" he asks. "I should try getting somewhere then, shouldn't I?"

"Maybe you should," I answer boldly.

He shakes his head at my over the top flirting. "I have a proposition for you," he begins hesitantly and I nod my head for him to continue. "I had a phone call from a friend of mine in Edinburgh this morning. She runs a venue during the Fringe all this month and one of her acts pulled out at the last minute. She wanted to know if I'd fly over and fill in for a few nights."

"Cool, when does she want you to go?" I ask, though I'm kind of disappointed that he's going to be away for a while.

"Tomorrow morning preferably," he comes and sits down beside me at the head of the bed. "Come with me?" he asks suddenly.

"To Scotland?"

"Yes, we've had a shitty week, with Aaron and last night's attack. A couple of days away will do us both good I think."

"But I have to work," I say to him. Disappointment fills my gut with the realisation. If I didn't have to bake every morning this week I'd be hopping right on a plane with him.

"Have someone fill in for you. Come on Fred, we both need this. Besides, I'm not going if you don't come too. I need my assistant with me after all, I'd be lost without her."

"Oh, you're a sly one," I grin, knowing he's trying to guilt me into this. "I'll make no promises, but I'll see what I can do. I might be able to get an old college friend to make my cupcakes while I'm away."

Nicholas wraps his arm around my shoulders with a triumphant smile, and I finish eating the food he made for me.

Later on I call up Aoife, a girl who was in my class in college, to see if she's available to fill in for me this week. She had a baby and got married as soon as she finished her degree, so she's been a stay at home mother ever since. I had her do my cupcakes for me once before when I was sick with the flu. Over the phone she tells me she'd be happy to take on the work and I do a little dance of excitement as I'm reminding her of the recipes and what not.

She takes notes and we hang up about twenty minutes later. Then I call up the charity shop and see if anyone would be willing to take my shifts. With that all sorted I send Nicholas a quick text to let him know that all systems are go. He writes back saying that he's going to book the flights and hotel online.

I've never been to Edinburgh before, but I've heard the Fringe Festival is supposed to be *amazing*. Needless to say, I'm as excited as a ten year old on Christmas Eve.

Nora rolls her eyes at me as I hurry around the apartment, putting on a shit Scottish accent a la Mrs Doubtfire and trying to get my clothes packed for our flight in the morning. She tells me that she's invited Richard over for dinner tomorrow evening and quite casually asks if I could possibly leave her a fool proof recipe for something to cook.

After I've had a good laugh at her ineptness for food preparation, and she is at the end of her tether with my jibes, I write down the ingredients needed for lemon chicken with mushrooms, as well as instructions on how to make it. It's simple, so there's less of a chance of her screwing it up. For dessert I tell her to make Eton Mess, since it's one of the easiest desserts on the planet.

She gives me a long suffering look and tells me that *she'll* be the judge of how easy it is. I tell her to send me pictures so that I can have a laugh at the *mess* she makes of Eton *Mess*. See what I did there? I should quit baking cupcakes and take up writing jokes professionally.

I call up my mum and let her know that I'm going away for the week with Nicholas, because I am a good little daughter like that. I haven't told her much about him so far, other than the fact that he's my neighbour and a new friend of mine. I can tell that she wants me to elaborate, as she keeps asking me roundabout questions, such as: *So is he a friend like Harry is your friend, or is he another kind of a friend?* Oh mother, do you really think it's going to be that easy to get me to talk? I laugh cynically to myself.

I avoid her questions as best I can. It's difficult to classify my relationship with Nicholas for her when I can't even classify it for myself. I can hardly tell my mum that I work for him because he's a drag queen and that we say we're best friends, but really we want to get inside each other's pants. She'd probably have a heart attack by the time I got as far as the drag queen bit.

Speak of the devil and watch him appear. Just as I hang up with Mum I get a text from Nicholas informing me that our flight is at a quarter to eight the following morning, and that he's going to drive us to the airport at six. I set my alarm for five and send him a quick message back, which reads:

Noted. C u in the morning sugar tits <3

To which he responds:

Sugar tits? Really Fred? U r giving me naughty ideas.

To which I encourage:

Oh. Feel free 2 elaborate :-0

To which he answers:

I wouldn't want 2 scandalize u like I did b4 ;-)

To which I venture:

If I recall correctly, I quite enjoyed being scandalized :-D

To which he scolds:

U r killing me, Fred.

And then orders:

Come 2 my place. Now.

To which I decline:

I'm afraid that would b inappropriate.

To which he declares:

Being inappropriate with u is my favourite thing

Fred. x

I sigh and throw my phone to the end of my bed. I really don't know what to say to that. And as usual, it's my own fault for starting it in the first place. A minute later my phone beeps with a new message. I scramble for it and open the text. It reads:

U r so fucking beautiful.

Oh wow. I bravely type back:

So r u.

He repeats his earlier request:

Come 2 my place. Plz. I have 2 kiss u.

His message makes me breathe heavier. I reply:

I can't. Need my beauty sleep. C u 2moro. x

I half expect him to ask me again, but he doesn't, he simply says:

OK darling. Sleep well. <3

My heart is going ninety. I'm never going to be able to get an early night now; his texts will just keep on repeating in my head. I go into Nora's room and ask her for one of the sleeping pills I know she keeps hidden at the back of her bedside dresser. She hands me the happy little pill and I grab a glass of water from the kitchen before swallowing it down. I make sure all of my stuff is ready for the morning and then I hit the hay once I feel the drowsiness of the pill kicking in.

Chapter Thirteen
Ukuleles and The Polka Dot Twins

I throw my bag in the boot of Nicholas' powder blue Nissan Figaro and then hop into the front seat beside him. It's six o'clock in the morning, but since it's the summer it's already bright out. I got a great night of sleep thanks to Nora's magic snooze pill, so I'm raring to go.

I'm wearing a peach coloured pencil skirt, a cream short sleeved t-shirt and cream flats. Yeah okay, I put in the effort, but it's not every day that I find myself travelling to Scotland with a drag queen.

It takes us just under twenty minutes to get to the airport. Nicholas leaves his car in the long stay parking lot and we head inside. Once we've checked our bags and gone through security we have a little fun in the duty free looking at all of the designer handbags.

Nicholas throws a dark red leather one over his shoulder and struts over to the mirror, doing his Vivica Blue walk. I've noticed they have different strides. Nicholas' is smooth, masculine grace, while Vivica's is lighter on the toes and contains more movement in the hips

Then we stop by a café where we have croissants and coffee for breakfast. When we board the plane I'm pleasantly surprised to find that Nicholas has booked us in business class. I flop down into the massive seat with relish.

"I thought you said you were going to try to be more frugal with your money Viv," I comment, even though I'm glad that he splashed out. I've never flown anything other than economy before, so it's a thrill despite the fact that the flight is going to take less than an hour.

"I said I *should* try. I never said I was going to," he corrects. "Anyway, I wanted to treat you."

"Aw, you're the best boss ever," I tell him happily.

I order a vodka and orange juice from the air hostess as she passes by our seats. When in Rome, as they say.

"Isn't it a little early to be drinking?" Nicholas asks with a wry grin.

"I'm on holiday Viv. Morning alcohol is allowed when you're on holiday."

"This isn't a holiday, it's a work trip." He reprimands, and seems to be enjoying doing so.

I scowl at him. "Semantics." I pause to sip on my drink. "Are you getting firm with me, boss?"

He lets his head fall back against the seat, his eyes trained lazily on my lips and slowly reaches out to run his hand over my knee. "Maybe. Do you want me to be your boss now instead of Viv? I think I can pull that off."

I draw my knees together when his hand makes a move to wander between my legs. "Nah, I think you should be Viv. We don't want to get ourselves thrown off the plane for indecency."

He glances at the fluffy clouds out the window. "We're airborne, Fred."

I raise my glass to him. "Exactly, Viv."

He laughs. "Are you drunk already? You've only had a few sips."

I shrug. "I could be. Alcohol affects me stronger this early in the morning."

"In that case, no more screwdrivers for you."

I laugh loudly. "*Screwdriver*, that's a funny word."

Oh my God, I'm tipsy. This is a new record. Usually it takes me at least a couple drinks to get this far.

I put down the glass and pull a cookery magazine out of my carry on bag. Yes, I read cookery magazines. Sometimes I'm partial to a bit of food porn. I love looking at the pictures of the finished recipes. It gives me good ideas about what new food I'm going to try and cook next. About a year ago Nora and I got into the habit of playing a game where we'd open a cookery magazine on a random page and I would have to try and make the recipe, no matter how difficult or bizarre. One time I made Heston Blumenthal's snail porridge. It was actually quite nice. Okay, stop complaining. I warned you there were more tangents on the way. I'm done now.

Nicholas motions for the air hostess to come over and asks her for a bottle of water. I don't fail to notice them flirt back and forth before she goes to get him his beverage. To be honest, I can't really blame her for flirting with him. He's one of the prettiest men you will ever come across. Still, it irks me that he flirts back.

I have no right to be irked, but such is life.

The air hostess comes back and twists the cap on the bottle of water open for Nicholas, before pouring it into a glass with ice and a slice of lime over the rim. I want to cock my eyebrow at her and remark, *Overdoing it a little, aren't we love?* But I seal my lips tight. I don't want to come across as a jealous psycho. Even though, let's face it, when it comes to Nicholas I am a bit of a jealous psycho.

She leaves to take care of another passenger and Nicholas leans in, resting his shoulder against mine while he peruses my magazine. The page is currently open on a recipe for homemade chicken stew.

"Do you remember some of the things you said to me last night?" he asks casually, his breath brushing against my ear.

"Unfortunately yes, but I have a feeling you're going to remind me anyway." I sigh and turn the page.

"You said you were going to kick the arse of the next punter who tries to get up on the stage and fondle me," he tells me, with a big delighted grin on his face.

"Alcohol makes me think I'm tougher than I really am," I explain. "You seemed a little shaken by the whole thing. I wanted to make you feel better."

He picks up his water and takes a sip. "Well, thank you for that. But I suppose I can't really complain about it. It's just something I have to deal with. Take the rough with the smooth. Most performers in my profession would kill for the packed out venues I get. If I started bemoaning the fact that some men can get a bit "handsy" then I'd come across as an ungrateful diva."

"There's no doubting you're a diva Viv, but you're certainly not ungrateful. Every night you pull out all the stops, giving the audience a performance they'll never forget. You make them feel a part of something special for a small moment in time. You put your whole self into your singing, portraying emotion through your on-stage persona. The least you can expect in return is for the audience not to disrespect you or turn you into an object."

He gestures with his hands. "This is why I like you so much. Most women would turn around and say I should enjoy being objectified simply because I have a penis. You see past that."

"Yeah well, that kind of thinking pisses me off. Some

people think that men are never the victims of sexual assault. Men can be raped too, you know," I say, waggling my teacher finger at him. A moment later I regret having said it when I look up to see some strange emotion on his face. Some kind of pain. Crap, maybe I went a little too far.

"Sorry, I didn't mean to offend you or anything," I apologise and focus back on the magazine.

"Don't be, I like that you say what's on your mind. You just brought back a bad memory, that's all."

Oh no. I don't want to think about what that memory might be. God, I really want to hug him right now, but that might make him uncomfortable. I've always known that Nicholas must have experienced a dark past, mostly because his cheerful demeanour is often punctuated with periods of sadness, but also from these little things he says. Like how he told me he's had to suffer for his passion that time when we were walking up Grafton Street.

"I'm sorry that you've got bad memories," I tell him, not knowing what else to say. I'm not going to come right out and ask him what the memory was. Some things you need to let people tell you themselves if they want to, and if not, you let them keep them hidden inside.

"Every memory makes me who I am right now, in this moment. Good or bad, all experiences shape you."

"And I like how you're shaped," I say, turning to give him a peck on the cheek. It's a sweet little gesture that I know he wasn't expecting. He smiles at me and turns to look out the window at the passing clouds. I focus back on my food porn for the rest of the flight.

If I had to pick two words to describe Edinburgh, I would tell you that it's majestic and beautiful. Really, really old, but somehow more alive than any other place I've ever been. Perhaps that's just because there are people everywhere for the Fringe. Every single sign post is covered with posters for shows. Around each corner there's a different street performer ready to show you something new. To dazzle you with some unusual and captivating talent.

I almost stick my head out the window of the taxi to get a look at a woman who's walking by in shorts and a tank top, with tattoos and piercings covering almost every square inch of her body. I'm thinking the words *cool* and *ouch* all in the one thought.

Nicholas gets the taxi driver who picked us up at the airport to drop us at The Royal Mile outside the Radisson Blu Hotel where, I shit you not, we are going to be staying. Okay, so if you've never seen this hotel before then you aren't going to understand my amazement. It's like a massive medieval looking fortress right there in the middle of the busiest street in the city. On the drive here I found myself astounded by the fact that around each corner there could be a castle waiting to surprise you. Or a historical building that shoots up high into the skyline.

When we get inside the hotel I find that Nicholas has booked us into a suite. A suite! This must be costing him a bomb, but he did say that he was quite comfortable money-wise, so I'm not complaining. I run inside the room and hop onto the bed. Then I look around and realise it's the *only* bed. So I'm going to have to share with him. Oh no, what a travesty. The idea simultaneously sets my body alight and paralyses it with nerves.

"Viv, you calculating little devil," I call as Nicholas puts his bags down in the lounge area of the suite.

He glances at me for only a second through the doorway, a carefully constructed innocent look on his face with his hand raised to his chest. "Calculating? Moi? Whatever gave you that idea?"

"A one bedroom suite in the fanciest hotel going, business class plane tickets. Need I say more? Better women would be naked and spreading their legs for you as we speak. It's a good thing I'm not materialistic," I raise my nose to the ceiling and fold my arms.

Nicholas' laughter filters in from the lounge. "Oh Fred, would you give me a hand out here with this bottle of champagne?"

I jump up and rush out, but there's no bottle of champagne in sight. Nicholas gives me an appraising look. "Not materialistic in the slightest," he raises an amused eyebrow and clucks his tongue.

"Fine, you have me sussed. I'm a fickle, materialistic, easily bought hussy. Now pop out the champers Viv, we haven't got a moment to lose."

"Maybe later, we have work to do first."

"Work? What's that? Never heard of it." I fall down onto the expensive couch and slip off my shoes.

"Take a look out the window and tell me what you see," he instructs.

I pad my way across the thick, soft carpet and look out. "People, people everywhere, but not a drop to drink."

"And what are the people doing?"

"Not much."

"Wrong answer," he says, coming to stand behind me.

"You see those two over there," he points at two guys wearing mariachi band outfits, wielding their flamenco guitars and playing for a group of people who have the look of tourists about them.

"Yeah, I see them."

"They're doing promotion work to get people to come to their show. That's what you've got to do during the Fringe. There are hundreds of shows going on at any one time. You've got to sell yourself, make sure people come to yours."

"Right, so you're saying that we have to go outside and sell Vivica Blue."

"Exactly," Nicholas squeezes my shoulders. "Now come and help me pick out something to wear," he lifts up his suitcase and lugs it into the bedroom, before plopping it down onto the bed.

Nicholas leaves me to assemble an outfit for him, while he prepares to have a shave. He's sporting a bit of a five o'clock shadow. I prefer him with stubble rather than clean shaven, but a drag queen with a beard just won't do.

"Go make that face as smooth as a baby's bottom," I tell him, as he grabs his toiletries bag and heads into the bathroom.

"Oh, it's not just the face that'll be smooth, I have to wax my legs as well," says Nicholas.

"Fun! Can I help?"

"No you cannot. A lady has to keep some things sacred," he says in a high pitched voice as he swings the door shut.

I laugh and dump myself onto the bed to sift through his costumes. I select a pair of barely there sheer black tights, bright red six inch heels and a navy blue form fitting lace dress. Nicholas comes out of the bathroom about a half an hour later wearing one of the complimentary hotel bathrobes. When he sits down beside me I lean forward and run my hand over his leg.

"Whoa, those are some smooth pins. You'll have to show me what products you use."

"Vivica Blue doesn't reveal her beauty secrets," he tells me with a wink.

"Speaking in the third person, Nicholas, you really are turning into a diva," I chide.

He takes the clothes I've set out for him, hangs them up in the wardrobe and we get to work on his make-up. He decides not to wear a wig today, so I use some wax to style his hair into that Jamie Lee Curtis slicked back look, like the first time I'd seen him perform.

We decide on this really dark lipstick that looks almost black and I find these cool diamond-esque body jewels at the end of the make-up case. I convince Nicholas to let me put them around his eyes and cheek bones.

A little fairy of a woman stops by the hotel room just as Nicholas is almost ready. She's got feathery white blond hair, is about 5 foot and looks like she weighs next to nothing in the most appealing way possible. She makes me feel like a giant, and at 5"6 I'd never considered myself to be unusually tall.

"This is Catelin, Fred. She's the friend I told you about, the one who manages the venue I'm going to be performing in tonight."

"Hi Catelin," I shake her hand. "It's lovely to meet you."

"The same to you," says Catelin, in a light Edinburgh accent. "I just came to drop these by. I take it you're both heading out to do some promo work now?" she asks, as she sets a stack of flyers down on the coffee table.

They've got a great picture of Nicholas on the front wearing a gold dress and a long black wig. The caption reads, in shiny silver font, "Miss Vivica Blue, singing sensation, returns to Edinburgh for a limited last minute run."

Nicholas gives Catelin a massive hug and thanks her for the flyers. It's a really warm hug too, a familiar one. I wonder if they're old flames? It seems like the only reason he doesn't kiss her on either cheek is because he'd get the dark lipstick all over her. They sit on the couch and chat for a few brief minutes. I go to the bathroom to freshen up and by the time I come back out, Catelin is gone.

"You two," I say to Nicholas, waving my finger at the door to signify I'm talking about Catelin, "you used to go out, didn't you?"

He smirks. "Very prudent Fred, how could you tell?"

"I don't know, just a feeling. That and she seemed unusually pleased to see you. Maybe she wants to get back together."

He looks at me in a smugly satisfied way, and I hate myself for having said any of this because it reveals so much of how I feel about him. "We were lovers for a short while, nothing serious," he gives a casual shrug. "And she's married now to a man named Barry, so there's nothing to be worried about."

"I'm not worried. Why would I be worried?" I ask, in the most unconvincing tone imaginable.

"Of course you're not," he smiles. "Come on, let's go get some work done."

Nicholas holds my hand as we walk through the hotel lobby, without as much as a raised eyebrow from the staff or other guests. They must be used to seeing people in strange attire during the month of the Fringe.

I have the flyers stuck in my handbag and Nicholas is holding a stack himself. He stops in front of a group of women and introduces himself, giving them a little pitch about his show. I idle just behind him and suddenly find a man and a woman who look freakishly similar to one another standing in front of me.

The man is wearing a pink dickey bow and a black and white polka dot shirt, while the woman wears a pink polka dot fifties poodle dress and her black hair is styled into a Betty Page do. She's also holding a ukulele. Ukuleles kind of annoy me, because they remind me of the hipsters back home who carry the tiny instruments around to make themselves look all subversive and kooky.

"Hello little lady," says the man, in a Liverpudlian accent. "I'm Bob and this is my twin sister Bobby. Together we're the Polka Dot Twins and we'd like to cordially invite you to our show, a musical comedy extravaganza of the filthiest kind," Bob hands me a flyer that tells me when and where their show takes place. It also states that it's free.

"Oh, are you really twins?" I ask, admiring Bobby's shoes that have little kitten faces printed on the toes.

Bob motions me closer, and whispers theatrically, "No, not really, but don't tell anyone. It would ruin our image."

"My lips are sealed," I grin.

A second later Nicholas has finished chatting with the group of women and comes to stand beside me. "Hey, I hope you two aren't keeping my assistant from her work," he jokes.

"Oh, I'm so sorry fair maiden," says Bob, giving Nicholas a sweeping bow. "I didn't realise this beautiful Irish molly was your assistant. Allow myself and my sister to play you a song as a gesture of goodwill."

"Go ahead," says Nicholas smiling.

Bobby begins strumming her ukulele and Bob bursts into an alternate rendition of "Hello" by Lionel Richie. He's changed up the lyrics to make them dirty and absolutely hilarious.

When they've finished we give them a round of applause and I pull one of Nicholas' flyers out of my handbag. "I tell you what, if you come to our show tonight, we'll come to yours."

Bobby takes the piece of paper from me and eyes it with amusement. Nicholas' show finishes at nine and theirs starts at ten-thirty, so it's doable.

"It's a deal," says Bobby, and we shake on it.

The Polka Dot Twins sidle off to sing for another unsuspecting passer-by, and Nicholas and I set about pitching his show to as many people as possible. By the time three o'clock comes around I'm exhausted. I have about twenty flyers in my handbag from other performers who all managed to pull me in and ask me to come to their shows.

I'll never possibly have enough time to go to them all. The whole day gives me a real glimpse into how competitive the Fringe is when it comes to getting punters in to see you perform.

When we get back to the hotel I go to run a bath in the fancy tub and Nicholas calls for room service, before getting out of his drag clothes and removing his make-up.

About five minutes into my soak there's a light knock on the door. Nicholas saunters on in a moment later. I went a little wild with the bubble bath, so none of my bits are on show. All the same, I grab a hand towel and lay it over my chest.

Nicholas sits on the edge of the tub and absent mindedly runs his fingers through the water.

"I ordered us both the steak," he says quietly.

"Sounds good," I mutter.

Neither of us is mentioning the fact that I'm basically lying here naked. I've never been more aware of another human being in my life. The fact that I'm nude in a bath of water and he's sitting there fully clothed in a t-shirt and jeans is strangely erotic. I feel vulnerable in the best possible way.

We're both quiet for a long time. I use my foot to turn on the tap and let more hot water into the tub. Nicholas' eyes are glued to the movement.

"Let me wash your hair for you," he says in a soft voice.

I look at him and hesitate to answer. For some reason I'm terribly nervous that he's going to try and hop in here with me. That would be trouble in a big fancy box with a bow on top. Delicious, wonderful trouble.

"Okay," I say finally, holding the hand towel firmly to my chest and turning around so that my back is facing him. Nicholas picks up a jug and fills it with water, before raising it and pouring it over my hair. The water trickles from my head all the way down my back, like a waterfall.

He grabs the tiny bottle of hotel shampoo, squeezes some out onto his hand and begins massaging it into my scalp. I focus on the pressure of his fingers as they move against me. It's a soothing sort of pressure and I relax, leaning back against the rim of the tub. I hear Nicholas suck in a breath. He makes a lather with the shampoo and then rinses out all the suds.

"There," he whispers. "All finished."

"Thanks," I manage to croak out. He doesn't move from his position next to the tub as I lift my leg and take a soapy wash cloth to run over it. Before I know it, Nicholas is pressing his lips to the hollow of my neck and purring, "Do you know how much I want to fuck you right now?"

I exhale and mumble, "Shut up."

"No," he says, as he reaches around me and yanks the hand towel that had been covering my chest right off me. He grabs one of my breasts and moulds it with his hand, then pinches the nipple. I moan and when I turn to look at him he's standing up and pulling his t-shirt off over his head. He's just about to pounce on me again when there's a knock on the door of the suite.

Nicholas groans and runs a hand through his hair. "Fucking room service would have to arrive at the worst possible moment."

"Go answer it," I say to him, trying to pull myself together after that very brief moment of bliss.

"Fine," he grumbles, and leaves the bathroom.

I quickly get out of the tub and dry myself off, before wrapping up in a bath robe. When I come out there's a tray with two covered plates and a bottle of wine on the table by the window. The member of staff who delivered the food is gone. Nicholas' gaze burns me. He's standing by the couch, devouring me with a single look.

I make a move to go to the table where the food is waiting, but he cuts me off and drags me into the bedroom, throwing me down onto the bed. He hasn't put his t-shirt back on yet. He pulls my legs around his hips so that I'm straddling him and gently tugs at the tie around the waist of my robe.

Before I know it the whole thing is open and I'm bared to him. He takes his time perusing my body and then begins planting little kisses over my breasts, murmuring words I can't decipher. I'm too lost in the sensation of his tongue as it snakes out around my nipple.

Slowly, he kisses his way down my stomach and when he reaches my mound my breathing stutters. He looks up at me and grins. I strain beneath his hold, as he places his hands flat on top of my thighs. He looks back down, at the most intimate part of my body.

"Prettier than I even imagined," he whispers, just as he pushes my legs wider and touches his tongue to my clit, feather light.

I let out a loud gasp that fills the room. A hundred tiny explosions go off inside my body. He begins licking me harder. I tangle my fingers in his hair and grip tightly. He pulls his head up to look me in the eyes again, and the expression on his face is evil.

"That's it honey, hold onto me. You feel amazing against my tongue," he says, his voice low and gravelly.

"Fuck," I bite out.

"All in good time, Freda," he promises, and then returns to licking. Jesus Christ. I've never had a guy do this so well before. There's no teeth or stubble with Nicholas, just soft lips and tongue. I close my eyes and push my head into the pillow as I feel an orgasm start to build deep inside of me. All I can see behind my closed lids are fireworks and shooting stars.

He brings his thumb up to circle my clit as he kisses and licks. I'm just about to explode with the pleasure, but not quite, not yet. Soon.

He reaches up then with both of his hands and massages my breasts. I look down at his head between my legs, his tongue going at me, his hands on my breasts and his eyes locked with mine. In that exact moment I fall part. I cry out his name, coming hard against his mouth. Several waves pass through my body.

"That's it, so sweet Freda, so fucking sweet," he says, watching me come.

My body goes limp, and I smile to myself as I turn my head into the softness of the pillow, high off the chemicals of my own orgasm.

"I'm going to feed you now," he says, and leaves the room swiftly. What the hell? I hear him go inside the bathroom and turn on the tap. There's running water for a minute or two.

Then the bedroom door opens and Nicholas carries in the tray with our dinners on it. Oh right. He's going to feed me. Makes sense. I pull on the robe to cover myself, and my face feels like an inferno is blazing just beneath my skin. Did that really just happen?

Nicholas lifts the silver covers off the plates to reveal fillet steaks on a bed of sautéed mushrooms with a tiny dollop of mash potato on the side and some Béarnaise sauce.

He slices off a piece of the steak, dips it in the sauce and raises it to my mouth. Okay, did he somehow figure out my ultimate sexual fantasy to be gone down on and then fed a five star quality meal? Perhaps it was just instinct. Or a lucky guess.

I take the steak into my mouth and Nicholas smiles approvingly. He then slices a piece off from his own plate and does the same.

"So, this must have been a special circumstance," I say casually, referring to our conversation a few weeks ago about lady gardens when Dorotea had been leaving his apartment.

He grins. "Your vagina is a very special circumstance."

I laugh loudly. "That's what I'm going to call it from now on, "my circumstance". It has a nice ring to it."

"You come really beautifully too," he goes on, his expression intense, as I'm taking my plate and placing it on my lap. "All little sighs and tremors."

I don't say anything, but I do breathe heavily as a deep red colours my cheeks.

He puts his hand to my reddened face. "What's this for? Are you embarrassed? It might be wrong, but I find that to be a fucking huge turn on."

"It's very wrong," I mumble, stuffing a forkful of mushrooms into my mouth.

He laughs. "Eat up Freda, you're going to need your energy because I'm dying to fuck you."

I cough on the mushrooms and he pats my back so that I don't choke. He pours me a glass of wine and I gulp it back.

"I don't think we have time for that," I reply finally. "You've got to be at the venue for seven and your show starts at eight."

"It's only four, we've got plenty of time."

"You're going to make me die of mortification,

Nicholas. Can we slow this down?"

He eats a slice of steak and frowns at me. "If that's what you want."

I put down my plate and crawl over to him, taking his mouth in a soft, barely there kiss. I pull back and look at him. "It is. Thank you," I whisper.

He smiles warmly. "How about we snuggle up in bed and watch a pay per view movie?"

"Sounds like a plan," I answer in relief.

I think it's the anticipation of sex that makes me nervous. If he had of said nothing and just sprung it on me then I would have gotten caught up in the moment. The fact that he's giving me some warning makes me try to wriggle my way out of it.

After we've finished eating we do indeed snuggle up on the bed. Nicholas picks out a movie for us to watch. It's some American comedy, but I can't find the will power to concentrate on it. I'm too aware of his body behind mine. He's sitting up with his back leaning against the head board and I'm sitting between his legs, my head resting just below his pecs.

I turn my head to the side and plant a little kiss to his bicep, where it's all inked up with the tattoo of his mother. I shift my entire body to the side so that I can study it up close. I run my fingers over it.

From all of the conversations we've had over the past few weeks, I get the impression that Nicholas idolizes his mother in some strange way. He mentioned something about her being the inspiration for him to sing and perform, since she was a performer herself. He also keeps a few of her dresses in his wardrobe, all tucked away and preserved like relics.

I think the fact that I'm touching him is turning him

on, because I can feel him slowly get hard behind me. It presses up against my back. With a surge of bravery, I turn around to face him before trailing my fingers over the bulge in his pants.

"Fred," he breathes, looking at me with fire in his eyes.

"Don't talk," I say quietly, as I zip down his fly and pull him out of his boxers. This is the first time I've seen his manhood in all its glory. I'm both impressed and daunted. I whisper my lips over the head before giving it a little lick. Nicholas exhales.

"What are you doing?" he asks, his voice strained.

"Returning the favour, I guess."

"You don't have to. Fuck," he swears, and I take him fully into my mouth. I keep my eyes open and watch him as he shifts his body and clutches onto the bed sheets.

I move my mouth up and down the length of him, before swirling my tongue around the head, which seems to make him go crazy. Who is this brazen woman? I wonder to myself. Usually I'm all talk when it comes to sex, but here I am giving head to my boss/friend in a fancy hotel suite. Nicholas brings something out of me, something I never knew I had.

I stop sucking him for a minute to run my tongue up and down his length. I keep my eyes locked on his as I do it, just liked he'd done when he'd been going down on me.

Then I take him back into my mouth and he grabs a hold of my hair, wrapping it around his wrist firmly.

"You're really fucking good at this Fred," he groans.

"I must be a natural," I try to say with him still in my mouth.

"Oh God, keeping doing that. Talk while you're sucking me, the vibration feels good."

I stop and glance up at him. "Why Mr Turner, are you asking me for a hummer?"

He pulls on my hair, and it's just on the cusp of being painful, which feels really, really good.

"Shut up and do it, you're killing me," he mutters.

I oblige him, making sounds at the back of my throat as I suck him off. A minute or two later he comes right into my mouth. I know that a lot of girls like to swallow, well, I'm not one of them. As gracefully as I possibly can, I let it drip out of my mouth and onto the bed and then I hear Nicholas groaning.

"Oh sweet Jesus," he says in a low voice. "That has to be the sexiest thing I've ever seen."

"I thought men preferred it when girls swallowed." I wipe my lips with the back of my hand, like the classy lady that I am.

"I don't know, there's something erotic about you spitting it out like that."

I laugh and slide up the bed to cuddle him. "We're going to have to call for the maid to come and change these sheets. I feel terrible now."

"Don't. I'll make sure to leave her a generous tip."

"Ever the gentleman," I smile up at him and he runs his fingers over my lips.

"Best blowjob ever," he whispers.

"Oh shut up." I look away, embarrassed.

He grabs a hold of my chin and turns my face so that I meet his eyes. "I'm serious, Freda."

I nod and grin. "Well okay then. I'm going to be feeling very smug with myself for at least the next fortnight."

"And so you should," he says, fitting his palm around my neck and massaging it.

I cuddle him close and shut my eyes. We just lie there like that for the next hour, soaking up the feel of one another.

Chapter Fourteen
Black Outs and Shopping Carts

Nicholas' show that night goes off without a hitch. The venue ends up filling out nicely, perhaps because of all the effort we put in today out on the street doing promotion. The Polka Dot Twins show up just like they said they would, and towards the end of his set Nicholas calls them both up onto the stage to sing Tom Lehrer's "Masochism Tango" while he plays it on the piano.

I didn't even know he could play until tonight; he never mentioned that he could. Back home he's normally accompanied by The Wilting Willows, so there's no need for him to play himself.

Afterwards Nicholas gets changed and then we go with Bob and Bobby to the venue where they're doing their free show. For some reason they have a shopping cart with them and it's all decked out in cushions, with ribbons weaved through the metal bars.

Bobby hops into it and Bob pushes her along, like she's a baby in a pram. Since most of the streets in Edinburgh are cobblestoned, I really don't see the appeal. It looks like too much of a bumpy ride for my taste. I guess it's a little quirk they feel the need to maintain, so that people can say, *there go The Polka Dot Twins again with their modified shopping cart, the eccentric bastards.*

About halfway through their gig, which is in the upstairs room of a tiny pub, the electricity cuts out. It's eleven o'clock at night, so the entire place goes pitch black. Nicholas and I are sitting close to the window, and when we look outside it appears that the entire street's electricity has gone. For a few seconds I experience what complete and total darkness feels like, and it's slightly thrilling. Then people begin taking out their phones to use as sources of light. I do the same since mine actually has a mini torch function.

"Okay," says Bob, shouting from the stage since his microphone clearly isn't going to work at the moment. "It looks like there's been a power outage. Everybody stay seated and I'll talk with the manager to see what's happening."

He hops off the stage, illuminated by the accumulating light from the sea of mobile phones held by the people in the audience.

Nicholas puts his arm around my waist, holding me close in the dark. He's been more tactile than ever tonight, and throughout his whole show earlier he kept on seeking me out in the audience where I'd been sitting with Bob and Bobby, looking at me with a little secret smile. I still can't believe that what went down between us earlier today actually happened. It seems like a dream, a really, really good one.

We've been skirting around each other for weeks; I just never thought we'd actually get to where we are now. I thought we'd simply continue to tease one another with words and subtle touches for the rest of our sexual tension filled lives.

He presses his lips to the side of my mouth and moves his hand over my thigh, before pulling me over onto his lap. The people all around us chatter with nervous excitement.

What is it about power cuts that turns people into slightly more child-like versions of themselves?

Suddenly you start getting ideas about breaking into sweet shops and stealing all of the candy. *Without electricity the alarms won't be working, and therefore we will never get caught, mwah ha ha*, the little devil on your shoulder urges you. It's funny how easily people will turn to law breaking when the fear of getting caught is removed.

Nicholas' hand moves beneath the hem of the calf length black dress I'm wearing. He hitches up the material and runs his hand between my legs. When he reaches my underwear he presses his fingers hard against me.

Breathing heavily, I whisper to him, "Stop it. The lights could come back on."

He smiles with mischief. "That's kind of the point."

"Don't," I hiss, but he doesn't move his hand, and from the way his pressing fingers are making me feel, I don't want him to. Sparks and tingles consume me as I bite down hard on my bottom lip to keep from making any noises. His fingers move in a rhythm against me.

A blissfully anxious minute or two pass, then Bob returns to the room and announces to everyone that there has indeed been a city wide power outage and therefore the rest of the gig will have to be cancelled. By this point Nicholas has slipped his hand beneath the material of my knickers and I'm coming in waves against him. He takes my mouth in a lazy, wet kiss, his tongue caressing mine.

He pulls back and whispers, "Good girl."

It feels like my body doesn't have any bones, and I can't think clearly enough to say anything in response. Did we really just do that in public? I've had a couple drinks tonight, but not *too* many. Perhaps I'm just drunk on Nicholas.

Bob and Bobby make their way over to us, and in the dim light I can see that Bobby has a litre bottle of vodka under one arm and her ukulele under the other.

"We're going outside to have some fun in the dark before the power comes back on. Do you two want to join us?" asks Bob.

"Sure," Nicholas answers, pulling me up by the hand.

We go downstairs and head out through the pub. Bobby silently takes a swig of the vodka before handing it to me. I take a gulp and then hand it back to her. God, it burns good.

The girl rarely utters a word. It's like Bob does enough talking for the both of them because he never fucking shuts up. I mean, I think he's cool and all, but he could do with shutting his motor mouth every once in a while. He's currently going on and on to Nicholas about how he gets great vintage outfits off EBay for cheap.

I walk side by side with Bobby, and it's kind of nice. We both know we're never going to see each other again after this one night, so we don't bother with any of the getting to know you girl chit chat. She repeats the pattern of taking a sip of straight vodka and then handing it to me. This is the last thing I can remember doing before I find myself drunk off my face, being pushed down one of Edinburgh's many steep, hilly streets in Bob and Bobby's cushioned shopping cart. Seriously, it's up a hill, down a hill almost everywhere you go here.

Bobby is pushing the cart, while Bob and Nicholas run along just behind us. I look straight ahead as we gain a little too much momentum. Why the hell did I agree to this? Although since I can't remember how I got into this situation it could very well have been me who suggested the whole thing. Vodka does strange things to my IQ.

We're going way too fast now, and all I can hear is the echoing laughter of the three people around me as I think, *I'm going to die in a shopping cart when it inevitably crashes into either a wall or an oncoming vehicle.*

I squeeze my eyes shut as one of my knees bashes off the metal. Ouch. That's going to leave a bruise. The cart is going too fast as we near the bottom of the hill and Bobby loses her grip on the handle bar. The wheels bump against some cobble stones, causing the cart to become airborne, and for a few heart stopping moments I am sailing through the air in the dark, hurtling towards a busy road that's lit up with the headlights of moving cars.

Before I can blink Nicholas has grabbed the end of the trolley with both of his strong hands and is swinging it around to stop me from crashing into a car. It bangs hard against the curb and comes to a painful stop. The cushions go flying and it seems like every part of my body is knocking against the cold metal. I'm going to be in a lot of pain in the morning, I think through my vodka soaked haze.

Nicholas and I stare at each other, our eyes connected like never before, and all I can think is that he looks positively furious with me and I fucking love this man. He just saved me from getting killed or severely injured because of my own drunken idiocy. And I love him. *Love* him. Oh God.

"Fuck," he swears.

"You saved me," I gasp.

"You're drunk."

"So are you."

"Shut up, Fred. That was a stupid thing to do." He's seething, seething like I've never seen him seethe before.

"What? You were running along with me. I could hear you laughing with Bob and Bobby."

"I wasn't fucking laughing. *They* were laughing. *I* was shouting at Bobby to stop the cart."

"Oh."

"Oh is bloody right."

His face is hard, but then when he looks at me again it softens. He gently pulls me up and out of the cart, just as Bobby comes running over to us apologising like a maniac.

Nicholas throws some cutting words her way and she visibly pales.

"I'm fine, I'm fine," is all I can remember mumbling to her repeatedly as Nicholas somehow manoeuvres my legs around his waist and my arms around his neck to give me a piggy back ride to the hotel. We lose Bob and Bobby somewhere along the way, and although they were sort of fun, I can't say I'll miss them.

The electricity still hasn't been properly restored, but thankfully the hotel's generator has kicked in so we don't have to fumble around in the dark trying to find our room. Nicholas flicks on the light and carries me straight into the bathroom. He settles me down on the closed toilet seat and then goes to turn on the shower. I let my head fall back against the wall behind me, because it feels too heavy to hold up on my own.

I focus on the noise of the shower head, as water

gushes out of it. Nicholas comes to kneel in front of me and methodically begins removing my clothes. He starts with my boots and knee high purple socks, before moving onto my dress. I watch him and I can tell that he isn't anywhere near as drunk as I am. His eyes are too focused. I'm going to be so embarrassed about all of this in the morning.

When he has my dress off he stands me up and unhooks my bra, then he works my knickers down my legs. He guides me into the shower and I stand under the water. He yanks off his own clothes, lightning fast, and comes to join me.

What happens next kind of knocks me for six. He washes me, shampoos my hair and soaps my body with such care that it makes my heart ache. He doesn't try to make it sexual except for when he kisses me under the hot stream of water as though he's trying to memorize every corner of my mouth with his tongue.

We get out and he wraps us both in a big towel. He hands me a toothbrush with some toothpaste on it and I brush my teeth while he brushes his. We haven't breathed a word since we got back to the hotel room. When we're done we climb under the covers, completely naked. I would never be brave enough to sleep with him naked if I weren't plastered. But I am, so I do. I fall asleep to the smell of his clean skin and the feel of his hard body wrapped around my soft one.

When I wake up my legs are tangled with Nicholas' and he is sporting one hell of a morning boner. It's early and the events of last night come crashing down on me in startling detail. It had indeed been me who'd convinced Bobby to let me get into the cart while she pushed me down a hill. For some reason I'd thought it was a fabulous idea at the time.

Nicholas had told me that he'd kill me if I stepped foot in the cart, but I hopped in too quickly for him to stop me and shouted at Bobby to start pushing me. She was drunk enough to oblige, laughing excitedly as Nicholas chased after us. We probably wouldn't have been so dead set on it if he hadn't given us chase.

And Jesus, now I can remember my thoughts from last night too, when I'd come to the realisation that I love Nicholas. All it took was for him to save me from being mangled by a car.

But I know that's not the only reason why I love him. I love him because he makes me laugh when I don't feel like laughing. I love him because he challenges my view of what a man is. I love him because I know I shouldn't love him and that he'll break my heart. I love him because he's a complete and total anomaly. I love him because I want to kill the sadness inside him more than I want anything else in the world.

While I'm drowning in these thoughts of love, Nicholas stirs beside me. His arms are tight around my waist and my face is pressed into the hollow of his neck. I move my lips against his skin, giving him a good morning kiss. We are both stark naked, and it feels warm. I like how his body feels against mine, smooth skin and tight, ripped muscles. We're complementary opposites.

"Morning," I whisper, just as he's opening his eyes.

It takes him a moment to realise that I'm in bed with him and we both have nothing on, but once he does he flips me on my back and positions himself between my thighs. He reaches up and brushes my messy hair out of my face, and looks at me with a marvelling expression.

He's not smiling, but he's not frowning either. He's staring at me like I'm a puzzle he's trying to solve.

"What is it about you..." he trails off.

I swallow down a gulp of saliva, because his erection is pressing against my inner thigh and I'm quivering from the inside out. When I do a little shimmy to get more comfortable beneath him he lets out a breathy groan.

"This is...dangerous," he says, eyes tracing the planes of my cheeks, the curve of my lips.

"Probably," I whisper in reply.

He leans in closer. "I want to be inside you Freda."

I bite my lip. "Mm hmm."

"What do you want?" he asks.

"I think I want the same as you."

"Fuck," he mutters, and it comes out sounding like a vow.

A moan escapes my lips when he nudges the head of his penis against my core. He's not even wearing a condom, but I can't think straight enough to care. It's a good thing I've been on the pill for years. He did mention to me in passing that he always wore a condom when he'd been with women in the past. I hope he was telling the truth. He takes my mouth in a soft kiss, sucking on my bottom lip, just as he pushes into me. He fills me slowly, pulling away from the kiss to stare into my eyes. I can feel the explosions again, only now they're going off deep, deep inside of me.

"Wow," he mouths, watching me, taking in my every expression. "You feel so tight, so good."

He slides himself in and out slowly for a long time. I lose track of the minutes as I fall into an abyss where there is nothing but him. We just keep holding each other's gaze like we'll die if we let it drop. I arch up into him. He curses and makes noises that I really, *really* like. Then something lustful takes us over. He starts moving faster until he's pounding into me and I'm gripping onto the bed sheets and crying out in pleasure.

"Nicholas," I moan, and he keeps going harder, faster.

As he's fucking me he bends down and takes one of my nipples into his mouth, swirling his tongue around it in the most beautiful way. He pulls himself up again, moving his flattened out palm over my collarbone. When he gets as far as my neck he grips it softly, like he means to choke me, but not quite. The possessive gesture makes me gasp. The fact that he's gripping me in such a vulnerable spot makes me feel his pounding even more intensely, shattering through me.

"I love your body," he tells me. "I love your breasts..."

"Please," I moan.

"You like this?" he asks.

"Mm hmm."

"I like it too."

"I need you," I whisper.

"I need you too," he mutters.

His breathing quickens just before he comes, pouring himself into me. He sucks on my ear lobe and plants kisses all along my neck, telling me that I'm the most beautiful thing he's ever seen.

We lie there for ages, satiated, all limbs and skin and sweat and heaving chests.

"I'm clean, by the way," he says, after a long, long stretch of contented silence. "I don't want you worrying about all that stuff. Are you...are you on the pill or anything?" He bites his bottom lip. "I'm not normally so careless, but I just really wanted to feel you without anything in the way."

I nod and kiss him on the chin. "Yeah, and I'm clean too, just in case you were wondering..."

"I know you are," he interrupts, looking at me seriously. "You are so fucking clean I don't deserve you."

For some reason I feel like he's not talking about my sexual health anymore.

"Oh," is the only reply I can come up with.

He smiles and it lights up his entire face. "Oh," he repeats, and then kisses me hungrily as he slips his fingers between my legs.

"So wet," he says, slowly circling my clit before rubbing down over my folds and back up. I tilt my hips into the bed and press my feet down on the soft mattress, as I drift away into the blissful build to orgasm.

Over the rest of the day we barely leave the bed. We order room service and Nicholas fucks me again. Twice. I try not to think about how it feels more like making love than fucking. I feel like my body is a malleable mass of flesh and bones by the time the evening comes around and we have to get ready for his gig. He tells me he doesn't think he'll ever tire of fucking me and I want to scream that I'm in love with him. But I don't, because I don't know if he feels the same way. Perhaps this is all just lustful obsession for him, as opposed to the L word.

I'm sipping on some tea and sitting by the window as he packs up his costume for tonight's show. I stare out the window at the passing crowds, while intermittently texting Nora about her dinner date with Richard.

Apparently there was some heavy petting in the living room afterwards. I tell her she better give the couch a good dry shampooing before I get home. She texts back telling me I have my shit in bucketfuls. I laugh to myself.

The electricity is up and running again in the city, but we still don't know what caused the black out since we spent the day in bed. I don't think I really care about the reason for it. All I know is that I'll never forget Nicholas with his hand inside my pants in the dark in that pub when we'd been surrounded by oblivious strangers.

"You're slacking," he teases, as he steps by me and pinches me on the nose.

"I'm relaxing Viv, don't be such a slave driver. Didn't any of your previous assistants take a break every now and again?" I ask.

He laughs like he has a secret, and goes to open a bottle of water from the mini fridge in the corner. He takes a sip and I watch the movement of his Adam's apple as he swallows, finding it strangely seductive. God, look at me, a day of earth shattering sex and I'm finding every little thing Nicholas does a turn on. Actually, that's nothing new.

"What's that laugh about?" I question, narrowing my gaze.

He grins so wide you'd think somebody just told him he'd won the lottery. "Nothing," he answers, with a coy expression.

"Spit it out Viv, I'm not liking this secretive side."

He drinks some more water, his grin has died down to a smirk. "You really want to know?"

"Yes, tell me," I say, slamming my palms down on

the upholstered arms of the chair I'm sitting on.

He scratches the back of his neck. "Okay, but promise not to go crazy at me."

"I promise. Spill."

"I've never had an assistant before."

"What!?"

"It was something of a ruse," he grins again, this time like he's a super villain with the world's greatest plot. When he sees the expression on my face he goes on, "Now, now Fred, you promised not to go crazy."

"I'm perfectly sane, you're the one who's crazy. Why would you lie about having assistants?"

He shrugs and walks across the room to stand in front of the window beside my chair. "As I said, it was a ruse."

"A ruse?" I question, my brow furrowed.

"I wanted to spend more time with you, so I pretended I needed an assistant."

Oh my God, the scheming little...I don't know whether to be angry or flattered.

I stand up and push him lightly on the chest with the palms of my hands. He falters back a bit, laughing at my indignation.

"That's devious Viv, terrible. I never even suspected."

"I needed to get to know you. It was the perfect way, don't you think?"

I raise an eyebrow. "Hmm, I don't know about that. You could have just made friends with me and gotten to know me the normal way. It's not like you were never going to see me. I live right next door."

"I know that, but I kind of wanted you to be around me when I was working. That way I'd know if you liked both sides of me, the Nicholas side and the Vivica side."

"Okay, I'm sort of getting where you're coming from now," I say, and go to sit back down.

We don't speak for a minute or two. I'm still reeling with this news that he conned me into being his assistant under the false pretence that he simply couldn't get by without one. Then I feel delighted that he went through all the trouble to have me around. Then I feel wary that he can maintain a lie so easily. Then I feel grateful that he lied since I got to experience a world I never would have experienced otherwise.

It's after another minute or two goes by that I come to my final conclusion about his little secret. "I have to say Viv, you are just too fucking cute."

"I'm not cute, I'm dark and sexy," he protests with humour.

"That too."

He gives me a comical little growl and then tells me to hurry up with my tea because we need to leave for the venue pronto.

"I had a dream about you once," I say to Nicholas as I'm brushing some blusher across his cheeks in the dressing room before his gig.

He's sitting down and I'm standing up, which leaves him in a good position to squeeze my bottom, which is what he's doing right now.

"Oh really? Tell me more." He gives me a devilish grin.

"It was a while ago, before we ever, you know kissed or anything. You had make-up on and you were wearing a bra and boxer shorts. It was weird because in my dream I found it really sexy."

He lets out a deep chuckle. "Are you hinting that this is something you'd like to try?"

"No!" I exclaim loudly in embarrassment. "I was just telling you about my dream. Get your mind out of the gutter."

"You're the one who said you found it sexy; what am I supposed to take from that?"

I shake my head. "That's not why I told you. I told because of what you said at the hotel about needing to know that I like the Nicholas side of you *and* the Vivica side. I think the dream was kind of symbolic that I do like both sides of you."

"Stop Fred, you're making me blush," he pinches my bottom and I let out a yelp before slapping his hand away.

"In that case I might as well forget about this then," I say, moving to put the blusher brush away.

"Don't be cheeky," he says, pulling me back and raising my wrist to his face. He uses my hand holding the brush to put it on his own cheekbones, while staring at me adoringly.

I pull the brush away and toss it into the make-up case. "There you go Viv, you're all beautified. Now go give them a show to remember."

He whispers his lips across my jaw and gives me a smouldering look, which works just as well in his Vivica outfit as it would in his normal clothes to make me melt. It doesn't matter what he's wearing. I like the him that's underneath the clothes and the painted face. I'd like him no matter what he wore.

When he's gone I look back at myself in the mirror, and there's a little streak of red lipstick across my jaw from when he'd put his lips there. I smile and wipe it away.

I don't go out and watch Nicholas' performance tonight, because I'm way too hung over and sore to be dealing with the noise of the crowd. After my little stunt in the shopping trolley last night I'm sporting my fair share of bruises and aching muscles.

I stay in the dressing room, flicking through some magazines and drinking herbal tea in the hopes that it will somehow cure my thumping head. When Nicholas emerges through the doorway after his show he stands there with a heated expression on his face.

I'm wearing jeans and a loose t-shirt, so I don't really get why he's looking at me the way he is, like I'm lying naked across the dressing table or something. He prowls toward me, slipping off his heels as he does so.

I back up in my chair. "Hey now Viv, don't be getting any ideas about my circumstance," I say to him jokingly.

"Too late, I have way too many ideas about your circumstance to be deemed healthy," he says, just before he lifts me up out of my chair and places my bottom down on the surface of the dressing table.

He pulls my legs apart and holds them on either side of his hips. Then he leans forward to kiss me fiercely and I'm done for. I reach up and pull the black wig off his head and then fumble with the zipper on the back of his dress. When I have it open I push down the shoulder straps and pull him closer to suck on his collarbone.

He shimmies out of the dress and kicks it halfway across the room.

He unbuttons the top of my jeans and shoves his hand down my pants. I gasp loudly while his other hand pulls my t-shirt off over my head and unsnaps my bra in a matter of milliseconds. He bends down and takes my nipple into his mouth. I look down at him, his face smeared with make-up and his mouth on me, and I don't think I've ever seen a more erotic sight.

He stands back and begins pulling down my jeans as I do the same to the tights he's wearing. I hear the sound of material ripping just before I realise that he's torn my knickers off me in his hunger to get me naked. I'm too turned on to be irritated by that and a second later his cock is pushing hard inside of me and I'm gripping onto his shoulders, practically clawing at his skin with my fingernails.

My eyes are focused on his strong neck when I hear him say, "Look at me Fred."

I look at him, losing myself in his bright blue eyes. His body moves and I try to maintain my balance on the dressing table. He lifts me up and slams me into the nearby wall, still pounding into me as I cry out. The music out in the club is loud; loud enough so that nobody can hear me screaming.

He keeps a firm hold of me and I lock my legs around his waist. He fucks me up against the wall like he can't control himself, but I don't think I want him to control himself right now. One look at his hot stare when he'd come into the dressing room before and I was immediately wet.

He lowers his hand and presses his thumb against my clit, making circles. The combination of his cock inside me and his thumb moving is almost enough to undo me completely. I clench my thighs harder around him and he groans, still looking at me, always looking at me.

"Need you," he pants, "need you so much, like this, just like this."

"Nicholas," I breathe his name and it's more air than sound.

"Say my name again; I need that too."

"Nicholas..." I trail off, losing myself in the sensations that are pulsing through me, building to something I'm dying to feel.

"Come on, Freda, come for me," he says, eyes scorching me now.

I feel my body quicken, and he keeps going with the pounding and the circles and it just about becomes too much as my body explodes. I shake against him as an orgasm shatters through me and I feel him come at the exact same time.

He pulls out and carries me over to the chair, where he sits down and cradles me in his lap, repeatedly stroking his hand down my hair.

"So, I take it you were pleased to see me," I joke, curled up naked in Nicholas' lap.

"I'm always pleased to see you honey," he answers seriously.

When I catch sight of myself in the mirror I can see that my mouth is smeared with Nicholas' red lipstick.

He moves his hand from my hair to my breast, where he cups it in his warm palm.

I rest my head against his shoulder and niggling questions consume me. What is this that we're doing here exactly? Will Nicholas still want me tomorrow as much as he wants me today?

"What are we doing?" I ask, unable to help myself, my voice quiet.

"We're enjoying each other Fred, making each other feel good."

"Oh."

"Isn't that what you wanted to hear?" he asks softly.

"I don't know. I'm not sure what I wanted to hear."

"I love being with you Fred, don't try to label what we are or put expectations on it. All that only poisons things. What we have is raw, it's real. It's the best thing I've ever felt when I'm inside of you and you're looking in my eyes with this expression of absolute rapture and innocence on your face."

"Oh," I say again, proper words failing me.

He chuckles and wraps his arms tight around me.

"Silly little Fred, what am I going to do with you, huh?"

"Um, I think you've done enough for one night," I say.

He chuckles again.

A few silence filled minutes later we go and clean ourselves up, then we make our way back to the hotel. We're both so exhausted that we crawl into bed and fall asleep as soon as our heads hit the pillow.

Chapter Fifteen

A Familiar Face

The next day Nicholas and I resume our street canvassing, pulling out our best convincing smiles in order to talk people into coming to see his show.

By lunchtime I've spoken to so many people that I feel like my voice box is going to fall out, if such a thing were possible. I resolve myself to one final pitch and select my target, which happens to be two men in their late forties wearing sharp business suits who are currently walking in my direction.

Nicholas is on the other side of the street, chatting up a group of young men who look positively smitten with him. Poor things. I know what it's like to feel the full force of Nicholas' dazzling smile when he lays it on you.

The suited men don't look like the usual clientele you'd normally come across at a Vivica Blue show, but I decide to chance my arm anyway.

"Hello gentleman," I say. "Can I interest you in a musical treat the likes of which you have never seen before?"

One of them blatantly eyes my cleavage, while the other smiles warmly and replies, "Maybe, what sort of musical treat are we talking about?" He's got a Scottish accent, so I take it that he's a local.

"Well, to put it quite bluntly," I say, gesturing him closer and putting on my most charming grin. "It involves a man in women's clothing with the best singing voice you'll have heard all year."

The suit laughs and his friend smiles wryly.

"I don't know if that'd be my cup of tea, lass," he answers.

"Oh rubbish. Vivica Blue is everyone's cup of tea. She's a rising star set for big things, you mark my words."

"Will you be there?" asks the friend, with a leery expression.

"I will indeed," I reply, even though he's being a bit of a creep and spoke to my chest instead of my actual face.

"In that case you can count us in, have you got a flyer?"

"I most certainly do," I answer and dig in my handbag, only to discover that I've run out. "It seems I'm all out gentlemen; follow me and I'll get one for you right away."

I guide them across the street to where Nicholas is just saying goodbye to the group of young men.

"Hey Viv, I need some more flyers," I call as I approach him.

He gives me a flirty grin. "Run out already? You must be working extra hard Fred. I'll have to reward you for your efforts," he winks mischievously.

He hands me a few flyers and I turn around to give them to the two men. When I do, Nicholas' eyes lock on the one who hadn't been ogling my tits, and his face literally falls to the ground. He stumbles backward on his high heels and I have to grab a hold of his elbow to keep him from hitting the pavement.

"Are you okay?" I ask with concern.

He turns his face to me absent-mindedly, his eyes are miles away, but he manages to blink himself back to the present. "I'm fine," he whispers, looking embarrassed about whatever just happened.

The two men eye him curiously. I hand them a flyer and they continue on their walk.

"Are you sure you're fine? You don't look fine."

He pulls his elbow out of my grip. "It's nothing. That man just bore a freakish resemblance to someone I used to know." His voice sounds pained and it's scaring me a little.

"Okay, maybe we should go back to the hotel now and have something to eat. How does that sound?"

He just nods and we turn in the direction of the hotel. Once we get back I order us some sandwiches and tea from room service and Nicholas goes to take a shower. He hasn't breathed a word since the incident out on the street. He didn't even flirt and ask me if I wanted to join him in the shower, which is odd in itself.

I kick off my shoes and tuck into the food once it arrives. It's been a half an hour and Nicholas still hasn't emerged from the bathroom. I leave it another fifteen minutes before I go to check on him, but when I try the door handle I find it locked.

"Nicholas," I call softly. "Are you all right in there?"

"I'm fine, just shaving," he calls.

I know he's not shaving. He shaved this morning.

"No you're not, let me in."

He lets out an audible sigh and a moment later I hear the lock flick over. I open the door to find him sitting on the edge of the bath tub, his hair is wet and he's wearing a bathrobe. I sit down beside him.

"What's going on?" I ask in a gentle voice.

He raises his eyes to mine and they look tired. He once told me that he's either happy or he's sad, that he doesn't have a middle ground. I'm guessing this is one of the sad periods. They're certainly less frequent than the happy ones, but when they come it kind of makes me sad too.

In a way I have this strange maternal-like protective instinct towards Nicholas. I want to kick the arse of anyone who messes with him, and I want to wrap him up in cotton wool and make sure that the world never gets him down.

"Who did the man in the suit remind you of?" I whisper.

His gaze drops. It takes him a long moment to answer. "A friend of my father's."

"You didn't like him?"

"Not even a little bit," he whispers, rubbing his palms against the towel fabric of his robe.

I want to ask him more questions, but I don't. Instead I take his hand and lead him into the bedroom. I sit him down on the bed and then go out and put a sandwich on a plate for him. I pour him a cup of tea and bring it in to him.

He nibbles on the sandwich, but doesn't really eat it. I lie back on the bed and turn on the television, keeping the volume low. Nicholas remains with his back to me, his shoulders slumped.

It surprises me when, after a couple of minutes pass, he begins speaking over the low murmur of the television, still not facing me.

"When I was a child I was always a little bit different," he mutters. A second passes and then he launches into a long speech. "I became even more different when I found my mother's old clothes in the attic and got this weird idea into my head to wear them as if they were my own. I'd prance around the house singing in dresses and lipstick when my father wasn't around, which was often. I basically had the run of the place, which is why I became so comfortable in my odd little habit. I suppose I did it because I'd watch old recordings of my mother and she just seemed like this wonderful, beautiful person; she was the complete opposite of my father. I never wanted to be like him, all cold and unemotional, so instead I decided I would be like her, literally."

He stops and turns around in the bed. I sit up a little, riveted by his story.

"I'm sure psychologists would have a field day with me," he remarks morbidly.

"This went on for years," he continues. "It was my secret because I knew that other people wouldn't understand my need to be beautiful, to sing beautifully and be something that wasn't my father in every way. I didn't know what killed my mother back then, but I always knew it was somehow down to my father's coldness, like I could sense it. She was stuck in a loveless marriage and she was miserable. Later on my aunt would explain to me that my mother died of an overdose. She'd basically been taking a whole medley of anti-depressants and eventually her system just failed."

I scoot across the bed to sit closer to him. I wrap my arms around his waist, but I don't breathe a word. A tear streams down his face.

"Being beautiful like her was my only happiness. At school I was bullied constantly by the other boys, because I preferred to play with the girls. They possessed the characteristics that I wanted to emulate – beauty, softness – that's why I liked to be around them.

When I went home I could be alone and be somebody else. I could be a woman like my mother was and not a weird boy who couldn't seem to fit in. It was my father's friend who ruined everything. They worked together and he was bringing some paperwork over one day when Dad was out. I was in the living room singing in front of the mirror in a dress, so you can probably guess how mortified I was to be caught by some man I barely knew."

"What happened then?" I ask, hardly a whisper.

"He destroyed me is what happened then. I'd never gotten a good vibe from him in the first place. He was a bad person, sick. When he caught me doing what I had been doing, he had something he could use to control me."

Nicholas pauses and I squeeze tightly on his arm, knowing what he's going to say next but not sure if I can take hearing it. Memories flit over his eyes.

"He started coming over regularly then when Dad was out. He told me that if I didn't tell my dad about his visits that in return he wouldn't tell him about what he'd caught me doing. He always made me be a boy with him though. I could wear the dresses in my own time, but that's not what he wanted from me when he came over. He fucked me up, did a number on me. I was a fourteen year old kid and he fucking ruined me Fred, pushed me into doing things that were for grown-ups. If it hadn't been for him then I probably would have outgrown my little obsession with the dresses and the make-up. He turned being a boy into something that I couldn't stand, so that being a woman was my only escape."

"Oh," I breathe, everything falling into place.

"This blackmailing went on for years, but when I turned eighteen I resolved myself to telling my father. Only I knew that simply telling him about what Kelvin had been doing to me all those years wouldn't be enough. He wouldn't believe me. So I had to *show* him. I told Kelvin to come over one day when I knew my father would be coming home early. I made sure that Dad found us in a compromising position so that there would be no refuting it. He nearly killed Kelvin that day. I hadn't been prepared for the violence. I had to drive Kelvin to the hospital and leave him at the entrance to A&E. When I returned home I found my dad crying in his study. Crying. It was the first and last time I'd ever seen him cry. I couldn't believe that finding out his best friend had been systematically raping me for years would be the thing that would finally get him to show some human emotion. I told him everything then, how it started, how it had been going on for years. He looked so broken and it made me so angry, because I was the one who was broken, not him. I packed my bags that night and that was the last time I ever saw him. It was years later that I got a phone call from my aunt telling me that he had died."

"Nicholas," I breathe, folding my arms so tightly around him that I'm worried he might suffocate.

He doesn't seem to hear me; he's lost in the past. He continues speaking, "I ran away to France first, and for a year I did nothing but drink and take drugs and try to forget who I was. Then I pulled myself together and started experimenting with shows in tiny venues and the whole thing grew from there. I created the Vivica Blue persona and I haven't stopped travelling and performing since. I get that some men want to dress up as women because they want to be a woman. I don't want to be a woman though, at least not when I'm off the stage.

"I perform for the catharsis, because it's freeing. It's the opposite of what Kelvin wanted me to be, so it's also a strange sort of protest. Every time I put on a dress I'm sticking two fingers up at what he did to me. In the same way that an actor needs to become another person when they act, I need to become another person when I sing. And now, when I'm Nicholas, I can truly reclaim myself when I can get lost in a woman like you because you could never be anything like *him*. I can be a man with you, strong, in control, not a scared little boy."

My heart thumps hard and fast against my ribcage.

"So, this is me darling, a complete and total contradiction. A fucking mess." He smiles sadly.

"A beautiful mess," I proclaim.

"But a mess nonetheless," he adds.

"Hey, that rhymed," I laugh.

"It did, didn't it." He doesn't laugh, he hasn't got it in him yet.

We sit in silence. Nicholas breaks it when he says, "I don't think I'll ever be the man you deserve Freda."

"You already are."

"I'm not. I have issues a mile long. Issues that might sink into the recesses, but never quite go away."

"The fact that you think you're not good enough just shows how good you are Nicholas." I say. "Do you know that you're the first man who's ever looked at me and actually *seen* me? When you're fat your whole life you get fairly used to people looking through you, dismissing you simply because you don't fit with their aesthetic ideals. So I either get men looking through me or men looking at me because they think I'll have low self-esteem and will be easy to manipulate. You didn't do any of that. You made me feel like a woman, a woman worth getting to know."

"You're not fat Freda," he says shaking his head.

"Maybe not to you because your beauty standard is different from the norm. But put me standing next to someone like Nora in a night club and I might as well be a part of the furniture. So don't you see, you are the man I deserve. You saw me, changed my life, made it better, and I'm completely fucking in love with you." I clamp my hands over my mouth after I say it. I can't believe I just said that; I hadn't meant to.

I stare at Nicholas and several agonised emotions pass over his face as he looks back at me.

"Oh Freda, honey, no," he says sadly.

I feel like I've been hit with a truck. The tone of his voice immediately tells me that I shouldn't have told him that. We've only been having sex for two days, what the hell was I thinking? Oh yeah, I wasn't. I was just letting my stupid mouth run away with me again.

"You don't love me," he says, still staring at me, as though trying to convince himself. "I'm not the person you should love. I'll let you down."

I stand up and wrap my arms around myself. "I – I didn't mean that," I mumble like an idiot.

He narrows his eyes. "You didn't mean it," he repeats my words back at me, disbelieving.

"Yeah, I um, I was trying to make you feel better."

"By lying and telling me that you're in love with me?" he raises his voice.

"It just came out," I whisper.

"Okay," he says, his temper simmering down and a

pained look crossing his face. Why doesn't he want me to love him?

"This has been a long day," he sighs and runs his palm over his face. "I tell you what, you take the night off. I'll do the show by myself. You can go and see the sights or something."

His voice is closed off now, like he's intentionally trying to hide away and ignore the fact that I love him. He knows I meant it when I said it. I know I meant it when I said it too. Now it's this pink elephant in the room that we both don't want to acknowledge.

God, I'm such an idiot. This was probably the worst possible moment to tell Nicholas how I feel, after he's just relived all of the awful things he went through as a young boy.

"I'm going to go for a walk," I say, needing to get away from him and my own pained emotions.

He simply nods as I go to slip on my shoes and grab my handbag. Feeling like I'm in a trance, I leave the hotel room and make my way outside. The Royal Mile is crowded with tourists as usual and I start walking uphill until I find myself at the entrance to Edinburgh Castle. I decide to go inside and have a look around, thinking it might distract me from my confusion over what just happened with Nicholas.

He basically spilled his guts out to me and I ended up loving him even more once I'd heard his story. But then I'd tried to hand him my heart and he'd looked at it like it was a dead rat he didn't want to see. He turned away from me and my helpless female need for his love in return.

I knew this was going to happen all along. From the very beginning I'd told myself to stay away, but I just couldn't seem to help falling for him. I saw how he treated Dorotea when she tried to make things serious with him and he basically ended up hating her for it. Why the hell would I be any different? I'm practically sucking back tears when I get to the ticket booth and pay the entrance fee to the castle.

In the end I don't even go that far inside. I walk to a wall lined with black cannons that looks out over the city and sit down, staring at the buildings far below me. Tourists of every nationality potter around me, taking pictures and chattering. I stay there like a statue, lost to my own misery and feelings of rejection.

Perhaps it's because of what he's been through that he can't accept love or anything more than the simple gratification of sex. Surely being molested by a man your father's age when you're only fourteen years old would do a number on a person. Maybe he'll always be like this, seeking only the rush of initial attraction and nothing more, just like Dorotea had warned me.

When I get back to the hotel hours later the room is empty. I order some dinner and sit eating by myself at the table, comforting myself in the only way I know how: with food. The trouble is, everything tastes like nothing and all I feel is the aching that's radiating out from my heart and seeping into the rest of my organs. Everything in my middle hurts. I can barely breathe.

I lie in bed for hours, remembering the details of Nicholas' story in my head and trying to figure out why he looked so pained when I told him I love him. It's nine at night the next time I glance at the clock. Nicholas will be just going out on stage now, I think to myself.

I need to see him, talk to him, figure him out. I spring

up in the bed, throw on some clothes (because I had been wallowing in my PJs like a complete and total lovesick stereotype) grab my handbag and rush out the door.

When I get to the club Nicholas is sitting by the piano, playing a song I've never heard before. It's not his usual upbeat number, it's slow, the lyrics introspective. The place hasn't filled out as much as it did last night or the night before, but there's still a good number of people here to see him.

It takes a few minutes for him to see me standing there. He looks through me and away, focusing on the people sitting in front of the stage.

He remains sitting at the piano when he speaks into the microphone. "This next song is for someone who told me they loved me today. It's called "I Don't Care Much" from *Cabaret*."

My heart sinks, my organs hurt more than ever, as Nicholas starts to sing. He makes a point of looking directly at me for a brief moment, *right* at me, so there's no mistaking who the song is meant for.

He tells me that he doesn't care much whether I go or stay.

He tells me that if he kisses me, if we touch, warning's fair, he doesn't care very much.

I die inside, not a little bit, but a lot. Before he's even finished the song I run out of the club like I'll suffocate if I stay. I can't even remember how I get back to the hotel; all I know is that there are tears running furiously down my face and when I do get back I begin shoving my things into my suitcase.

Why did he do that? Why the fucking humiliation of a public rejection? Does he hate the fact that I love him so much that he had to tell me he didn't care in the cruellest way possible?

He really is a beautiful mess. A beautiful mess that sucks you in and messes you up too. If I fly too close to the sun, I can't exactly expect anything other than to get burned.

I leave the hotel and hop into a taxi, instructing the driver to bring me to the airport. On the drive I call up Nora and sob my sad little story to her down the line. She tells me to buck up and that everything is going to be okay, but those kinds of words mean nothing when your heart is breaking.

In the end she goes online and books me a seat on the next flight back to Dublin, which isn't until six o'clock tomorrow morning. I end up spending the night sitting on a chair in the waiting area, my face red from crying and constantly dabbing my nose with a piece of tissue. I watch as planes take off over on the runway through the massive glass windows.

When I woke up this morning in bed with Nicholas I couldn't have been any happier. I never expected things to change so drastically.

A little old woman comes and sits down beside me at one point. She has a face that looks like a smiling potato. After about fifteen minutes of her sitting there, she randomly reaches over and gives my hand a squeeze.

"You'll have lots of that crying business to come if you ever have children," she says, her accent northern. "Save your tears for the ones that matter most."

Then she stands up and walks away. I don't know how she could tell that I don't have any kids yet. I want to scream at her that I'm crying for the best person I've ever met, but that he might also have been the worst. But I don't, I just continue to sniffle into my tissue. I think the world is a cruel place when it can show you such happiness and then just snatch it right away again so soon.

I drift off to sleep and wake up when I hear my phone beep with a text. It's from Nora, it reads:

Just had a strange phone call from Nicholas. He asked where u were and then hung up:-/

I immediately dial Nora's number. She answers, sounding sleepy and annoyed.

"What Fred? Nicholas already woke me up and now you too."

"What did he say?" I ask.

She takes a minute to answer, and I can tell she's doing a big, open-mouthed yawn. "Oh um, well for starters he sounded really distraught, then he asked me if I'd spoken to you. I said yes I fucking well did and told him he's the world's biggest dickhead. He didn't seem pleased, but then again he didn't try to defend himself either. Then he asked where you are now. I told him you were at the airport waiting for a flight home. He just said "Good" and then hung up. Rude much?"

I sit there, speechless. Good. That's all he had to say to the fact that I was leaving early after he publicly rejected me?

"If you ask me, you're well shot of him," says Nora, not put out at all by my silence.

"I wish I could share your enthusiasm," I mumble.

"Oh look, we'll talk about it when you get home. I'm going back to sleep," she clips out, being her usual straight talking self.

"Okay," I whisper and tap the end button.

Chapter Sixteen
Broken Hearts and Sugary Tea

When I finally get home it's just after nine the next morning. Nora comes to the door and I break down crying. I can tell by the expression on her face and her stiff body posture that she's not sure how to handle me. During the three years we've lived together I've never had an emotional breakdown on a par with this. Sure, I'd have days when I was a moody cow, but not full on bawling my face off like I am now.

God help her, she does her best to comfort me, but she's not the greatest person at making people feel better. Especially now, since I know she's all loved up with Richard. She's been texting me about him ever since their dinner date on Monday night, and she's had nothing but good things to say.

In the end she makes me a sugary cup of tea and sends me to my bed for the day. I call up my mum and tell her everything, from start to finish, because she's the only person I know who'll be able to comfort me and give me proper advice. At first she's surprised that all this has happened without her knowing about it, because normally I tell her everything that's going on with me.

Mum is a good listener, she doesn't butt in and try to talk down to me, telling me I should have known better than to get involved with Nicholas. She just listens quietly and then asks me if I want to come stay with her and Dad for a few days. I thank her for the offer, but decline. I need to be able to deal with these sort of life situations without running home to Mummy and Daddy like a twenty-five year old baby every time something doesn't go my way.

A week and a half goes by. I return to work and try to slip back into my old routine, as well get used to not being at The Glamour Patch with Nicholas at the weekends. A few days after I got home from Edinburgh, Nora told me that she bumped into Nicholas out in the hallway. She said he looked the same as usual, but that he only said hello to her politely before going inside his apartment.

The fact that he looks fine and I'm a blubbering mess says it all really. I need to pull my shit together. We weren't some kind of once in a lifetime romance, we were friends who had a couple mind blowing sex sessions and that's it. (No matter how much I try to convince myself that I believe this, it still doesn't stop my heart from hurting all the time.)

I spend an evening over at Harry's and after I've told him all about my Edinburgh heartbreak, he quite reluctantly reminds me that we still have the group trip to Electric Picnic in a fortnight to contend with. I've already paid for the ticket, and apparently I can't get a refund. Since Sean and Harry are still an item and Sean is good friends with Nicholas, neither one of them wants to take sides, and Nicholas is still dead set on going.

If I hadn't spent so much on the ticket I simply wouldn't go, but wasting all of that money just doesn't sit right with me. I resolve myself to ignoring Nicholas and simply enjoying the music, and fingers crossed, the good weather. Although you can never rely on it to be sunny in this country.

My plans for ignoring Nicholas are momentarily

thwarted when Harry informs me that Nora is going to be sharing a tent with Richard, who is now coming too, and his brother Colm is bringing his work friend Eric. That leaves me and Nicholas the odd pair out. I decide to invite Anny along at the last minute so that I can share a tent with her. She's all up for it when I call her. Nicholas can sleep in a tent on his own. Fuck, he can sleep in a porta-potty for all I care.

Two days before we're supposed to leave for the festival I get a surprise visit from Phil. He steps into my apartment all casual, as if it's a normal occurrence for him to come and see me.

"How's it going Fred? We've missed you down at the club."

I sit down on the couch and he joins me. "I'm okay. Hasn't Nicholas told you what happened?"

Phil frowns. "He did. I'm sorry about that, but I've known him a long time and I've never seen him the way he is now. It's like he's lost his spark or something."

I purse my lips. "Nora saw him and she said he looked fine."

"Nora doesn't know him like I do."

"I'm not trying to be rude Phil, but why are you here?"

"I came because I think you should try and speak to him. Nicholas isn't exactly the easiest human being to navigate. He's got his demons more so than the average person."

"I know that. He told me about what it was like for him growing up," I say in a quiet voice.

"Then you know that it isn't easy for him to accept a person's love the same way it is for others. I don't mean to be crude, but that man has fucked his way across

Europe half his life. All of a sudden he comes to Dublin to settle down and the first woman he meets makes him laugh and does something to him that no woman has ever done before. All he's ever known have been simple, short term relationships and I know he doesn't deserve your forgiveness after the way he behaved; between you and me I wanted to give him a slap upside the head when he told me, but if you could just find it in yourself to give him a chance, I think you could be *it* for him Fred."

"I'm not *it* for him, he doesn't want *it*. I'm not sure if he ever will."

"He wants you, I know that for a fact. The man never shuts up about you; his face instantly brightens when you walk into a room. Since you two had your falling out he's been going on about all the times you spent together. He's driving me crazy like a broken record."

I stand up and fold my arms across my chest, feeling uncomfortable with this conversation. I can't seem to determine how I feel about Nicholas in this moment. I hate him, but I also know that he's dealt with some fucked up situations in his life, and that makes me want to take care of him. I wish he could just be out and out bad, that way I could hate him and that would be that.

Phil grabs my hand and pulls me back down to sit. "Listen, I'll tell you something that you probably don't know. A couple of weeks before you two met I had to drag Nicholas out of a really deep depression. He'd been living in a shit hole apartment in Berlin even though he has the money to buy a penthouse if he wanted to, drinking all day long, doing crazy, sloppy performances at night. I got a call from a mutual acquaintance of ours telling me about what was going on. Nicholas had been a really loyal friend to me for years, stuck by me through some tough times, so I didn't hesitate to jump on a plane and pull him out of there. He's had high points and low points over the years, and this was one of the lowest.

"I brought him home to Dublin with me, helped him to clean up his act and then gave him a job at the club. He got himself back on track, rented out the apartment next to yours and had all of his things moved there. Then he met you and I can tell you Fred, I immediately saw a change in him. He told me that he had found a new friend, someone who makes his life better, and I was so relieved that he had someone to keep him on the straight and narrow. At the same time I was terrified, because I could tell that you were much more than a friend to him and I was worried that something could go wrong and Nicholas would go back to the drinking and the depression." Phil pauses and lets out a heavy sigh.

"You need to talk to him Freda. He loves you back, I know he does. He's just completely incapable of dealing with the emotions he's feeling because he's never had occasion to feel them until you came along."

"Christ," I whisper.

"He needs you," says Phil softly. "But you need him too."

"If he needs me so much then why haven't I heard from him in three weeks? Why hasn't he tried to make contact? He lives right next door, Phil."

"Because I told you, he's confused. He doesn't know how to accept your feelings for him and his for you."

"I need some time to think, I don't know what to do right now." I pull on a curl in frustration.

Phil puts a hand on my shoulder. "Just don't leave it too long, hun," he tells me, then gets up and lets himself out.

The closer it gets to the festival, the more nervous I become. The things Phil told me have been swirling around in my head ever since. I understand that Nicholas might not know how to accept love, but Jesus, that doesn't mean he had to ignore me all this time. It doesn't mean he had to push me away in such a cruel and callous manner either.

I pack up my sleeping bag and clothes the night before, deciding to bring boots and loose cotton dresses, since they're the easiest thing to wear in a camping situation. Harry has gotten a loan of his cousin's Volkswagen van so that he can drive us all there together. Fucking joy.

I plan on going to see as many bands as I can fit in, on my wish list are The Killers, Elbow, The Cure, Crystal Castles and Patti Smith. This will ensure that I won't have any time to be lingering around Nicholas.

In the morning the sun is shining, which puts a small smile on my face. I throw on my knee high brown socks, cream flower print dress and my heavy brown leather boots. I leave my freshly washed hair down while I still can, since I'll probably be wearing it in a ball on top of my head by the end of the festival, what with the limited washing facilities and all.

Anny arrives at our apartment with her two man tent that she's going to be sharing with me packed up in a bag in one arm, and her ruck sack in the other. She and Nora have gone for the whole short shorts, t-shirt and Wellingtons festival look. I avoid this look, because it only really looks good on the super thin and pixie-like types.

We catch a bus over to Harry's place in Drumcondra, where we find Richard and Colm out front, loading camping stuff into the back of the van. The two men are getting on like a house on fire, which doesn't surprise me. Nora may be smitten, but I can tell that Richard is just as vain and shallow as Harry's brother. Yes that's right, my world view is even more cynical these days since I'm miserable over Nicholas. It irks me that Nora is all loved up, so I'm taking it upon myself to dislike Richard.

Colm looks me up and down and gives me a leering grin when he sees me coming, to which I roll my eyes.

"Hey Fred, let me take your bag," he says loudly, not hiding the fact that he lets his knuckles graze over my boob as he pulls the ruck sack off one of my shoulders.

"I can do that myself, thanks," I say grumpily, yanking my bag away from him.

"Whoa there little lady. Got out of the wrong side of the bed this morning, did you?" he asks and laughs.

My reply is a hate filled scowl and a simple. "Piss off Colm, I'm not in the humour."

"Oh, *burn*," says Richard, to which Nora lets out a little giggle. Good lord. I was definitely right about him, Richard and Colm are two peas in a pod.

I push past them and go inside the house, where I find Sean sitting on a stool by the kitchen counter, injecting a bunch of oranges with vodka. The sight lifts my spirits after dealing with Colm and his boob grazing knuckles.

"What on earth are you doing, trying to get the oranges drunk?" I ask with a laugh, going to sit down beside him.

He has one full syringe stuck in his mouth, while he plunges another into a piece of fruit. He puts down the orange and pulls the syringe out of his mouth.

"I'm hoping they'll be more inclined to shag me if I ply them with alcohol," he quips.

I grin. "Seriously though, what are you doing?"

He puts the orange into a plastic bag containing a bunch of other oranges. "You know the way they don't let you bring your own drink into the festival?"

"Uh huh."

"Well, this is my way of outsmarting them. There's enough vodka in these babies to keep me and Harry going for a night or two. It'll save us spending extortionate amounts on awful pints of beer from the stalls at the festival. Plus, these are so juicy and more-ish."

"You're a genius," I exclaim, laughing.

"I'll let you have one when we get there," he winks and goes in to Harry, who's calling him from the bedroom.

It's then that I hear a flush coming from the bathroom and a second later Nicholas emerges. He's wearing hiking boots, jeans and a long sleeved t-shirt. He looks amazing. I hate him. He stops in his tracks when he sees me sitting there.

"Freda," he breathes, his tongue lingering on the syllables, like he's been dying to say my name since he last saw me, which doesn't make any sense since he was the one who saw fit to drive me away. Time seems to slow down as we just stare at each other, drinking one another in.

"Hi," I croak out and look down at my short

fingernails. He continues staring at me just as Nora, Anny, Richard, Colm and Colm's friend Eric come into the house, laughing their heads off about something.

"What's so funny?" I ask, in an effort to ignore the fact that Nicholas is burning me with his gaze.

"Oh, Anny fell over trying to squeeze her bag into the back of the van. It was hilarious," says Nora.

Anny slaps her on the arm. "Hey! I could have really hurt myself."

"That's what made it so funny," Colm puts in and Anny gives him a flirty, half-hearted scowl.

Harry and Sean come out of the bedroom then. "All right, is everybody ready to hit the road?" Harry asks, to which we all make noises in the affirmative.

As we're making our way out to the van, I feel someone grab gently onto my elbow. I turn slightly to find myself looking up into Nicholas' gorgeous blue eyes and my icy heart melts just a little. I try to steel myself against the effect he has on me.

"Can I talk to you for a minute Fred?" he asks quietly, eyes searching mine; taking in my every feature like a man dying of thirst. Again, he has no right to look at me like that after what he did.

"I have nothing to say to you," I whisper.

"Please," he begs, some kind of desperation in his voice.

"Come on you two," Harry calls. "We need to get a move on if we want to snag a good camping spot."

I pull my arm away from Nicholas and hurry on out to the van, only to find that since he delayed me the only two seats left are side by side at the very back. I slide in next to Eric, who's occupying one of the window seats and Nicholas, the last to climb in, takes the final seat beside me. I'm piggy in the middle, sitting far too close to the man my heart is aching for.

Sean, who's sitting in the front beside Harry, turns on the radio, which makes things a bit less awkward. Unfortunately, Nicholas has no such plans for making the hour long journey ahead of us comfortable in any way. He bends his head down, and I can feel his breath whisper across my neck.

"You look great, by the way," he says, moving his knee so that our legs touch.

I ignore his comment, determined not to talk to him. I pull my leg away and turn my head to stare out the window.

"I've really missed you Fred," he says, so quietly that I'm the only one who can hear.

I swallow back the tears that want to come out and glance back at him. "You didn't want me, so why would you miss me?" I ask, unable to help myself. I can never stick to a vow of silence, even when I'm really angry with someone.

His eyes go sad. "I always want you."

"I can't talk about this now," I snip at him, folding my arms over my chest.

He doesn't argue, he simply replies, "Okay, maybe later then."

I pull my iPod out of my handbag and shove the earphones in my ears. I put Dead Kennedys on at full volume and make a concerted effort not to look in Nicholas' direction. He moves his knee again, touching his leg off mine. I don't bother to pull away, because he'll just keep moving closer if I do. And yes, some small part of me is soothed by the contact.

I rest my head back against the seat and close my

eyes. I don't open them again until I've listened to at least five songs. When I do I find that Nicholas' gaze is focused on my chest. A blush colours my cheeks and I breathe heavily at the look in his eyes.

I want to slap him right now, because he knows what his looks are doing to me. He gives me a very subtle grin. My mouth opens involuntarily, but a second later I clamp it shut. Nicholas trails a finger over my hand and then grips it in his own. I squeeze my eyes closed, pushing away the emotion. He twines his fingers with mine and I just lose it. I rip my hand out of his hold and pull my earphones out.

"Stop it," I grit my teeth. "Stop making this difficult."

"You won't talk to me. What do you want me to do?"

The others are chatting, not noticing our row, but I think Eric knows that there's some sort of tension between us and I feel bad for making things uncomfortable for him. However, since he's a friend of Colm's he probably deserves it.

"I just want you to leave me alone. You've done enough damage."

"I know that," he whispers. "Believe me, I've been hating myself ever since the night you left. But I've been thinking a lot too, and I have some things that I need to say to you. But I can't do that if you won't hear me out."

The sadness in his expression is what softens me. As I might have mentioned before, I'm a bit of a pushover when it comes to feuds.

I let out a long sigh. "*Fine*. We can talk later, somewhere private after we get to the festival. Good enough?"

His face goes all soft and he nods. "Yes, that's good

enough," he says, and then turns his face away from me.

We sit out the rest of the journey in silence, the radio and everybody else's voices filling the van.

When we get to the camp site we all get to work setting up our tents. Well, everybody else gets to work, while Nora and I sit on Harry's fold out chairs and eat one of Sean's vodka enhanced oranges. I'd feel bad about leaving Anny to put up our tent all by herself, but I don't because she's practically getting Colm and Eric to do all the work for her anyway.

Nicholas has a tent of his own, and I can't help myself but to watch him as he works to set it up. The movement of his shoulders beneath his long sleeved t-shirt is the part that I (grudgingly) like the most.

"What was going on between you and Nicholas in the van?" Nora asks in a hushed voice.

"Oh yeah, did I not thank you for that yet?" I reply sweetly. "You and Harry know that things are strained between us, yet you leave us with no other option but to sit bumper to fucking bumper in the back seat."

Nora gives me a sheepish look. "Oh. Sorry about that. I didn't think."

"Of course you didn't, you were too busy slobbering all over Richard, who by the way, *is* a poser as it turns out." I tell her sourly. Since I'm in a bad mood, Richard is just going to have to bear the brunt of my bitchiness.

"He's not a poser. You'd realise that he's actually really cool if you bothered to get to know him." Nora sucks on her half of the orange.

I gesture with my hand over to where Richard is shoving a length of pipe inside the lining of their tent. "Is he or is he not wearing a black wife-beater and camouflage army pants over there?"

"It's sunny. Men wear wife-beaters when it's sunny out," Nora defends his choice of outfit.

"Poser men who want to show off their muscles do. And the only people who should be wearing army pants are people who are *in* the actual army."

"Jesus, you are not in a good mood today Fred, are you? Can't you just tell me what happened with Nicholas and quit criticising my boyfriend?"

I huff and give in. "He wants to talk. I told him I'd hear him out later, somewhere away from prying ears," I say, reaching over and tugging on Nora's ear lobe.

She slaps my hand away and laughs. "Hey, stop that. Your hands are all sticky from the orange."

I pretend I'm going to shove my hand in her face just to tease her and she pulls her chair another few inches away from mine. Anny comes over and sits down on the grass by our feet, tying her straight blond hair up in a ponytail.

"I'm thinking I might shag that Eric guy. He's hot," she states.

Typical Anny, mind always set at the lowest common denominator. If she knew how condescendingly I think of her in my head, I don't think she'd want to be my friend anymore.

"Oh yeah, hot to trot, go for it," Nora encourages her.

"Just make sure you do it in *his* tent," I put in. "I don't want any unsavoury liquids getting onto my sleeping bag."

Anny lets out a loud hoot of a laugh and Nora giggles. It garners Nicholas' attention, who glances over in our direction.

"What are you three giggling about?" he asks with a

smirk.

"Unsavoury liquids," Anny answers. "Fred doesn't want me getting any on her sleeping bag when I shag Eric." She nods her head in Eric's direction, who thankfully is too far away to hear her.

I pinch Anny on the arm. Nicholas laughs and shakes his head.

"So he's a foregone conclusion is he?"

Anny gets a predatory look on her face. "Of course, who could resist all this?" she says, running her hand down her hip.

"Who indeed," Nicholas agrees, just before his eyes land on me.

"You can share my sleeping bag if anything happens to yours," he says, his hot gaze locked on mine.

"I'll survive, thanks," I reply cuttingly.

"Have it your way," he mutters, turning to finish putting up his tent.

Once everyone's done setting up camp, I stick my ruck sack and sleeping bag inside mine and Anny's tent and then set off to do some exploring. The great thing about this festival is that it's small enough, so it's not as stressful as the big ones. I mosey around the stalls selling various bits and bobs; jewellery, band t-shirts and the like. There's even one where you can get a henna tattoo done.

I get a sandwich and a beer and sit down on a patch of grass to eat. I wasn't in the mood to stick around the others, because I'm sombre and they're all full of excitement for getting drunk and seeing the bands. When a pair of boots stop in front of me, I glance up and find Nicholas standing there holding a hot dog and a Coke.

"Mind if I join you?" he asks, smiling, but it's not his usual carefree smile, it's an insecure one.

"Do I have a choice?" I grunt and sip my beer.

"You always have a choice Fred," he answers in a low voice.

I look back at him and gesture at the spot of grass before me. "Fine, sit. It's a free country."

He sits down, all grace and lithe muscles, placing his Coke on the grass.

I eye the beverage. "No alcohol for you huh?"

"I'm trying to avoid it to be honest. It's never been something I could enjoy in moderation anyway."

I remember what Phil told me, about Nicholas wasting away in some dive in Berlin, drinking himself into a stupor every day.

"That's good then, that you're avoiding it." I whisper quietly.

"It is," he agrees. "Is this a good time for us to talk?" he asks, eyes wide and hopeful.

I just haven't got it in me to be mean to him right now. I'm too emotionally exhausted. Mum always told me that even when someone puts you down, you should always try to be the better person and kill them with kindness. So that's what I'm trying for now, to kill Nicholas with kindness, let him feel guilty for how he rejected me.

"When you said what you said to me Freda," he begins, "you have to understand, despite the way I reacted, it was the happiest moment of my life."

He's referring to when I told him I loved him in the hotel room in Edinburgh. "Seemed more like it was the saddest," I mutter. "You didn't look happy at all."

He puts down his hot dog and takes my hand into his.

"I was sad because I was sad for *you* Fred. I know I joke about wanting to corrupt you, but that's all that it is, a joke. You are so pure and clean and I felt like I was soiling you by being the person you fell in love with. Women have told me they loved me before, but it wasn't real, it was just momentary lust mistaken for love. When you said it to me I could tell that you truly felt it and it terrified me. That's why I sang that song to you when you came to the gig to see me; I needed to drive you away somehow. I've never had a time in my life when I've been consistently balanced. I've gone from being on top of the world for months, performing in amazing night clubs the world over, to living in my own filth and losing myself in a bottle of whiskey. I was scared that if you fell any deeper in love with me that I'd end up reverting back to one of my low points and dragging you down with me."

I bat away my tears. His words lacerate my insides, because they are so heart-wrenchingly honest. I don't want him to be honest with me, I want him to be a bastard so that hating him is easier. I'm torn between forgiving him and shouting at him that being afraid isn't a good enough excuse for what he did. I mean, I was terrified too. Sometimes feeling fear is an indicator that you're really living life.

"Phil visited me. He told me about what you were like before he brought you to Dublin." I say, my voice comes out jittery, portraying how difficult it is for me to hold in my emotions. Having Nicholas sitting right beside me is actually painful, because I haven't seen his face in weeks. I'd almost forgotten how beautiful he is.

His eyes widen and he drops my hand momentarily. "He told you that? When?"

"About two days ago. He came to my apartment trying to play cupid and urged me to go talk to you because you'd lost your spark, as he put it," I reply.

He shakes his head, silently cursing Phil for interfering. "I'm sorry he bothered you like that. I promise I didn't send him with a sob story to try and win you over. I didn't want you to ever know about any of that."

"So it's true then, what Phil said?" I prompt.

He scratches his head. "Yeah. Phil's rescued me from shit situations my whole life, and I've returned the favour for him a few times too."

"I understand why you get down," I say to him, meeting his eyes even though it hurts. "But don't you think that maybe if you allowed yourself to be with someone then you wouldn't be so sad anymore? Human beings aren't designed to be alone. And I know that you're hardly alone when you're performing for clubs full of people every night, but sometimes you can be in a room packed with others and still feel absolutely isolated." I stop to take a breath.

He takes my hand back into his. "I know that now Freda. That's what I've come to understand. These past three weeks without you have been the worst of my life. Even worse than when I'd been a comatose drunk. I'm not going to ask if you'll take me back, because we were hardly together long enough to properly define what we were. But if you could just find it in yourself to give me another chance I promise I won't let you down again. If you think you can't forgive me enough to be with me the way we were in Edinburgh, then please consider just being my friend again. My life is shit without you in it."

I pull my hand away. "You seriously fucking hurt me Nicholas," I whisper, my throat getting full with tears.

He reaches forward and caresses my cheek. "God I know I did, and I hate myself for it." He searches my face, trying to figure out what I'm thinking. I don't know what to say, so I don't say anything.

"Listen," Nicholas finally speaks. "You don't have to give me an answer right now. I'll go away and you can think on it. Come to me when you know what you want."

His voice is gentle. I love how his mouth moves when he talks. I look at him and nod; time to think seems like a good option. He nods back, gives my cheek one last caress, picks up his food and walks away.

Chapter Seventeen
Zen Gardens and Buddhist Monks

My phone starts ringing. It's Nora. She's probably wondering where I've gotten to. I'm not really in the mood for company though, because my brain is filled with Nicholas telling me his life is shit without me in it. Nobody can have something like that said to them and not feel at least a tiny bit special afterwards. Did he tell me he didn't care about me through that song back in Edinburgh to try and disguise the fact that he really does care?

I let my phone ring out and then get up to have a wander about. I'm lost in thought. I find myself standing watching some drama group put on an art installation, while a bunch of people stand by and watch. Some guy right behind me sidles up and tries flirting. I can't even rally up the energy to be polite. I just shake my head at him and walk away.

After that I bump into Harry and Sean, who pull me along to some place called the Zen Gardens, which are, in my opinion, an effort to replicate the whole Woodstock hippy thing. At first I'm wary, but after a while I find myself taking part in a yoga session and having a great time relaxing. I end up sitting drinking chai tea and talking about life with a guy who may or may not be a Buddhist monk. I'm not sure whether or not it would be rude to ask.

I spill my guts to him, telling him all about Nicholas and my broken little heart. At the end of my rant he simply gives me a serene smile, says something in Chinese, and then walks off to refill his teacup. A fat lot of good that did me. Then again, it did feel relieving to get it all out.

It's around ten-thirty by the time we get back to the camp site. It's relatively quiet since most people haven't started making their way back for the night yet. Harry and Sean have started to get all lovey-dovey, so I leave them to it and head over to the tent I'm sharing with Anny. It's only when I get close to it that I realise I'm hearing sex noises. Just great. I warned her to go to another tent with Eric, but did she listen me? No she bloody well didn't.

I sit down on the grass in the dark and drop my head into my hands. I let out a little manic laugh and rub at my temples. All the calm I took away from the Zen Gardens is quickly dissipating.

I hear somebody zip open their tent just before Nicholas' voice asks, "Fred, are you okay?"

I turn around to find him sticking his head out of his tent; his hair is messy and it looks like he'd been sleeping.

"I'm fine, except for the fact that Anny is shagging somebody in our tent when I told her not to. What are you doing here? Didn't you go with Nora and the others to listen to some music?"

He scratches his head. "I wasn't really in the mood. I'll go see some bands tomorrow though. Where have you been?" he asks.

"Harry and Sean took me to do yoga. It was actually kind of fun."

Nicholas crawls further out of his tent. "Now that's something I regret missing," he mutters in a low voice.

What does he mean by that?

Anny's currently making these high pitched yipping

sounds and our tent is shaking from side to side. The girl really has no shame. I feel kind of bad that I've never had a deep enough conversation with her where she could have told me what caused her to become so slutty. Perhaps she has daddy issues. As I said, she's only ever really been a casual "going for a night out" sort of a friend.

I let my face drop into my hands again. "Jesus, I can't believe all my things are in there," I mumble. "Thank God everything's zipped up and I didn't take out my sleeping bag yet. I guess I'll just have to wait until they're finished."

I glance back at Nicholas and he's glaring in the direction of my tent. "She shouldn't be leaving you with nowhere to go like this. It isn't right." It looks like he's grinding his teeth in anger.

"Anny doesn't exactly think with her brain all too often; she's more inclined to go where her knickers tell her. I've only got myself to blame for organising to share with her anyway."

Nicholas stares at me now, taking me in. "Come and stay with me for the night," he says softly.

"Nicholas, I can't..."

"I don't mean like that," he interrupts. "I just mean to sleep. I've got the biggest tent out of all of us and there's only me in it. I've got more than enough room."

I glance at his tent. It's true, it is the biggest. It could fit at least four people. I turn back to him. "Okay then, but I haven't got any of my things."

"I'll go and get them," he offers, walking towards the shaking tent where Anny is still being way too noisy. You'd swear she was in there with Enrique Iglesias or something. I can't imagine Eric (or whoever she's with) is *that* skilled of a lover.

I stand up and pull him back by the arm. "You can't go in there, they're still..." I trail off and gesture animatedly at the tent.

Nicholas smirks. "I don't care what they're doing Freda, I'm getting your bags for you. Now go get in my tent. I'll be back in a minute."

I nod and crawl inside, and God the whole place smells of him. It's almost too much to take. His sleeping back is spread out on top of a mat and it's slightly crumpled. So he *was* in here sleeping. I find the idea of Nicholas trying to get some shut eye while the young people are out getting wild and drunk so incredibly adorable. This big sexy man going to bed early. There's a discarded t-shirt in the corner. I check to make sure he's not on his way back yet and then pick it up and inhale deeply. Look, I'm not trying to be creepy, I've just missed his smell so much.

I hear him approach and then shove the t-shirt back where I found it. He crawls inside the tent with an amused expression on his face.

"What? What happened?" I ask, curious to know what he saw Anny doing.

Nicholas shakes his head and makes a show of zipping his lips. I can't believe he's not going to tell me what he saw. He hands me my stuff, then slips off his boots and jeans before getting back into his sleeping bag.

"Nicholas!" I exclaim. "You can't just not tell me. It isn't fair, now I'm dying to know."

He turns over and props his head up on his arm. He sucks on his bottom lip for a moment. I watch the movement with riveted attention. He has really nice lips. And he broke my heart. I have to remember this.

"She has two guys in there with her, Colm *and* Eric," he answers finally.

I put my hand to my mouth in shock. "Oh my God. This is a new extreme for her," I say in surprise, and to be honest, a little edge of disgust. Two guys aside, she's only just met them. Plus, Colm's a sleaze bag.

I glance at Nicholas out of the corner of my eye. "I knew something was up, she was making an awful lot of noise. What were they doing?"

"I'll leave that to your imagination, I think," he answers with a grin.

"Fine, I guess I don't really want to know anyway," I say, and begin pulling off my boots. I open my bag and pull out my night clothes. Nicholas is watching me.

"Turn around for a minute would you?"

He sucks on his lip again and I have to clench my thighs together, because just watching him do that makes me tingle between my legs. It reminds me of when he went down on me. After another second he shakes his head and turns over. I pull my dress up and over my head and then shimmy into my shorts and t-shirt. I leave my socks on because it will probably get cold later. I'm busy tying my hair in a bun when I glance up and suddenly realise that Nicholas has turned back around.

"What are you doing?!" I exclaim indignantly.

He smirks and shrugs his shoulders. "I thought you were finished."

"I would have told you if I was finished," I huff and roll out my sleeping bag, before zipping it open.

"It's not anything I haven't seen before," he whispers.

"That's not the point," I whisper back.

"Do you want to know what my favourite part of your body is?" he asks, leaning forward.

"I'll take a wild guess, shall I?" I roll my eyes and nod to my chest. There are goose bumps on my arms. Goosebumps I'm having a hard time ignoring.

"Nope, though they are a close second," he says, looking smug and playful. I love him when he looks playful. I hate that I love him when he looks playful.

"Go on then, enlighten me," I say, trying to sound bored. It's not like I'm *dying* to know or anything.

He reaches forward and traces his hand over my stomach. "This part. It's all round and soft. I'd love to fall asleep right here."

He flattens his palm out low on my belly, the ends of his fingers are a little *too* low, brushing the top of my knickers which are beneath the shorts.

I suck in a breath and try to regain my composure.

"Good to know. You can move your hand now," I breathe, my husky voice betraying me. Nicholas telling me that his favourite part of my body is the part I'm most insecure about is too much, too close.

He rubs his thumb over the skin peeking out of my t-shirt and then pulls his hand away. I lie down and try to get comfortable, but when I close my eyes all I can see is his face, all I can feel is the memory of his hand on my stomach. I shift my sleeping bag over a little so that there's more space between us.

"Those two nights we spent together in Edinburgh were the best of my life," he whispers into the darkness of the tent. I can hear far off noises and music, but that doesn't negate from how quiet it feels right here, how strongly his words mark me. "I've never been with a woman that intensely before. It feels like forever since I was last inside of you."

My breathing becomes heavy. "Let's just go to sleep, Nicholas," I whisper back. "I'm exhausted."

"I'm not sure if I can sleep with you right over there."

"You're going to have to try." There's pleading in my voice. I hope he can hear it.

He lets out a long breath. "All right, sweet dreams Freda." I hear him shift in his sleeping bag and then he doesn't say anything more.

It takes me ages to get to sleep, but I drift off eventually. When I wake up it's morning and there's condensation built up on the roof of the tent. I glance over to the side to find that Nicholas' sleeping bag is all rolled up and he's nowhere to be seen.

I dig in my bag for a make-up wipe and rub it over my face. It'll have to do as a replacement for washing. I put on a dab of moisturiser, not bothering with make-up because I'm too tired. I quickly change into some clean underwear, a new pair of socks and a dark green cotton dress. Then I grab my toothbrush and toothpaste and crawl out of the tent to go in search of one of those temporary sink units they have at festivals.

After I've brushed my teeth and relieved myself in the cleanest porta-potty I could find (which wasn't very clean at all if you must know) I head back to the camp site.

Everybody is sitting on the grass eating breakfast and soaking up the morning sun, except for Anny, Colm and Eric.

"Fred, I got you some food," Nicholas calls and pats the space beside him on the grass.

I sit down and say, "You didn't have to do that," as he hands me a steaming paper coffee cup and a bacon sandwich. I take them and place them down on my lap. Apart from the small shadows of grey beneath his eyes, he doesn't look like he just spent the night sleeping in a tent. He's got a clean t-shirt on and a pair of low hanging jeans. His hair is neatly combed. I have this strange urge to reach over and mess it up.

He tucks a stray curl that's fallen out of my bun behind my ear, as I take a sip of coffee. I can't stop myself from closing my eyes and savouring his touch.

"Did you sleep okay?" he asks in a gentle voice, not failing to notice me close my eyes.

I nod and take a bite of the sandwich. It's salty and warm and tastes really good.

"At least one of us did."

"You couldn't sleep?" I question.

"I slept some, but I wanted to watch you. This could be the last chance I'll get," he answers, his tone sombre. My gut squeezes.

"Nicholas..." I trail off then, because Anny interrupts me as she comes crawling out of her tent, moaning loudly about having a thumping headache. I glance over at her to see she's wearing a t-shirt, boy shorts and her Wellington boots.

Nora turns in her seat to see what's going on and I snicker when I see her jaw drop open at the sight of Colm and Eric coming out of the same tent as Anny.

She glances at Richard, her eyes widened as she mouths, "Oh my God."

Richard smirks and shrugs his shoulders.

"Well, well, well," Harry chimes. "What do we have here? Three in a sleeping bag and the little one said roll over, was it?"

Anny scowls and crosses her arms over her chest.

"Shut up, Harry."

Colm and Eric look half embarrassed, half proud of themselves that everyone knows they participated in a threesome last night. Ugh. Colm spots me and gives me a little eyebrow waggle, as if I should be impressed with him or something. I don't bother hiding my disgust.

The three of them get a change of clothes and go to buy some breakfast for themselves. When they get back they sit down with the rest of us and chow down. There's a couple moments of awkwardness, before everyone starts chatting and it disappears as if nothing out of the ordinary happened in Anny's tiny little tent last night.

I'm just finished up with my sandwich when Colm starts talking to me from across the way.

"Hey Fred, are you planning on flashing some of the bands later on?" he asks with a wink.

I can feel Nicholas instantly tense up beside me at the remark.

I sneer at him. "Why would I do that?"

"For fun. Just make sure you give me a heads up so I can reserve myself a front row seat."

I muster my best condescending tone. "Colm, we're at a music festival for yuppies in the countryside, not a cock rock video from the eighties. Oh yeah, and there was something else, what was it again?" I rub at my chin ponderously. "Oh right, that was it, go fuck yourself."

Everybody laughs. Colm wipes some ketchup from the corner of his mouth and grins, not backing down.

"I've been trying to get you to fuck me for the last two years. When are you going to do me a favour and put me out of my misery?" he asks.

I think he might still be a little bit drunk from last night. He's normally a dickhead, but not this much of a dickhead.

Nicholas leans forward on his elbows. "Shut your mouth, mate," he says in a low voice. He sounds threatening.

Colm lets out a big, sputtering laugh and gets to his feet. "What are you gonna do about it if I don't?"

Harry winces and says, "Colm, please just sit down and stop offending people."

"No Harry, I want to know what that lady boy thinks he can do to shut me up."

The irony of Colm calling Nicholas a lady boy in front of his openly gay brother doesn't escape me.

Nicholas raises an eyebrow and casually remarks. "I'm not the one who spent the night having a three way with another dude."

Colm's jaw drops open and he sputters, "What? No I - I never touched him, we were both only doing shit to her," he throws an arm in Anny's direction.

"That's not what I saw," says Nicholas with a shrug. I glance at him and grin.

"You saw nothing," Colm hisses.

Nicholas laughs. I adore that sound. He raises his hands in the air. "All right then mate, I didn't see anything. But if I hear you make another comment like that to Fred I think I might remember that I did see something."

What did he see? Or is he only trying to spook Colm?

Colm gives Nicholas a look that could kill and then marches off to dispose of his rubbish in the nearest bin. Harry shakes his head at his brother's retreating figure and then carries on with the conversation he'd been having with Nora and Sean.

I lean in to Nicholas and ask, "Did you actually see anything?"

He turns and shifts close to me, placing his hand flat on the grass about a centimetre away from my bottom. "Not really. He's a fuckwit though, and it pissed me off how he spoke to you. Hopefully now he's learned his lesson to shut up and keep his hands to himself."

I don't mention that Colm never tried to touch me. I suppose the intention was there.

"I'm grateful to you for sticking up for me and all, but you didn't have to do that."

He moves his hand and presses it lightly to the base of my spine. "Fred, I will never like the idea of another man touching you or making innuendos about you. In fact, I am very much opposed to it, hate it even."

"I hate the idea of another woman touching you," I whisper in response, unable to hold back.

Nicholas presses his hand harder into my lower back and replies, "Well then, we're both on the same page."

"I still need time though," I say to him quickly. "I'm still not sure..."

He puts a finger to my lips. "Hush. I know. I'm willing to wait until you decide what you want from me. Friends. Lovers. Nothing. It's your decision." His voice seems to catch when he says the word "nothing".

"Thank you," I reply, moving my mouth against his hand.

It takes him a minute for him to pull his finger away. He watches me as I involuntarily lick my lips after he does so.

"Spend the day with me?" he asks, his tone unsure.

I hesitate, before nodding. "I think everyone's going to stick in a group today anyway. You can help me to ignore Colm if you like."

Nicholas' grin lights up his face. "Done and done," he stands and pulls me up with him.

Once everybody's ready to go we make our way out of the camp site and towards the main stage where there are bands playing. The friendly atmosphere from yesterday isn't as prevalent today. Anny, Colm and Eric are carefully avoiding one another. I don't get why people enjoy having uninhibited, drunken sex when they have to deal with the embarrassment the next day.

Harry is throwing his brother harsh looks every chance he gets after the way he behaved earlier, and Colm is sending negative vibes Nicholas' way by bumping into him and talking over him, *supposedly* unintentionally. Nicholas seems to be making a concerted effort not to punch the guy in the face.

All of this I notice, yet it pales in comparison to my awareness of Nicholas as we stand in a field close to the back of the crowd at the main stage and watch some band called Wild Beasts play. Harry and Sean go to get in a round of drinks for everyone. Nicholas tells them that he'll just have a bottle of water. He must still be trying to stay sober. In a way I'm proud of him, especially now that I know about his past drinking problems. I also feel a little ashamed of my own excessive drinking while in his company.

The grass is a bit more muddy and littered than it had been yesterday, so there aren't as many nice patches to sit on. Richard sits down and Nora perches herself on his lap. Nicholas offers for me to sit on his and I'm not sure whether I should. In the end I shrug and sit down, because I don't want to get my dress dirty. He puts his arms casually around my waist and rests his hands lightly on top of my thighs. We let the music wash over us.

I try to forget the decision I need to make about whether I want us to be friends, or lovers, or nothing. I just soak up the contentment his closeness brings me.

Sean hands me a beer and I ask him what happened to all those oranges from yesterday.

"All gone I'm afraid," he says, with a sad little sigh.

"I'm definitely going to do that trick if we come back next year," Nora puts in.

"If we come back next year I'm bringing a watermelon," Harry announces.

Nicholas' hand on my thigh moves by the tiniest fraction. It's almost nothing, yet I feel it so intensely. I move a little in his lap and take a sip of my beer. I can feel him breathing heavily against the back of my neck.

Everybody's currently having a conversation about what other fruits you could inject alcohol into.

"What do you think of the band?" I ask Nicholas, turning my head to him a little.

"Not really paying attention to the band Fred," he answers, so low I almost don't hear him. His thumb brushes against the fabric of my dress.

I swallow hard. "Well you should, I think they're good. They kind of remind me a little bit of Muse." I manage.

"Mm hmm," he mumbles, his thumb now lazily rubbing against my thigh.

I feel a pulse of electricity shoot right from my lungs to down between my legs.

"What do you think Fred?" I suddenly hear Harry ask

me.

"Huh?" I glance over at him and he gives me a secret knowing smirk. "About blueberries, do you think it would be worth the effort?"

"Um, that depends on how dedicated you are to the cause," I quip. Nicholas hasn't stopped moving his thumb, damn him, it's edging closer to my inner thigh now.

"I think blueberries are out," says Sean. "Nobody has that much time on their hands."

"You should just stick with oranges," Anny speaks up. She's been unusually quiet today. I wonder if she feels happy about her threesome last night, or dirty. Probably dirty. Eric is sitting close by, but she looks like she just wants him to get away from her.

I catch Colm's eye then, and he's sneering openly at me. I guess he doesn't like the fact that I'm sitting on Nicholas' lap. Even though I still have mixed feelings about our relationship, I'm happy that Nicholas spoke up to him at breakfast. The last thing I need is for Colm to keep chancing his arm all weekend.

"You're so beautiful," Nicholas murmurs, pulling me out of my thoughts. His mouth is now a bare inch from my neck. I tense up.

"I'm sorry, I just had to say it. I want to say it whenever I look at you," he goes on.

I turn my head to him and the question I've wanted to ask him for weeks spills out, "Why did you say you didn't care about me?"

His arms tighten around my stomach and he takes me in silently for a time. "Sometimes we're cruellest to the ones we care about the most."

That's true, I guess. I know my parents mean the

world to me, but there have been times when I was younger when I said cruel things to them. Mostly because I was hurting on the inside and I wanted them to hurt too. To understand the hurt I was feeling.

There's a long stretch of silence between us.

"So you do care about me then?" I ask shakily.

"I care about you more than I care about myself, Fred."

"Don't say that."

"It's the truth."

I can't seem to think of anything to say in reply, so instead I take one of his hands into mine, interlace our fingers and rest my head back against his shoulder. It's all I can manage right now to show him that I care about him just as much, because words are failing me.

Chapter Eighteen
Holding Hands and Perfect Days

For the rest of the day we wander around the festival, taking in as many of the bands as we can. Nicholas stays close to me at all times; there's a lot of subtle, barely there touching going on between the both of us.

I keep thinking of how he said he cares about me more than he cares about himself. It was wonderful to hear him say that, but it's not exactly what I wanted him to say. I wanted him to tell me that he loves me as much as I love him. Even though he hurt me, I can't deny that my heart still yearns for him.

When we get back to the camp site that night I don't even bother to argue about sleeping in Nicholas' tent again. I couldn't bring myself to stay where a threesome just took place the night before, but more than that I need Nicholas' presence. I need his eyes on me. I need to be able to put my eyes on him.

Anny has disappeared off somewhere anyway, so who knows what new bed partners she'll be bringing back with her later on.

The sexual tension between me and Nicholas is skyrocketing, but neither of us is brave enough to make the first move, fearing what will happen if we do. We quietly undress and get into our sleeping bags.

I'm so tired that I can hardly keep my eyes open. I yawn as I lie down and try to find a comfortable position.

"I had a really great day with you Fred," Nicholas says quietly.

"Me too," I reply.

He reaches out across the space between our two sleeping bags. "Give me your hand," he whispers.

I glance down at his outstretched fingers, then I slowly reach out too and interlock mine with his. He rubs his thumb back and forth over my wrist, and I fall asleep to the calming motion of his touch.

When I wake we're still holding hands, though a little more loosely. It's early morning and Nicholas is still asleep. I decide to get dressed and go get him some breakfast, since he got mine yesterday. I repeat the same routine as the previous morning in getting washed and dressed and then go to grab us some food. When I get back to camp, the others still haven't gotten up. I put the breakfast down on the grass and zip open the tent.

When I crawl inside I come face to pecs with Nicholas' naked chest.

"Hey," I say, sucking in a breath at how good he looks without a top on. I miss seeing him without his top on.

He smiles, which makes his face even more handsome. "Hey yourself. I was just coming to see where you were," he pulls a clean t-shirt on over his head.

"I got breakfast, come outside," I tell him and then quickly retreat.

He follows me out, looking smug. He knows that I liked what I saw of him in the tent just now. He thanks me for the food and we eat in companionable silence.

"I want to spend the day alone with you Fred," he says as I'm sipping on some coffee.

My heart seizes, but I try to disguise it by simply replying, "Okay then."

He gives me a grin that could melt the knickers off of

a nun. I can feel myself slowly warming up to him again. Oh, what I am I talking about, I'm practically burning for him. I mean, you have to forgive people sometimes, right? He's been open about his reasons for why he pushed me away like he did. He hasn't tried to paint over the cracks; he's exposed them to me in all their twisted, dysfunctional glory, and I have to give him credit for that.

I make a decision to tell him that I want us to be together again before the end of the festival. Today is the last day and we'll be going home tomorrow morning. That gives me twenty-four hours to summon up the courage.

Nora is still asleep, so I send her a text message telling her that I'm going to go see some bands with Nicholas today. She writes back about an hour later, asking me if that's a wise idea. I tell her I'll be okay.

Nicholas and I stroll through the crowds side by side. I want to reach out and hold his hand, like we held hands all through the night. We stop at a jewellery stall and he buys me a silver necklace with a little bird pendant on the end of it.

"Here, let me put it on for you," he says, as the woman hands him the chain.

He turns to me and fastens it around my neck, letting his fingers trail down my skin to admire the pendant.

"It really suits you," he comments, eyes on my chest.

"Thanks, I like it," I reply on a swallow.

He takes my hand into his, and his touch relieves me. "Come on, let's go listen to some music."

We while away the hours going from stage to stage. It's funny how I had planned on avoiding Nicholas this whole time, yet I've actually found myself constantly in his company. He is such a complex creature, but I'm coming to think that his complexity is what I love about him. He has suffered in his life, and it's created this wonderfully flawed man who I don't think I could live without.

We sit on the grass and eat crepes for our dinner. He pinches me in the side and tells me I have amazing hips. Hips that you just want to grab a hold of. I tell him to keep his hands to himself, while secretly hoping he doesn't.

When we've finished eating we head back to the main stage, where Elbow have just started playing. It's late evening, quickly drifting into night time. Nicholas stands behind me and slowly weaves his arms around my waist, pulling my back flush to his front. He rests his head next to mine and sways us to the music.

The intro to "One Day Like This" begins to play, with a string based melody that seems to touch my heart. The lead singer, Guy Garvey, tells the audience to sing the opening lines. Nicholas starts to turn me in his arms so that I'm facing him. He's not looking at the stage or anywhere else, just at me. Only at me. He pulls me close, his lips nearing my ear.

The multi-coloured stage lights flash around us, and even though there are crowds of people all about, I feel like I'm in a capsule where there's only the two of us. He stares deep into my eyes and starts singing into my ear. His voice is low and husky. I can feel it pierce right into me, vibrate through me, his beautiful, beautiful voice.

Even after Guy has taken over from the crowd who had been chanting the lyrics, Nicholas continues singing to me. It's the most perfect moment of my life; I want to put it a jar and shelve it, keep it forever.

He asks me what made him behave that way, using words he never says?

He can only think it must be love..

He asks me to kiss him like it's the final meal, kiss him like we'll die tonight..

He says that holy cow he loves my eyes..

That only now he sees the light..

He says to throw the curtains wide, that one day like this a year will see him right..

I pull him closer to me. I hadn't realised it until now, but there are tears streaming down my face. I couldn't be any more in love with this man if I tried.

He pulls back to look down at me. "I love you Freda," he breathes. "It feels like nobody in the history of the world has loved another person as much as I love you. I love you so much it hurts. You make me smile, you make me laugh, you make me *burn*."

Whoa. What do you say to that? In the end all I can manage is to wipe at my tears and simply whisper, "I love you too. I want you, need you."

My voice almost fails me, and then I pull his mouth down to mine. We kiss and it's like fireworks. Shooting stars. The rainbow that comes after a shower. Every single wonderful thing the world ever thought to spit out to counteract all the ugliness it creates.

His tongue slides over mine, and all I can feel is him, all I can taste is him; all I can hear is the music pulsing through me, the strings and the guitars and the drums. He draws back from the kiss, panting, blue eyes shining just like they shined on the first day I met him.

His lust filled expression turns into a huge smile, and then his huge smile turns into musical, gorgeous laughter. He puts his hands on either of my cheeks and holds my face up to his.

"This feels right," he tells me. "So perfectly right."

"It does, doesn't it," I reply, with a weird nervous laugh that melds into his gorgeous one.

His hands drift down from my cheeks, his thumbs giving me just the right amount of pressure on the base of my neck so that I feel it all the way down my spine.

"I belong to you. I've belonged to you since the beginning, since before I even knew that I did," he rambles. "I'll never hurt you again. I'd rather die than to hurt you."

I quiet him with another kiss. We fumble for each other in the dark, surrounded by drunken, happy revellers. My hand travels up his t-shirt and over his abs. His hands travel low to cup my bottom.

"Let's go back to the tent," I breathe past his kisses.

"Good idea," he says huskily and grips my hand.

We run through the crowds, Nicholas pulling me along with him faster. I have to stop to catch my breath, but also because I'm giddy with laughter. I hold onto my stomach, unable to stop giggling. He watches me with so much love in his eyes that it almost hurts. I recover and we continue back to the camp site at a more manageable pace this time.

When we get inside the tent Nicholas opens up his sleeping bag and spreads it out across the floor. He takes my hand and pulls me close to him, placing a soft kiss on my lips, the tip of my nose, my chin, my neck.

"It's too dark in here," he whispers and pulls out his phone. He switches on the torch and places it on the floor. "I have to be able to see you."

His hands graze down my sides, resting on my hips

and squeezing. I gasp into his mouth as he kisses me. He lifts up the skirt of my dress and trails his hand over my inner thigh, before rubbing between my legs.

"More," I whisper against his lips.

His mouth tilts up at one side in a grin. "More what, baby?"

I don't have to answer him because he's already slipping a finger inside my underwear and sliding it over my wetness.

"Yes," I pant. "Like that."

He draws his hand away and I almost groan in frustration. He unzips the back of my dress and pulls it over my head, then buries his face in my breasts.

"I missed these," he mumbles into my skin, like he's worshipping at an altar.

He removes my boots, socks and bra, all the while I'm trying to unbuckle his belt and pull down his jeans. I need to feel his skin against mine, taste it. Once I'm wearing nothing but my knickers, he practically rips off his t-shirt and pulls his jeans down the rest of the way. He lowers me carefully onto the outspread sleeping bag and kisses all down my stomach, briefly dipping his tongue into my belly button and then continuing his descent.

He takes hold of the side of my knickers and pulls them over a little to expose me. He licks me once and yanks the fabric against me hard. I cry out. With deadly eyes he grins and drags them down my legs before pulling them off. He's kneeling between my legs now, his erection starkly obvious inside his boxer briefs.

I lean forward and kiss his collarbone; a gush of breath leaves him. I run my hand over his toned stomach and he groans. Then I take his cock into my hand and rub him gently. He watches my every movement with parted lips and heavy breathing. The next thing I know I've pulled him down and switched places so that I'm straddling him and he's lying flat on the sleeping bag.

"Freda," he says, some kind of warning in his tone.

I put a finger to his mouth. "Quiet, let me take the lead," I whisper.

He visibly swallows and nods, closing his fluttering eyelids for a second. I pull him free of his boxers and raise myself up, before slowly lowering myself down onto his stiff cock.

"Oh fuck," he swears and grips me by the hips.

I start moving up and down slowly on him, then I quicken my pace, working him towards his release as I work my way towards my own. I kiss and lick at him everywhere. I feel powerful like this, like I'm marking him as mine. We've been dying to touch one another for days, the tension has built up to boiling point that it doesn't take long for both of us to come in unison.

Nicholas holds my wrists tight to his chest as he spurts into me and I shake against him. I collapse on top of him and he turns us so that he's cradling me in his arms. We stay like that for innumerable minutes and then he begins kissing my neck and fondling my breasts.

"I need you again, honey," he says softly into my ear.

I can feel his erection hard and pressing against my bottom. He manoeuvres me onto my hands and knees and positions himself behind me. He caresses my neck and then grabs a tight hold of my pony tail. He pulls on it gently, dragging my face around to look at him. He puts his other hand palm flat to the hollow of my throat and then sinks himself into me.

God, he feels good from this position, deep inside of me. His gentle tugging on my hair with each thrust of his hips is like pure, undiluted pleasure mixed with the sharp tang of pain. This seems to be his thing, hair and neck holding; almost like pulling, almost like choking, but not quite, always on the cusp. I can tell that he enjoys seeing me from this vulnerable sort of angle because his eyes are practically glowing.

I never would have thought to ask him to do this, but I know that I like it.

He fucks me hard and fast, holding onto my hair and neck as I dig my fingernails into the fabric of the sleeping bag. He lets go of my neck to pinch one of my nipples and I moan.

"That's it Freda, give me your noises. I want them all." He encourages me.

I moan again and again until he's coming inside of me and my body feels like liquid. We sink to the floor, lost in one another.

Later on he uses some tissue paper to clean me, and even though it's a little embarrassing, I still let him. I need the intimacy it brings like I need air to breathe. He puts me in my night clothes and unzips my sleeping bag to throw over the both of us. I bury my face in his neck and fall asleep.

When I wake up I have three days' worth of sweat and last night's sex all over my skin, but I've never felt better. I turn to my side to find that Nicholas had been watching me.

"How long have you been up?" I ask, rubbing at my sleepy eyes.

"Only a little while," he says, leaning forward and

giving me a kiss on the forehead. I can hear movement outside the tent just before Harry calls out, "Come on you two love birds, rise and shine, we've got to get packed up and out of here."

I crawl forward and unzip the tent, before sticking my head out. I yelp when Nicholas pinches my bottom and then I turn around to give him a look of warning. He raises his hands in the air in surrender.

"What time is it?" I ask, squinting up at Harry in the morning light. He's standing there fully dressed, as the others pack up their camping gear behind him.

"Almost ten o'clock. Now come on you've already overslept. Tell lover boy to get his arse moving too."

My eyes widen infinitesimally in surprise. "Yes, that's right." He goes on, whispering now. "Sean and I came back early last night and heard everything. You put on quite a show. Well, an audio one at least." He winks at me.

I go completely red in the face, tell Harry to shut up (to which he laughs) and then zip the tent closed again. Nicholas and I get dressed. It takes longer than usual because we keep getting caught up with kissing or teasing one another. After that Nicholas packs up the tent in record time and we follow the others back to where the van is parked.

He holds me all through the drive back to the city. I notice everyone looking at us questioningly out of the corners of their eyes, but they don't ask what's going on between us. I'm glad they don't, because it's none of their business anyway. What I have with Nicholas feels so precious and fragile right now; I don't want anybody else to even know it exists.

Back at the apartments Nora announces that she's

going to her bedroom to catch some shut eye, complaining that she slept awfully in the tent the past few nights. I'm just about to follow her into our apartment when Nicholas pulls me back and practically shoves me in the door of his place. He pierces me with a sexy grin and turns over the lock. We spend the next hour having the most amazing shower sex ever. He presses me up against the wall and goes down on me. We kiss beneath the spray of water. He slides himself into me and I get lost in the sensation, in the feel of him.

When we get out I change into one of his clean t-shirts, before crawling into his bed.

He looks like he's just about to pounce on me when his phone starts ringing and he turns away to answer it. I text Aoife, who had been filling in for me again with the cupcakes this morning since I was still at the festival, to check if everything went okay.

She writes back saying it went fine, just as I hear Nicholas exclaim over the phone, "They said what?!" He paces back and forth at the foot of the bed.

"All right, so some stranger paid them fifty Euro to throw a brick through the window of the club and rough us up a bit, what the fuck Phil?"

Oh my God, he must be talking about the attack at the club from before we left for Edinburgh. The police are only getting back with information now? Talk about slow. I'd completely forgotten about it since I've been so miserable over Nicholas the past few weeks.

"Wait, wait, wait, describe him to me again?" he says, his voice calmer now as he rubs the back of his neck. I crawl forward and grab him by the hand while he listens to Phil on the other end of the line. I tug him down to the bed and plant little kisses all along his shoulder.

He winds his hand through my wet hair and nuzzles my neck with his nose, then pulls me onto his lap as he hangs up.

He leans in and presses his lips to my throat, just before he says, "I think we might have a bit of a problem on our hands."

"You do?" I question, furrowing my brow.

"That was Phil, as you probably heard. The police came to the club yesterday to tell him that they caught one of the thugs who attacked us the other week. This guy is about twenty years old and known to the authorities; he hasn't been in jail before, but he's been arrested more times than they can count. When they brought him in for questioning about the attack he ended up telling them that some man paid him and his friends fifty Euros each to do it."

I suck in a breath. "Are you serious?"

Nicholas nods. "And that's not all, the guy the thug described sounded an awful lot like Aaron. Medium height, blond hair, prim and proper dress sense."

"Oh shit! We need to tell the police it was him then," I let my face fall into my hands. "Oh God, oh God, this is all my fault. The attack happened right after Aaron came to the club that time and stormed off. He must have done this as his twisted idea of revenge."

"Well, you did say he wasn't the full shilling," Nicholas adds. I like it when he uses my Irish phrasing back to me. "I'll call Phil in a minute and tell him what we know, then we can go to the station and tell them about Aaron."

I'm just about to agree, anger consuming me, when

suddenly an idea surfaces. Okay, so I know it's not the mature, *legal* thing to do, but I kind of want to get my own back at Aaron before we turn him in to the cops.

I put my hand on top of Nicholas' and ask, "Can we wait just one more day before we do that?"

He eyes me curiously and puts his phone down on the bed. "Why?"

"I have a devious plan," I tell him.

He pulls me closer on his lap and trails a finger down my arm.

"Oh really? Do tell," he says, eyes alight with interest, and I explain to him what I have in mind.

Chapter Nineteen
Thelma and Louise

Have you ever tried to laugh silently when your whole body just wants to break out into a furious bout of giggles? Well, it's no easy feat, let me tell you.

It's two o'clock in the morning as Nicholas and I creep around the front of Aaron's nondescript, red brick house, where his pride and joy sits, all shiny and clean. A black Ford Mondeo that he's had since he was in college.

He has a weird OCD thing about this car. Even though it's kind of old and he has the money to replace it, he never does. He just continues to keep it in pristine condition. Aaron doesn't like change; I guess that's one of the reasons why he started stalking me after I broke up with him in the first place. He couldn't seem to move on to someone different. I'd feel sorry for him if he weren't so cruel and calculating on top of it all.

We had to go to an art and craft supply store, as well as a DIY warehouse, to get what we needed for my devious, and yes slightly whimsical, but also very much illegal plot for getting our payback. I dip the paint roller into the bucket containing a mixture of wall paper paste and gold glitter, before running it over the hood of the vehicle.

Nicholas is busy plastering rainbow stickers all along the bumper, quietly snickering like a kid sneaking candy in the middle of the night. That's right, we're turning Aaron's car into a poster vehicle for gay pride.

Okay, so I know what you're thinking, isn't it going to be a little bit obvious that it was us who did this? And yes, it is going to be obvious. Perhaps that's the point. The thing is, I know Aaron well enough to predict that he won't be reporting our little vandalism to the police, since he is strange and proud. Crazy proud, emphasis on the crazy.

He'd rather let us get away with it than have the police come to his house and see what a delight we have made of his car. He would never in a million years draw attention to himself or make a spectacle for his neighbours to see.

I pick up the bag of silver star shaped cut outs and spread them over the hood so that they'll stick to the glittery paste. Nicholas finishes with the rainbow stickers and begins painting the tires luminous shades of pink and orange. A flutter of glee goes through me. I feel like a mischievous pixie carrying out a prank with an aesthetically pleasing result. Of course, that all depends on your personal taste, because I'm sure Aaron won't be finding it aesthetically pleasing in the slightest.

Once we're done we stand back and admire our handiwork, not forgetting to take a few pictures on Nicholas' phone so that we can show Phil proof of our secret revenge. We dump everything into black bags, making sure not to leave a speck of evidence, just a dazzling, multi-coloured masterpiece of a Ford Mondeo. We even put a big purple bow on the roof of it.

Aaron drives this car into work every morning, so he's going to throw one hell of a hissy fit when he strolls out his front door and sees what we've done. I wish I could be here to witness his reaction. And anyway, it serves the bastard right. In fact, he deserves a lot worse. One of those scumbags could have seriously injured any of us that night. The brick had almost hit me in the head. I could have *died*. This little prank is nothing compared to what he deserves, and I hope that once we turn him in to the police tomorrow that he gets his comeuppance.

We drive out to the nearest landfill site to dump the evidence. We haven't stopped laughing since we got into the car and drove away from Aaron's street. It must have been the hour we spent holding it all in that's caused it to build up to us giggling to the point of delirium. Every time our laughter starts to die down we simply glance at each other and it starts up all over again.

We're almost home by the time we finally manage to come to our senses. Nicholas reaches over and takes my hand into his.

"You know what Fred, even if Aaron did decide to turn us in, I would happily go down with you for such a wonderful crime."

"Oh no no," I declare, as he raises my hand to his lips for a brief kiss. "They'll never take us alive Viv, we'll drive off the edge of a cliff - Thelma and Louise style."

He laughs and looks at me with a warm expression and a short, thoughtful silence ensues.

"You colour my world, Freda," he whispers into the quiet of the car, just as he parks and cuts the engine.

It's funny that he says it, because I had always considered it to be him who coloured mine.

"Ditto," I say. My tone goes serious when I tell him softly, "I love you."

"I love you too," he answers, before pulling me out of the car and inside the building.

Later on I rest my head on Nicholas' shoulder as we

sit in his living room in front of the television. He picks up the remote control for the old VCR player he bought and presses the play button. A moment later the video starts running; the camera work is a little shaky. The spotlight is on a woman on a stage in a small club. Nicholas' mother. She's sitting by a piano and playing a slow, jazzy song intro; a minute later she starts to sing. Her long black hair is resting on one shoulder and she's wearing a pretty velvet dress.

In this moment I genuinely understand how Nicholas could have seen this as a young boy and wanted to replicate it. She's beautiful and so is her singing. I take his hand into mine and rub my thumb down the centre of his palm. We sit back and watch the rest of the video, immortalizing a moment in the life of a woman now gone from the world.

It's two weeks later to the day that we hear how the guy Aaron paid to attack us identified him to the police and now Aaron's being charged. It's the same day that there's a party going on down at The Glamour Patch to celebrate its six month anniversary since opening.

Nicholas and I are planning on getting dressed up and having a night to remember. In fact, I've been having a lot of memorable nights lately. I've hardly slept in my own bed since coming home from Electric Picnic. Draw your own conclusions.

True to form, Aaron never said a word about what we did to his car. Phil nearly had a heart attack he laughed so hard when we showed him the pictures.

I've gone back to being Nicholas' show assistant, even though I now know that the whole thing had been a sham from the beginning. The thing is, I love feeling a part of his performances and I don't want to give it up.

Tonight Nicholas is wearing black trousers, a crisp white shirt and a thin grey tie. He's leaning back on my bed, looking like he should be on an advertisement for expensive men's cologne, as I step out of the shower and into the room, wrapped in a towel.

I go to have a look through my wardrobe for something to wear, then I feel myself being yanked backwards and thrown onto the bed. Nicholas kisses me softly on the lips before announcing, "I'd like to dress you tonight."

I raise a sceptical eyebrow. "You want to dress me?"

"Yes, you dress me all the time for my shows. It's time for me to return the favour."

Now, normally if a man wanted to choose my outfit I would tell him where to go, but since Nicholas probably has better taste in women's clothing than I do, I shrug my shoulders and agree to let him have his way with me. It's after I do this that a devilish grin shapes his lips and he pulls a bag out from under the bed.

"What's that?" I ask, eyeing the bag that looks all too much like it contains new lingerie for my liking.

"A present," Nicholas replies.

He pulls my towel loose so that I'm naked. His eyes peruse me slowly, but he doesn't touch. Instead he opens the bag and pulls out sheer lace stockings, suspenders, and a lacy black matching set of bra and undies.

"Mr Turner, you're making me blush," I joke, as he comes toward me with the bra.

"Don't worry darling, I love it when you blush," he returns, and then proceeds to dress me in the lingerie he bought, copping several feels along the way. It all fits perfectly, and when he's done I stand in front of the mirror, wondering who this woman is before me, all decked out in sexy under garments.

The next thing I know, Nicholas is pulling that red dress he got for me weeks ago out of my wardrobe and slipping it on over my head. It feels like it's melding to my body as he zips it up at the back. He trails his hand across my stomach and then wraps his arms around me.

"You look stunning. Now all we need to do is get to work on your hair and make-up."

"You know Viv, most men try to get their girlfriends *out* of their clothes, not *into* them," I remark cheekily and he pats me on the behind.

"I think we both know that I've never been most men," he answers, running his fingers through my hair and tilting his head to the side as though trying to figure out what to do with it.

I turn around and kiss the side of his jaw. "No you're not, you're better," I say, rubbing up against him.

He groans and mutters, "If you don't stop doing that I'm going to become most men and tear this dress off you. Then we'll miss the party and Phil will pull a strop the next time we see him."

"Fine," I mutter, nipping at his bottom lip and turning back around.

By the time he's finished with me my hair is clipped up in a twist, with pieces falling down around my neck. Nicholas paints some gloss onto my lips and dabs dark eye shadow onto my eyelids. He then sits me down on the bed and pulls out the *pièce de résistance*, which is a black shoe box containing a pair of silver high heels. He has a grin on his face, indicating he finds this positively hilarious.

It's been our little activity over the last week or so for him to continue teaching me how to walk in heels. I've made progress, but by no means am I a pro. He rubs my calf with one hand as he kneels down on the floor in front of me and slips one of the heels onto my foot. He quickly puts on the other one and pulls me up.

"There," he says. "Perfect."

I walk as gracefully as I can manage over to the mirror to admire how the shoes make my legs look shapelier.

"Not too shabby," I say, grinning at him through the mirror.

"Beautiful," he adds, handing me my clutch bag and then leading me down to the waiting taxi.

When we get to the club the place looks amazing; there are streamers and balloons everywhere. Three drag queens up on the stage are doing a dance routine and miming to an old Madonna song. Nicholas isn't performing tonight, so he leads me up to the bar and orders me a glass of wine. He gets an orange juice for himself.

I haven't seen him touch a drop of alcohol since our trip to Edinburgh. I was going to ask him about it, but I decided not to. Making a big deal will just put more pressure on him to stay sober.

We join Nora and Richard, who are sitting at a table by the stage with Harry and Sean. Nicholas keeps his arm around my waist as we cheer on the performance and sing along. When the song ends one of the drag queens starts calling for Nicholas to come up and sing something. He waves her away at first, but after her endless encouragement he gives in, kisses me once on the lips and steps up onto the stage.

Instead of going to the microphone stand, he walks over to the piano and sits down. He plays a few notes and then gestures for the sound guy at the back of the club to adjust something. Once he's happy with it he rubs his hands on his trousers and turns to address the audience.

"I want to play a song for the woman I love," he says. "She doesn't even realise it, but she saved me." There are several "aws" from the crowd, as well as some guy (who I suspect to be Phil taking the piss) shouting up, "lucky bitch!" Everybody laughs, but Nicholas only smiles and shakes his head. "I've sung to her in the past," he continues, letting his fingers play a soft little tune on the keys, "but the sentiment hadn't been honest. So now I'll play something that's true."

His fingers glide effortlessly over the keys as his lips hover close to the mic and he starts singing "Your Song" by Elton John in a low, husky voice. He seems like he's singing to nobody for a moment, like he's looking inward. Then he brings those blue eyes that I adore up to me.

He says I can tell everybody that this is my song.

That he hopes I don't mind if he puts down in words how wonderful life is now I'm in the world.

I can't help it, but my heart is beating fast and my cheeks are blazing red. I stare down at my hands, before forcing myself to meet his gaze. He doesn't look away from me through the entire song. He sings like he's making a vow. It frightens me.

I'm living one of the most sentimental moments of my life and yet I'm scared to death. It's terrifying when you're staring the person you know you want most in the world dead in the eyes, and knowing that they belong to you unequivocally. I soak in the words, the truth of them, how special they make me feel in front of all of these people.

Nicholas and I are far from perfect, but we are heartbreakingly in love with one another and although this may seem like the happy ending of our little tale, it's only the beginning. I want to grow old with this man. I want to have his children. I want to hold him when he's sad and laugh with him when he's happy. I want to put him in dresses and see him become a woman on the stage. I want to keep each and every one of his smiles, mould them into a tangible thing and store them in a box.

I want to heal him with each and every one of our kisses. With every time we make love. Make him see that despite the past, the future holds mysteries that we can explore hand in hand. His melodious voice pulls me out of these thoughts. He looks at me and smiles as he presses down on the final note. I hold his gaze and blow him a kiss.

Epilogue

Dublin, Ireland, Present day.

Clean warm sheets cover Nicholas' body as he stares down at the beautiful woman lying naked and sleeping in his arms. She is the embodiment of all that is female, and all that he strives to replicate as an artist. She doesn't know it yet, but she is his muse now, his everything.

He recalls their first meeting, as the sounds of her deep breathing calm his mind. She'd been soaked from the rain and frustrated, but she'd still shone for him that day, made him laugh. That's what caught him, he thinks to himself, her unending humour, how she could render the world both light and dark with a simple joke.

He runs a hand through her silky, golden brown curls, relishing how every part of her fascinates him. He thinks of the little boy in the dress; the boy he used to be, a lost little boy. Now he can be a man in a dress, but he isn't lost. He has his golden eyed girl to lead his fractured soul through a world that once seemed dark and empty. In the present there's nothing but bright, wonderful sun light.

And even if bad times come, he knows he'll have her to share them with, so they won't really be bad at all. Her acceptance and love is something he didn't even realise he'd been searching for, but now that he has it he knows that he'd die if it got taken away from him. Every time he loses himself in her body, a little bit of the pain gets erased. She washes it away.

He holds her tight, promising himself that he'll never,

ever let her go.

END

Thank You For Reading
♥

About the Author

L.H. Cosway is a self-employed writer, editor and proofreader. She has a BA in English Literature and Greek and Roman Civilisation and an MA in Postcolonial Literature. She lives in Dublin city. Her inspiration to write comes from music. Her favourite things in life include writing stories, vintage clothing, dark cabaret music, food, musical comedy, and of course, books. You can follow her on twitter at twitter.com/lhcosway and you can contact her at lhcosway@gmail.com. You can also read her blog at lhcosway.com.

Printed in Great Britain
by Amazon